The Crown Estate

By

David Titmuss

The following are actual quotes by Prince Harry. Everything else you are about to read is entirely a product of my imagination. Occasionally, everyone asks themselves, 'What if..."

> *"For me personally, as I said, I want to serve my country ... I feel as though I should get the opportunity to do it again."*
>
> *"You've got to give something back. You can't just sit there."*
>
> *Prince Harry*

This book is dedicated to my mother. Years ago, she gave me a framed quote which hangs on my study wall. Rudyard Kipling's "If" has guided me through the ups and downs of my life. It applies to many men, even Royalty. In writing The Crown Estate, I found the final verse especially significant:

If you can talk with crowds and keep your virtue,
Or walk with Kings—nor lose the common touch,
If neither foes nor loving friends can hurt you,
If all men count with you, but none too much;
If you can fill the unforgiving minute
With sixty seconds' worth of distance run,
Yours is the Earth and everything that's in it,
And—which is more—you'll be a Man, my son!

The Crown Estate

King George III faced financial ruin in 1760. The King could no longer meet the cost of the British government and its Army and Navy. Bankers demanded repayment of loans and refused George III further funds needed to maintain a military presence in America, Britain's most valuable colony. The debts amassed by George III plus those of former war-mongering kings finally overwhelmed the royal family's enormous financial resources.

The British monarchy risked collapse; King George III desperately searched for a long-term solution to separate the costs of the state from the monarchy.

Under the Civil List Act 1760, George III agreed to transfer his assets to the 'Monarchy' as an institution. Henceforth this would become known as 'The Crown Estate.'

Under the Act, George III and all subsequent Kings and Queens would receive an annual income known throughout the centuries as the 'Civil List.' The arrangement met the expenses of the monarch and senior members of the royal family. The Civil List met the cost of the construction and maintenance of royal palaces, living costs and ceremonial duties. It also allowed each King or Queen continuous use and control over all transferred assets in perpetuity.

Two-hundred and sixty years after the establishment of The Crown Estate, it remains the UK's largest landowner. The Estate owns most of the UK shoreline, shopping centres, farming land, industrial estates and many parts of one of the most expensive cities in the world, London. Buckingham Palace and Windsor Castle are part of the Estate and are the most extensive and valuable residential properties in the world.

Other assets include the vast treasure trove known as The

Crown Jewels. The collection, housed in the Tower of London, includes over twenty-three thousand gems. The world's biggest bright cut diamonds, the Cullinan I and Cullinan II, adorn the British monarch's sceptre and crown, respectively.

The Royal Art Collection amassed over centuries by the Kings and Queens of the United Kingdom, feature paintings by almost every major artist of the last 700 years. Works by Rembrandt, Canaletto, Rubens, Raphael, Van Gogh, Caravaggio, and others adorn the walls of royal palaces, royal residences and museums. The Leonardo da Vinci collection housed at Windsor features 600 life drawings, their value thought to exceed £1 billion.

The value of The Crown Estate is said to be incalculable. The monarch 'inherits' the estate on succession to the British throne which then passes to their heir when they die.

Should Great Britain become a republic, The Crown Estate would cease to exist as a legal entity. The deposed King or Queen could justly reclaim the assets of The Crown Estate. Others may disagree...

Prologue Harry - A Lonely Funeral

The world mourned and the nation wept for my mother forty years ago as I walked behind her coffin with my brother, father, and grandfather. This time I walked alone.

Today, thousands of people watched me, but no one jostled for position. The coverage – this time – broadcast to millions, not billions. The people, press and politicians saw us as a relic of the past; a Royal Family eclipsed by celebrity. An institution no longer relevant in the modern world.

King William, Queen Katherine and their children were not allowed a 'state' funeral procession, yet another royal funeral seen as excessive in times of economic turmoil.

As I retraced the route to Westminster Cathedral, my gaze remained upon the five coffins carried by slow-moving hearses; traditional gun carriages were ruled out by my government. Fronting the procession, ten mounted-soldiers I knew led us, dressed in our regimental uniform which gave me a degree of comfort in the absence of state regalia. Mr Crippley, our Prime Minister, was resolute; there would be no state paraphernalia and I would have to pay for the funeral.

I continued to walk; my solitude complete. Meghan, and the children, would meet me at the Cathedral. She worried about their safety, rightly so, given the terrible events just weeks before. Nevertheless, I insisted the new heir to the throne, Archie, be present.

Since leaving the Palace, the drizzle became a hard unrelenting downpour. Water dripped from my army cap into steadily blinking eyes. Not yet halfway along the Mall, the straight road leading to Buckingham Palace, I saw a group of people protesting about the cost of the royal family. Their anti-monarchy slogans were blurred by the rain making their disfigured messages stand out, demanding to be read.

I expected protests. The previous evening, I watched the *'10 O'clock News'* on the newly nationalised ITV channel; it was clear the Government's republican agenda set the mood for the broadcast. Praise for my Grandmother were the only kind words spoken. Queen Elizabeth II reported as the *'last and the best'* monarch. Carefully selected reporters, and the behind-the-scenes news editors, ensured the socialist agenda came across loud and clear in every report.

By the time I walked under Admiralty Arch, converted to a

Marriott Hotel some time ago, I felt my resolve falter and my doubts increase. My grandfather's now vacant supporting hand was still heavy on my back as we passed underneath the building for support many years ago; I needed it then, and I yearned for his touch now.

The British royal family and the monarchy held a smaller place in people's hearts now. The United Kingdom, in crisis financially, alone in the world following Brexit, broken by Coronavirus, no longer held the respect of the world or the British people themselves. One commentator saw my brother's funeral as an event which marked a monarchy in demise.

I left a vastly different Britain six years ago after 'stepping back' from my royal duties with my American wife. As sixth in line to the throne, I was surplus to the Crown's requirements. However, we remained in the spotlight of a British press intent on marketing our lives as a product.

Our move to the US was blamed on Meghan, but it was my choice. Meghan gave me the balls and backbone to forge my own path. Contrary to popular opinion, my grandmother supported our decision, but my father and brother felt deserted, their displeasure made apparent by taking away my military commands and excluding us from royal duties in the UK or around the world.

William's death changed everything. I was dragged out of LA and forced to take a step up to fulfil my duty as the King of the world's oldest democracy. I had grown used to LA. I lived a quiet life with my children while Megan's career flourished once again. Our carefully orchestrated plans to build a new life in the USA were now in tatters.

As I continued along the path I took when I was twelve years old, I did so as the new King of the United Kingdom of Great Britain and Northern Ireland. Our Prime Minister had done everything since he was elected to make sure I was to be the last.

BOOK ONE - CRIPPLEY'S COMMITTEE

CHAPTER 1 - MR CRIPPLEY

Jarrod Crippley, the plain-speaking, radical left-winger, and labour activist, met King Charles at Buckingham Palace. The King invited him to form a government as the new Prime Minister following the landslide Labour victory in the general election.

Colonel Brenton Taylor, the King's Private Secretary, briefed Mr Crippley on the necessary protocol on meeting the King. "Mr Crippley, go in, the King will remain seated. The King will ask you to form a government and he will initiate the conversation. King Charles will ask you some questions and give you his thoughts and opinions. Once the King is finished, he will go silent. You should bow once more and walk backwards out of the room."

"Walk backwards? Why?" answered Jarrod Crippley.

"Because it is the way it is always done," the Colonel said, a little surprised Crippley wouldn't know this already; perhaps he did?

Crippley followed the Colonel to the King's formal stateroom. The door opened in front of him, where he could see the King seated in a gilded baroque chair about to replace a cup on its saucer; the small table that received it as regal as the King himself. There was only one chair and it supported King Charles's heavy stare.

King Charles remained seated as Crippley entered; neither spoke. The King eyed Crippley who gave the briefest of nods after an awkward pause although he decided, ahead of the meeting, he wouldn't bow his head.

"T-thank you ... f-for inviting me to the Palace."

Charles' left eye twitched as he noted Jarrod Crippley's omission; failing to address him as 'Your Majesty.' Naturally courteous, Charles smiled a placating smile. "Congratulations, Mr Crippley. I would like you to form a Government."

"I will. T-thank you."

"I have a few words of advice. First, I note you have a robust mandate from the British People as they have returned a substantial majority for your party. While this is the case, I would urge you to consider our history. I find, as my mother did before me, radical changes can be unsettling. Take your time to find your stride and try to take *my* people along with you."

Crippley took his time to reply, "I was, we were, voted on a 'change' manifesto. There is a lot to do and achieve. You'll find I'm not a man who likes to wait...for any man."

King Charles remained silent.

Crippley let the silence draw out as he waited for an answer. Recalling the Colonel's words, he realised the meeting was over. He turned away with purpose and walked to the door, his back to the King.

Meeting Crippley on the other side of the door, Colonel Taylor held his hand out to congratulate the new Prime Minister of the United Kingdom. "I trust it went well, Sir," he said.

More composed, Jarrod Crippley shook the Colonel's hand. "Colonel, thank you for your help. You'll find many of my meetings with *your King* will be as brief."

"Our King, Mr Crippley."

The new Prime Minister said nothing and withdrew his hand, leaving the Private Secretary to the King staring after him as he left the room.

Jarrod Crippley made his way out of the Palace to the government's official car, a Jaguar. Robbie McNee's outstretched hand greeted him. "Congratulations Jarrod, Mr Prime Minister."

Crippley smiled. "Now the real work begins." He tried to make himself comfortable by loosening his tie and unbuttoning his top button as he looked over to his chief advisor and friend of over thirty years. "I wasn't going to wait for Charles to lecture me on the environment, employment, taxes, even fox hunting for God's sake. What sort of age do we live in when someone must bow his head to another? Just because he was born to the most over-privileged family in the world. It is time to get rid of them. Strip them of their palaces, their jewels, the art, everything."

It was futile to attempt to stop Jarrod Crippley as he continued his tirade all the way to Westminster. As Crippley finally ran out of steam, Robbie interjected, seeing his chance to move the conversation along. "Never mind them, there's too much to do," he said. The expletives continued until they caught sight of Number Ten Downing Street; Jarrod Crippley's new home for the next five years.

Robbie McNee followed the Prime Minister into No.10. They were met by the team responsible for the successful 'Socialist Labour' campaign.

Robbie worked with Jarrod Crippley, drank with him, and considered him a friend. Their closeness allowed Robbie to read the new PM's mood. The anger of the Mall had not subsided, he could tell despite the outward appearance of a man pleased with himself and his achievements.

Once the reception was over, tired campaigners and party officials returned to their houses up and down the country. An hour later, only Jarrod and Robbie remained, each nursing a whiskey in the small apartment the PM would call home.

Robbie looked at Crippley and said, "They'll be wondering what you're going to do first? Of course, we have the list of people who expect to be appointed ministers tomorrow. But what are your priorities? You set the country alight with your radical manifesto. What first?"

Crippley relaxed back into the large leather armchair next to the open fire, made up and lit before they arrived in the apartment. As the light of the fire reflected on the PM's crystal tumbler, McNee waited; it was rare to see him quiet and reflective.

"The Royal Family are the root and cause of the class divide. It is why the people of the United Kingdom are not united. Some citizens have £20million houses while others live in crumbling flats unable to feed their children. It is led from the top. It is no use treating the symptoms of inequality, we must administer the cure to the cause, the reason why everything is so unfair. Without rooting out this cancerous infection, we can never be equal. Superiority trickles down from the royals to the aristocracy, the private schools, the private clubs and to parliament, where we are supposed to bow down and walk backwards in their presence. This land deserves better, an elected head of state and the fair distribution of all wealth. Robbie, the most important thing we must address is the dissolution of the monarchy, the distribution of their wealth and build a new republic."

McNee cut in at the pause, as he always did, "Surely they are irrelevant. We have so much to do. The economy is in trouble, the country stands alone in the world and Europe, even the USA seem to be against us."

Crippley stood and rested his arm on the mantlepiece. He fixed his gaze on his advisor. "No, this issue needs to be tackled," he started again. "It will take time. The dissolution of the monarchy, taking away their powers, distributing their wealth and removing their privileges will help solve the problems our nation faces. It will demonstrate to the people of the country, and those doubters abroad, we mean business. The new Socialist Labour Party is the people's party. The fawning Labour leaders before me were dazzled by the royal family. For fuck sake, they were blinded by them. I can see what they are - parasites on the British people. Our parliamentary majority is the highest ever seen in British politics. This hammer of power will destroy Charles and the greedy family he supports." Crippley continued, driven by the fervour of his own diatribe, "I want to form a committee. We will meet down at Chequers, so we are out of the way from prying eyes. McNee, they have their informants everywhere.

"There will be five of us, and you, of course. There we will plan our attack on the Royal Family. I want someone with a military mind, a tactician. We need a money man too, someone like Felix, the hedge fund man. A lawyer will be integral to our plans. I hate to say it, but we need a Cambridge don, a historian will be useful, someone with an insight to the jiggery-pokery the family are famous for. I want a member of the aristocracy, someone who thinks like they do and has their insight. We need to peel back the secrecy too, so we must have intelligence, someone from MI5 leaving you and me. We will be a tight, watertight, group with no one from the benches, no politicians. We must keep this as close to our chest as possible. Our strategy needs thinking through. We will need the resources of the government, but no one should know what we are up to. It will take some doing, but it has to if we are to rescue the country and once again be strong."

The whisky burned the back of McNees throat. Jarrod Crippley was barely five foot eight. He carried a lot of excess weight; his three-piece suit was a size too small. The new PM's rimless glasses reflected the fire and glowed red, giving him a demonic appearance. McNee liked being close to power and Jarrod Crippley radiated it. His impassioned speech came from his heart and impressed him. After the years working with Crippley, McNee’s chest was heavy with honour at sharing the room with him. Jarrod's burning passion burned brightly this evening following his election success. Robbie didn't believe the Royal Family was such a big problem but, if Jarrod did, so did he.

"I will get right on to it, Sir." McNee stood and left the room, leaving Crippley staring into the fire.

Outside, the elation at winning the election receded, maybe because he was so tired from the two-month campaign. The image of Crippley's glasses glowing in the reflection of the fire came to mind as the government car drew up to take him home. A cold shiver ran through him; how well would Jarrod Crippley be able to manage the power he now possessed?

CHAPTER 2 - REPORTING FOR DUTY

Arthur Thiskwood missed the Army. The retired American five-star general yearned for the cut and thrust of the politics between Washington and the Pentagon. The Army taught him discipline and strategy, while politics sharpened his mind and allowed him to hone his knowledge, using it where he could to his advantage.

After leaving the Army, Thiskwood initially felt lost until he decided to write a 'tell-all' book; 'Balls to the Walls.'Writing his explosive memoirs pulled him out of the void of obscurity. His book gave the General the satisfaction of having his own views in print even though it upset many of his former friends and colleagues.

There were far more stories to tell than he could ever have included in his autobiography. It took six months of hard negotiating with the Pentagon and Washington to get the full text approved. The best lawyers came crawling out of his wife's deep pockets, a luxury he wouldn't have been able to afford on his own. They argued every proposed redaction and each request to delete references to both living and dead colleagues in the army and influential politicians in the Nation's Capital.

The book was a moderate success and led to the General being interviewed on several major national talk shows in America. Media lapped up his stories of overspending, incompetent politicians and life and death mistakes on every battleground. Chat show hosts enjoyed exploring the General's right-wing views on homosexuality, extramarital affairs and sought further examples of non-politically correct observations expressed in the seven-hundred-page tome.

Senior figures in the military closed ranks to ensure Thiskwood understood he was no longer welcome among them. Most objected to the scandalous content, for breaking the unwritten rule; a code of honour, battleground secrets. Many former colleagues agreed the book gave a poor reflection of the General's massive achievements and it devalued his reputation as a great tactician.

McNee's fifth call to General Thiskwood was answered by the General. Prime Minister Crippley sent him a note asking him to talk to his chief political advisor. Thiskwood met Jarrod Crippley at a diplomatic event organised by the former Ambassador to the UK, concerned the pigmy politician would one day come to power in the UK. They'd enjoyed the discussion at dinner despite their opposing views. Thiskwoood was intrigued by the approach, but he wanted Crippley to ask first, not his bag man.

"General, thank you for taking my call."

If McNee was frustrated by his unsuccessful attempts to contact him, it didn't show. 'Typical English' he thought, as he answered a clipped reply, "Jarrod asked me to talk to you."

"I am Chief Political Advisor to the United Kingdom's Prime Minister."

Thiskwood laughed, "I know, the communist?"

McNee ignored the remark. "Mr Crippley and I have an interesting proposition for you. We need help on a delicate matter and wondered if you would were up to it."

"What on earth can a retired army man like me do for the Brits?"

"We have an interesting project which requires careful handling," said McNee. "We need a robust strategy to ensure its success. Our contacts over there mentioned your name several times, and The PM remembers meeting you. You appear to be the man we are looking for."

It was 8am when the phone first rang, and he'd hardly had time to get out of his bathrobe. Most people would see an image of a former fighter, still fitter than a man half his age and meticulously neat. Thiskwood was far more critical; his grey moustache needed a slight trim and his once blond hair was slightly unkempt, not the precise crew cut he was known for. In his prime, he stood at six foot four and was built like a tank, but even Thiskwood recognised those days were over and he grimaced at the older man he now saw in the mirror.

Since the furore over his book died down, General Thiskwood found himself again without purpose, bored. So, to say this conversation had him intrigued would be an understatement. "Go on."

"I can't really tell you anything until we meet, General. This is a delicate matter of the highest importance to Mr Crippley and the British People."

The General turned away from his reflection. "I'm an information guy, McNee."

McNee answered, "General, we have different systems of Government. Which one is the better way of governing?"

"Ours, of course. It has flaws but to have someone who heads your country because they were born to it is madness."

There was a silence before McNee answered. "This subject is

one of the PM's favourite topics."

Now it was time for the General to go silent. His larger than life persona sometimes gave the false impression he wasn't a great thinker, but he was. He was pleased he researched both Crippley and McNee ahead of the call. Crippley would have been locked up in the McCarthy era as a raging red communist. Information on McNee was harder to find, but the man had the same radical left political leanings as his boss.

Intrigued the General said, "So what do you want?"

McNee paused, his breaths beating into the receiver, then said, "We would like you to come and see us over here. We have a few people we are putting together to build a plan to change things for the better over here. I am afraid I can't say more at this time. Of course, we'll arrange travel unless you are busy?"

The General had an inkling of what this was all about and agreed to make the trip. Life at home suffocated Arthur and his wife, Carolina, would like him to be out of her hair.

Thiskwood walked into his bathroom and hung the dressing gown on the hook by the door. Naked, he studied his reflection again in the floor-length mirror and threw back his shoulders and stuck his chin out. He winked at himself and smiled. He would enjoy the trip over to the UK. While Thiskwood recognised publishing his book lost him most of his friends and the respect of former colleagues, he secretly enjoyed their outrage. The delight of unloading his opinions on the ineptitude of weak men and flawed politicians more than made up for years spent following orders and respecting rank. However, he needed to do something with his time, the request interested him.

General Arthur Thiskwood decided to put on the dark olive service uniform he kept pressed, ready always. Carolina had found someone to tailor the new suit for his press tour. The feel of the material and the shine of his brown leather oxford shoes readied him for the action to come.

Fully dressed, General Thiskwood returned to the mirror and saluted himself. “General Thiskwood, Reporting for Duty,” he said in a low, confident, voice.

CHAPTER 3 HARRY -BLACK SPIDER

I tuned into the BBC TV news every day from my home in Los Angeles. Witnessing the decline of Great Britain since our move to America made me feel like I'd abandoned a sinking ship. The news showed pictures of uncollected garbage, strikes and the dramatic decline of the economy. Meghan told me not to look back; our future was in the USA. I took to watching the news from my study to avoid her comments and hid my growing concern.

The UK's exit from the European Union, and the shock of the Coronavirus pandemic, weakened Britain and changed the political direction toward socialism. I found myself calling friends we left behind who told me more about what was going on, giving me a feel for the mood of the country still dear in my heart. Britain eventually requested a bail-out from the World Bank to help restore the nation's finances as unemployment passed the twenty-percent mark. Investment in Britain dried up as companies moved away and assets amassed by the baby boomer generation were in freefall, decimated by a near forty per cent drop in the value of housing. The decline reached every walk of life and everyone in the United Kingdom apart from one: King Charles.

My father made mistakes despite the years he spent 'training' for the role after he acceded to the throne. He publicly criticised the ultra-left-wing Socialist Labour Government elected to power six months following my Grandmother's death. He was unforgiving of their plans and policies designed to bring about a new economy and a revival of the country's fortunes. My father used his Christmas address to express his personal views; something the Queen never did. He also gave frequent interviews to the press, critical of government decisions.

In a way, looking at Britain from afar helped me with my perspective. While the people saw King Charles using the Royal Train, Plane and Helicopters, they heard him say they should use more public transport. Increasing numbers of people could no longer pay mortgages on their valueless homes. At the same time, their King had a choice of several palaces.

I missed most of the critique levelled at my family. While my new life isolated me from the country of my birth, even I could see the growing disparity between my father's lifestyle and 'the man on the street'.

Meghan couldn't care less about the rest of the family's portrayal as she obsessed over our own in the media. Initially, immensely popular, public sentiment turned against us, with poor Meghan receiving almost universal criticism as people blamed her for our move to the US.

Our father remained passionately committed to keeping the same standards he was born to. Privately we saw a man who changed clothes four times a day helped by three servants who organised his wardrobe and dress. I know William urged our father to make savings, remain quiet and turn the Monarchy into a low-key institution at least while the country suffered. Unfortunately, papa lost the respect of the people as well as politicians.

Jarrod Crippley became the Prime Minister in the first year of my father's reign as the leader of the recently renamed 'Socialist Labour Party.' His views were so, so far to the left, it would have been fairer to rename it the Communist Party. Mr Crippley won the most significant parliamentary majority in history with four hundred and ninety seats. This gave him carte blanche to bring in radical policies designed for 'a fairer Britain.'

Weekly, I read reports of Crippley's dramatic changes. He nationalised major industries without recompense. Gas, Electricity, Water, Rail, the Internet, and several large enterprises were absorbed by the state. To be fair, Crippley's election campaign promised many of the fundamental changes his majority Government was able to make. Initially popular, Socialist Labour increasingly came under pressure as the stock market crashed ruining individual investments and pension fund values. The communist ideal resulted in what some people called the 'most significant financial mismanagement in UK history.'

Some of my income still came from my father. Years before, he insisted on paying for our security but the pound to dollar exchange rate plummeted so much I felt the pinch and cut staff to manage.

William found it hard to accept our departure from the Royal Firm. For months, contact came through intermediaries and messengers. The bond between William and I remained, though. Our shared history meant it was only a question of time for us to start to communicate. The Queen's death brought me home, and, when I met William for the first time, we both acknowledged the need to reconcile.

William called me one day after a meeting with our father. He asked me to visit him, something he rarely did. I booked a ticket, even Meghan supported my unplanned trip home. The idea was to spend the day together on a shoot at a friend's estate, an hour from London, knowing we would have the time to talk without interruption.

William resented our decision to seek a life in the US. Meghan, ever the sceptic, said William preferred our being out of the British public's eye. I suppose she was right in part as we often attracted more publicity.

The death of our mother cemented our close bond. My move to LA stretched our relationship to breaking point. Still, our brotherhood remained, and you could hardly cut that out. Over time, we became friends once more. Our wives and families opted out of this new arrangement. Meghan spent most of her time working on her TV show. Kate, who I called 'Mother Earth,' kept herself happy with her children and being a model Queen in waiting. William and I forgot about trying to mend the rift between them. In the end, our wives were different people with nothing in common save for their link through us.

William met me at our friend's estate. As I stepped out of the car, he rushed over to me and we embraced. William held me for a second longer than usual.

We planned our shoot ahead of our meeting. My flight from LA was delayed by the air traffic controller strike currently paralysing British airspace. The shooting party, long since departed, meant we could go into the house and be alone.

William said, "I thought even you would show up on time. We've missed the shoot."

"There'll be another."

"Perhaps."

I waited for him to continue. I'd long ago learned William scripted out what he had to say if something was important.

"Father told me we face some pretty big issues regarding finances."

I was surprised; we never discussed money in our family,

others sorted out finances. I patted the chair next to mine and William sat down with a low grunt, something I saw him do increasingly often.

"There is no money. We won't get any money from the government this year, Harry."

William had to care about finances and Meghan earned more than enough for our relatively everyday lives, so I was nonplussed. "No money?"

William regarded our move to LA, still, as a temporary affair. We didn't. Our lives were more than comfortable, and, to a large extent, the Royal finances weren't my business anymore.

William relaxed back in the chair and looked me in the eye. I knew that look. A shiver ran down my back. Solemn, alone. His eyes were dead.

"You know the Royal Firm gets twenty-five per cent of the profits of the Crown Estate."

"Yes,'" I replied, waiting for more.

"Last year, the Crown Estate made a loss, a big loss. Given the state of the economy, Mr Crippley refused to subsidise us at all. Father has known about this for some time and believed it was not a problem at first. He thought it could be sorted."

"I must confess," I said to William, "I'm not sure how it all works." I'm not embarrassed about this at all as I'm 5th in line to the throne and would never see any money. Sure, we lived a millionaire's lifestyle in the States but lived on far less money than it took to run a Royal household.

When William became Prince of Wales, he took over the Duchy Estate which usually generated over £25m cash a year last time I looked. Both William and I were taught early on how vital the 'Duchy' was. The Duchy of Cornwall Estate, founded in 1337, owns about one per cent of the United Kingdom landmass.

"It's OK, you have the Duchy," I said, smiling. "It was worth over a billion pounds, right?"

William looked down, he'd been keeping things to himself, and was recently reoccupied when we chatted on the phone. "All is not well there, Harry."

Once again, I waited. I reached for the bell to summon a butler; I fancied a drink. *Needed* a drink.

"Don't Harry, let me get this off my chest, we don't need an interruption." I pulled back and sat in the chair, wanting that drink even more. "Besides, it is too early for a whiskey."

"Last year the Duchy also went into loss. The money I've been using is from our investments."

"I should have connected the dots, Harry. The Duchy is much smaller than the Crown Estate, but we have the same issues, the same problems the whole bloody country is having. When I was summoned to the palace, I was going to raise it with the King, *father,* hoping he'd be able to sort something for us," said William, leaning forward. The King had replaced father in his words. William spent more time with his family than our father liked. They were frequently at odds regarding sharing responsibilities. Even though he'd had so many years 'in training,' our father became more reserved and crotchetier, burdened by the position he now held. I didn't talk to him as often as I should; we had a lot on with our life in the US.

William continued, "He sat me down and went through the finances in detail. In fact, in more detail, than I'd ever seen. The King said we'd been getting some £100million a year until a few years ago. It's our twenty-five per cent of the profits of the Crown Estate. It pays for the palaces, maintenance, the Royal Household, everything. OK, it doesn't pay for Balmoral or Sandringham, they belong to him, but they cost buttons in comparison. For the first time in centuries, the Crown Estate isn't making money. Even the wind farms we built offshore, the shore the Crown Estate owns, have stopped paying the Crown Estate rent."

I tried to think of a response, "What about Mr Crippley, can't he help?

William reached over and pressed the bell himself. A butler came in, I shook my hand as if holding a glass, "two large ones please."

As the butler left, William lent forward as if he'd got to the real issue which. "The King and Mr Crippley had a frank and open discussion. Father wrote one of his famous 'black spider' letters! Our father's habit of writing long letters in thin, black, barely legible handwriting. "When our father complained about finances, Crippley suggested he visit Number 10 to discuss the matter."

I couldn't believe it. "He summoned the King?"

"Yes," said William. The disbelief apparent in his voice, our father went nowhere for anyone, especially if he was asked to do so. "He ignored Crippley's request and, eventually, the PM asked for an audience."

"Who told you?" I asked,

"Taylor." Colonel Brenton Taylor was our father's Private Secretary, he handled most matters between the Royal Household and the Government.

I raised my eyebrows; Taylor hardly ever gave anything away.

"Anyway," William continued, "The PM came over and read the Riot Act to the King."

"I can't imagine anyone reading the Riot Act to papa!" I said, deliberately using the name we both called him when we were younger.

William smiled. "Papa was *told* the government was facing a revolt by 'the people.' He said they are demanding the Royal Family be reined in - excuse the pun. The conversation got heated when Mr Crippley mentioned "Moving Times," and, "The Need to Modernise."

I'd met Crippley a few times; an intense, dislikeable and repulsive man. My estimation of him may have been too high. The PM, short, fat, and bald with thick rimless glasses, the resemblance to Churchill stopped there. People were surprised when Crippley got elected to the leader of his party. He worked for years on the party machine to get to the position. A friend told me he had 'black' files on people who mattered. He came to power because of what he promised and a weak opposition, unable to muster support given the faltering economy. The manifesto assured the electorate of more money, a fairer society, a statutory minimum of six weeks paid holiday a year and many other treats they couldn't resist.

William stood and wandered around the room. We both had our drinks, I couldn't remember the butler even coming in. He continued, "Papa called Taylor into the room on some or other pretext, you know how he hates being cornered. Taylor told me a better account of the meeting than father did, he said he thought there are moves to review our role. Someone high up in the government told Taylor they'd been asked to examine the 'function, purpose and cost of the Royal Family in modern times.'

Even in our Grandmother's day, there were times when the public sentiment turned against the family. This time though, I felt a sense of something more substantial. Here we had a broken Britain, people on the streets combined with a powerful PM with strong anti-royalist views.

"Are you surprised?" I said.

William saw things differently to me; it was his future, "This family has been at the helm for centuries, I'm sure this will pass." Still, there was the slightest doubt in his eyes.

"It might do William, it will," I tried to reassure him. When our father became King, the celebrations were short, insincere, and deflating. People loved the Queen. They didn't have the same feelings toward our father. Megan often said the idea of a monarchy didn't fit with real democracy. I'd learnt to ignore her, the UK was my country, my heart never left the land of my birth.

"More immediately," William said, "we have a real problem to contend with. The Duchy and the Crown Estate are solid, set in stone, but we can't take any capital."

I didn't know as much about how it all worked, "So where will the money come from? Doesn't it cost about £60 million a year to run the family firm?

"Father says we'll have to spend our own money."

While the value of the Crown Estate and the Duchy of Cornwall were immense, the private royal finances were healthy but much smaller. The Queen passed down over £900m when she died in investments plus there were Balmoral and Sandringham and her own jewels which were valued on her death at over £190 million. I recalled William and my father discussing this recently, I guessed the personal fortune had also been dented by recent events.

William continued, "You know our kitty has been hit, I'm not sure we could last many years if we had to pay for everything. We'll have to sell something. Until then," he paused, looking embarrassed, "I may have to ask you and Meghan to help us out financially."

I stared at my brother and didn't answer. I was trying to figure out how I would persuade my wife to part with some of her money. Meghan's income surpassed the Crown Estate but, given her feelings for my family, parting her from some of her new wealth wouldn't be easy.

CHAPTER 4 - THE COMMITTEE

Jarrod Crippley walked into the dining room slightly late from a session in the Commons. Addressing the assembled guests, he said, "Gentlemen, Lady, welcome to Chequers."

Taking his seat at the head of the table, he continued, "Did you know the Grandson of Oliver Cromwell once owned this house. Later, I will show you around the collection celebrating Cromwell's life and works. His greatest act was to sign King Charles I's death warrant. He ran this country in one form or another for seven years until, foolishly, King Charles II was put on the throne. I tell you this because of the plan I, no, the plan WE need to put in place to rid ourselves of this ancient constitutional monarchy and form a modern Republic. Mark my words, the Royal Family feeds off the United Kingdom's resources to the detriment of every man, woman and child in our nation."

Crippley picked up a glass of red wine and placed it to his lips while studying the room, eyeballing the members of his new Committee while they absorbed his words.

There was a stunned silence. Heather Taylor-Todd spoke first. Her wealthy aristocratic upbringing gave her the confidence and, she believed, the right to be heard first. "I like it. What a plan."

Jarrod Crippley smiled at the sister of one of the UK's largest landowners. McNee told him she was proud of her ascent to the pinnacle of the education system as Oxford University's Professor of History and Public Policy. She refused to be called Lady Heather Taylor-Todd. She would flatten anyone who used her title with a withering look and a caustic comment.

John Amery smiled at his Cambridge acquaintance. They'd met at the famous University but weren't close. It struck John she might be an excellent connection to seek new investors in his hedge fund.

Heather was one of the great beauties of his Cambridge days. A little over five feet five, what she lacked in height was more than compensated by her commanding presence. Heather was raven-haired, her eyes were sapphire blue and her figure which looked the same as in her university days; stunning. Had she been a few inches taller, she'd have made it as a supermodel, although she would hardly consider the role.

John met Heather in Freshers Week ahead of their first term at Cambridge called 'Michaelmas.' The week was filled with parties and events designed to ease new students into life at the University. John was attracted to her, yet nothing happened. The rush from party to party, from pub to pub and dinner to dinner - all in a haze of alcohol - made them ships passing in the night. On one of the last evenings, he'd caught up with her in a group of first-year students. She looked ravishing; dressed in tight short shorts and a fashionably torn T-shirt. Her group was full of earnest, spotty youths captivated by what she said or how she looked, maybe both. As she spoke, her views misted his rose-coloured glasses. Her ideologies were so different from his own he guessed there was little point in getting to know her more intimately; they wouldn't get along.

Smiling, he caught Heather staring at him from the opposite side of Crippley's grand dining table. She looked away, embarrassed.

John was glad Roger Casement cut in. "There'll be a massive number of challenges. The Royal Family has ruled this country for nearly a thousand years, save for the brief Cromwellian period of course."

His peers regarded Casement as one of the most brilliant lawyers of his generation. His rise to the top of the British legal system drew much comment since he was black, born in Barbados to a single mother. His mother made her way to the UK in the 1970s and landed herself a cleaning job in a retired Judge's house. The Judge, who left the bench following a stroke, took a shine to the young Roger who'd often come with his mother who couldn't afford childcare. With no children of his own, the aged Judge took to Roger and paid for a private education. This put him on the path to a legal career, helping him to enter Cambridge University, and afterwards at a successful law firm as a trainee solicitor. Despite his success over the years, Roger Casement carried the scars of his time at Cambridge. The British elite objected to his presence there and students and professors alike inflicted racist abuse, excluding him from most social occasions.

The Judge continued, "You'll find it difficult to break a system so old and so firmly entrenched in the British way of life. Trust me, I know."

General Arthur J Thiskwood, the tall, heavyset American, leaned forward into the table. He cut Judge Casement off, "Crippley, what the hell has it got to do with me?"

Robbie McNee, who selected the Committee members, answered following the Prime Minister's glance at him, "General, gathered around this table are some of the most respected minds within their speciality. Your role is to devise a strategy, using all the resources at our disposal, to help defeat the system embedded in history. We think success is only possible by working with one of the greatest military minds." Robbie

chose his words carefully knowing the General possessed a massive ego.
The military man relaxed, sat back in his chair and looked over to the handsome man next to him.

Prompted by the General, John Amery looked over to the Prime Minister who nodded for him to speak. "I am not sure how I can help either if I am honest," said Amery, "I am a money man here. I don't see how this plan could get any input from me?" He stole a glance at Heather as he spoke and chastised himself for doing so as his heart leapt again. It would be much better if he didn't have to come back. He wasn't used to anything being out of his control.

Again Robbie McNee interjected, "As with all things in life, money is critical, particularly in this situation. When King Edward VIII abdicated, the only matter causing a problem was the private fortune inherited by him under the Primogeniture Act of 1701. King Edward's VII abandonment raised the question; who owned the royal estate? At best, the situation was hazy.

"Yes," Heather Taylor-Todd cut across McNee, "the Act stopped women acceding to the throne where there was a male heir, even if he were not the firstborn. It ruled out the Catholics too."

"King Edward, no doubt prompted by Mrs Simpson, focused on how much of the Royal Family's private wealth would remain with them," Robbie continued. "Eventually, the matter was resolved but not without some substantial sacrifices by the new King George VI.

"I understand the King's private fortune is relatively modest by today's standards," John Amery asked, "about £700million?"

Crippley stood up, anxious to retake centre stage. "You know how they've managed to keep hold of their great wealth? No? They've hardly ever paid tax. They, alone, escape the British tax system and it isn't fair."

"Hang on, I thought the Royal Family was one of the richest in the world. The Crown Jewels. The art. Hell, Buckingham Palace is in one of the most expensive cities in the world and must be worth a billion dollars alone."

Crippley smiled down at Thiskwood, "The Crown Estate encompasses it all. Some estimate it is worth more than £55 billion. However, the monarch merely has use of it while holding office. It is a deal made centuries ago."

Crippley walked around the table and placed a hand on Heather Taylor-Todd's shoulder, who flinched away from it. "Heather," he said, "help the General understand."

A silence drew out in the room, Crippley's touch made her uncomfortable. He sensed her concern and returned to his seat. He looked at her again until she said, "Oh, I see. Hold on a moment." She placed her fingers on her temples, a gesture her students knew well. After a pause, she continued, "Now I see. I see why you have brought us together. Well some of us, we haven't all been introduced yet."

Crippley leaned towards Heather Taylor-Todd. This issue was important; further introductions could wait. Dutifully, she continued, "In 1760, George III, King of England, signed The Civil List Act. The King bore the cost of Government, as such there were no taxes and he paid for the cost of the State. He owned lands and significant assets which were depleted by the ever-rising costs of keeping a democratic Government in place. Previous unwise wars drained the Royal purse and significant debts were incurred. The situation was made worse by King George III's unsuccessful and costly campaign to retain America as a British Colony. The Act allowed the King to exchange the assets in return for a yearly amount, called the 'Civil List,' paid to maintain the Monarchy and Royal Household. The Sovereign Grant Act 2011 was the last major overhaul of the system. The new act fixed the payment to the monarch at 15-25% of the profits of the Crown Estate. To give you an example, even back in 2010 the profits of the Crown Estate were £210million, resulting in £52.5 million distributed to Queen Elizabeth II and her family. Security and other costs are paid directly by the Government.

"OK, OK, you'll have to help me out here. I'm an American, what does this all mean?"

About to answer, Heather Taylor-Todd gave way to Crippley once more who said, "We have an issue here. It has long been my dream to turn the UK into a republic like the US, General. It isn't a secret; I've said it many times."

Amery interrupted the PM, "I'm not sure if I saw a mention of a republic in your election manifesto?"

Jarrod Crippley ignored Amery who looked down at the table, embarrassed. The PM continued, "When we become a republic, the Crown Estate could face a claim of ownership by Charles and his family. I mentioned the value was estimated to be circa £55 billion. However, the value could be more than £100 billion or even more. The Crown Estate has been massively undervalued in terms of assets."

Following a short pause, the PM slammed the table to gain attention. "The purpose of gathering you all today is to figure a way to rid ourselves of the monarchy without the cost of losing the Crown Estate. If we can't hang on to the Crown Estate, we may have to forget the idea of a republic."

CHAPTER 5 HARRY - SCREENING ROOM

Meghan and I were happy with our chosen place in life. The occasional family event in the UK aside, our base in the USA gave us even more independence than we ever expected. I ran our charities and Meghan worked; the children were happy in our beautiful house.

Against all the odds, our finances were excellent. When we decided to step down from our roles and move to Los Angeles, my father pretty much paid all our bills. I couldn't object at the time. Meghan had other plans. Her knowledge of the media and workings of TV and Hollywood came to the fore. The issue was I gave undertakings to the Queen not to 'cheapen' or 'demean' the Monarchy by signing overtly commercial sponsorship deals. I also promised not to use our HRH titles, something Meghan said she was okay with. Though, I wasn't so sure she was. Our fame and notoriety leant itself to reality TV, crass sponsorship deals and more. Meghan came up with the answer.

Meghan often complained about the deal I'd agreed with the family. Still, I remained steadfast. I was expecting another verbal thrashing when she said she had something to discuss after she got in one night. Fresh from a few days doing a voice-over for a Disney film, she had a glint in her eye and outlined her new idea at dinner after I put the children to bed. My reaction was 'no way!' and considered it the end of the matter.

One thing I should expect; Meghan never gave up. I shouldn't have been surprised when she invited me to the new Netflix Studio complex near Hollywood a few weeks later. We were shown to a small room laid out like a mini cinema where Megan said I'd be viewing a documentary film with a voice-over from her.

Meghan and I were alone when the screen lit up with a title sequence of a show which simply said; 'Meghan!' The chat show featured some big celebrities balanced out by interviews of everyday 'Heroes' who achieved something extraordinary. I remained silent throughout the pilot screening. Meghan did too, surprisingly.

The show was excellent, even for a pilot episode. Impressed by her intelligent questions, her empathy with the guests and her engaging personality, I could see people warming to Meghan.

After the show finished, we remained in the screening room. Meghan explained hosting her chat show would play to her strengths, allow her to set the agenda and help her avoid shorter-term deals which could blow up in our faces if mishandled.

Meghan explained how the deal with the studio meant she would own the format, giving her a significant share of the income made from syndication in the US and abroad. This arrangement also gave her editorial control, assuring me my guidelines would never be broken.

'Meghan!' became one of the most viewed daily chat shows in the world. Advertising and sponsorship deals blossomed and generated over $180 million profit each year for its single shareholder; my wife. I couldn't be prouder. She found a way through the complexity of her royal connections in a far better way than anyone in the royal family ever achieved. Her show entertained, intrigued, and added a massive dose of humour no one ever expected from my wife.

CHAPTER 6 - TOTALIS SILENTIO

The Committee members listened carefully as McNee told them they should sign a specially drafted legal agreement based on the Official Secrets Act.

Mr Crippley took over from McNee as the room grew silent, "Each of you will sign a binding document subject to the Official Secrets Act. You will also sign the *Totalis Silentio* addendum, this means total silence."

"Now you know the purpose of the committee you are bound by law to keep it secret, tell no one. If you decide to leave our committee, you will still be bound by its terms. The addendum means you will be financially ruined if you break its terms. Once you read it, you will also find your families are subject to the same conditions.

McNee, ever the diplomat, interjected, "Don't worry. We all have a lot to gain and the Totalis Silento addendum is there for 'belt and braces' so to speak."

"Don't threaten me, I am a fighting man," the General said in a low but powerful voice.

"Of course not, General, of course not. As I said, General," McNee gulped, "it is merely a mechanism which we can all depend on, including yourself."

"We will, as I said, meet regularly. McNee will brief each of you on your roles so, by the next meeting, we will have a lot to discuss. The addendum protects each of you as well as me."

Reading the room, Crippley smiled in an attempt to pacify the members of the new committee. The effect was minimal. "Gentlemen, let me introduce Heather Taylor-Todd more formally. You may be familiar with her from the historical documentaries she makes."

There were a few nods from the men in the room as Crippley continued. "Heather, your job is to carefully examine the Acts of Parliament, the rules - written and unwritten - and regulations governing the monarchy in the UK. Over the years, our constitution, never written down, is a collection of precedents and traditions. The middle ages and even the Victorian age, as we all know, have one thing in common: Royal scandals. One of the facts I want in our armoury, if possible, is to have the right of succession of the current monarchy put into question. We tend to accept the current status quo. I want you to use historical fact to overturn anything to enable us to question the current King Charles and his heir's claim on the Throne. Also, you will help in identifying all the Royal assets, many are long forgotten. Leave no stone unturned."

Turning to Roger Casement, Crippley waited until the judge swallowed the food in his mouth. "Mr Casement here is a highly respected Judge. Your central objective, Roger, is to examine the question of ownership of the Crown Estate. Needless to say, I carried out investigations through another party previously. I am concerned the family may attempt to take back the Crown Estate should they be deposed. You need to follow the trail from the point Charles III made the deal in 1760. Be careful though; dig as deep as you can and make sure you don't conclude anything other than that which has been demanded by the British People."

Judge Casement looked over to Crippley, careful in his reply,

"I'm sure I will be able to deliver the right conclusion. I'll make sure of it."

John Amery looked to Crippley, sensing his eyes were upon him, they were. "Mr Amery, you're one of the world's foremost financial experts. John, your role is to assess the exact value of the assets held by the Crown Estate. You should also include other items and rights held in the name of the Crown, such as the Royal Art collection and its value. You need to be a ferret, we all know about the wind farms and the palaces, but I'm interested in the art, the library contents, even the jewels. For heaven sake, the jewels alone are supposed to be worth some £4 billion. One diamond in the State Crown, the Cullinan I, is worth £600m. When we know the total value, I want to dispose of it for the good of the people. I don't care if Buckingham Palace itself is brought by a Russian billionaire or a Columbian drug czar, everything will be sold."

Amery watched as Crippley continued to talk about the Crown assets, the PM liked the sound of his own voice. While the fabulous wealth of the Crown Estate wasn't in question, its ownership would be if the monarchy fell. As with any forced asset sale, the value would be depleted and any issue of ownership could mean no sale at all. Amery asked the PM a question, interrupting his flow, "What about the debt situation?"

"What do you mean?"

Amery wiped his mouth slowly with his napkin. "As far as I can see, King Charles did a deal in 1760; sign over the Estate to the state in return for an income."

Heather Taylor-Todd looked perplexed, "Yes, we know, what is your point?"

John Amery recalled how cutting Heather could be. Calmly, he replied, "If you add up the income over the years, you could find the royal family were underpaid over the centuries."

Amery now held the committee's attention and continued, "It could be argued the income given to the family over the years falls far short of the original loan terms. I'll do the sums, but I have a feeling I may have a point here."

McNee noticed the red filling Crippley's cheeks. "Ok, Amery, you make a valid point, but we will need to work around this, include Heather and Judge Casement here before we come to any conclusions."

John Amery worried about working with Heather, given his sudden loss of control when he saw her this morning. Amery merely nodded in reply and turned to Roger Brereton as did the other committee members, given he remained the last person in the room to be included in the debate.

"I guess it is my turn here, Prime Minister?"

Crippley smiled, his anger dissipating, "Yes, dear fellow, your skills are going to be called upon by this committee. They will be, in my opinion, invaluable."

"In any particular direction?"

"Yes. We have covered off a lot here today; history, the law and we have even discussed the money, but we also need another string to our bow. Roger Brereton here is Deputy Head of Mi5. Roger, you will supply us with more information on King Charles. We need to find his intentions, what he is saying, what stresses and strains exist in the House of Windsor. You need to spy on the King."

CHAPTER 7 - I, SPY

Robbie McNee met Ronald Brereton ahead of the meeting and explained the purpose of the committee. Of all the attendees, McNee thought Brereton was possibly the most useful given his role as Deputy Head of Britain's Secret Service; Mi5.

Like most intelligence service professionals, Ronald didn't react as McNee explained the makeup and purpose of the committee. When McNee finished, he said to Ronald, "What are your views?"

Again, Ronald Brereton remained silent. His experience told him to wait for the Prime Minister's political adviser to continue.

"I see you are keeping your powder dry." McNee said, "I better explain another reason for joining us on the committee; to help us. You see, we need you and your resources if we are to succeed."

Ronald allowed himself to smile. The Arabian quarter of him was used to procrastination dressed as a courtesy. "Why should I join you? It could be viewed as treason. I swore an oath to the King—as did Mr Crippley."

McNee flinched at the mention of 'treason' but said, "I know you were surprised at your appointment.. We faced a lot of criticism; not only from the UK, our American friends questioned your appointment. The UK and its allies face the Muslim threat on the streets of every town and city. Of course, we proved to them you were the man for us, after all, you say you are a Christian, not a Muslim. You have proved yourself and your allegiance to the government again and again. We outlined your achievements and proved our case. Your Muslim heritage means we have the advantage in many cases."

"Why do you think I would help you?" persisted Brereton, waiting for the threat to come; thirty years' experience in spy craft taught him to.

Ronald remained silent, letting McNee continue, "Your son is at Oxford and has his whole future ahead of him. I understand he is a scholar? His skill as a rower will almost certainly help him get selected for the University's Boat Race team. Your rich wife, too; not only did she inherit money, but she also made a great deal more from anti-cyber-attack software. Of course, her company depends on government contracts. All I am asking is you do what the Prime Minister asks, help us if we need it and all your family will thrive."

Ronald looked at McNee with contempt, but he would do his job, which was to serve the government. If Crippley wanted help, he would help, his family was much more important than the royal family. "Why would you think I would want to do anything other than helping my Prime Minister and his government?"

"Now, Brereton, We'll need you to arrange for key information to be collected from a range of sources. I am glad we met beforehand to make sure this fits within your government role and remit."

Crippley called for the Chequer's butler for lunch to be brought in. The tension eased in the room as plate after plate of food and drinks were served. As the commotion of the assembled committee members increased, one member decided they must play this carefully; King and Country depended on it.

CHAPTER 8 - SHOW ME THE MONEY

John Amery left the Committee and climbed into his car driven by Ben, his butler-cum-chauffeur.

"Good afternoon, off to the airport as planned?" said the driver smiling broadly in the rear-view mirror at his boss.

"Yes," said John, clipping his seat belt in place, "Phew, what a surprise I met the Prime Minister."

Ben, a long-serving employee, enjoyed a good relationship with Amery, said, "You're moving up in the world."

"I guess you could say so, Ben. You know the Prime Minister doesn't really earn a great deal considering his responsibilities. Still, it sure helps to have a country house like Chequers thrown in with the job. The place is stunning."

Pulling out of the main gates to the house, Ben reached over to the passenger seat and passed a magazine over to John. "You are looking good in the magazine, John. I hope you don't mind, I read the article while you were in the house."

Amery reached over and took the magazine. "Ah, the Forbes piece. Bloody hell, the photograph, it's embarrassing. It looks a bit..."

"Pornographic maybe?"

"It sure doesn't look like a business magazine cover shot. Most of the businessmen I know would be a little embarrassed picking this up from the newsstand."

"Plenty will buy it."

"Perhaps. Right Ben, I must do some work. How long will it take to get there?"

"An hour, thirty usually but the traffic is heavy, so allow more like two."

"Great."

Ben read his boss's mind, "I'll leave you in peace." He pressed a button on his dashboard to raise the privacy glass.

John Amery looked at the Forbes Magazine cover; "John Amery - George Soros's Heir Apparent?"

Amery looked at his picture. He remembered the stupid amount of time the photographer spent in organising the shoot, he was pleased they did, he looked ok. The photo, taken at his Palm Beach estate in Florida, showed him in his swim shorts, fit, lean and dripping with beads of water as if the photograph were taken as he got out of the pool. Of course, it was a little fake, the pretty young assistant sprayed water on him as the photographer clicked away.

According to his PR, the idea was to make him look like the sex symbol of the financial world. At the time he thought the idea amusing. However, he became increasingly embarrassed as he read the article.

At forty-one, John Amery's body is lean and muscled, much the same as his days as a national swimming champion. He is six-foot-four, blessed with dark good looks, and worth a cool thirteen billion.

Amery, the son of a wealthy British surgeon, came top of his class at Cambridge University and Summa Cum Laude from the Wharton Business School in the States.

George Soros spotted Amery early in his financial career and offered him a rumoured one million a year starting salary. Amery flourished in Soros' secretive and complex world of Hedge Fund management. According to Soros, John Amery stood out from his other young Turks by keeping quiet, working hard and partying with people outside the financial community. Soros is credited with saying, "My fund managers spent so conspicuously they didn't notice Amery quietly climbing the ladder behind them. John ended up making more money than all of them."

Even Soros couldn't accommodate John Amery's ambitions leading to a split between the two. Amery set up his own fund, Red Diamond, named after the most expensive gemstone in the world at $1 million per carat.

According to reports, Amery extended the olive branch to George Soros and the two are often seen dining together despite the rumours of a bitter split. Soros said recently, "John's intellect and competitive nature drove him to the point where I lost a disgruntled employee and, eventually, made a lifelong friend."

While Red Diamond's funds now surpass £300 Billion, Amery limits the firm's size by his insistence on high ethical standards, both within his investments and from his clients. Wealthy family offices and sovereign wealth funds vie for the 'Diamond Touch.' Those who don't pass John Amery's high ethical bar are left out in the cold.

Despite his financial fame, not much is known about Amery's private life. Unlike other well-known financial goliaths, John Amery doesn't seek publicity. Occasionally he is seen with a beautiful woman at charity functions but few that last more than a few months....

Another picture of John and a former girlfriend sat awkwardly on the page, or so he thought. Whenever he looked at her or any of the other women in his life, the image of Mia came to him, making the other's pale in comparison. It was why none of the other women stood a chance.

Mia, olive-skinned, tall, beautiful, and vivacious would've made fun of the articles, then him in her Italian accent.

John and Mia attended nearby schools which merged their swimming squads to create an award-winning team. Seven of their team members were national champions in their chosen races, including John and Mia. The fifty-meter pool, one of the few in the UK, was based at Mia's School which meant long early morning bike rides for John, sometimes in the dark of the winter mornings.

Their relationship blossomed during their training sessions together with the team. John was men's Captain; Mia joined the squad following her parents' move to the UK from Italy. Initially, John thought Mia disliked him as she was quick to mock him in front of other teammates. He learned later she felt the same about him and Mia said she regretted the wasted months playing games with him.

The two schools were relatively liberal, with John's regarded as the more academic. Their relationship consisted of swimming twice a day in hard two-hour sessions and spending as much time as they could together in between. By the time each was sixteen, they'd had sex in the playing field behind the pool and regularly thereon. Mia was more worldly-wise and readier to share her emotions. John learned how to relax and enjoy his time with her.

In the final term of school, John saw less of Mia because both were revising hard. His father insisted on good grades, he was anxious not to let him or himself down. Increasingly Mia cycled over to his school in the evenings to spend the little time with John she could. There they found they could safely meet away from prying eyes in his school medical facilities. The rooms were seldom used.

One evening Mia failed to turn up. Mobile phones weren't allowed in school; only a few teenagers owned them so he couldn't contact her. The next morning, he rode to the pool, more than a little angry with Mia for not meeting him.

Waiting at the front of the pool, unexpectedly, was their coach, Nev Cross. He remembered the look in his coach's eyes as he cocked his leg over his bicycle and freewheeled to the bike stands near the door. Nev came over and told him Mia was knocked off her bike on her way to meet him the evening before. Although Mia lived for a few days, John wasn't allowed to see her.

As John relaxed in the car, an image of his father sending him off to the boarding school where he met Mia came to mind. Boarding school drove a wedge between him and his parents, making him self-sufficient and independently minded. While John gave credit to his expensive education in providing him with a foundation for his success, he envied the closeness Mia enjoyed with her parents.

He decided to call his father, "Dad, are you busy?"

"How did it go, son?"

"Interesting, I'm not really supposed to talk about the meeting. Thank you for putting my name forward."

"He's an odd fellow. I'm not quite sure how I met him, we keep bumping into each other at that cocktail bar you hate."

"The Mews, Mayfair?"

"Yes, don't see him so much since Babs and I got married."

"I bet she likes their speciality drink, The Mayfair Tart."

"John."

"Sorry. I'm sure your second wife loves you."

John's father changed the subject, it was getting uncomfortable. "Yes, McNee is an odd fellow. I don't agree with his politics, of course, but he is far better than his boss. Mary McNee and your mother got on well."

"How is mum, have you spoken to her lately?

"Still drinking, she texts me late at night, it doesn't go down well with Babs."

"I wish she would find someone else."

John's father lowered his voice, "I wish you would. All that money and no one to go home to at night. It can't be right. Are you gay?"

"Dad! You've asked me that so many times, no, I'm straight. Look, I have to go. Before I do, I notice your portfolio with Red Diamond is doing well."

"You've made me a wealthy man, son. You might not be a surgeon, you might not save lives, but you're good with money, I'll have to give you that."

John cut the call after saying goodbye. While his father appreciated the money John made him, it would never be as good as being a surgeon.

Ben honked his horn to get someone out of the way. John smiled to himself, his trusty driver was as impatient as he. Amery's mind returned to the Committee meeting and wondered if he wanted to get involved. However, it was an honour to be asked. He guessed, given he signed the *'Totalis Silento'* addendum, he had no choice even though he was more than busy with Red Diamond.

He'd need to do a lot more research on the Crown Estate. Finding in-depth information would involve more than a Google search on Wikipedia or an airline magazine article read on some transatlantic flight taken god knows when.

Using his iPad, he turned first to Google, the global library. He was due to return to his Florida home, but he wanted to get on to this straight away. The flight over would allow him to write a brief for his research team based in New York.

The fabulous wealth of the Crown Estate was something he'd never given much thought to. After reading the yearly report published by the Crown Estate Commissioners, he could see they managed the holding well albeit conservatively. The organisation escaped many of the ravages of the last few years. Still, income declined similar to many business organisations in the UK. The Crown Estate included fifty-five per cent of the British shoreline. The Commissioners invested heavily in wind energy showing some foresight into the potential of the renewable power source. The investment paid off, and Crown-owned wind farms became the most significant player in a valuable market.

Like most of the British public, John knew the Crown Estate included Windsor Castle and Buckingham Palace. Still, it surprised him the assets included Regent Street in London, hundreds of thousands of farmland acres and several shopping centres. Google threw up some unusual Crown estate Assets; John had no clue as to the value of all 'naturally found oysters and muscles in Scotland.' By his rough calculations, the total worth of the Crown Estate amounted to some £35 billion. Some assets with overt Royal connections such as the palaces would fetch twice their commercial value, so the amount could be £40 billion, more? He imagined the rush of Oil-rich Arabian investors anxious to acquire Buckingham Palace.

The value of the Crown Jewels, which included over twenty-three thousand gems, were pure conjecture. Russian Oligarchs would surely pay many more times their valuation. Wikipedia placed a value on the Jewels above £4 billion. One expert put an estimate of £ six hundred million on the Cullion I, the world's biggest clear diamond set in the royal sceptre. Its slightly smaller sister, Cullinan II, adorned the state crown and the two added up to over £ billion.

The value of the Royal Art Collection included works of most of the prominent artists of the last 700 years. Windsor Castle housed a collection of more than six hundred Leonardo Da Vinci life drawings. The valuation of the Royal Art Collection was estimated at over £10 billion.

Amery pictured some of his art dealer friends climbing over each other to earn commission selling the Canaletto's, Rembrandts, Van Gogh's and more. Even the Royal Philatelic Collection, old postage stamps, was worth over £100million.

The further he dug into Google, the more the money added up. Rights over lands in foreign countries, untapped oil, and mineral reserves, even the Royal Tableware collection could fetch £ Millions.

Now entering Farnborough Airport, Ben interrupted John by lowering the privacy screen, "We're here John. I'll take you straight to the plane."

"Thanks, Ben. I'm not sure how long I'll be in New York or Florida. Will you do something for me?"

"Of course."

"I'd like you to visit all the Royal Palaces. Take your wife and kids if you like. Stay over if you need to, I'll cover the cost. Are the kids at school?"

"They've got a break coming up next week."

"Good, it will give them something to do. I'd like you to take pictures. Not set ones, I can find them on the internet. Give me an idea of their state of repair. The surveying degree you spent four years studying for might get an airing. Look at the Palaces as if you were looking at them from a real estate point of view. Send me a report on each one."

Ben looked at John once again through his rear-view mirror, "Of course, we'll enjoy it. You must be doing better than I thought at Red Diamond John, are you buying Buckingham Palace?

"No, but I might be the one who sells it!"

Ben laughed as John got out of the car. He called back, "Ben, don't rule it out."

On entering his aeroplane, John was greeted by the Captain who told him they were ready to go. Once seated, John declined the drink offered by the only stewardess who had little to do for the remaining flight. The onboard internet connection allowed him to carry on his research.

Google reminded John it was King George III who relinquished control of the American colonies giving them their independence. Retrospectively, this looked the worst move a monarch could have ever made. The 'Mad King' as he was later known, really had no choice in the matter. The establishment of England as the supreme power in the Americas attracted not only many British immigrants but also people from all over Europe. The massive natural resources attracted young and healthy people formally held under virtual servitude by European Aristocracy. Their ambition and energy to build a new life also led to a political movement intent on claiming independence. It was only a matter of time before the people united against their former rulers.

In 1760 King George III, struggled with debts built up through wars waged by his predecessors. The reigning monarch collected taxes and paid for the Government of the country. As Britain's population grew, the government machinery, the debts and other costs became crippling. The Civil List Act was signed transferring the expenses and the rights to collect taxes over to Parliament. In return, the majority of the King's assets were transferred to a trust preserving their value. Both parties recognised the transferred assets had considerable value; the King considered it a loan in perpetuity for succeeding monarchs. Once signed, the 1760 Act provided for an annual payment to the reigning Royal Family to pay for the upkeep of the monarch and other items such as maintenance of the palaces and running costs.

In 2011 the Sovereign Grant Act became law to formalise the amount the reigning monarch could receive from the Crown Estate. From 1760 to 2012, the amount paid was by negotiation between the Government and the Royal Household. The amount fluctuated according to government finances and the popularity of the King or Queen at the time.

Under the new Act, the Government fixed the sum given to the Royal Household at twenty-five per cent of the Crown Estate's profits. By setting the amount, the subject of the Grant was seldom mentioned in the news until recently.

John decided he should catch up on his sleep and moved to the bedroom; a luxury his previous Jet didn't have. Despite his best efforts, John couldn't sleep and continued with his search, turning to the news coverage.

Crippley's new socialist Government was the first to question the Sovereign Grant Act. During his campaign at the last election, it became a subject of much discussion with Crippley claiming it was unfair to the people. Once in power, it took little time for Crippley to act on the Grant. He persuaded King Charles to forfeit payment; 'due to the state of the economy'.

Looking at Crown Estate accounts online, Amery saw the organisation recently reported losses; the first in modern-day times.

Amery was disturbed by the Captain's voice coming over the intercom. "Thirty minutes to land Mr Amery." John looked at his watch, surprised by the time.

He decided to try and finish his briefing document before he landed. There was one factor remaining. In a court of law, it could be argued the purpose of the Civil List Act 1760, was to effectively 'lend' the estate assets to the Government. In return, the Royal Household would receive a yearly payment and allow the monarch to retain the rights he or she had. If the Monarchy was abolished, the King might be able to unwind the agreement.

John wondered if cancelling the 'deal' could allow a claim by a deposed royal family to the previous income derived from the Estate they didn't receive? In addition to the actual Crown Estate reverting to the monarch, the King might be able to claim over £60 billion in unearned income.

Amery, polite and well-spoken, looked out of the window and said to no one in particular, "For fuck sake, we're talking about over £150 billion at least." If John were King Charles, I would be more than a little worried about what a left-wing bastard like Crippley would do to get his hands on the money.

CHAPTER 9 - FAT DUCK

Roger Casement's invite to Chequers from Jarrod Crippley intrigued him given where they'd left the last matter between them. Why would Crippley invite him to the inner sanctum of Government, the country house retreat of the Prime Minister?

Casement's last letter from the Prime Minister was to chastise him on a decision he made as High Court Judge. The PM criticised his decision to free a man who Crippley strongly suspected was misleading the court. At the time, the Judge decided it was better not to reply. The CEO of a large pharmaceutical firm was a greedy and immoral man but not a criminal.

As Casement travelled home from Chequers on the train, he made copious notes despite his near faultless memory. The last time they met in person, Crippley was still the leader of the opposition. The two enjoyed a lengthy discussion regarding the class system, during a tedious reception for foreign notables hosted by King Charles. It turned out both agreed the 'system' in the UK was corrosive and unfair. While Casement enjoyed the debate, the zeal in Crippley's eyes was discomforting, to say the least.

Lances of sunlight flashed between the trees lining the train line. The Judge relaxed and closed his eyes deep in thought; why choose him? Constitutional law wasn't Casement's specialist area, it wasn't even financially rewarding. Roger's law practice, before becoming a Judge, ran along strictly commercial lines. His success as a lawyer bought recognition and increased the size of his bank balance.

Seeing his mother clean houses until the day she died, Casement focused on his finances as much as his law practice. Success came naturally for the black lawyer and recognition in legal circles was a biproduct that came in spades. Was he just a box to tick? Proof they were not elitist nor racist? Of course, many lawyers were both.

Celia, Casement's wife of over 30 years, pointed out he was welcomed to legal society functions but not their homes. The mother of his four children often helped him find his way to the crux of an issue.

On returning home from Chequers, Celia was watching TV and smiled when her husband walked in. She had a large glass of beer on the table by 'his' chair, knowing he'd come in and sit with an audible sigh reaching for the alcohol at the same time.

He gave Celia the rundown on each attendee, and what was said, not sparing detail on their reactions. When he finished, he sat back and drained his glass, quickly replenished by Celia.

Walking back into the room, after her customary ‘thinking time,’ Celia said, "So, this Cromwell Committee... you're up for it?” She was always the careful type, each word and thought mulled over before she said it. “I know what you think about the elite in this country."

When she sat down, handing him his beer, she sipped her own. "Chin, Chin," he said with a smile.

Celia sat close to him on the sofa and raised her glass. She waited for her husband to answer the question.

"This might be interesting. I'm used to dealing with older laws and precedents, but nothing this important or complex. You know me, I like challenges and I'll have to read up on constitutional law; hardly my subject."

Celia nodded in agreement. The man she married completed the Times crossword before 12 every day, she was proud of him. "But do you believe in what our Mr Crippley has in mind?"

Roger took the first sip of his refuelled glass of beer. "I'm not a monarchist...or a republican. The British system is flawed, for sure, but it works. The legal system is one of the best, although money can buy you better lawyers. Crippley wants money, you've seen how he is managing to mess up the economy. Many hold the view republicanism might be a way to make the UK a fairer society, equal the chances for everyone. I was lucky. I'd like to see unlucky people get a better playing field."

"So, you're on board?"

They were alone in the house, their four children now having successful careers and homes of their own. He swallowed dryly. They had good friends, a great life, a stunning, charming cottage. Would it be wise to upset this all? He thought and then said, "I don't really have a choice. I'm not keen on our Mr Crippley, there's something dark about his character."

"Not as dark as you Brother." she laughed to herself.

Roger leant in and grabbed her hand. "I love you. You lift my mood when I need it most. I'm going to do what he wants."

"So, what's the issue?"

Her laugh was infectious now as it rippled out of his own mouth; his wife's ability to read him was exceptional. "The problem is my findings may support the King, not the PM. We may find Mr Crippley's quest for the golden egg might turn into a big fat duck. He won't like it; I worry about how he'll react."

CHAPTER 10 -THE HISTORY GIRL

A year after their mother died, Earl Hazlehurst died peacefully in his sleep. They left behind their children; twenty-one-year-old Heather, and Oliver, who was a year younger.

Despite being firstborn, Heather could never be as important to her parents, the staff at their ancestral home or their school friends and teachers. Heather's brother inherited the Earldom, their Stately Home, and the family fortune. The law passed many centuries before ensured male heirs took preference.

Oliver was blessed with good looks, charm and charisma and possessed their father's good nature which eluded Heather occasionally. Oliver's reputation also gained him many friends since he excelled at cricket, not to mention his popularity with women and his skill as a mathematician. The family fortune was safe in his hands. Oliver understood the business world.

Heather's brother married his school sweetheart. Their son, Michael, was born nine months after making both parents happy, especially Oliver, who secured the line of succession for the Earldom.

Oliver cared deeply for Heather and considered her more than his equal. Heather was brighter, quicker and more gifted than he, but no one noticed, least of all their parents. Their parents favoured Oliver and 'poor Heather' remained his shadow for much of their youth.

No matter how hard she tried to impress her father, Oliver received more attention. Her casual acceptance of her future, in her youth, soured as she grew older. Heather's solution was to embrace schoolwork, to the detriment of all other pursuits. She won a place at Cambridge University, took part in student rallies and joined the Labour Party.

Following graduation, Heather decided not to take a gap year and secured a job as a lecturer at Oxford University. Increasingly she led a solitary life; even more so after she became one of the youngest ever Dons at the University. Her interpretation of the secret scrolls of Hasabana gained international recognition, leading to a whole scale review of the story of the Beduah people. While her sheer determination and focus fuelled her academic excellence, it was at the expense of her social life.

The turning point for the Earl's daughter came on the eve of her thirtieth birthday. Oliver found her one evening at the family home standing on the battlements looking ready to jump the one hundred feet into the moat. Oliver calmly talked his sister down clutching her hand with caring desperation. Dressed only in her nightgown, Oliver found his sister could barely speak, the little she said made no sense. At their doctor's insistence, Heather was persuaded to enter a private mental health unit to seek help and to ensure she didn't harm herself. With the help of psychiatrists and the attentive mental health nurses, Heather embarked on a long journey of psychoanalysis to rebuild her self-image and self-worth.

Heather Taylor-Todd's road to recovery met some potholes. She surprised her family and colleagues when she fell for a handsome PhD student, who was under her employ. Friends didn't warm to Charlie when they married, least of all Oliver. He objected to the union not because Charlie DeWaltud was a communist activist; he simply didn't like the man. After only a year, Heather realised she neither wanted nor loved Charlie either. The divorce was messy, given she refused Oliver's suggestion of a prenuptial agreement. Charlie demanded half of the small fortune their father left Heather on his death. Socialism was thrown away in favour of the fortune he'd seen in her possession. Oliver told Heather he would fix it. Eventually, Charlie dropped all claims and disappeared from her life. Heather never asked Oliver how he sorted the matter or what the price was.

A few years after the divorce, Heather burst out of obscurity when she reluctantly agreed to front a TV show in the UK, a month after her thirty-fifth birthday. The University Proctor was desperate to raise the College's profile. He expected Heather to pay him back for proposing her to the college board as head of her department in the face of some opposition. As the writer and presenter of 'The History Girl', she charmed the nation with her upper-class accent, hippy appearance, and relatability. Never one to be concerned about how she appeared, Heather was sharp enough to know her good looks played a part in her success. The first show led to bigger productions such as 'The History Girl v The Popes', 'The History Girl v Islam' and 'The History Girl meets her Maker.'

Unfortunately for Heather, the failed marriage fuelled her distrust of men and a series of relationships withered to nothing. Seeing John Amery at Chequers in the committee surprised her. More surprising was her reaction to seeing him; his presence knocked her sideways. The man was sexy. Her cheeks reddened when she looked at John although she tried not to for fear of showing him how much his presence affected her.

McNee met Heather socially on a couple of occasions. Mary McNee went to university with her and made him watch each one of her documentaries. In their last conversation at a fundraising event organised by his wife, he recognised the same de-sire to change the class system. When he set about forming the recommendations for the committee, Heather Taylor-Todd was first ahead of other candidates.

The Prime Minister asked to meet her privately following the committee meeting to get the measure of her. As they walked the Long Room at Chequers, Crippley noted Heather's interest in the paintings, particularly of Cromwell, where they came to a stop. As both looked up at the portrait, the PM said to Heather, "I liked your programs on the TV, especially the one recently, it caused a stir. I am surprised they commissioned it."

Still looking at the oil painting, Heather replied, "I know. The silly buggers gave me carte blanche on the subject, so I went for it. Surprisingly, they were pleased with the result as it drew in a new audience and increased their numbers. It kept their name in the news as well; all publicity is good publicity, as they say."

"I'm not sure, anyway, I enjoyed it. Remind me, was it Netflix or Amazon Prime?"

"Netflix."

Turning to Heather, Crippley said, "Yes, Netflix. You upset people when you concluded God was a figment of our imagination. How you linked God to the centuries-old capitalist agenda is a novel concept, one I hadn't considered."
"Thank you," she smiled. "Coming from you, that's a compliment. Yes, God was invented to tame people and keep the elite - whoever they were at the time - in their place."

Not one for small talk, Crippley changed the subject, "Are you with us in our endeavour? After all, you are one of them."

"I expect you mean I'm part of the aristocracy. The daughter of an Earl?" she replied.

"Yes"

Heather took a step closer to the Cromwell portrait and peered at the signature, buying some time while she considered how she should reply. "I can't read this."

Crippley answered, "Hans Holbein, the Younger."

"The class system is unfair; the whole thing is about privilege. I can't help who my father is, but I can help change this country into a fairer place to live."

"So, it is nothing to do with you being the firstborn, denied from inheriting anything because you are a woman?"

"You've done your homework," Heather said as they continued, pausing to look out onto the gardens. "My lineage doesn't control me. In answer to your question, I'll have fun with this. As you know, I'm perfect for the job. I'll help the old Judge with his background material. I expect I'll pick up some meaty morsels which will help us."

"'Us,' I like the ring to that."

"Thank you. My mind is doing cartwheels. One avenue I'm sure we'll find of interest is the actual line of succession. The Royal Family has a lot of skeletons in their closets, they're not exactly known for their fidelity. You never know, we might find the Crown, or the Crown Estate, is not Charles's after all."

The PM laughed. "Heather, I'm sure we'll find we get on together. Harry isn't exactly the image of his father, is he?

CHAPTER 11HARRY - THE LAST CALL

Given his age, my father had limited time on the Throne when the Queen died; it turned out to be less than a year.

Following tradition, my father's Coronation was planned for a year following his ascension to the Throne. Unexpectedly, Buckingham Palace issued the news King Charles suffered a minor stroke one month before the Coronation was due. The ceremony would take place once the effects of his stroke became more manageable.

William and I agreed to keep his actual condition secret; our father was incapacitated. He lost his ability to walk, speech unintelligible and his cognitive ability was in doubt. The doctors were incredibly upbeat; nevertheless, his lack of progress and a further stroke a few weeks later confined him to his bed. I visited my Papa shortly before he died, I wouldn't leave our relationship as it was, or so I thought. I caused him so much grief by moving to the USA and turning my back on my family. Not being able to hear him forgive me would forever be my biggest regret.

The pace of change with my father dying and William becoming the new King, within two years of the Queen passing, unsettled the UK.

My grandmother held the British Throne for over seventy years. Winston Churchill served as the Queen's first Prime

Minister, and she met every President of the United States from Truman onwards. An experience not rivalled in history. Her diplomatic skills steadied the British ship through a range of right and left-wing governments. She also managed to keep the commonwealth together, admirable since they were the countries of the former British Empire.

My father was forever in his parents' shadow. His pioneering views on agriculture and architecture gathered fans over the years but not enough. He had little time to make a mark on the Monarchy since his reign was over in the blink of an eye.

The Queen's opulent and grand State Funeral was attended by the leaders of the world. Commentators at the time called it 'Britain's Last Big Show,' sensing the winds of change which would follow.

In contrast, King Charles' funeral, held within the grounds of Windsor Castle, was a muted affair. Mr Crippley's Government insisted the expense of another State Funeral would face heavy criticism among the British public. I suspected he had another agenda at the time, but I could do nothing about it, nor could William.

Rarely on speaking terms, Katherine and Meghan made it challenging to mend bridges and the two families seldom met in private and never ventured out in public. Katherine insisted William forge his own identity. Meghan felt Kate actively encouraged her husband to distance himself from us both.

Our father used his short time as King to make unexpected and out of scope remarks on many issues of the day. His views were often the mirror of Mr Crippley's and public sentiment in general. King William reverted to our grandmother's style; he never commented on any political issues nor became involved in anything controversial. Given the distance - physical and emotional - I was in no position to promote a more active role in him. William took the Throne in a new direction. He passionately believed in a slimmed-down monarchy, a lower profile. He made sure the wider Royal family were left out of official duties.

I missed Great Britain. While our new home in Los Angeles suited Meghan, I felt at a loose end. Our contract with Netflix excited me at first but my part in it diminished over time. Meghan's chat show became too big a success making the joint projects we planned unnecessary. As fourth in line to the Throne, my position was still considered expendable. William's children were growing up fast. His older son, George, was given lessons to make sure he would be able to handle the position of Prince of Wales when he came of age. By all accounts, George was a fine young man, but I rarely saw him.

I am a red-haired man full of energy. The busier Meghan became, the less I had to do. It was difficult, to say the least. I loved our children and spent a lot of time with them. Archie played baseball well and liked to watch sports on TV with me. Although still young, Philip was academic and delicate. A contrast to each other. It fascinated me how this could happen coming from the same parents.

Sometimes my energy felt barely contained. Secretly, I yearned to find a proper role, a role for a man. My wife's success with her TV show should not threaten my masculinity, but it did.

I picked fights with Meghan, and, although I'm embarrassed to say it, with some of our house staff. I loved a drink and party occasionally but one or two pictures of me leaving a nightclub in the early hours soon made their way across the web. The British people increasingly resented Meghan and me. We were often critiqued, poked fun at and derided. My night time activities merely fuelled the fires burning in the UK.

King William took opinions and advice from many quarters. Mostly, he listened to Kate; her aim in life was simple, family-orientated and children focused. William's reasonable and diplomatic mindset became fuddled as he sought more and more opinions, paving the way for a peaceful decline in the status of the Monarchy.

William sold Balmoral for over £300million to a member of the Saudi Royal Family. In my opinion, this bastion of privacy should be the last personal asset to go. William used the money to endow a charitable trust overseen by Queen Katherine. The remit of the Trust was to distribute money to the needy and deprived people of the United Kingdom. This briefly helped the Royal PR machine, but the effects lasted less than a few months. I told William the money released by the sale should be used to fill the royal fortune, to protect us in our uncertain future. William dismissed my opinion and the thoughts of his closest advisors. William was 'well-meaning but weak,' a sentiment I blurted out to him in argument. The relationship between our households weakened subsequently.

Meghan appeared to grow stronger, certainly less in awe of my family. However, her 'exclusive' interview with Oprah Winfrey some months after my father's death caused me several problems. She said King William heralded a new era and could imagine a new role for us taking on some international royal duties.

No one was more surprised than me when I saw the interview. Kate called me minutes after the interview aired in the UK and offered a little advice. "You and Meghan can't move back to the Royal fold, William wanted you to know."

"Tell him to 'man up' and speak to me himself."

I remember slamming down the phone and cursing Meghan and waited to talk to her when she got home. I arranged to have the nanny look after the boys to give us time to talk.

That evening Meghan was later than usual. She came in and threw her bag on the table in the hallway, expecting someone to pick it up for her and take it to her dressing room.
She didn't see me at first so I said, "Meghan, what made you do that interview?"

"Oh, H, you scared me. Don't creep up on me like that. What interview?"

"Look, you know what I mean. The one about my father, about William."

Her demeanour altered, gone was the tired expression she wore as she entered the house, replaced by most dazzling smile. "I owe so much to Opera. She came up with the idea for the show. You know her, she's been here a few times, I thought you two got along?"

"That's nothing to do with it. You know we can't say anything about the family without passing it by them first. Hell, you should have spoken to me about it."

Megan decided to remove her smile and passed me as she walked to the kitchen. "Where are the children?"

"They're fine. Meghan, you simply can't go on record about my family. You know that."

"I thought I was free of all of this." She turned back to me, "Harry, she asked me as a friend. It was a five minute piece, that's all."

"You said you could see us joining Royal life again, take up a more formal role. Kate is raging, apparently William isn't happy at all."

"You are mad, aren't you? Did your obedient wife break the rules? Should I have one of your PR men to keep me from talking?

"Meg!"

"Meg nothing. I'm fed up with you walking on eggshells with your family. Anyway, I thought you'd like me to put in a word, so to speak. Since the show started you don't seem to have anything to do. You could surely do some good, become involved again with your family, officially I mean."

"I've told you..."

Meghan cut me off, "You *told* me?

"We agreed, no interviews, no off-the-cuff remarks."

I could see the wheels turning furiously in Meghan's head, her expression changed once again. "OK. I'm sorry. Look H, since the children are taken care of...shall we go upstairs?"

Meghan knew how to handle me. I made my point and the thought of going upstairs with my wife began to seem much more important. "I'm sorry, let's put this behind us. Yes, let's go."

Meghan smiled at me again. "I'm sorry too Harry, now come on."

The following day I apologised to Meghan again. To be fair, she also said she was sorry for doing the interview.

I assured Kate by phone the next day that Meghan was sorry about the interview and about her promise to me not to do another. Kate was gracious enough to thank me for my apology, but I doubted her sincerity.

The last call I made was to William. I wanted to rebuild the bridges between us. Unable to sleep the night before, I came to the simple conclusion I'd been busily blaming Meghan, William, Kate and others for my unhappiness. The fact was: I pushed my family away when we moved to the USA. William was my life-long soulmate, so I was a little ashamed to have pushed him away more than anyone. William dragged me through my twelfth year following our mother's death, played with me as kids and drank with me as adults. I realised I spent my adult years telling William how he should be leading his life and what he should do to improve the Monarchy's standing. I decided to seek his advice for the first time since I married Meghan.

I made the call but didn't get through and never would again.

CHAPTER 12 HARRY - AIRFORCE ONE

I received a call in the early hours of the morning from our security detail, housed in a small cottage at the end of the driveway to our Beverly Hills estate. "Dak Henshall would like to speak to you urgently."

My head, foggy from sleep, struggled to understand why I was being disturbed. "What's wrong?

"Nothing is wrong, you're safe, but Dak is coming to the main house, Sir. He tells me it is important."

I answered the door in my dressing gown while Dak wore his usual dark jeans and T-shirt. The air was humid and warm. Beads of sweat glistened on Dak's forehead. "Sir," he said in a subdued voice, "there's no need to worry, you're safe. May I come in?."

I merely stepped aside to let the six-foot-four former SAS major come in. I detected a slight hesitation; still, my head was clearing, I might have imagined it. I followed him into the hallway. "Dak?" My voice was hoarse, still waking up.

Dak hesitated slightly, "There has been a terrible terrorist incident in the UK, Harry."

Since he joined our staff, I insisted on first name terms. Hell, we'd served together and partied together.

With a sense of foreboding, it was hard to speak. "The news

is still coming through, but something has happened at Sandringham."

Immediately pictured the vast fossil of a house in rural Norfolk used extensively by my grandmother, loathed by my father, now William's English country home. "What! Tell me?"

Dak, hardly a sensitive man, placed a hand on my arm. "It is the King, the family..." He stuttered, unable to make a sentence... "They were out at the beach, taking photos of the kids having a great time. With their security, of course. An inflatable came in from the sea. They, the men on the boat, had guns and shot the two security men dead. A third security man was shot but barely hurt." He looked down.

"And?" I said.

"They shot them, them all." His grip tightened. "Harry, they're all dead."

My legs went weak, Dak moved in to steady me. "I am so sorry. So sorry"

We struggled to the library, where we had shared more than a few whiskeys together. Dak sat me down in the heavy winged leather chair near the fake fire Meghan liked so much; I hated it. I looked at Dak and let out a hollow scream. Tears rolled down my cheeks. All I could say was, "No, no, no."

Meghan came running into the room dressed in her silk nightgown, alerted by my scream. Dak filled repeated his story as I sobbed. She came to my side, "Harry, oh poor Harry. Dak, leave us alone for thirty minutes. Sort out the security. Someone needs to protect the King."

In my sorrow, it took me a minute to understand what she said. My one true friend, my brother and Kate, the children; they were all dead. The implications were far from my mind. Always the quick thinker in our relationship, Meghan pointed out the obvious. Our life, the happy place we made for ourselves here so many miles from London and the Crown was over. Years ago, I stepped back from my Royal duties. Now it was time to step up. With the realisation coming to me as Meg said 'the King' my pain doubled, and I collapsed in front of my wife.

An hour after being told about William, the house was surrounded by police and officers from the FBI. Meghan, the children and I were in our bedroom. The noise and lights outside woke the kids up. They became distressed by the activity outside and, I'm sure, the vibes both children picked up from us.

My phone rang incessantly. Calls came in from old friends, unknown numbers and the text messages made the cell phone beep continuously; I turned it off. I gave Dak instructions to contact the Prime Minister and take guidance and advice from him. We dressed and tried to distract the children with cartoons on the TV while Meghan and I talked.

"We have to go back," I said.

Meghan, miserable with concern for me and our kids, said, "I know, H. I know, we'll have to go back for a while to deal with the fallout."

"It will be for more than a while."

Meghan hugged me tightly. In a small girl-like whisper, she said, "I know, I know. Why can't your family, your Country, leave us in peace. We've been so happy."

Meghan, typically, saw the events of the last few hours on her terms, what it would mean to her, the children and to me. I said, "It is my family, it is my Country. Meghan, I can't deal with anything else. I have to deal with what's happened to William, Kate, their children."

Meghan merely hugged me tighter, as if letting go would make events happen faster. Her tears wet my shoulder; they were joined by mine. Her tears were for us. My tears were for my brother and his family.

Dak came into the room and said the President of the United States was on the telephone. I was surprised, I hadn't spoken to him for over a year. In his eyes, my position as King of their most important ally meant I'd be talking to him more regularly from now on. I took the phone from Dak and waited for the White House switchboard to put me through.

"Harry," he said in his bombastic loud voice, "the American people, and I, commiserate with you, Meghan and the British People. You have been dealt a terrible blow as have everyone in the United Kingdom. I am truly sorry."

"Mr President," I said, using his formal title, maybe to remind him he'd not used mine. "Thank you so much for your call." I was yet to speak to the British PM or any other official, so I was surprised my first call was from the President.

"Now listen," he said, "we have Airforce One on its way to Los Angeles Airport. You can't use an ordinary plane; we don't know who may be after you. We need to make sure you and your family get to the UK as soon as possible."

Ever the Englishman, I said to the President it wasn't necessary, we could sort out the arrangements ourselves, but it was kind of him. In response, the President said, "Now listen, the world is in free fall. Stock markets are down, Britain is locked down and Europe is on high alert. I won't take no for an answer. "

I was annoyed by President Cuomo trying to take over. Still, at least I didn't have to worry about how to get home. I handed the phone back to Dak and told him how strange it was to receive a call from the President and not Mr Crippley. I mentioned this to Meghan, she didn’t like the PM, and that was only after having met him once. She said, "Be careful, Harry. He might not let Airforce One land."

CHAPTER 13 RAF NORTHOLT

Crippley watched the TV at his office desk in No. 10 as a frail Princess Anne waited to greet the new King at RAF Northolt. Hours before, the PM called the President to object to Harry's use of Air Force One, suggesting they could wait until an RAF plane could be flown over. Typically, the President told him to stay put with his old plane, after all, Harry already accepted his offer.

Princess Anne climbed the Air Force One steps, and the TV commentator said, "The situation is unusual. The new King will step on British soil from an American President's aircraft."

Crippley's Butler, watching the King said, "How strange, coming to Britain in an American President's plane."

Crippley slapped down the remote control on the table. "Yes, on Air Force bloody One for fuck sake. The cheek of Cuomo. He did this on purpose. Harry played right into the Italian thug's hands."

The Butler looked puzzled. "Will there be anything else?"

"Get out."

CHAPTER 14
HARRY - DARK FORCES AT WORK

As I climbed the Grand Staircase past portraits of my ancestors, my head reeled from the events of the last 48 hours.

Airforce One was a comfortable pleasure. Meghan appreciated it more than I. The American in her. Apparently, it was a dream come true for a US national. The staff aboard the 747 were pleasant and helpful. I was brought up with well-trained but reserved servants, it amused me how friendly the crew were. I wondered if they were the same when the President travelled? I suppose so.

We landed at RAF Northolt and my Aunty Anne, Her Royal Highness, The Princess Royal, to use her formal title, came aboard. She shocked me by curtsying as soon as we met, our relative seniority had changed from my last visit.

"Your Majesty."

"Anne, don't curtsey." I kissed her on both cheeks, surprising myself how emotional I felt.

"I might as well get used to it, so should you," she said, typically to the point. "Meghan, good to see you."

"Likewise," Meghan said quietly. She once told me she thought Anne was the hidden enemy. I told her she was paranoid, there was little warmth between the two. They dutifully kissed.

"I know we spoke on the phone, but could we talk about Will..." Unexpectedly tears came to my eyes. "I'm sorry, seeing you, coming home."

Meghan moved closer to me, linking arms. "Don't worry about him, I've got it."

I looked over to Meghan. Oddly, I felt she was trying to claim me, hold me back as if seeing someone from my family was a threat. "Meghan, can you sort out Archie and Philip?"

Megan instantly uncoupled her arm from mine, "Sure."

Anne watched her walk away. "Meghan has taken this well, she has been a great help."

"I'm sure she has."

"Come, sit, tell me, is there any more information?" I pointed to the seats usually occupied by the press when the President was travelling.

"They caught up with the gunmen on a boat headed for Belgium. The Navy cornered the ship they were using but were too late to capture the five men who blew themselves up, sinking the boat in the process. Like I said on the telephone, it is assumed they were Islamic terrorists; members of the newly resurgent ISIS 'state'."

"Assumed?"

"There's something decidedly fishy if you want my opinion. You were not around when Uncle Dickie got blown up by IRA terrorists. Those were dark times and, in many ways, the assassination didn't come as a surprise. The IRA was very active at that point, Northern Ireland virtually a no-go zone."

"I've read about it, father often spoke about him, never about him being killed though."

"ISIS, Islamic terrorists, I haven't seen them in the news here recently. They appear to have drawn back from their activities in Europe since the war between Iran and Iraq flared up a couple of years ago. No, it is different. William's assassination came out of the blue."

"Have you spoke with Crippley?"

"Your Prime Minister, Harry?"

"I guess he is, I'm not sure about him."

Anne looked up as one of the crew walked by us, waiting until they disappeared. "Yes, I've spoken to him, not our greatest fan, is he? Mr Crippley assured me the people behind the murders would be found and their leaders called to account. Not sure if I believed him, he will not try that hard. The way he is running the country, he is doing more damage than terrorists ever could. I assume you're up to date on how it is going here? It is a mess, Harry. Welcome home, you have a lot on your plate here." Anne lent over and put her hand on mine, it surprised me, "Will you be OK?

"Thank you, Anne, I will be, I have to be. I'm not sure Meghan will cope so well."

Anne looked at me, about to say something. Instead, she made a move to get up. "Come on, Harry, time to be King."

I wanted to ask more of her but Meghan came back in with the Children. Philip looked very tired, I went to pick him up, but Anne stopped me. "Your photo will be taken as soon as you exit this plane. The image will be on the front page of every newspaper and pictures on every screen in the world. Let Meghan look after the children. Walk out of here with your head held high."

I looked over at Meghan, who nodded. I went towards the

door and threw my shoulders back before I stepped out to face the press.

As we approached Windsor, I saw the Castle from a fresh perspective; it was effectively my home, or at least one of them. The imposing presence of the round tower could be seen from miles away even though the rain poured down, reminding me I must get used to English weather again. I mentioned the rain to Meghan who merely rolled her eyes; there wasn't much my wife liked about my country, unfortunately.

At Windsor Castle, we were met by George, the Master of the Household. We were shown into the private apartments, last visited when my grandmother was alive. My Papa and William only ever met me at Buckingham Palace on my infrequent visits back to the UK.

William told me the private apartments at Buckingham Palace were made over by Camilla once my father became King. The decor was exactly as I expected, pictures of horses, country style furniture and a keen smell of dogs. However, I found the Camilla touch missing in Windsor. There were still worn carpets and old sofas the Queen insisted on keeping way beyond their expected lifespan.

George D'Languil, the first-ever black Master of the Household, led us inside and we sat down to brief us on arrangements. George, a Frenchman, spoke to us in an accent I found hard to understand initially. William made George's appointment; it was so like him to make a conscious effort to help people of all races and colours.

Despite his formal and somewhat archaic title, George is the Chief Operating Officer for the Royal Firm, all staff reported to him. He seemed nervous, unsettled. "George, how are you, this must have been a shock to you and the entire staff."

“Your majesty, we ‘ave been through bad times but never as dark as this. My condolences to you and her majesty,” said George who briefly looked at Meghan.

“Thank you. Have you made arrangements for us and the children?”

“Yes, of course, Sir. We ‘ave the private apartment ready for you. If you are in agreement, we ‘ave made plans for you to stay at Windsor. The security is better ‘ere than at Buckingham Palace.”

“Yes, that is fine, let’s go up, the children are tired. I am too. Meg?”

Meghan spoke for the first time, “Yes, let’s go, hoist the drawbridge.”

I began to smile but stopped myself, it occurred to me my wife was trying to make a point.

George sensed the situation and changed the subject, “The Prime Minister will be here at nine a.m., Sir. He will be joined by other members of the Accession Council to formally declare you our new King.”

“Oh, you’ll have to guide me through all the formalities, George. I didn’t have the training my brother received.”

As we walked up the stairs and along the long ancient corridors of Windsor, Meghan and the boys followed in silence as George used the time to outline the diary for the next few days.

As George went on, my mind zoned out. The details and the tasks ahead were mind-boggling. A few days ago, I was playing with the children in our garden in LA, not really a care in the world. Now I felt the world on my shoulders. I don’t mind saying, I feared for our lives as well. As my grandmother once told me of my mother's death, "There are powers at work in this country about which we have no knowledge."

CHAPTER 15
LIGHTING THE FUSE

Robbie McNee landed in a British Government plane at Hyde Field, the closest private airfield to Washington, for his meeting with General Thiskwood. He expected to see General Thiskwood waiting for him. As he got into a waiting car, a nondescript driver in plain clothes merely said, "General Thiskwood is expecting you. It will take forty minutes to get there."

Robbie, tired and already feeling the jetlag, replied, "Where is there?"

"You'll see, there's no need to bother you with details, the General wants a quick meeting and I'll bring you straight back."

McNee didn't bother to reply, a little disappointed he would have no opportunity to do some shopping for the children. They would be expecting something from his trip given he was forced to miss Rosemary's birthday. His daughter was five today, something he and his wife, Mary, thought would never happen; the little girl caught meningitis the year before and it was touch and go for some time.

Robbie sat back in his seat and stared blankly at the unimposing buildings passing by. He dozed off for a few minutes before hearing the engine stop.

"We're here, Mr McNee."

Robbie opened his eyes and looked at a grey office building,

"Here?"

"Yes. You'll find the main door open. Take the stairs located by the elevator to the tenth floor. The General will meet you there. The elevator is out of service.

McNee entered the faceless office block which looked unoccupied. The carpet tiles, dirty from years of use, smelled faintly of mould and there were faded pictures of other office blocks on the walls of the entrance hall.

As McNee climbed, the sweat stained his shirt, his breathing laboured.

"Come on, man. What's taken you so long?"

McNee looked up, panting, as the General stood above him, "General, so good...to see you."

"You should exercise more," Thiskwood said as they shook hands.

The small corner office contained a few computer monitors and a couple of chairs obviously leftover from previous tenants. The General walked to the window and, with his back to McNee said, "Sit."

General Thiskwood turned around from the window and walked over to a large board. Silently he wrote 'Operation Catesby' on the heavily marked whiteboard in a red marker. McNee briefly wondered if the pen was permanent, a mistake he'd made too many times.

The General remained standing, and said, "Robert Catesby was the instigator of the catholic plot leading to the failed attempt to blow up the Houses of Parliament where Guy Fawkes was captured. While Catesby was forgotten over time, Guy Fawkes is remembered each November 5th where people burn fires, let off fireworks and some burn effigies of him.

"Your Mr Crippley, you and others want to destroy the Royal Family, the British Monarchy, like the Gunpowder Plot of 1605, 'Operation Catesby,' is, therefore, a suitable code name."

McNee could see the General was pleased with himself, it made no difference save for the need for secrecy and anonymity for him and the PM.

"Here, have some water. You're still sweating. You back-office types think you can go on and on without taking care of your health. I sprinted up those stairs."

"Thank you," McNee replied, thinking how self-righteous Thiskwood was.

"I've studied most of the major battles since the Second World War. I have a library in my house in Louisiana where I've built a treasure chest of some of the best and most valuable battle strategy documents and plans. Eisenhower, Rommel, Patton and historical figures such as Napoleon and Alexander the Great - they're all there, I've read all their battle documents."

As McNee relaxed and found his breath, he became a little calmer; he was happy for the General to rattle on. The research provided by the intelligence team attached to No. 10 gave him all he needed to know about the General. Thiskwood referred to 'his' house. The magnificent Louisiana Mansion belonged to Carolina Thiskwood, the valuable documents in the library were bought with Carolina's money.

McNee discovered Thiskwood's colleagues respected him and appreciated his talent, but they didn't like him. The research confirmed the General possessed an uncanny ability to predict an enemy's response. His vision earned him the name 'the chessman' such was his skill at planning out moves and countermoves.

The General continued, "Of course, I've been involved in our own Battles. Remember McNee, I've been at the heart of successful campaigns like the Gulf Wars. Operation Catesby needs time to work. If you are to get the support you need, we must take our time. I know we are looking at other factors; the line of succession, the money, and the law but your monarchy's survival, as I see it, depends on the goodwill of the people. Of course, this has ebbed and flowed over time, but it has remained remarkably stable over a long period."

McNee was impressed, "General, you have it spot on."

"You Brits don't like collateral damage, but there has to be some to change this view, we need the British public to fall out of love with their Royal Family."

"What do you mean, collateral damage?"

The General took a seat in front of McNee, his form silhouetted against the bright light pouring through the window behind him. "The thing we all signed, the Totalis Silento, binds you as much as me, right?"

"Yes, of course."

The General pushed the folder marked 'top secret' over to McNee. Inside the front cover, the first page was entitled "Operation Catesby."

McNee started to open the next page but was prevented by the General who placed his big hand over his. "You'll find this hard to read. When it comes to getting something done here, we need to act without sympathy. Our targets need to be set fast and hard. There's no room here for no man's land, no room for prisoners. Are you sure you want to read this?"

As the General moved his hand away, McNee turned the next page. At the top of the page "King Charles" was underlined and emboldened. A list of simple bullet points followed:

- Unpopular

- Poor Comparison to QE2
- Quirky
- Interfering
- Blood Pressure
- Susceptible to Stroke
- Administering the drug
- Immediate result; Stroke (possibility 80%)
- The expectation of survival; (5%)
- Deniability; (95%)
- Cost of operative; $150,000

McKee looked at the General who smiled in return. "Is this..."

General Thiskwood looked hard into McNee's eyes and nodded slightly. McNee felt sick, had he signed up for this?

CHAPTER 16 HARRY - SEX, LIES AND VIDEOTAPE

I finally entered Westminster Abbey, it was packed with family and friends, heads of charities and dignitaries. As this was not a state funeral, heads of state and other world leaders were absent. Out of respect to our family, however, many sent senior representatives. Minutes before I set off from Buckingham Palace, Jarrod Crippley's office issued a statement declaring the PM indisposed through illness.

Meghan and the children were by my side as we watched the five coffins carried up the aisle and placed before the altar: two large, three child-sized.

As the music filled the Abbey, images of William filled my mind. My tears came, I wasn't too embarrassed to cry at my brother's funeral.

The chair provided for me for the service was hard and unforgiving. A slight twinge in my back brought me back to the present. I looked over to Meghan as the Archbishop of Canterbury headed towards the end of the funeral service. The life we both fought so hard to build thousands of miles away was over for me. Looking sideways at Meghan, I wondered as she held each of the children, how long she would stay by my side.

The Government wanted us to keep the funeral to St George's

Chapel at Windsor. Crippley told me it was my father's wish for his funeral to be held at St. George's Chapel, and I should follow the format with William's funeral. I didn't believe my father would ever indicate his wishes to the PM and doubted Crippley's words. At the time I disagreed, William eventually put his foot down and our father's funeral was also held at Westminster Abbey. Crippley was nothing if not consistent.

Given the muted reception of people outside the Cathedral, he may have been right. Nevertheless, the funerals for our father, grandmother and past monarchs to King Edward the Confessor were conducted here. Some stayed entombed here, but later Kings and Queens were buried at Windsor.

It was presumed, after the death of our father, King William's reign would last many decades like our grandmother's; the longest-reigning monarch in history. William's reign was a month shorter than our father's. He didn't make it to his coronation either. George, William's son, would never get the opportunity to become King. Fresh tears came to my eyes as I looked at his small coffin next to his brother and sister's.

Although I helped organise the funeral service, the succession of choirs and readings made my mind wander. Images of William came to mind, I pictured the whole family playing in Windsor's private gardens back in happier times before I broke away from the family firm.

William's accession to the throne naturally increased the popularity of the Royal Family. The newspapers and online headlines repeated their assertion of a new age. William, forever kind and thoughtful, was rightly popular. His decision to sell Balmoral was received well by the press and the people. The money helped Katherine, often in the shadows, to flower as the head of the Queen Katherine Charitable Trust.

William occasionally called me to fill me in on his reforms. He reduced the number of staff, cut the King's flight to one helicopter, and opened more rooms in the palaces to the public. Britain's multicultural population received the news the King would no longer be the formal head of the Church of England; a move which gained him plaudits around the world. Kate and William travelled overseas less frequently, dramatically reducing costs which gained favour in a nation struggling in post-Brexit and Coronavirus times.

Meghan and I were based in America most of the time. Our painful separation from the royal household behind us. Meghan's TV show received a cold review from the British press and, while it received excellent ratings in the UK, it was a sign we'd sold out. Friends told me they felt Meghan was taking the spotlight and I should be careful I didn't let Meghan eclipse me. I was happy to stay in the shadows, it suited me after spending all my life in the glare of flashbulbs and blinding TV lights.

Of course, none of this helped me with my family. While William and I repaired our relationship and spoke frequently, our wives didn't speak at all save for the few trips we made back to the UK. My contact with the rest of the family reduced considerably and, with Meghan, non-existent.

Toward the end of his first full year as King, the public's attitude toward William soured considerably. The family was rocked by the publication of intimate pictures of Queen Katherine with her royal protection officer. William told me the images were fake, I believed him. Meghan laughed, saying "Kate hasn't got enough passion," but the public took their publication as a further reason to doubt the 'value' of the Royal Family. There was some further damaging news about Prince Andrew's past activities and poor press regarding his daughters 'cashing in' on their status. Bad news came weekly. The revelation our grandfather, Prince Philip, kept a mistress for over thirty years shocked the nation and me. There was a constant flow of negative stories online, on TV and in the newspapers. Kiss and tell stories about improper behaviour of palace officials caught looting presents and selling them on-line became a TV sitcom based on 'true events!'.

My brother was accused of selling a few forgotten paintings from the Royal Collection to a wealthy Japanese investor and pocketing the proceeds. Of course, William denied this, but no amount of reassurance from him could rescue the situation. Indeed, the PM mentioned a full 'review' of Crown assets would take place to assure the public no further items could be sold off by William. I believed William, the people didn't.

William's year grew worse when phone calls between him and Katherine were published online by Wikileaks. I heard them, the whole world did. They argued, both accusing each other of infidelity. My sister-in-law, customarily reserved, sounded chillingly cold and startlingly malicious as she threatened to live apart and take the children with her. I phoned William when I heard the news, he refused to answer my calls, but he sent me a note, telling me the calls were fakes as well. The evidence was so overwhelming, I found it hard to believe him. I dropped the matter diplomatically, a first for me.

By the thirteenth month of William's time as King the monarchy was a mess; finances were in disarray and the family's popularity at an all-time low. Nothing my brother said could heal the rift between the public and the royal family.

In previous years, in past decades, the monarch received undying support from the PM. However, William received little help from No. 10. Crippley would fan the fires, not put them out. His statements to Parliament erred on the side of doubt. In one of our last conversations, William said he was sick of the PM. I told William he was paranoid. He pleaded, "I need someone to believe me."

I should have.

Upon our arrival in England, this time with me as King, I consumed newspapers, watched TV and looked online to try and gauge the extent of the decline in our family's popularity. Meghan concluded, "Harry, you've inherited a bag of worms. The last few years, your father's years, your brother's, they've done a fine job of making this family a laughingstock, a stock the public no longer wants to buy."

I wasn't so sure. As a well-informed outsider to the royal firm in the last few years, the constant stream of bad news looked orchestrated. Maybe it was I who was paranoid?

It was time to leave, but I couldn’t tear myself away from the coffins, tears filled my eyes. I cried for my brother and remembered Kate from when we were close. The sight of the three smaller coffins was shocking but, as I mourned my brother's family, I felt anger growing from the pit of my stomach; I wouldn't let this happen to my children. I recalled my grandpa saying to me before Afghanistan I needed to trust my gut instinct and it would keep me safe. Now my gut was telling me something was wrong, very wrong, and I didn't feel safe.

CHAPTER 17 -THE BUTCHER KING

Heather Taylor-Todd called Robbie McNee on the secure telephone given to each member of the committee following their first meeting. "Robbie, how are you?"

They were all told to only use the safe cell phone relating to 'Operation Catesby'. Heather Taylor-Todd considered it a little clandestine to have an operational name. It occurred to her the code name should be a bit more circumspect; still, apart from her and other historians, most people didn't know who Catesby was.

"Fine, fine," he said, sounding distracted. Heather wasn't surprised, the recent general strike led to unrest. Garbage, uncollected for weeks, piled up on the streets in the country. The streets of Oxford and Cambridge became rat-infested and smelt dreadful. "Heather, what can I do for you?"

"Robbie," she said, using his name again to get his full attention. "There is little new regarding the line of succession not already in the public domain. The further one goes back, the less I believe or can prove. I've been thinking about this, I think we need to work in the present. I can work on my other project with John." By far, the most essential part Heather had to play was to track down the history of the Crown assets. Her task was to find out what they were and how they were obtained. This would help John Amery's evaluation of the Crown

Estate and assist Casement in his deliberations.

"So, you've found nothing at all?"

Heather sighed, realising McNee needed a little more proof she was doing her role correctly. "Possibly the most convincing story traces back to the War of The Roses; a fight between two branches of the same family in the fifteenth century. We found a centuries-old claim Edward IV was illegitimate, meaning the succession should have passed to the 'Loudoun' family. Simon Abney-Hastings, 15th Earl of Loudoun, dismissed the idea he was the true King of England. He's a butcher in Australia and is happy with his life there. Given the trials and tribulations of the British Royal Family, he may have a better life chopping meat."

"Ok. Have you got plenty of time? Are you looking hard enough?

Heather detected McNee's frustration; it matched her own in being questioned on her ability to perform the task. "The Cambridge University Library contains over nine million items; I know where to look! I have four of my PhD students helping me. I assure you, Robbie, we've researched every snippet we could find regarding the British Crown's line of succession."

"Ok, I'm sure you have done a thorough job, Heather. Let's work through the current heirs. It is obvious Charles is Queen Elizabeth's son. Concentrate on Harry, we've all heard the rumours about him.

"James Hewitt?" Heather asked.

"Yes, Princess Diana and Hewitt were lovers for years; the likeness between him and Harry is undeniable. I don't think it will unsettle King Charles but, let's face it, he has been getting bad press of late."

"True, it isn't going well for them, is it?" McNee replied. Heather noted the irony in his voice. She figured out another player in the Catesby Group, probably Ronald Brereton, was busy with the anti-monarchy fake news machine.

"I will get on it. I'm sure we can obtain some of Harry's DNA one way or another. I might need Brereton's help. Now, is there anything else?"

"How are you getting on with Amery? He'll need a lot of information from you."

Heather felt her patience with McNee finally running out and answered "Fine, I'm speaking to him later."

On hanging up, she readied herself for the next call she had to make this afternoon to John Amery. The information was ready, the list questions he gave her a few weeks before was more than satisfied. The next call would be by secure video on their safe cell phones. Absentmindedly she wondered where he would be and what he was wearing this time?

CHAPTER 18 HARRY - A FRENCH LETTER

Windsor Castle loomed ahead of us, disappearing each time the wipers crossed the screen. The four of us were in the back of the ageing Bentley limousine given to my grandmother by the company years ago. Archie and Philip were asleep, snuggled next to Meghan who stared ahead, stone-faced, deep in her own thoughts.

The plan was to transport the coffins to Windsor later, so they'd arrive after us. We left them safe and under guard at Westminster Abbey.

William and his family would be interred outside St George's Chapel with a temporary memorial marking their resting place. St George's was full of resting former monarchs. I planned to have something built as a lasting memorial, I wouldn't forget William, Kate and the children. I was determined to future-proof their lives. To immortalise them.

I didn't want a wake for William and his family due to the nature of their death. Also, they were all too young to be mourned over canopies and wine.

As the Bentley drew up to the doors of the Castle, a tiredness swept over me. Meghan took the children to their rooms once we reached the private apartment. Despite the changes Camila made elsewhere, it was still pretty much the same as when the Queen lived here. It was much more comfortable than at Buckingham Palace, it reflected my grandmother's tastes; chintz everywhere. I went straight to the cocktail cabinet, the one new addition William made when he became King. I liked Vodka mostly, but tonight I chose a whiskey, the day called for a sharper drink.

Alone for the first time that day, I finally took out the piece of paper given to me by the French Ambassador's wife. Virginia Dumont, an American, married her French husband over thirty years ago. Formally a successful executive, she was glamorous and the epitome of sophistication. Virginia agreed to help me with the French authorities to gain their support for Invictus, the 'Olympic games' for disabled ex-servicemen I founded. I met her on several occasions, I liked her. I was more than happy she came up to us after the service was over despite it being a surprise; it wasn't exactly the right etiquette for the occasion.

"My dear Harry," she said, "my heart goes out to you and your family" as she leaned forward kissing both cheeks. At the same time, she placed a small note in my hand. "Please," she said quietly, “don't read this until you are alone." She looked at me, I nodded, and I put the note inside my pocket, forgetting it until now.

The note was handwritten, presumably by Virginia. As I read, Meghan came in and I put it in my pocket; I would follow her wishes.

"They're down. Asleep already," Meghan said. "Pour me a Jack Daniels please, I need one after today."

I did as I was told and handed the glass to her, making sure it had ice and Coke, as she liked. She was an infrequent drinker, and an advocate of my cutting down, or even stopping. Not likely, especially given my new responsibilities.

"Harry, when do you think I can get back, Michelle is a temporary host although she is doing a great job."

Meghan seldom surprised me. On the day of my brother's funeral, she was thinking of her career. When Michelle Obama said she'd stand-in for her, she was so pleased. Ratings for my wife's show went up, driven by the publicity the Obama name generated in the USA and beyond. I guessed Meghan might be a little jealous. We'd been caught up by the whirlwind of the last two weeks. Neither of us had the time or wanted to discuss the future. Meghan dropped the subject of our lives in America until now.

I hesitated, trying to think of an answer to placate her. To me, it was a foregone solution; our lives in the US were over. I went to say something and stopped. I really didn't have the words. She just sipped her drink, crossed her legs and gave me a long, unwavering stare. I felt a little ashamed as the prospect of sex went through my mind, she had great legs.

"Well, Harry?"

Again, I said nothing. I stood there, a deer in the headlights of a speeding car.

She took one last sip of her drink. Meghan placed the glass down on the table in front of her and stood to leave. I think I heard her say something but didn't catch the words. I should have gone after her, but I was too tired and I didn't know how to handle the situation.

As she walked out of the room, I collapsed in a chair, exhausted. I felt the note in my pocket and pulled it out. It said, "Someone wanted Charles and William out of the way. Your father was poisoned. Protect yourself from your Government. I can't tell you anymore as it will endanger my family. Be careful, my friend. V."

CHAPTER 19 - MR CRIPPLEY'S CHALLENGE

The PM called Robbie McNee at midnight. "Tomorrow, before 8. The chequers, we need to catch up," was all he said .The late-night call caused another argument in the McNee household. Mary McNee resented the PM's constant call on her husband's time.

Sat alone in the Great Hall, McNee surveyed the valuable art and sumptuous decor. Crippley loved Chequers and took on a 'lord of the manor' air when he was here. He used the house extensively for business and pleasure. However, the PM's love of the country estate was at odds with his socialist beliefs. While the nation suffered and significant assets were sold off to the highest bidder to help the country's dreadful financial state, the PM never mentioned selling Chequers. Most ministerial houses were sold to Marriott the previous year including Dorneywood, usually the Chancellor's country residence. In all, fifteen country houses belonging to the nation were sold, bringing in £50 million. The amount was enough to fund 30 minutes of UK Government Expenditure which topped a trillion pounds for the first time.

Robbie looked down at his feet and noticed his socks were slightly odd; one dark blue and one black. He rushed this morning, woken by the car sent to collect him. Mary had moaned at him to turn the light off and he really couldn't see what he was putting on. His tie didn't go with his shirt either. She would often say his mind was too busy to have the time dress appropriately. She was right as this wasn't the first time he came to a meeting with odd socks.

McNee jumped as the PM came into the hall. He stood, "Good Morning, Prime Minister."

"I'm sorry you weren't included in my little weekend party McNee. I have something for you to do. I didn't trust the telephone," said Crippley.

McNee replied, "Of course, what do you need me to do?" From the outset of his Premiership, Crippley treated Robbie McNee as the friend who stood by him over many years. Gradually their relationship changed, their personal closeness becoming more employer/employee, more formal. McNee liked to think he remained the same man. Jarrod Crippley's position changed him; the old Jarrod would have at least said hello.

Crippley sat and Robbie chose the seat opposite. He waited while the PM settled himself. When he came to power, the Prime Minister carried extra weight, he was at least twenty pounds heavier now.

"I want to make sure Judge Casement is still on board. He sent me this report yesterday, have you seen it?"

"I haven't, I'm sure he was thorough?"

"Typical lawyer, he gave me all the arguments but didn't come down on one side or another. We need him to give us a definite steer, we won't have another chance. Make sure his heart and mind are on this. We chose Casement because of his background, his beliefs. I can get any lawyer to do an essay on the ownership of the Crown Estate, I need one who is going to find how we can get at it, take it completely out of their hands. I don't need arguments for and against."

McNee sensed another speech and cut in; he wasn't called to Chequers for this alone. "I'll go and see him today. Was there anything else?"

Crippley smiled, the benefit of working together so long was each read each other's thoughts. "Yes. Now listen here, this thing is going far too slowly. I like the General's plan, I think we chose the right man for the job. We've made progress, but the simple fact is we need more action. The country doesn't grasp or understand our ideas as much as we would like. It needs to speed up. In fact, Robbie, I wonder if you are the problem?"

McNee's face reddened, he tried to splutter a reply. "I, I..."

Crippley stood slowly, "No matter, I'm sure you are doing your best. I need you to get in touch with all the committee members again. I expect a lot more action before we meet next Sunday. Use the information we have on all of them. Get someone to visit Ronald Brereton's son to give him a little message, so their father pulls his finger out. Threaten Heather Taylor-Todd, see if we can make her think we will engineer a withdrawal of her university funding. Use the Financial Conduct Authority to lean on Amery's firm. Roger Casement's been looking for a peerage, maybe a little bad news could be organised, so he gets the message too. I want each of them to arrive next Sunday with a flea in their ear. The days of being calm and collected are over, let's pressure each of them."

McNee wasn't at all surprised, "The General sir, you missed him out?"

The PM, was already on his way out, but stopped and said, "The General likes what he's doing. He can't wait until the next stage. A simple 'well done' will suffice but tell him the plan needs to be brought forward."

"Yes sir, of course." The door shut quietly. No 'hello' and no 'goodbye' thought McNee. Alone, he wondered why the PM was so tolerant and trusting of the General. It wasn't like Jarrod at all. Perhaps his old friend was wary of the American; maybe he should be a little more careful in dealing with Arthur Thiskwood as well.

CHAPTER 20 - SENDING A MESSAGE

Alex Brereton loved life at Oxford University. His was a small group who went up to Oxford from Millfield, a sizable private boarding school, noted for its sporting achievements. Alex was on the school's rowing team, his ambition was to row for Oxford, an honour and very good for his future career. He was fit, tall and strong, the perfect profile for the elite university team.

Initially, Alex partied hard at university, making the most of his first taste of freedom coming from a boarding school. Recently, he was concentrating more and more on getting his place on the University team. The pre-dawn training sessions in the cold mornings ruled out drinking and partying the night before.

One morning, returning from an early training session on the river, Alex found the University security officers located outside his rooms. They allowed him to enter where he met a man in a suit sitting down on his sofa. There were several small plastic bags set out in front of him on the coffee table. The man asked who he was and when he was told, pointed to the items on the table.

"We've discovered Class A Drugs in your rooms here, we've been informed you are selling to other students."

The warmth drained out of him, as he said, "I've never seen these before."

The man stood and smiled. He didn't introduce himself and walked towards the door. Turning back briefly, he said, "You'll be asked to attend a disciplinary meeting with the Proctor in a week. I would suggest you return to your family home, make sure you tell your father, you'll be sent details of when and where to go for the meeting. We have taken the decision to inform the police following the hearing. It is our standard practice."

Chip Stourbridge, Chief Financial Officer of John Amery's firm, was called to attend a meeting at the Canary Wharf offices of the FCA; the Financial Conduct Authority.

Chip was used to meeting the FCA, usually held in Red Diamond's offices. The sudden directive from the firm's supervisor at the FCA to attend a meeting at their offices the next day surprised and worried him. The last time he'd locked horns with the FCA was because they objected to Red Diamond's use of private polling in and around the Brexit vote. Red Diamond gained significant financial advantage having predicted, correctly, the British people would vote to leave the European Union. This knowledge allowed them to take massive short position against the British Pound. The profits they made were significant; the highest one-day profits in Red Diamond's history.

John Amery directed the firm to be far more aware of the FCA's powers and invest in compliance personnel. Chip, the other directors and all the Red Diamond staff worked hard to prevent the firm from being picked on again by one of the most potent financial authorities in the world.

Chip took the decision not to bother Amery with the news and attended the meeting alone at the unusual time of seven in the morning the following day.

Told to arrive alone, Chip found the tall glass building almost empty. The typically buzzing office block in Canary Wharf was silent with one solitary security guard handling reception. The guard expected him and gave him a visitor pass in return for his passport he'd been told to bring. Again, this was far from ordinary. As an American living in London for over five years, handing over his passport made him feel insecure, at risk.

Chip double-checked his tie and suit in the elevator's mirror as he rode up to the top floor conference. Business dress at Red Diamond called for smart chinos and a good shirt. However, he never held a meeting with the FCA without a suit. Even his shock of wiry red hair was combed as best he could.

Stourbridge headed for the large conference room at the corner of the building. He'd been here a few times, usually for group meetings and once a formal evening drinks event to welcome the new supervisor for hedge fund firms. He knocked on the door which was opened by one of the support staff he recognised from a previous visit.

Sitting alone at the large conference table was a woman he never met before. The letter said he was to meet his usual supervisor, a man.

"I've been waiting for you. I am Carly Sharp."

"I hope I am not late; I don't think we've met before, I was expecting...."

Sharp cut him off, mid-sentence, "Take a seat. This won't take long. I am chief of Cyber Security here at the FCA. I've been told your systems and procedures surrounding your computer operations are not up to the standard required by us."

"We have invested millions, our Supervisor, he will..."

Again, Carly Sharp interjected, "Red Diamond may have to

cease operations while we conduct a thorough review. I suggest you message John Amery and get him to take this seriously. Tell him we met and the FCA is concerned about the lack of security. Make sure he gets the message as soon as possible. Tell him I've even communicated my concerns to the Cabinet Office. We'll be in touch by the end of the week." She stood and left the room without saying goodbye or shaking Chip's hand.

It was Chip's strangest meeting with the FCA; before hours, with someone he never met before and they were usually polite. More importantly, the most significant warning sign a British host could use; no tea or coffee was served. Chip felt a cold shiver run down his back. This was too hot to handle alone, so he remained in the conference room and called John Amery. He couldn't remember if John was still in the UK or the States, Chip hoped he wasn't about to wake him in the middle of the night. Still, he was anxious to get this red-hot potato off his hands and into his boss's.

Tim Lenman, Roger Casement's clerk, welcomed Sally Benfield into his office. The appearance of the tiny bespectacled lady in her late fifties belied her role as inspector of finances, an influential role.

Tim said, "Welcome to Judge Casement's chambers, Mrs Benfield."

Sally Benfield's expression hardened, "Ms," she corrected him.

"Sorry, Ms, your call yesterday evening was a surprise. Our annual review is due in four months, isn't it?"

"Something has come to our attention and we felt it required an extraordinary visit. We have analysed your office finances, there is an anomaly."

Tim's stomach tightened. He had been with Judge Casement

for years. The Judge, a brilliant man, avoided administrative tasks in favour of the cases he was handling. Each morning Casement would arrive and throw any receipts he remembered to keep on Tim's desk. In the last 'administrative' meeting Tim held with the Judge, he pointed out his ongoing claims needed to be reviewed and brought up to date. "Ok, perhaps we can discuss it. Can you leave details with me to find out any issues and I can come back to you?"

"I am afraid not, Mr Lenman," said Ms Benfield, "there is too much here to brush under the carpet. I will be staying here and will need a desk and access to all your files, your administrative files."

"Surely there's no need for this? The Judge has a busy schedule, we are swamped. The amount of money must be insignificant. We all know the Judge prefers to concentrate on his cases, not administration."

Ms Benfield slowly took off her glasses, revealing her small beady eyes. She looked at Tim Lenman in the eye to catch his attention, "Mr Lenman, over five hundred thousand pounds is missing. The Judge has signed several capital expenditure requests, we cannot identify the items he authorised."

Expecting the Judge in less than an hour, Tim excused himself citing the need to go to the restroom. As he walked to the toilet, he rang the Judge, something was strange here and Casement needed to be made aware.

CHAPTER 21 - JALFREZI TO GO

John Amery took Chip Stourbridge's call mid-flight on his way back to the UK. As Chip relayed his meeting with the FCA, Amery was struck by the strain in his voice.

The phone rang again as soon as he put it down. As much as he wanted to, he couldn't ignore Heather Taylor-Todd. "Hi Heather, can I call you back a little later, I'm dealing with something."

As if not hearing John's request, Heather said, "I can't believe this John. They are threatening me with a withdrawal of all my funding. I'll have to close down my department and disband the three teams I have in place. It could be the ruin of fourteen bright young PhD student's careers. For god's sake, aren't we supposed to be on the inside here?"

"Slow down, Heather. Start at the beginning. What happened?

"I got an unexpected visit from the University's finance manager. He told me a whole load of crap about 'tightening of finances, the need to streamline, my department was the least valuable in terms of contribution.' Out of the blue, he said I needed to give a full justification, or the department is gone, the History Department, or my section of it, its history, so to speak."

John paused, gathering his thoughts, "Why call me?"

Heather laughed on the phone, "Come on, John. This is Crippley, he is sending me a message. What I want to know is, why now? I've been hard at work; we've found out some pretty useful facts. Why have I been singled out?"

"I don't think you are the only one." John didn't want to relay the conversation he had with his Chief Financial Officer; it was market sensitive. He hesitated but decided Heather could be trusted. "I think they're doing the same to me, us, at Red Diamond."

"In what way?"

"It's stuff to do with the FCA, they are concerned about our systems. It came out of the blue too; it can't be a coincidence. We are being sent a message here. They want us to be on our toes when we meet later this week. Crippley wants us all to know we are under his control; he pulls all the strings. He must be worried about something."

"It is pretty bad here. The pound is down again, there are national strikes, the NHS is critically underfunded. A poll has come out about Crippley's popularity, or lack of it. Even Margaret Thatcher in her last days of government didn't get as low a rating as Crippley."

"Heather, can we meet today? I land in two hours. I can come to Oxford from Farnborough and be there by three in the afternoon. I think we have more to discuss than we thought."

"I am busy this afternoon," she sighed. "Why don't I come down on the train later and meet you in London? You could buy me dinner if you like."

"I may have to watch my pennies."

Heather laughed. "You've more than enough. How about an Indian meal on Brick Lane? I don't think anyone we know will see us there. Besides, it is cheap."

"Ok, I'll buy the food, you get the drinks."

"Other way around, I've heard about how much you drink."

"Deal. I'll book a place and send details. See you at eight." John put down the phone and found he was looking forward to seeing her.

The Bengal Village on Brick Lane looked more like a Greek restaurant than an Indian. John Amery found it online, he trusted the Evening Standard food critic Fay Maschler who called it the 'best Indian in London'.

He sent Heather the details a few hours before and told her he'd have a car waiting at Paddington Station, so she didn't have to fight the commuters on the Tube. His driver called forward to say she was slightly delayed, so John went into the restaurant as it was raining outside.

The table at the back of the restaurant was reserved. Even though it was near the kitchen, they could talk in private here. The waiter took him to his seat and John ordered his favourite drink, Tiger beer. His eyes were a little heavy. He planned to sleep more on the flight over but the succession of calls and papers he needed to read before arriving made it impossible.

The last call before landing was to Chip Stourbridge who couldn't understand why John was seemingly unconcerned about the FCA threat. John told him he would sort it by the end of the week and that he needed to trust him on this occasion. There was a note of relief in Chip’s voice, glad that John would be sorting out the problem.

The coded threat from Crippley wasn't a surprise. The PM's reputation for blackmail and coercion were infamous. But why had Crippley felt the need to use it against him or Heather? They were on with the job in hand. His team produced a comprehensive report in less than a week, confirming his quick valuation of the Crown Estate.

While John waited for Heather, he re-read a report sent by his Head of Research, Ajay Sadeky. He confirmed they were on the second list Heather supplied, detailing the other assets such as the feudal rights collected by the monarchy over the centuries. Sadeky also listed valuable gifts given to the family so they could be called part of the overall Crown Estate.

Like all financiers, Amery skipped to the last page of Sadeky's report, looking for the total: £165 Billion so far. It was an amount which would put King William at the top of the world's wealthiest people. It was also equal to sixteen per cent of the UK government's yearly expenditure or less than ten percent of the national debt. While the assets would take time to sell, the proceeds would be of tremendous help to the UK's treasury. With Crippley's economic strategy in tatters, it would buy him time to mend the government finances if the public voted to become a republic. Several polls published recently suggested this was a real possibility.

Disturbed by the door opening at the front of the restaurant, John looked up and saw Heather walking towards him. Dressed in a sapphire blue trouser suit, her luxurious black hair pinned up, a real picture. He rose to welcome her and kissed her on both cheeks.

"You look wonderful. Well."

"I'm a little overdressed for an Indian restaurant on Brick Lane, I know. I promised a girlfriend I'd drop by her charity event after and support her."

John saw Ben outside, waiting under the umbrella he used to walk Heather to the restaurant and nodded his dismissal. The driver would be back in less than an hour; more than enough time to eat and to catch up with Heather.

As the waiters fussed over her and laid a napkin on her lap, it gave him time to look closer without being noticed. Small beads of rainwater glistened in her hair. She wore a delicate gold and diamond necklace which plunged down between her breasts. He looked away to his menu as she looked up.

"What Charity?"

"The Cystic Fibrosis Trust. My friend has supported them for years. Life is hard for CF sufferers having to take thousands of pills and need daily physiotherapy to keep their lungs clear. Many spend months in hospital, I'm more than pleased to help where I can. I think my brother being an Earl helps, he'll be there."

"I won't keep you long." He said brightly, trying not to show his disappointment.

"By the way, John, I've been thinking on my way here. Why are you helping Crippley, what's in it for you?"

"Typical Heather." He smiled. "Straight to the point, I'm a republican,"

"You're whatever you need to be to make you even wealthier."

"Ouch," said John, "That hurts."

"So?"

"They've promised my firm will be involved in the sale of the assets."

"Let me see. My brother gets a nice little commission when his firm is involved in a sale. You must be on to collect at least 1%."

"Not far off," John said, picking up the menu, hoping she'd move on. "We have more than enough to discuss before Cinderella has to go to the ball."

Heather Taylor-Todd laughed, "I have a good-looking brother, not an ugly sister in sight."

John smiled, "Let's order. We have a lot to talk about."

The waiter took their order, John asked them to bring another Tiger beer. Heather asked for the same.

"Lady Heather Taylor-Todd, drinking an Indian beer. My word."

"Drop the 'Lady,'" she said with a slight edge to her voice.

The violet of her eyes seemed to pierce him. "Tell me more about the funding, Heather."

Heather recounted her conversation with the University treasurer and filled in on some of the people she'd disappoint, especially the young post-graduate students hoping to gain their doctorate. John filled her in on Chip's meeting with the FCA. He explained to her how it could seriously affect his firm's ability to operate not only in the UK but in Europe and perhaps the USA too.

"Why does Crippley feel he has to do this? I'm more than doing my end of the deal. I'm sure you are trying your hardest as well," she said, goading Amery.

"I'm doing better than you, Lady,"

"John!"

Amery winked at Heather without thinking about it and smiled. She smiled back. His face grew more serious, he continued, "In the States, it is all about money and who has leverage. Here in the UK it is all about political influence, the money helps, but it is 'favours for favours'. Apparently, according to my team, Crippley is a master of it. His 'modus operandi' is to use a carrot and a stick. My carrot is the enormous financial rewards, what are yours?"

Heather declined to answer at first. The waiter brought them poppadums, which gave her the excuse to momentarily change the subject. "My great grandfather worked for the Viceroy of India back in the Empire days. It helped the family fortunes somewhat."

"See, it is who you know."

"I guess so." Heather took another swig of her beer, "Two reasons really. My post-graduate students are selected on merit. I had to take on a sub-standard student because my hands were forced by the 'old boy' system. It is how it works in Britain. You know it. The class system makes Britain unfair."

Amery couldn't help but nod.

"Crippley and his sidekick, poor Robbie, know what I stand for."

"Why 'poor Robbie'?"

"I'm not sure about him. He is married, but the man is clearly in love with Crippley. Not because they have similar beliefs. Perhaps it isn't love, maybe he is infatuated by the man. McNee would never be able to stand up either on a debating platform or in the House, he doesn't have the confidence or gravitas. Crippley mistreats him. McNee always comes back for more with his ill-fitting suit and odd socks. Mind you, McNee is no intellectual slouch, Crippley is lucky to have him at his beck and call."

"That's pretty much my take on McNee. In a way, I think he helps Crippley in smoothing out his more radical views. Tell me, what is the other reason, you said there are two," John said. He snapped a poppadum in half and spread lime pickle liberally on one piece before he put it in his mouth.

"My word, your breath will stink tonight. How can you eat that stuff."

"And the other reason?"

"My Brother is a good man. Successful. He carries a lot of responsibilities, takes a lot of pressure with his business and the estate..."

"And?"

"Two years ago, he did something out of character. Crazy you could call it. It was all hushed up at the time by the family's PR machine."

John looked at her, "What?"

"It is hard to say. In fact, would you mind if I told you another day?"

"Ok. But if Crippley has something on him, why threaten you with the withdrawal of funding?"

"They know I love my brother. Of course, he is my younger brother." Her face grew more serious. "I will have to check with Oliver on where he is with his...er...problem. I think they want to pile the pressure on."

John decided not to press Heather. "My team did some behind the scenes work on Crippley, asked a few questions, spoke to a few people. People we could trust mind you. They say he is like a chess grandmaster; he calculates every move and makes sure he is prepared for anything. He won't want us to speak to anyone about this, now or in the future. He must feel his 'Totalis Silento' clause in the documents we all signed needed to show its teeth. The UK is tanking in the global markets, Crippley really needs this to work out for him. Of course, he also believes in what he is doing. He is a true socialist."

Heather snapped her own poppadum, mirroring John's actions moments before. "Are you saying I'm not a socialist?"

John sipped his beer and left a pause slightly too long for emphasis. "I am not so sure."

"It doesn't matter what you think, Mr Amery."

"True, it doesn't. However, I do think you look stunning tonight, comrade."

Heather blushed, she took another sip of her beer to give her time to reply. "Flirt."

"A name I've been called before. I'm only giving you a well-deserved compliment."

"Only... that's a disappointment."

"Now you're flirting."

"My train journey was eased by three glasses of cheap railway wine. Now I'm drinking beer. I could make some bad decisions here".

"I hope you do. Another beer?

Both Heather and John were saved from answering by the arrival of the second course: Chicken Jalfrezi. The waiters fussed about them, giving them both time to think.

As John watched Heather concentrating on her food, a feeling he long since parked to the back of his mind came to him; he wanted to spend more time with this woman, he wanted her in his bed.

Heather caught John looking at her, "John, you have something on your chin, messy eater." Heather reached over with her napkin and dabbed his face softly, removing the small spot of curry sauce. As she did so, he gently touched her wrist and felt a shock. Their eyes met and they held each other's gaze.

Heather eventually broke the silence, "John, we, um," she stumbled.

"We should..." His mind raced.

John still held Heather's wrist and moved his hand into hers, they intertwined their fingers.

Heather tightened her grip on John's hand but said, "I have to go to the thing...the charity auction."

"Why don't I give you a ride, Ben is outside."

Heather pulled her hand away at last but did so gently. "I, I've had enough to eat, I'll be late. Yes, I... I'd appreciate it."

John reached for his wallet and counted five ten-pound notes out and placed them on the table. Paying by American Express would take too long, he wanted to keep Heather in the moment. Apparently, so did Heather, who stood grabbing her bag. He helped her with her coat. They walked out of the restaurant to the car parked on the street nearby. They surprised the driver by opening the door as he watched something on his phone.

As John closed the privacy screen, something made him look back at a man on a motorbike taking selfies. A thought occurred to him; why was the man in a blacked out helmet taking selfies in the dark of night?

CHAPTER 22
HARRY - CALLING IN THE TROOPS

I couldn't hold a coherent thought after reading the note. I stayed up trying to find reasons not to trust the information the letter contained. Maybe Virginia Dumont liked the idea of playing with my mind, my emotions?

I got to know Virginia when someone suggested I asked her to help with my Invictus Games organisation. I needed the French on my side, I found there was no one more capable persuading the sometimes-obstinate French to come along with my plans. Virginia cleverly won the French and many other countries to lend their support. She genuinely cared for the Invictus men and women, I trusted her.

After several whiskeys, I decided I should believe the information contained in the note; someone poisoned my father. They caused his stroke in the sure knowledge it would bring about his demise in a short shift. Could she be right about William? I wanted to believe she was wrong, besides, how could she know? If there was the slightest possibility she was right, someone must be behind this, could it be my own government? How far up did this go?

Over the last few years of both my father's reign and William's, the PR machine was brought into question. My family was being targeted from all directions. The brutal murder of William and his family left no doubt someone was eager to destabilise the UK. Credit went to Islamic extremists for the assassinations, which I believed until I read the note.

My mother said we'd be manipulated and controlled by the family and the courtiers to the Royal Household and the politicians, so it was essential to develop a sense of self. She told us so-called friends would let us down and to make sure we placed our trust in only a few people who demonstrated their loyalty. Just a few months ago, William and I discussed the very conversation. He complained about one of the Palace mandarins suspected of leaking false details about his marriage. Our mother's wise words came back to me then, I told William he should go with his first reaction and to fire him. He agreed but said he found it difficult to trust anyone, maybe that was why he called me more in the last few months.

I needed an ally. If the note from Virginia was correct, who could I trust? I inherited the same people close to both William and my father at the Palace and in Westminster. Some were close enough to slip something into my father's food or drink, maybe even inject him with a substance to bring about his stroke. If Virginia was correct, the same people could be behind William's assassination.

I felt trapped; boxed in on all sides. It made me think of my fighting days in Afghanistan, especially the time we were in Helmond taking flak from the Taliban; that same fear from that time visited me again.

I spent ten weeks in Helmond undetected by the press or by the Taliban. While I was passionate about serving in the field of operations, I had to accept I would be a valued prize for our enemies. I served Queen and country as Harry Wales for ten weeks in Afghanistan; the first time in my life and felt ordinary, never freer.

The top brass helped me get to Afghanistan without being noticed. The news blackout held fast until a German rag leaked the news of my posting. I fought with the Gurkers, the group of elite Nepalese soldiers under the wing of Major Chancre Bahadur Pun during my tour of duty. The soldier I remembered most was Colour Sergeant Raj Rai because he saved my life.

In Helmand province, the war was aggressive and bloody. Each day our patrols were targeted by the Taliban. I made such a great effort to be there and to serve with my regiment I could hardly ask to leave when the going got tough. I won a lot of praise for my time served in one of the world's most bloody conflicts. However, there were more than a few occasions I would happily board one of the Royal planes to get out of the hot hell hole of a place.

One such time, Raj Rai and I were out on an afternoon patrol; the hottest and most dangerous part of the day. We were sent to a small village five miles from the barracks to check out reports of men seen hiding in nearby hills. I had no idea where the intelligence came from, we followed orders. Five of us travelled out in a wreck of a Land Rover which should have been taken apart for spares years before. Occasionally, I wished my presence would receive some sort of priority when it came to vehicles. I kept quiet, as Harry Wales would do; I was not HRH in Helmond.

Nowhere was safe in our part of Afghanistan. At least in the countryside, we could get some sort of idea of the perils. The small village, a few miles out from our base near Deshu, was war-torn; partially flattened by bombs and scarred by gunfire. With each bend in the street, a bombed-out building could pose a threat from hidden snipers and people willing to blow themselves up if we came close enough.

The villagers we saw on the streets as our Land Rover made its way through the town were either old or young children.

There were no men or women of fighting age to be seen. This was not unusual, but it did put us on our guard. As we turned the vehicle around, our exploration fruitless, I felt Raj Rai stiffen next to me. We're taught in the army to watch each other's backs; it was all about teamwork. While I was capable, I wasn't battle seasoned and seeing Raj Rai tense made my stomach tighten.

Ahead of us lay the remains of a religious building, the ornate brickwork of a former tower lay shattered on its side. We'd driven around it on our way through the town so would need to manoeuvre around it our way back. Without warning, I felt a brutal push in my side, knocking me down and out of the Land Rover. I landed on my elbow and pain shot up my arm in lances of white-hot agony. Raj Rai threw his body onto mine to stop me from moving. I'm a foot taller than the little man, but it felt his entire weight on me; I couldn't move or see anything. Split seconds later, an almighty roar boomed. A bomb. The sound of the explosion blasted through my ears, deafening me. Next, I felt my bulletproof vest being hauled up. I opened my eyes to see Raj Rai lifting me back into the vehicle. Two of our unit members lay next to the car, dead. Only three of us remained. Raj Rai threw me down into the back seat and jumped over to take hold of the steering wheel. Despite its condition, the Land Rover's engine roared into life and we set off. I recovered my composure and fired off shots into the dust cloud thrown up by the speeding vehicle. My finger never left the trigger, I continued shooting even though we were well out of range of the village and the bombsite. I loaded and reloaded my machine gun even though we soon reached the open countryside.

Eventually, we came to a stop overlooking a ridge which gave us excellent visibility. Raj Rai reached behind and laid a hand on my shoulder. He told me to stop firing. The third man, Tip Rai, offered to take over the steering wheel. Raj Rai hopped into the back and grabbed me firmer. I was shaking all over. I'm not proud of this, but I vomited into the sand. My mind flashed with images of our fallen men who lay dead, bloodied and battered by the bomb.

Raj Rai held me and didn't speak at the time. Neither did I. Later, as we limped home after calling in reinforcements and a clean-up squad, I tried to thank him. I couldn't find the words. He held his finger to his lips and made a 'shushing' noise telling me to stop trying. All he said was, "Harry Wales, I am sure you would do this for me. Here we are equal. We are a team. I would always protect you." All I could do at the time was smile and accept his words.

I went on more missions with Raj Rai, none so bad, but we became friends. Forbidden to ask me about my family, I warmed to him as he told me about his wife and children. Raj Rai married young; an arranged marriage which produced two children. He carried a picture of his family in his breast pocket and he had the habit of placing his hand there when he spoke of them.

When I was forced out of cover by the press, the top brass made the call to withdraw me from Afghanistan. I stayed in touch with Ray, as I called him. He left active service and did well in a training role, climbing the ranks and taking more senior positions. He travelled the world but eventually returned to Gurkha Regiment HQ; Shorncliffe near Folkestone in Kent.

Raj Rai received The Prince of Wales' Kukri in 2017, one of the Gurkha regiments highest awards for lower-ranking soldiers. My father was more than happy to comply with my request given I told him during my time in Afghanistan how Raj Rai kept me safe and out of the firing line.

The last time I heard from him was when the world learned of my brother's death. He was one of a few who had my cell phone number.

I dialled his number. Who could I trust more than someone who saved my life?

CHAPTER 23 - A GENERAL OBSERVATION

Carolina Thiskwood liked her routine. After an early start and a busy day, four in the afternoon was the time she reserved for herself. She usually drank iced tea on the veranda while reading. Today, Arthur was asleep on the lounger invading her space; his snoring annoyed her.

Carolina looked at her vast bulk of a husband sleeping in the shade on the terrace of their country estate outside Louisville, Kentucky. It amused her how different he was asleep. Awake, Arthur could never sit still. Even as he read his endless military texts, newspapers, and reports, he was never still. When not reading, he was moving, when he spoke it was a few decibels louder than anyone else.

"Arthur, Arthur!" She yelled, trying to wake him.

Thiskwood opened his eyes and reached for a gun which wasn't there.

"For heaven sake Carolina, why did you wake me up?"

"I'm sorry, I didn't realise you were asleep," she lied, "you never sleep in the daytime. Don't you have anything to do?"

"I'm busy enough."

Carolina said, "Yes, I saw the luggage in the hall. Are you off somewhere? You're not late, are you?" Carolina was afraid Arthur had begun a new book. She really couldn't stand another bloodletting on the scale of his first autobiography; 'Balls to the Walls'. Even the title offended her southern sensibilities. "Are you working on your next book Arthur?"

"No, something else."

"Share?" Carolina said, knowing the word annoyed him.

"Don't worry your head about it, it doesn't concern you," he replied. He got up from the lounger and looked out across the green fields of the ranch, his back to Carolina.

Carolina wished he'd leave the veranda and the house. Carolina signed up for the marriage to Arthur Thiskwood many years before, pretending to be disgusted by her father who arranged the whole thing. Her father didn't know a military husband was her ideal partner. As she predicted, he was away from the family for months on end, leaving her at Arkle Wood, the ranch her father eventually left to her.

Carolina's father's fortune, shared between her and her siblings, allowed her to be independent. She had lots of friends, mostly from the same background; people who shared her interest in horses and horse racing. A husband always away on service allowed Carolina the freedom she craved. Since Arthur's retirement, it was an arrangement she wished could be restored.

Arthur came home from time to time, enough to sire two children and convince her friends he wasn't a figment of her imagination. However, since his retirement, he was at a loss as to what to do. Unfortunately, Arthur was used to being the boss and he steadily encroached on her life after the furore caused by the book's publication died down. She didn't like it at all.

Their daughter, Darlene, was a girl after her own heart and she helped out at Carolina's successful horse breeding business:

The Arkle Stud. Bernard, ever a disappointment to his father, made his own way in the world, rejecting the idea of service in the Army as Arthur would have preferred. Carolina was proud of her son, who based himself in San Francisco. He recently made a lot of money on an internet venture, had a bayfront home and happy life. Bernard rarely came home, preferring to put as much distance between him and his father as possible.

Carolina realised neither she nor her husband had spoken for some time. She sipped her iced tea. "It would be good to have something to do. You know you get bored."

"I'm not bored. I'm off in an hour. I'll be out of your hair. You can get on with your horses. Anyway, I'm finished with writing books."

"Oh?" Carolina was glad he found something new to do with his time. The book was her suggestion. It was easy to get Arthur to jump at the idea after her campaign of mentioning how impressed she was with major autobiographies of famous people. It took a few weeks of subtle hints and suggestions. Arthur announced his intentions to write the book one morning over breakfast, a meal she much preferred to eat alone.

"Balls to the Walls" took over a year for him to write and a lot of Carolina's money to get published. While Carolina was prepared to support her husband, perhaps for selfish reasons, she didn’t expect the backlash from friends who shunned them such was the incendiary content of the manuscript.

Once involved in writing, Arthur hardly bothered her, and those fourteen months were as if he were back in service. The book tour took another six months, but when it was all over, he was home with her again. This time it was worse for Carolina. Arthur barely left the house as more and more of his friends and colleagues chose to freeze him out of their social circles. It was sad seeing a man like Arthur become isolated. It didn't surprise her; when she read his manuscript, she counselled him against some of the more explosive passages, but he ignored her as she expected.

Carolina witnessed her husband's spirits deteriorate. Too proud to admit he made a mistake, he continued to call and contact people only to be knocked back with messages they were not available. No one called back or got in touch by email.

Arthur tried to reconnect with Bernard by flying out to the West Coast. Sadly, their son had long ago given up hope of forming a healthy father-son relationship with his father. Arthur came back a little bruised, using Bernard's work commitment as the reason they only had one meal together; Arthur planned to stay for a week. He returned a few days later and was at a loss of what to do with his time. He sat alone in his vast library at the house, surrounded by militaria, photographs of his army times and books on military history.

Carolina noticed Arthur had a new project because he looked as though something was preoccupying his mind. The change in his general demeanour surprised her; he was happier. However, as time passed, the feeling in her bones told her all was not well given how driven and secretive he became.

"Where are you going? England again?"

Arthur turned around. "What do you know about England?"

"Oh, remember, you mentioned something the other day. No, wait, I'm sure one of the staff was looking for you. An important call, apparently. Long-distance, from England."

"Maybe?" He would leave the truth hanging. "Right, I'm off. I'll be away for a while."

As he walked into the house, Carolina wasn't surprised he made no attempt to kiss her or connect in any way. The truth was she didn't much like her husband. His treatment of young

Bernard was burned in her memory. Arthur would demand he play ball in the yard, try to teach him moves on personal defence and watch football games on TV when he was home. Bernard, ever accommodating, did as he asked but hated every minute of it. His love of computers and programming left Arthur cold.

As Arthur climbed the ranks of the Army, his trips home became shorter. Nevertheless, he tried to get all his parenting in the short breaks between duties. Bernard became increasingly resistant to doing anything with Arthur who took to calling his son a 'pussy' and a 'geek.'

Darlene wound Arthur around her little finger when she was young. Arthur doted on her. Sadly, their daughter increasingly shunned her father, not being able to face the way he treated Bernard . Their children were close, Carolina spoke to them often and Darlene would see Bernard at least five times a year in California, never at Arkle Wood. Carolina loved her son's easy-going manner and they would FaceTime each week. She looked forward to their chats as Bernard made her laugh with anecdotes about his life in San Francisco. Occasionally, she travelled out to San Francisco. Bernard always made those times special.

Arthur's renewed level of activity worried her. When he was working on the book, he would often give her updates and ask for her opinion: seldom given and never taken. He told her nothing about his latest project. He didn't say what the calls from Britain were about or mention who he was meeting. He could be gone for days giving no clue as to where he had been and why.

Carolina followed Arthur through the house in time to see her husband load luggage into his Cadillac.

"Have a good trip," she said. Arthur looked up and merely nodded as he would do a stranger and climbed into the car, not looking back. As she watched the large vehicle make its way along the long drive from the house, she decided; she needed to find what Arthur was up to.

The library at Arkle Wood was impressive. Her father built it and stocked it with books, but Carolina rarely saw him read. She was more than happy when Arthur adopted the space as his own, she seldom went into the room. The library was at the rear of the house and made dark and drab by the mahogany panelling and dusty books and drapes.

Sure he wouldn't return, she decided to spend an afternoon in the room. She told her staff not to disturb her as she needed peace and quiet as she had a migraine coming. She wondered why she needed to give them a reason as she never had a migraine in her life. Perhaps it was because she intended to go through every paper and document she could find. Arthur didn't use the computer save for emails and for watching the occasional military clip on YouTube. She was sure she'd be able to find something about what he was working on. Arthur kept a meticulous filing system and an orderly desk. He catalogued his own library so she would be able to find her way around.

Carolina seldom entered the library when her father was alive. If her father called her in, it was usually to be told off for something. When she and Arthur moved in, she was more than happy for her husband to claim it as 'his' domain. Carolina felt a chill run down her spine as she entered the room; the smell of Arthur's favourite aftershave lingered, adding to impression he had a presence here. Unlike the rest of the house, the light was subdued and distinctly masculine.

Carolina made her way to the large old English' partner' desk. She vividly recalled the image of her father ready to tell her off for spending too much time with the horses and not concentrating on her schoolwork. Carolina jumped as something moved, only to laugh at the reflection of herself in the gilded mirror hanging on the wall near the desk. She looked over and saw herself; a picture of wealthy elegance albeit 'pleasantly plump' as she liked to think of herself. Unlike many of her friends, Carolina didn't spend tortuous hours with a personal trainer and eating 'rabbit food' to maintain her figure. She wasn't lazy, her horses kept her more than active. Her greying blond hair was styled in a 'Grace Kelly' style adopted years before. Smiling at the reflection, she decided to sit in Arthur's chair and work on her task, determined to find out what her husband was involved in.

The items on the desk were set out precisely. The writing pad was pristine, two Mont Blanc pens were set out perpendicular to the pad as were the telephone, a calculator, and a hole punch. She noticed a full container holding the punched-out holes.

The two filing drawers which supported the table top were locked. Thinking, Carolina pushed the chair out and dipped under the table, hoping no one came in and saw her ass in the air. She reached to the furthest end of the desk and pulled a small latch, a little too small for her fingers. Years ago, they tackled the lock with ease. She and her sister would sneak into the room sometimes when they were young. 'Daddy's Room' fascinated them, mostly because it was usually out of bounds. Long ago they found the 'secret key' to the draws only to be continuously disappointed by the contents: boring papers.

The key, more of a lever than a real key, was tough to move. It hadn't been opened by either sister for years. She wasn't even sure her Daddy knew of its existence; she was sure Arthur didn't. She tugged again and again until it eventually moved with a thump releasing the locking mechanism.

Carolina made herself comfortable once more in the chair. As she opened the draw, she wasn't surprised to see the file labels in Arthur's neat hand. The subjects were a surprise, though. Printed in capital letters were a series of labels naming the most prominent members of the British Royal Family. Before she delved into any of the files, she took her time to open the other draws. One was full of clippings and notes neatly stacked and clipped together with a staple.

Returning to the first file she noticed, entitled King Charles, she picked it out and laid the folder on the desk. The King died a year back so it piqued her curiosity; why would Arthur have a file on the late King?

There were a series of papers, all nicely kept in place with a ring binder and sections, suitably headed with colourful tabs. The first section was entitled 'Drugs.' There was some sort of medical report, her eyes were drawn to a line highlighted presumably by Arthur.

'Methamphetamine will trigger a gradual increase in blood pressure and will accelerate the heartbeat. Methamphetamine, if administered in a large enough dose, may result in a stroke usually within twelve hours.'

The next section headed 'Medical' contained several pages. Carolina flicked through the sheets copied by someone in a rush, Arthur would have someone court-marshalled for sloppy copying. Her heartbeat quickened. Even though she had enough time, and no one would bother her, Carolina felt a rush of adrenaline and her face flushed. Many of the pages were similar, albeit with different dates. They were the medical records of the late King Charles. By the time she finished looking at the pages, it was clear the former King suffered from high blood pressure. She met him once, albeit briefly when attending a polo match with her sister in the UK. Carolina didn't speak to Charles, he wasn't the King at the time, but recalled his flushed cheeks and a ruddy complexion. Her sister said he might be a drinker. The medical records confirmed high alcohol consumption but not anything out of the ordinary according to the handwritten notes.

The penultimate section of the file contained typewritten sheets. Arthur used an old IBM electric typewriter convinced it added a level of security as it couldn't be hacked.

A picture formed in her mind she didn't care for. Carolina decided to leave the room and closed the files. Arthur's lingering presence in the room became overpowering. She decided to return once she was sure he was out of the country when she could be sure he wouldn't return.

On Carolina's return to the library the next day, the desk, the one she'd known since childhood, was missing from the room.

CHAPTER 24
STANDARD PRACTICE

Ronald Brereton was one of the few people with a direct line to the PM. He used it as seldom as possible and, usually, the calls went in one direction, from the PM.

On this occasion, Brereton called the PM safe in the knowledge it was the most secure line in the country. The two-way encryption introduced a momentary pause as each person spoke, not a problem in normal circumstances. It did mean the line worked only one way at a time, so Ronald used it to his advantage.

After the scarcely audible click, the Mi5 officer said, "How dare you use my son against me? Alex is not involved in either politics or espionage. He is just a lad who wants to do his best, for god sake, he stands a chance to row in the Boat Race or stood a chance, I should say."

The PM paused; Brereton could hear his slightly raspy breathing at the end of the phone line. Eventually, he said, "I'm sorry, Roger, what are you talking about?"

"Alex, my son. You've met him."

The PM paused again as he tried to recall the boy's face. . He had inherited his mother's beauty, tinged with the Arabic ancestry of his father. The lad, who he met eight months before at No.10 during a 'get to know you session' with his top civil servants and their families, stood at least a foot taller than his father. As they stood drinking cocktails at the reception, he noticed more than a few women looking at Alex. "Yes, I remember the boy, up at Oxford, no?"

"Not now. Someone planted drugs on him, they set my son up."

The PM waited longer than the line's pause required to answer the Mi5 Deputy Head, "Teenagers these days, they are so free and easy with drugs. They don't think anything about taking them, selling them even."

Trained in the art of subtle messaging, Roger noted the PM mentioned selling drugs. So, his instincts were right; it was a setup. He wanted to believe his son when he came crying on the telephone. Alex wasn't the model child; they'd had their fair share of issues in his early teens. Something in Alex's voice, enraged indignation, led him to believe his son.

This time Brereton held off answering the PM, not for effect, he wanted to think of the right response.

Jarrod Crippley beat the usually quick-witted Mi5 head by saying; "You see Ronald, we have to leave the police to their machinations. You know what the press would do with this; it would be a field day. If they found a senior Mi5 officer's son, an Arab no less, was a drug dealer, I'd have to bow to pressure and ask for your resignation. There would be a question mark, a more significant question mark, over your head.

"Prime Minister, you fought for me in the face of a lot of opposition so I will forever be in your debt." As Brereton muttered the words, bile tightened his throat. While there was nothing wrong with being an Arab, the PM framed it as an insult knowing Brereton couldn't, or wouldn't, say anything in return.

"I really want to believe you, Ronald, I really do. It's like playing a hand of poker where you know it is going in your favour. You want to take any doubt away, so you're 100% sure, you know what I am saying?" said the PM. He continued, "I'd like you to get in touch with the General before our next meeting, make sure you're doing all you can for our little project. Also, maybe drop the matter concerning the man who visited the palace."

Ronald suspected the circumstances of the King's demise. A known operator was caught leaving the country via the face recognition systems at the UK's biggest passenger ferry terminal at Dover, the port closest to France. His people traced the trail of the man back to London and, to the surprise of his analyst who reported it, the path led back to a Buckingham Palace diplomatic reception. Mi5 had files on the operative as a possible gun for hire, he was linked to a few cases of interest around the world. Without a doubt, the agent was dangerous. Rumoured to be a Columbian, he didn't have a mode of operation, but he left several people dead or harmed in his wake. Unfortunately, the authorities released the assassin due to lack of evidence.

Brereton cursed himself for bringing the investigation to the PM's attention through his weekly report. He should have known of Crippley's involvement. He should have put two and two together given the number of conspiracy theories on the internet following King Charles' stroke and his subsequent death.

Brereton realised he remained quiet for too long, "I will talk to the General Sir. I might be delayed as I must sort this mess Alex is in. After all, Sir, isn't it you who told me 'family comes first'? "

"Good, excellent, Brereton. I'm sure the problem will resolve itself. Make sure you speak to the General. Maybe arrange to see him ahead of our next full meeting. I believe you two could make a lot of progress, a team if you like."

Ronald left the office in the early afternoon to beat the traffic. Despite the hour, traffic was heavy. He got stuck on the Westminster Bridge overlooking the Houses of Parliament when his personal mobile rang.

"Thank you, Dad, thank you for sorting it."

"It is fine son, get on with your studies and stay out of trouble. Maybe get someone else to move into your rooms with you. You know, for the company and to stop this sort of thing happening again."

He could hear the relief in his son's voice, "Dad, I love you."

"I love you too, son," Ronald Brereton said and ended the call.

It was standard practice in his profession to have more than enough leverage on an operative to make sure he or she would do what was required. It was also standard practice to get enough in reserve to give their controller the option to ask more in future. He and Crippley agreed on a coded deal, so his son got to stay at university. His next job was to talk to the General to see what else he would have to do. Whatever it was, it was going to be a lot riskier for himself, his family and King William as well.

CHAPTER 25 -THE WALK OF SHAME

Heather Taylor-Todd woke up at dawn next to John Amery.

When she entered the car the night before he stumbled slightly as he followed her into the black limousine and sat down close to her. Both relaxed by the alcohol, they laughed and found themselves looking at each other, both growing quiet, aware of the electricity between them.

Heather leaned into John and he took her face in his hands, pulling her closer. Their lips were close, Heather made the final move by parting her lips to meet his. His embrace tightened and he found her tongue and kissed her greedily.

The streetlights flickered through the windows of the car as they kissed as they made their way toward West London. Heather could feel John's lust growing. She remembered being a teenager suddenly.

As the driver closed the privacy screen, Heather giggled. John's hand squeezed her breast, thinking it didn't take him long to get to first base. "You make me feel like I'm off to the school prom," she said, making him pull away slightly.

"You make me feel like I might have a chance of going further."

"Where are we going?"

"Where do you want to go? My driver can take you to the charity function or home, this is the right direction?"

"I'm an Earl's daughter, my sir, you won't find me an easy catch. I have my reputation to protect."

John laughed but stopped abruptly as Heather gave him a depreciative look.

"I, I'm sorry, I didn't mean..."

Heather stopped him by breaking out once again in a full laugh. "Don't be silly. I am joking. I think you'll find the aristocracy are more than willing to let their reputation take a back seat."

John smiled. "Heather, you bugger. You had me there." He leaned in again and kissed her tenderly. "I think we could carry on our discussions at home, there's a lot to sort out. I don't have too much time before I head back across the pond and I really don't like talking about this stuff on the phone, encryption or no encryption."

"My apartment is a mess. I am not taking you back there."

John pressed a button and the privacy screen silently lowered. The bright lights of oncoming traffic lighting the back of the car. "Ben, take us to Number One please."

Number One Hyde Park was a controversial development of super-luxury residences. Many of the apartments were classed as second homes and qualified for tax relief despite their average £20million price tag. Revealing the fact she had researched John Amery, Heather said, "Number One Hyde park, eh? Do you get tax relief on it like all those other despotic and corrupt former world leaders and gangsters who have an apartment there?"

"I class it as my main home. I pay all my dues. What about your charity function?"

"It is Ok, Oliver will cover for me. He's the one with the money, I'm the decoration. I'll text him."

Both went quiet as they turned into the Mall and headed towards Buckingham Palace, the shortest route to the penthouse on Hyde Park. Part of the visible austerity drive imposed on the UK by the International Monetary Fund meant all public buildings would no longer be lit at night. The Palace loomed large as they made their way down the Mall. The white stone facade emitted a glow of its own, the grandeur of the building could not be hidden even though the lights no longer shone.

The sight of the Palace sobered them both. They watched the building pass without a word. Quietly, the privacy glass slid upwards, Heather assumed the driver had sensed the need to put space between him and his employer again. She was glad. "John, we are doing the right thing here, aren't we? I know we have different outlooks. Mine is ideological, yours must be the money."

John said, "Crippley has his heart set on this. If it weren't us, he would have some equally able people to take our places. Don't forget, we are only supplying information and doing all the groundwork. We can give Crippley and McNee all the facts, how they use them is their business. Perhaps they are right and 'the system' needs to change, I don't have the issues you have."

Heather went quiet and placed her hand on John's leg and stroked it. His arm was still around her, drawing her closer again, they kissed.

As the car drew up outside the brightly lit portico of the apartment building, John turned to Heather. "We're here."

"We are."

"I'd like you to come in."

"To see your art collection?" Heather said, raising her eyebrows.

"You can take a look if you like."

"I read you have a few masterpieces in there."

"I do," John said, kissing her again.

The noise of the engine hummed in the background. The privacy glass made the back seat of the car feel warm and safe as Heather enjoyed John's tight embrace. "I want to come in."

"You are sure...?"

She put her finger to his lips. She heard his seatbelt unclip and saw him reach for the handle. "John, I...."

He turned towards her and put his finger lightly to her lips. "Trust me."

He was a dominant lover, it surprised Heather how much she enjoyed it. They'd dozed off, waking later in the early hours of the morning to make love again, this time much more tenderly. The contrast intrigued her.

After they finished for the second time, Heather lay next to John. Exhaustion gripped her now. The bed faced a floor to ceiling window overlooking the green expanse of the park. Lights twinkled; the air conditioning unit making the only noise.

"John, I'm cold."

"Come." He put his arms around her and pulled up the bed covers.

In the darkness Heather could see John's eyes reflecting the light from outside. "Mmm. I like this. It makes me feel..."

"Loved?"

Heather didn't answer. It was too soon to talk about love.

John changed the subject, slightly embarrassed, "Why are you involved with Crippley?"

"I'm beginning to wonder. Since King Charles passed, Crippley has become more focused, more demanding. The more the economy tanks, with all the civil unrest, the more Crippley applies pressure on us all to hurry Project Catesby along.

John flicked the light on next to the bed making Heather blink. "The money from the Crown Estate is nothing more than a sticking plaster over an open wound. It won't last for long."

"John, for heaven sake. Turn the light off. I'm no spring chicken you know, and you've made a mess of my makeup."

"You're beautiful," he said but flicked the light off, nevertheless.

"That's better, a lady needs to keep the illusion, a hundred-watt bulb doesn't help." Heather relaxed once again next to John and continued, "It doesn't feel right. There's something amiss with this whole thing."

"I agree. I'm thinking of getting out, dropping it. I don't need the money."

Heather stroked John's chest. "I like your chest. No hair. Do you shave it?"

"No I don't, do you shave yours?"

Heather pinched his nipple, making him yelp and said, "No!" She rubbed his nipple softly, "Sorry, John."

"Next time I'll have to play rough with you."

"If there is a next time."

"There will be."

"Don't be so sure." Despite her words, Heather kissed John again and said, "Maybe the system we have in this country isn't so bad after all. Inequality is wrong, of course. But Crippley is all about gaining power over people. I want to get out of this too."

"We may not be able to 'get out' as easily as we think."

Heather didn't reply. After a moment she began to stroke John's naked body, he moaned with pleasure and went to kiss her.

"Stay still, you've worked hard enough tonight. It's my turn, John Amery."

The morning sun shone through the windows as John slept on. Heather got out of the bed, the sheets rolled off John who was laying on his stomach, naked. She paused to admire his body shamelessly, despite being anxious to get on with her day. She searched for the bathroom and found the shower.

Heather put on her clothes from the night before after finding them over things, dropped in various places over the large penthouse. In the mirror by the front door, she saw her black hair was messy and tousled. Her clothes would look out of place when she made her way home, making it obvious she spent the night with someone.

Opening the door to leave the apartment, Heather decided the 'walk of shame' home would clear her head. Acting so out of character, letting John get so close was a mistake. It was a moment of madness, she needed to get away to make sure she didn't let it happen again.

CHAPTER 26
ASHAMED

General Thiskwood convinced Crippley to reduce the number of committee meetings, change his approach and encouraged the PM to strengthen his leverage on each of the participants.

Crippley met with McNee again at Chequers where most of their Operation Catesby discussions took place.

"You see, Robbie, the General was right. Putting a little bit of pressure on has bought us faster results."

"It has created a feeling of distrust, Jarrod. I've noticed most of the members of the group are becoming more guarded."

"Maybe, maybe," replied Crippley, "but results from each of the members are coming in thick and fast following the shot across their bows we gave them. John Amery did a great job of pinning down all the assets included in the Crown Estate, it looks like he and Heather are working well both in and out of the bedroom.

"I'm surprised," mused Robbie. "They're like chalk and cheese."

"Keep Amery on-side, Heather, as well. They've done a great job on the Crown Estate list but move Amery on to the next stage: finding buyers for all of these assets. Selling the Crown's national treasures will require an international view and some serious research is needed. He's the best man to do it."

"And Heather Taylor-Todd?"

Crippley's face darkened. "Heather dismissed the rumours Charles was not Harry's biological father; it turned out Harry is a true Royal. I'm sure she came to a conclusion too quickly. Do you trust her?

"I don't see why she shouldn't do a good job. Yes, I trust her."

"The General is right about you, McNee, you're too trusting."

"Oh, you've discussed me?"

Crippley looked at his notes on the desk which divided the two men. "Leave it, it isn't important."

"Is there a problem?"

"No. I said leave it, McNee. Give Heather a new task; I want her to map out the aristocracy in the UK and their influence over both the government and the economy. When we are ready to establish a republic, I need a plan to neutralise the second tier of Dukes, Earls, Lords and their families."

McNee, wondering why the PM and General discussed him, said, "The General's plan was spot on, I'm not sure I would have included the aristocracy."

McNee watched the expression on Crippley's face falter, a knowing sign er was gearing up to rant about something. Crippley began, "Wealthy families have created immense trusts which help them escape taxation such as inheritance and corporation tax. When we are ready to force through a republic, we need to make sure this powerful group is left without the means or the motivation to maintain the status quo. Ask the Inland Revenue Service to map out how much aristocratic money is hidden in trusts and tell them to cook up something so we can get our hands on it."

"Yes," replied McNee, "can we get some coffee?"

"Ring the bell yourself, who do you think I am?"

McNee did what he was told but wondered why Jarrod Crippley was so much more aggressive with him of late. "Yes, sir, would you like one?"

"Yes, ring the bell. Ronald Brereton has done a good job; I'm pleased with him. I didn't think he would be so productive. He's invented some real scandals for us, I like his creativity. How he manufactured the telephone call between William and Kate was brilliant. You'd think it was really them. The pictures too! - oh, the wonders of modern technology."

McNee noted the PM appeared to get more pleasure from the grief he was giving William and Kate than his grand plan for a British republic. "The word circulating on the street is a palace mole is responsible for the scandalous stories which come out regularly on members of the Royal Family. The Royal Family's reputation is taking weekly hits on TV and the press. The polls are reporting a staggering loss of support for the monarchy."

Crippley laughed, there was a broad smile on his face. He sipped some coffee bought in moments before. "The General has no loyalty to the Crown, which helps, his plans are working out well. He's a man of action as well; he sorted out King Charles. Where is the man?"

"The General has been delayed a little. I've asked them to show him straight in when he arrives."

Crippley searched for the General's document in a pile of economic reports, most of which were sent to him by his Chancellor, increasingly concerned about the worsening economy. "Where is Thiskwood's document, I better have it ready when he arrives."

"Remember, I haven't seen the whole document."

"That old chestnut McKee. I told you, the General wants to compartmentalise everything. Besides, you're better off this way. You don't need to know everything, you're not even in the bloody cabinet."

McNee looked down and picked up a document, pretending to find something of interest.

"Remember, McNee, I need some changes to bring about progress ahead of the original timescale. Make sure we focus on timescales when he gets here."

The doors slammed open, Thiskwood – the General – followed in. "Your air traffic controllers should be hung and gutted. I've been flying in circles for two hours waiting for those guys,"

"Good evening, General Thiskwood, good to see you."

Thiskwood ignored McNee, taking preference over Crippley's outstretched hand. "Now, can we eat?"

The meal for the three took place in one of the smaller dining rooms at Chequers. While the dinner was served, their conversation ran down the confines of daily affairs.

"I see the London stock market took another hit. New York is up, it's on fire. I bet my wife's brother is getting off on it as we sit here. 'Never met a man so focused on making money apart from Amery."

"One of the UK's biggest companies, BP, announced their decision to quit the country in favour of the Netherlands. Sky Television collapsed after Amazon Prime won the bid to screen all live football matches."

"Who asked your opinion, McNee?" Crippley glared back at him.

Thiskwood chuckled, relaxing back in his chair, hands clasped around his belly. "I've got to hand it to you Crippley, you've had a big effect on the UK."

Jarrod Crippley made a point not to answer and, instead, asking the butler to clear the dishes, “And leave us alone.”

Dinner clear away, a selection of brandies wheeled in, their discussion turned to more serious, private matters.

"The problem is I can't go to the people for another election yet. I will have to soon, but there is no guarantee I will have such a large majority. Public sentiment is slightly against us for various reasons."

"The understatement of the decade, Crippley. I should think you and your cronies are the most unpopular government in a generation. Some of Britain's most exceptional businesses are ruined. I'm not sure nationalisation has been your best move; I see unemployment levels are at a historic high."

McNee found his time to cut in with the PM’s face darkening. "The PM is set on making radical changes, there's bound to be some pain."

"McNee, I don't need you to apologise for me."

Thiskwood laughed, "The States and the rest of the world don't really care. Britain was once the fifth-largest economy in the world, it's ranking slipped below Mexico last month for God's sake."

Both Crippley and McNee remained tight-lipped, allowing the General to continue, "Look, you have to act. The best way to take people's minds off the mess in the UK is to give them something else to worry about. Hell, I've seen American Presidents declaring war on some poor country many times as they edged toward election year. I have to tell you Crippley, I'm not sure the money from the Crown Estate will make much of a difference."

Knowing Jarrod Crippley, McNee was surprised as the PM merely smiled at the General, who was now picking his teeth. "I enjoy our conversations, you know how to press my buttons, Arthur. You asked me on the telephone the other day why it still matters. Let me remind you why. The rest of the world is doing fine, their economies are strong. The value of the entire Crown Estate has been pegged at over $165 Billion, enough to fill the gaps made by some of our...err... less successful policies. Apart from the economy, the only other grudge on people's minds is the unfairness existing between them and the Royals. They live in their own world. William is a nice boy, but clueless. The sale of Balmoral gave him barely a week of good press."

McNee finding opportunity, cut in, again, "General, your plan to use the information we have is feeding this frenzy like you predicted. I'm sure the scandals have kept some newspapers in busin—"

"—All I am asking, General," Crippley cut in, "is for you to reconsider the final part of your plan. Bad news and scandal alone are not going to get them out, we are running out of time."

The General relaxed back in his chair. He lit a thick cigar, not because he really wanted it but because Crippley hated smoke. "What are you asking me to do Mr Crippley?

"We need to come up with something. Something major..."

"You're going to have to tell me what's on your mind, Crippley."
He tried to hide the wince at the familiarity of hearing just his surname used again and didn't react further. "I think we need a hammer blow, something which is going to end it all."

Slightly amused, Thiskwood decided to make the PM sweat a little more. "I can't think what you mean. A hammer blow?"

McNee said, "Despite the furore around William and Kate's decaying marriage, the public remains stubbornly committed to the King and his family. William has three heirs. Harry and

Meghan have cleared off and are doing well on their own. The people, according to the polls, have no time for Harry since he made his famous 'step back' comment years back. All they see is someone who turned their back on the beloved Queen and an American actress who used her marriage to further her position. She is one of the richest actresses in the world from her TV show. The British don't like them, not one bit."

The General decided it was time to say what they wanted. "You want me to come up with something to deal with William?"

"Yes, if we could engineer a way to get, no, force William to abdicate and rule out his heirs, there's no way they'd settle for Harry and Meghan."

"Are you sure your polls are correct? Harry comes across well. He is popular in the States. They've navigated their exit from British Royal Life well, some say," said the General.

"The United States of America is a country obsessed with celebrity," spat Crippley, finally showing his agitation with Thiskwood. "The British people tend to be a little more circumspect where celebrities are concerned. They are not popular here and never will be again. They walked away; the British don't like people who throw in the towel."

"Let's be straight about this. You need Brereton and me at Mi5 to create a shitstorm William can't ignore to force his hand?"

"If that's what it takes, yes."

On his way back to London having not been asked to stay the night, McNee called his wife, anxious to get hold of her before she went to bed, "Mary, hi, it's Robbie."

"I know. Your name comes up on the phone. Robbie, I'm in bed, I'm tired, the kids have been a nightmare. Can't it wait?"

"I'm sorry Mary...I..."

In a softer tone, his wife said, "Robbie, what's wrong?"

"It's just...when we started out, Jarrod and I, we had this dream of making the UK a fairer place to live. He isn't the gifted young politician I met at twenty-two. He..."

"Robbie, I'm still here."

"Jarrod will do anything to get his way. I'm ashamed of him, of me, what we are doing."

Mary replied, "Come home, Robbie. Wake me if I fall asleep. We'll figure it out."

CHAPTER 27 - CLEARING THE DECKS

Roger Casement reached Chequers an hour early. He drove himself and decided to wait out the time outside the heavily guarded Estate. He rarely left London and hardly ever drove himself, the trip to Chequers tired him out.

Parked on the hillside, he caught sight of one of the buildings at Chequers if not the building itself, he wasn't sure. He would dearly love to bring Celia to the house. His wife dragged him to various stately homes owned by the National Trust when she could. Thankfully, he had a group of friend to go with; he called them the 'Trust Junkies.'

Always worrying, Celia Casement prepared a flask for his 'long journey'. He appreciated it now despite telling his wife he didn't need it. He poured himself a cup of hot tea and reviewed his papers ahead of the meeting.

The information flowing from Heather Taylor-Todd surprised him. He doubted her expertise, maybe because she was so attractive. The Judge chided himself for thinking he, above all, should not discriminate. The Earl's daughter was thorough and insightful. It was clear she traced more Crown Assets than he could have discovered using researchers. He believed the documents she prepared were the best accounts of Crown assets in existence.

Roger's job was to analyse the ownership of the Estate. The de facto understanding was the Crown Estate belonged to the nation; he wasn't so sure.

Unexpectedly, Roger found it challenging to obtain the original text of the Civil List Act of 1760, a surprise as England and the United Kingdom kept exemplary records. The documents detailing Acts of Parliament from 1497 are held at the Parliamentary Archives in Westminster, with earlier records stored in The National Archive. Eventually, the text was identified, and he was able to read the content, albeit not without questions, why would a high court judge need this information?

By far the most straightforward explanation of the Civil List arrangement was made in Parliament by the Chancellor, George Osbourne. In 2011. He said, "*In 1760, George III agreed to surrender for his lifetime the full income of the Crown Estate to the Government in return for a civil list. That arrangement has been in place ever since. A clear demarcation has long been established between the private income of the royal family for their private expenditure and the publicly funded income, derived from the civil list, for the royal family's public duties.*"

Osbourne introduced the Sovereign Grant Act in 2011 to formally establish the financial arrangements between the Royal Household and the UK Government. Previously, each new King or Queen required a new Civil List Act passing within six months of their accession to the throne. Inflation and fluctuating costs, repairs of the palaces and so on required constant adjustments to the amounts given. Political pressure, either to increase or decrease the amount given to the monarchy, introduced more uncertainty. The new Act established a direct link between The Crown Estate profits and the amount given to Queen Elizabeth II and her heirs. Under the new law, the monarch would receive fifteen per cent of the profits. Should major restoration works be required, the percentage could increase to twenty-five per cent by agreement. Should a surplus build up in the Royal Accounts, a proportion would be returned to the Government.

The Sovereign Grant Act of 2011 established the definite principle of a direct link between Crown Estate Assets, the Sovereign and the State. This surprised Casement; an explicit arrangement or relationship never appeared in Civil List Acts text previously. It was understood, for sure, but not written. This gave Crippley's grand plan a fundamental weakness.

The alarm on his phone made him jump. He had fifteen minutes to get to the meeting with Crippley and McNee, enough time.

He considered the other side of the equation; Queen Elizabeth would never cross Parliament, it wasn't in her nature, but she was dead, so was Charles. Charles might have, he was a rambunctious old sod who went against convention whenever he could. William's modern view and kind nature reflected his grandmothers' and, likely, wouldn't cross Parliament either. If Crippley decided to sell off parts or all The Crown Estate, he should have a clear path. Indeed, public sentiment was with him on this subject if not on anything else, he couldn't remember a more unpopular PM. Thatcher's popularity plummeted in her final years but never as much as Crippley's.

The Judge started his car, an old Jaguar he bought years ago and seldom used. Jarrod Crippley and Robbie McNee expected him for breakfast, he was hungry.

"Good Morning Judge," said McNee, who met him at the entrance to the grand mansion.

"Good Morning Robbie. Am I overdressed?"

McNee looked the Judge up and down, then his own attire. He looked scruffy. "I am sorry I should have told you it would be informal. The PM is already in the dining room, you know he likes his food."

Roger smiled, he couldn't be annoyed with McNee; the tall, scruffy though he was, he was always pleasant. And Roger could deal with pleasant.

They walked to the dining room and saw Crippley eating bacon, beans, mushrooms, a fried tomato or two, sausages and eggs. Even fried bread: the full, traditional English breakfast. Laid out in front of him was a stack of newspapers, mostly with headlines taking a swipe at his Government for the latest unemployment figures and house repossessions; statistics released the day before. With a mouthful of food, the PM failed to look at him but said, "Tell him what you want," nodding at the butler standing by to attention.

Casement tried to hide his displeasure, abhorrent behaviour from a man of his standing, and he'd put on weight too. The buttons to his shirt looked like they struggled with every breath. He chose a seat one along from the PM as the papers covered the setting next to him.

The butler, ever respectful, asked the Judge what he wanted, he ordered toast. He didn't really want to spend much time at Crippley's table, the PM's lack of manners put him off his food.

Coffee was poured for Casement, he took a small sip before saying, "You asked me to update you, Prime Minister. I have come to a few conclusions, so your timing is excellent."

"You took your time. The clock is ticking, you know. Tic Tok. I expected faster results from you of all people."

"Of all people?" Casement asked, making Crippley explain himself.

The PM looked at the Judge for the first time. A small scrap of egg hung from his bulging lower lip. "You...your background. You're black, you're not from the ruling elite. I thought you might want this to happen a lot faster."

"Heather Taylor-Todd supplied some excellent information. It allowed me to dig much deeper into this for you," said Casement, ignoring the PM's reference to his colour and background.

"Go on. Tell me."

Judge Casement outlined his findings detailing his meticulous research. He planned to help Crippley understand by referencing famous cases which supported his view. He wanted to give his interpretation of the importance of the link made between the Crown Estate and the Sovereign in the Sovereign Grant Act. However, Crippley stopped him, "Ok, you can give the details to McNee. I will study it later. What is the bottom line?"

Casement paused, not for effect but out of a slight trepidation such was Crippley's mood this morning. "If the monarchy is dissolved in favour of a republic the deposed sovereign, King William at present, has the right to reclaim title to the Crown Estate. He would also be able to claim historical underpayments and the remainder of the assets, especially the Royal Art Collection and the jewels."

Crippley put down his fork, the Judge now his only focus. He remained quiet. Roger shifted in his seat, pulled at his collar. He continued, "My considered opinion is; King William will never seek this solution or outcome from a change to our constitution, the establishment of a republic.".

Silence stretched throughout the room. To fill the space, he took a bite of fried bread.

Suddenly Crippley is on his feet. "Thank you, Roger. I've no doubt you have done the best you could and have covered all the points. Good job, great job, well done. You're the only expert who has full possession of the facts. You are the only person who has been able, for the first time in our nation's history, to have come to this conclusion. I like your suggestion the King wouldn't dispute the Government's claim on the entire Crown Estate in the event of the republic being formed." The PM walked out of the room, leaving Roger with a half-eaten piece of fried bread, slightly nonplussed by the PM's departure.

McNee came to his rescue, "Don't worry Roger, the PM has a lot on today. I am sorry you came all the way over here to fill the PM in on your findings. I know he appreciates it."

Roger placed his fried bread back on the plate and carefully wiped his hands on his napkin. He stood, shook Robbie's hand, and said his goodbyes, anxious to exit the room and the house.

As the door closed, McNee recalled the PM's words. He was pretty sure the Judge took them as a compliment. Having worked with Crippley for so long, Robbie interpreted them differently. Judge Casement's conclusion wasn't what the PM wanted. Jarrod Crippley certainly wouldn't want the respected Judge to share his findings with anyone else.

Three days later, McNee spilt his morning coffee on the breakfast table, soaking the newspapers piled up beside him.

"For heaven's sake, you're all fingers and thumbs these days, Robbie.".

"I'm sorry, Mary. Look, I'll take them all to work. Here, I'll put them in a shopping bag or something."

"Good, I'm fed up with them filling up my recycling. Rosemary, fetch your father a bag."

The McNee's daughter jumped up and went to the pantry where her mother kept the plastic bags. "How many?" she shouted.

"Rose, one should do," Robbie answered, a warm smile for her when she returned. "You stand there, I'll put the papers in. Open the bag wide."

"Why do we get so many newspapers, Daddy?"

"It's my work, I have to read them. Here you go."

"You're always spilling something." Mary took over. "Worse than the children."

Robbie McNee patted his wife's bottom as she loaded the papers into the bag. Rose had already left. "Hang on, there's one there I have to read. Give me the Daily Mail, it's in your hand."

"Can't you do that at the office?"

"Give it to me."

Mary looked at her husband and handed the newspaper to him, it escaped most of the spilt coffee.

Robbie McNee stood, took the paper from Mary and went into his study. After closing the door, he re-read the smaller headline at the bottom of the front page; 'First Black Judge Dies in Horrific Road Accident[DS31].'

Robbie's heart skipped a beat. Yesterday he read the news Ronald Brereton, Deputy Head of Mi5, was found by his son at home, dead, hanging from a rope in an apparent suicide. The coverage was extensive. Some commentators surmised Brereton may have killed himself because he was suspected of being a spy.

McNee sat at his desk and turned to the main article on page five. The picture of a burnt-out car dominated the page. The well-written article summarised the Judge's career. It gave further details of how a bystander saw the Judge trying to get out the burning vehicle. Another column reported the heroic efforts of an off-duty fireman who tried to free him, receiving terrible, life-changing burns in the process.

McNee sat back in his chair, he read enough. There were few people able to do the maths on both pieces of news. His boss, his friend of many years, must be behind this. Why didn't he know? Crippley was clearing out the committee members, it was obvious the PM intended to keep McNee out of the loop. McNee wondered who would be next but dismissed the fleeting thought it might include him.

BOOK TWO - THE GENERAL'S BATTLE PLAN

CHAPTER 28 A FOREIGN TOUR

Carolina Thiskwood booked her yearly trip to Europe a month early. Each year she treated herself to a month-long break to visit major stud farms, many of which were owned by her friends.

Her sister often accompanied her, the annual tour of Europe becoming a tradition. Arthur was usually busy, but she didn't even ask. She was sure it suited him, and, besides, she was happier without him.

The money Carolina and her siblings had in trust was sizable. Her brother, Marcus, turned the $100 million their father left them into $700Million. Over the years Carolina expanded the Stud into one of America's most successful breeders of racehorses. In time Arkle Ranch became more than self-sustaining and Carolina became well known in the horse racing world. Her reputation spread abroad as she improved her bloodstock by the yearly buying spree of young horses from notable studs in England and France. Carolina was well known not only for her wealth but as a knowledgeable horsewoman and for a bright, engaging personality.

Arthur Thiskwood practically ignored his wife's success; talk of horses seldom came up between them, he wasn't interested. When Carolina announced her trip would be brought forward, he didn't ask why.

The disappearance of her father's old desk in the library

caused an infrequent argument between them. Carolina, even though afraid of her husband's wrath, took a harsh stance with him over that mystery. By focusing on the desk's personal value to her, she hoped to divert any discussion about its contents. On reflection, Carolina guessed someone at the house told Arthur about her visit to the library. Arthur, dismissive of Carolina, may have concluded Carolina no threat to his plans as she neither possessed the motivation nor intelligence to figure it out.

Her husband was wrong in thinking Carolina cared little about the contents of her father's desk. Since seeing the information regarding King Charles, her mind couldn't settle. The contents of the other files, the ones she never got to see, worried her more. What was Arthur up to?

The one person she maintained contact with from the Army was Pierce Brice, Arthur's former personal attaché. She developed a warm relationship with Pierce over many years since being introduced by her husband. Pierce's family also came from Louisiana and were still involved in the horse industry as they owned a small stake in the Delta Downs Racetrack. Pierce, also retired, ran a relatively new stud, and would solicit her advice.

The day following the removal of the desk, Carolina telephoned Pierce. She suggested she visit him at his ranch to have a look at his progress. Delighted, he asked her to come the next day because he was expecting a new gelding from a stud in Spain.

The Delta Stud, an hour's drive from Arkle Ranch, stretched from a beautiful river to the hills behind. Pierce and his boyfriend had established a small vacation business, the grounds were dotted with authentic-looking cabins.

Pierce opened her door as soon as she arrived. "So kind of you to come to this two-bit operation Carolina. Lance is travelling this week; he sends his regards."

"Ah, I don't give a damn about you or the young gelding either. Lance is why I came!"

Pierce laughed. "I like how you get on with my boyfriend."

"Yes, Pierce, he always seems to be away. Is everything ok there?"

"He has to visit his sister each month. She's lovely, they get on so well, but she's had her troubles, Lance likes to be there for her."

"As long as you don't get lonely. You've had enough pain. I like the new cabins; they look as though they've been here for years."

Pierce reached out to Carolina and hugged her. "Thank you, Carolina. You're a true friend. You've helped us so much."

"More than can be said of my husband."

"Yes, Arthur thinks himself a 'man's man,' I told you I didn't expect him to take it well when he found out. I'm happy. Why are we talking about this again? I'm sorry, Carolina, I must bore you."

She rested her hand lightly on his arm. "You do, a little."

"You minx. Thank heavens I found you again at the Horseshoe Ball. I was lucky Arthur wasn't there. You didn't think I'd ever leave the Army from the look on your face; Arthur keeps things to himself, doesn't he?"

Carolina ignored the invitation to talk about deeper things and continued, "Our friendship is our secret. I don't see any reason why Arthur should know, after all, he cut you out of his life and the Army. I'm grateful to you as a friend and a fellow stud owner.

Although interested in the new gelding being displayed in the ring, Carolina's purpose of coming over was to ask Pierce's advice. She couldn't steer away from the subject any longer. "Arthur is busy again. I think he is helping out some folks in the UK at the moment. I am not sure what it is all about."

"He needs something to occupy his mind," said Pierce, "look, his hindquarters Carolina, classic form, no?

"You'll need to be careful when exercising this one, look at the slight hesitation when he turns, see?"

Pierce's eyebrows pinched together. "You have a point. What's the best thing to do? Regular hydrotherapy?"

"Yes, it will do no harm. Don't worry, I've seen this before in horses leading the field and winning races."

Pierce smiled as he opened the gate so they could get a closer look.

Turning to Pierce, Carolina said, "Listen, we are friends, right?"

Pierce looked perplexed, "Of course, why?"

"Can I seek your advice on something?"

"What?"

"It is about Arthur.".

He looked back at the gelding, saying nothing for a moment. He asked, "I'd rather you asked me something about the stud!" He seemed to tense up. "I am sorry, go ahead."

"Do you think Arthur is capable of doing something criminal, something wrong?"

He paused again, then said, "Arthur Thiskwood is a skilful man, a soldier."

"Not an answer, Pierce. Do you think my husband would break

the law, going against orders?

Pierce put his hand on Carolina's arm gently, as if to console her. He said in a quiet voice, "Arthur Thiskwood is a major force, his strategic mind equal to the greatest military minds in history. For a long while, I was in awe of him. I still am really. However, he is one of the most ruthless men I've ever encountered. General Thiskwood will destroy anything getting in his way. I'm sorry, Carolina, I love you, but I wouldn't recommend trying to delve too much in what Arthur has and hasn't done. You should watch out. Trust me, leave it well alone."

"Are you sure? I'm worried."

"I've said enough, so have you. Carry on with your life and let Arthur lead his. I've seen him in action, you haven't, leave it."

On her way back to the Arkle Ranch, Carolina went cold, jittery at what they'd discussed. Pierce wasn't himself when he talked about Arthur. The length of time the two men worked together gave Pierce a unique understanding of her husband. It is the fear in him that frightened her the most; after all, Pierce would know best about Arthur. Was it a fear she needed to share?

Carolina phoned Arthur who answered after two rings, the unusual dial tone meant he was still out of the country. "Arthur, I've been thinking. I'm going to be in Europe and, since you are spending a lot of time there, why not join me for a few days? I can't remember the last time we spent time together on vacation. We could book the Ritz in London and the George V in Paris. I'm sure my sister would be thrilled to see us both."

Arthur sighed before saying, "Thank you, Carolina. I'm buried right now. I might still be in London when you arrive, so why don't we take it from there."

"Oh, Arthur," she layered disappoint in her tone, "you are supposed to be retired."

"Now Carolina." He chuckled, a little. "You're the one who doesn't work."

"Ok, I'm in the car, we can talk later." She took care to keep her tone light. The Arkle Stud made over $12 million a year in straight profit, the breeding stock alone worth over $200million, not bad for someone who didn't work.

"I'll be in the UK for a while. Call me when you get here."

"Ok darling, keep in touch." Carolina pressed the button on the dashboard to cut the line, relieved they wouldn't see each other any time soon.

Following a few days of issuing instructions to household staff and in the business, Carolina made her way to the airport. Usually, she would travel with her head trainer and his wife; Richard and Karen Glover. Given her change of plan, they were unable to accompany her meaning she was free to come and go as she pleased.

On boarding the plane, she made herself comfortable. Using the onboard Wi-Fi, Carolina opened her laptop and set about creating a new online Gmail account. Something about Arthur's behaviour in the last few weeks made her especially concerned about her security. Despite what Pierce said to her, she couldn't imagine Arthur harming her if she got in his way. However, it wasn't beyond him to spy on her.

Their marriage lasted many years because it suited them both. Arthur, away a lot of those years, did whatever he liked and so did she. Pierce's words forced her reassess their relationship after so long. Was he really the man she knew? Many of her friends who married below them, in financial terms, at any rate, were divorced. Sure, Arthur liked the money, but there was more than enough. In the earlier years of their marriage, Carolina used her freedom to pursue a series of torrid affairs and assumed Arthur did the same. Occasionally he asked her to attend Army functions, Arthur reciprocated by attending the annual Horseshoe Ball and a few others when he could. Their kind of marriage worked well for both. The problem was, it may no longer be so useful for Arthur, especially if she got in his way as Pierce warned. When Arthur left for the UK, he didn't kiss her, even on the cheek, a first.

Using her sister's address, she wrote an email requesting they meet in London.

Virginia remained in France when they visited all those years ago and established a life for herself there. Carolina's sister met her husband during their teenage trip to Europe. Like many American's, they travelled the length and breadth of Europe finishing their trip first in Paris followed by London where they would catch a flight home.

Phillipe Dumont walked confidently to the two girls in a smoky bar in the Montmartre district of Paris and introduced himself. He cut a dashing figure, accurately fitting the profile of the sort of man the girls dreamed about meeting before their travels. Carolina witnessed the immediate sparks between the two and graciously departed the bar.

Unlike most student travellers, the hotel they stayed at was five stars paid for by their father who worried about the girls' safety and comfort. While they never had to sleep rough or share bathroom facilities with twenty other students in a hostel, it made it hard to meet other travellers. Carolina worried when Virginia didn't return until the small hours of the morning. Ready for an argument, the look on her sister's face when she returned made it pointless. Virginia spoke endlessly about Phillipe Dumont with a glint in her eye Carolina never saw before.

When the time came to move on to London, Virginia refused to accompany Carolina. Within weeks her sister married, sending their father into an apoplectic rage when Carolina returned to the Arkle Ranch alone.

Despite her and her father's concerns, Virginia and Phillipe's marriage turned out to be successful and as solid as a rock. Unlike Carolina's relationship with Arthur, Virginia's was warm and passionate. Her sister enjoyed being part of her husband's nomadic diplomatic lifestyle. Phillipe came from a respectable family and his passion for diplomacy culminated in him being appointed as the French Ambassador to London. Carolina marvelled at the places her sister and her husband travelled in his diplomatic duties and was vaguely jealous of the people she met and the contacts she made. Carolina didn't hold this against her sister because Arkle became her passion and horses her life. Both remained close through their correspondence, lengthy telephone calls and yearly visits.

Virginia met Carolina at the airport, expecting smiles and hugs. Instead, her sister looked tired and drawn. "Carolina, what has happened?"

"It is Arthur," she said with a heavy sigh. "I'm afraid he is not the man he used to be. He is involved in something here in the UK, I'm not sure I know what to do."

Virginia, escorting Carolina to a waiting car. "Don't worry." She hugged her tight "We will figure this out. Wait until we get in the car and tell me all about it."

Years ago, Virginia told her sister she wasn't overly keen on Arthur Thiskwood. Phillipe shared some shocking stories about Thiskwood supplied to him by his diplomatic connections. Carolina told her about the unspoken arrangement she and Arthur where he led his life and she hers. She told Virginia not to worry, but she did. Her visits to Arkle and Carolina's visits to Europe didn't involve Arthur. She kept the General away from her husband since they clashed on the few occasions they did meet up as a four.

In the car, Carolina outlined the information she found in their father's desk. Virginia couldn't fain surprise given her knowledge of Arthur's various activities over the years. "If true, Arthur has outdone himself this time."

Carolina looked at her, one eyebrow raised.

"I told you a long time ago, Arthur is a bad egg. I see no point going over what I know about your husband, but he takes no prisoners."

Carolina jolted at the reference to 'prisoners.' Pierce used the same exact phrase to describe Arthur. She looked at her sister. "Someone else said the same to me recently. What do you mean?"

Virginia said, "Arthur Thiskwood could be considered a war criminal if anyone was able to find the evidence. He murdered people who got in the way of his plans, not only his enemies, his colleagues as well. Phillipe told me about this years ago and even more stories when Arthur's god-awful book was published. He is a dangerous man, Carolina. I know you have closed your eyes to this for a long time but wake up. Don't Cross him."

CHAPTER 29 -HARRY - WHO TO TRUST?

Raj Rai answered my call despite the hour, "Good morning, Ray."

"Hi Harry, it is a particularly good and early morning. My sympathy Sir, your brother was a good man."

I felt guilty because I hadn't spoken to him for a long time. Ray was the one who recommended I take on Dak as the head of my security in America. He made sure the American team was up to the task on his last visit to see the family and me. "I am sorry I haven't been in touch."

"No problem Sir."

"Harry!"

"You are the King, Sir. Can we please settle on 'Sir?'"

"Fine. Listen, I need to talk through a few things with you, Ok?"

"Fire away," he said. I was amazed by how bright he sounded at two in the morning. I'm sure I woke him up.

"No, come here, please. To Windsor. Will it be ok at a moment's notice? I think I will need you for some time."

"Sir, you are the King. You can ask anything of the Armed forces. Contact Major D'Rayt, I will send you his number right away. I would suggest you call him directly and mention this to no one else. You can trust him, I do."

I sensed Ray snapping into his professional mindset after detecting the concern in my voice and answered him, "I will, Ray, thank you."

The text with the Major's contact details pinged on my phone, so I called him. He wasn't as bright or ready to accept a call from the new King of the United Kingdom in the small hours of the morning. I merely told him I needed to second Raj Rai to my service, he readily agreed. He was aware of the connection between Raj Rai and I and was happy to assure me the matter was between us when I asked.

I decided to try and sleep, I would need my wits about me. Training as a soldier had taught me to get sleep whenever I could. I didn't want to disturb Meghan, so I lay on the sofa in front of the fire. I could sleep on a washing line and it wasn’t long before I was asleep again.

Meghan woke me up the next morning with a kiss. “What time is it?” I asked, groggily. Our life in LA was frenetic, Meghan's TV show called for early starts, I rarely saw her on weekday mornings.

"Gone eight.” She raised her eyebrows. “It's not like you to sleep this late."

The children were up, I could hear them as they ran around the apartment from room to room, excited. Archie, the big brother, was good with Philip and I could see my firstborn was trying to make him busy enough not to fret, something we'd noticed in Philip more than once.

Meghan looked more rested. Dressed in casual sweatpants and a T-Shirt, she looked gorgeous as ever if not exactly like the new Queen of Great Britain.

"Why did you sleep out here, H?"

"I couldn't sleep, it hasn't exactly been easy the last few days with the move and the funeral. I'm due to attend meetings later to get a full briefing from George D'Languil."

"I like him, he is a brother," Meghan joked, referring to the black Master of the Household.

I laughed; her spirits had recovered overnight. Meghan was down one minute, up the next.

"Meghan," I said, "How are you feeling? I am sorry I haven't given enough thought about how this has affected you."

"I'm fine, absolutely fine. Everything is on an 'even keel' as you British would call it. I'm tired, you are too. It's been a hell of a few weeks."

"Don't worry, I'll sort everything. William's death will mean heightened security, so we won't be expected to show up everywhere. We can take our time. George is a good fellow; he'll be able to guide us. He's not like my grandmother's army of old stuffed dogs, he has a more relaxed approach."

"Mmm," she said, "Your version of 'relaxed' is different to mine. We left because of those vipers. They didn't protect us; I'll never forget it."

"Remember, you are the Queen, my consort. You set the agenda at home. All I'd ask you to do is to respect them and their history as I'll ask them to respect you and your back-ground." I was worried Meghan would take a hard-handed ap-proach with our new staff as she had when first married.

"I'll be easy with the staff, don't worry. Go, get dressed. I'm hungry, the children must be too."

I needed a shave. The thick stubble on my chin was signifi-cantly more abundant than the hair on my head nowadays. It wouldn't be long before I was as bald as my brother... as my brother was.

As I was shaving, Meghan came into the bathroom and touched my back. I felt a shiver of excitement go through me.

"Harry, you're always on heat. Stop it."

"Why not, we have at least five minutes."

"I remember when you'd settle for nothing less than fifteen," she said, looking at me as if giving it some consideration. Her look altered, she continued in a different tone, "One of the butlers, Francis I think, came in. Can we set some rules here? I want some privacy, some boundaries."

"I will sort it, why, what did he want?"

"Apparently you've asked to see someone called Ray. I peeked through to the Drawing room. He is tiny, dressed in uniform but I don't recognise his regiment."

"My friend Ray, Raj Rai. He serves in the Gurkha regiment. I've asked him to come and help with security, he'll be around a lot."

"I remember," she said. "Surely this has all been sorted by... by someone, I guess?"

"Meghan, they will have sorted security, but it is my job to look after you and the children. I must look after myself, too, there are too many dead kings around here. I don't want to be the next for some time."

She looked at me seriously, "You're right, of course. Anyway, 'Ray' is waiting. Once you've finished, maybe introduce me. It sounds like I need to get to know him a little."

Out of habit, I had a swift Army shower, turning the water off while I soaped myself. It made me smile, I was the King of one of the oldest monarchies in the world and here I was saving water. Ray wouldn't mind waiting, all Gurkhas are patient men. I dressed choosing my jeans and a T-shirt someone laid out for me, another thing I'd need to change; people would expect me to wear a suit more than a T-shirt which said 'Bruce Springsteen and the E Street Band Tour - 2016.'

As I walked in, it made me incredibly happy to see Ray standing looking out of the window onto the courtyard below. At 5'2, he didn't look like the trained killer he was.

"Ray, welcome to Windsor!"

The diminutive Gurkha soldier turned around slowly, he smiled at me, "Sir, how good to see you."

"Well, I'm still in one piece," I said as I walked over and shook his hand. Ray wouldn't go for a man hug like so many men these days.

"I came as soon as I could. I think you surprised General D'Rayt, he called me right after you contacted him. He said I'd be with you as long as you need. I'm pleased to be of help I can for as long as you want."

"Let's sit here." I indicated to the two chairs by the second window. "I'll explain why I called on you."

Ray took the seat opposite me. "First off, how is your beautiful wife and baby?" I learned his wife gave birth to their third child a year before. I sent him a card and a small gift at the time.

"They are well, Sir. They are in the UK too."

"We'll get on with the details in a minute. However, it may be best if you ask your wife if she would like to come here, to Windsor."

"I am sure she will be honoured, Sir."

"I'll sort out suitable accommodation for you. Can you call your wife after we've spoken so I can get someone to make the arrangements? It will all be handled for you."

The usually stoic Gurkha gave a slight smile telling me he was pleased. I suspected the Colour Sergeant's current accommodation was basic. I'd make sure they had one of the Grace and Favour apartments in the Grounds of Windsor castle itself. It would be better for them and for my family and me.

"Now, to business. No doubt you've been reading the papers and watching the news. Our family is going through some pretty bad times, of course, the whole country is. I'm afraid there's another dimension to this. The terrorist who attacked my brother and his family… the ones who killed them," I said, still with a tightening of my throat, "are assumed to be Islamic Terrorists."

Ray caught my intonation. "Assumed Sir?"

"Yes. Yesterday, at the funeral, someone passed me this note." I took out the note from my jeans, I hadn't let it out of my sight yet. I did not show it to Meghan. I decided to keep this to myself as it would only worry her. Also, Meghan was not beyond calling in her own guards and trying to take the situation over. I continued, "Please read it."

Ray took the note from me and scanned it. He looked up, growing concern on his face. He remained silent, waiting for me to speak next, to explain the note.

"If this is right, I think I have to be prepared."

"Who is it from?"

"It is from someone I would, on balance, trust. I have no reason to do otherwise".

"Of course, Sir."

"Ray, I will tell you. You must understand my head is swimming with this news, I only got the note yesterday."

"It is perfectly fine, Sir."

"I wish you would call me Harry."

Ray looked me in the eye and said, unexpectedly firmly, "We established this in our last conversation. If I am to work with you, your staff, politicians, everyone must know I am your personal security officer."

I sat back in the chair and nodded my agreement. Ray was right. I continued, "If the note is correct, the natural leap is to put the accountability for the death of my father and brother at the same door. I could be next."

"I would agree. The question is, how do we deal with this? Why did you call me of all people, Sir? You are the ultimate commanding officer of all the armed forces in the country."

"You know why I called you."

The Gurkha's face flashed grim, then serious. "Yes, I think I do. You believe I saved your life."

"You did, Ray. You are the one person in this world who I trust not only with my life but my family's too. There are many good people around me, but I do not know who to trust. If they killed my father in the way the note says, someone must have been able to get close to him. I would like you to remain close to us, watch out for us, help me navigate my way through this minefield like you did in Afghanistan."

"I can review all the security arrangements. I will question your officials every time you have to step foot out of Windsor. We'll have to improve the arrangements here; I noticed a few weaknesses when I arrived. I will help protect you and your family. But, Sir, you will need to find out who is behind this. I'm not sure I can help you there."

"I know you will do your best; I already feel safer with you around." I couldn't hide my sigh. "Now the funeral is over, I have time to grieve. The mourning period also gives me time to think this through. I will have to trust others, but I need to be careful."

Ray looked down, finding the words, "Grief takes time."

With him here, and those words, my sadness worsened. "Ray, you must be tired. I have already asked George D'Languil, the Master of the Household who greeted you, to sort out a room for you. If your wife agrees, a larger set of rooms will be made ready for you and your family." I stood and shook Ray's hand again. "Thank you, Ray, for coming, we'll talk later. Hopefully, I will have a little more information for you."

"Thank you, Sir. If it is OK with you, I will ask George a few questions so I can get started right away."

I smiled as we walked towards the apartment door. I pitied poor George; Ray would grill him on everything. The Gurkha was a thorough, considerably intelligent man, which matched his bravery and skill in the line of fire.

As I closed the door behind Ray, I put my mind to Meghan. She could be a great asset. However, depending on which way she took the news about my father and brother's murderers, she might be a liability as well. I made a decision: I would run a tight ship; Meghan would be told when she needed to know. Nevertheless, I am sure she could help me without knowing it.

Raising my voice, I called her, "Meghan, where are you?"

I heard one of the children laughing and went to the children's room where Meghan sat on Philip's bed, laughing with him. All three were still in their pyjamas. "Meghan, have you a minute?"

The children cried out in unison, "Papa!" I walked over to Archie and scooped him up and plonked him on Philip's bed where he lay with a broad smile on his face.

"Now you two, get dressed. Your Mom and I need to sort something out."

They were good kids, Archie took the lead and jumped off the bed shouting for Philip to follow him into the bathroom to brush their teeth.

Meghan followed me out of the room. "How did your meeting go?"

I forgot to introduce Ray to Meghan, "I will introduce him to you this afternoon, OK?"

"OK. So, what did you want?"

"I've been thinking about our discussions. There is a lot to sort but, for the meanwhile, I want to make sure you are comfortable here at Windsor. We have to stay put for at least a month to show respectful mourning, it will suit us, for now."

She grimaced, "I suppose." She wasn't happy, but even Meghan would leave it a few days for the trauma of the funeral to pass.

"I have an idea. I'd like to create a sort of transatlantic bridge for you. How about asking American women living in the UK here for lunch or something. You can't live here in a tower like Rapunzel, you know. It would be good for you to make you feel less trapped."

Meghan laughed; I could still make her smile. "Mmm, yes, a good idea, ok."

"Do me a favour, ask Virginia Dumont, the French ambassador's wife. She helps me with Invictus. She was at the funeral."

"Of course, she seems like a nice lady." I didn't know why Meghan turned away from me to answer. I was to learn, later, she saw Virginia slip me the note at the funeral.

CHAPTER 30 - THE GENERAL'S 5 STAR PLAN

General Thiskwood was enjoying himself, care of the British. Crippley paid for him to travel first class on their newly nationalised national carrier, British Airways.

The General dismissed the dutiful steward after he bought another tray of food and drinks. He didn't waste his time watching the films nor drinking the champagne, he was enjoying reviewing the progress of Operation Catesby.

Establishing the committee was a mistake, but it was one Crippley made before Thiskwood came along. It took several long telephone calls to change the PM's view before he finally relented. The PM dug his heels in because he was a stubborn old coot and didn't like the implied criticism from him. In wartime, the fewer people aware of operational plans, the better. Operating in cells was more secure; making sure you got what you wanted from key people without them having a view of the whole picture.

The hardest person to cut out was McNee, the PM's trusted sidekick. The look on the odd fellow's face when he first saw the General's plan was enough for Thiskwood; the sooner he was out of it, the better. McNee had no balls and he doubted his reliability.

Removing McNee from the 'inner circle' was the General's primary objective. He noticed Crippley took too much advice from McNee and it was slowing everything down. With McNee out of the way, Operation Catesby could progress with more speed.

The money secured by Thiskwood from Crippley to fund his operations was a delight to the General. It allowed him to employ several operatives needed to fulfil each part of the plan. There was so much money in the black accounts in the Grand Cayman Islands he could form a small army. It might even allow the General to take a few million dollars off the table. It would be good to have his own money and not have to rely on his wife's.

He decided the best way to sort out Judge Casement was to tamper with his old Jaguar. The only issue was to get him to use it once the car was rigged; the man took cabs and official vehicles everywhere. Getting him to drive out to Chequers provided the answer. He got Crippley to set a meeting early morning making train travel less of an option. The operatives who planted the device in the car's tank did the job beautifully. The British authorities were strangely lax in checking into the crash which burned the Judge alive in his seat. It had to be done, Crippley agreed. The Judge came to the wrong conclusion; they couldn't afford for Casement to turn rogue on their Operation. Both Thiskwood and the PM agreed they could see the Judge telling the King about his claim over the Crown Estate.

The heavily guarded deputy chief of Mi5 proved a little harder to neutralise. In a way, the General felt a little sad about his demise. Roger Brereton performed his tasks better than any other committee member. Using his team of 'off the book' specialists, he was able to spy, with impunity, on the leading players. He had to credit Brereton with his ingenuity as well.

Brereton couldn't find anything on William and Kate. Thiskwood told him to 'manufacture' the evidence they needed for the greedy British press. The General told Crippley that King William would never deny the stories publicly, he was proved correct.

Unfortunately, Brereton was becoming increasingly difficult to handle. The Mi5 man changed his attitude towards both Thiskwood and Crippley after they'd threatened his son's future. His removal from the picture was the next, natural step.

Roger Brereton was found hanged at his home in an apparent suicide. At Crippley's insistence, the authorities eventually agreed to declare the case a suicide driven by 'personal circumstances'.

The team Thiskwood hired to organise the Mi5 man's suicide performed their job to his satisfaction. However, the man's son, still at University, continued to insist his father wouldn't kill himself. He was demanding a more thorough investigation. The problem was this: Operation Catesby could be exposed if they looked too hard. Alex, the son, may have to be dealt with at some point given he wasn't above going to the press.

Thiskwood was glad the PM agreed to keep the plans for the committee members from McKee. Crippley and Thiskwood discussed the remaining members of the committee; Heather Taylor-Todd and John Amery. The last time they called each other was about these two. There was no agreement on their fate.

Crippley argued, persuasively, he needed Amery for the next phase. They would need the money man to orchestrate the financial part of the plan and help liquidate the Crown Estate. As the economy worsened, Crippley increasingly focused on the money at the expense of the ideological purity of forming the Republic of the United Kingdom.

Ahead of his demise, Brereton reported Amery and the 'History Girl' were spending more time together and sent him pictures of them kissing in a car. They also snapped Heather Taylor-Todd coming out of Amery's apartment building in the early hours of the morning. While Heather was expendable, the psychological analysis provided by Brereton convinced them Amery could become dangerous if his new 'squeeze' was eliminated.

Thiskwood let Crippley get his way. Surely the two would figure out the link between them and the deaths of their former committee colleagues, and this should keep them onside. If not, the problem could be dealt with at any time.

As time progressed, the British Prime Minister became frantic, looking for a way out. His radical changes, based on a long-held socialist ideology, were catastrophic. Foreign investment in UK business dried up as anxious investors saw significant parts of the economy being nationalised. Uncontrolled government spending under the guise "Investing in the British People" eat away at Britain's prosperity with hardly any long-term benefits. Large infrastructure projects were left incomplete, the most prominent example being the abandoned M100 motorway linking the East to the West of central England. It was described as the 'road to nowhere.' Someone had the idea a bridge between Scotland and Northern Ireland would improve the economies of both nations only to abandon construction a year later as funds dried up.

The General realised Operation Catesby was viewed as the 'golden key' to Crippley: the solution to all his worries.

As the plane descended, Thiskwood realised he failed to read the report sent by his British operatives and opened the file. The General was surprised by its contents; McNee went home to his wife and children last Friday evening after work and disappeared. Reading between the lines, he could see the agent he employed failed to stay on the job assuming McNee would return to Westminster after the weekend. He decided to hire new investigators and sack the man who was unable to follow his assignment through. He considered the threat from McNee minimal as the PM's aid was complicit in Operation Catesby and, if he chose to expose the PM, he would implicate himself. McNee lacked the backbone for any altruistic revelations. That said, his elimination would obliterate the risk entirely.

When he landed, the General was escorted from the plane by two of the PM's security detail, he had met them before. A nondescript saloon car waited on the tarmac and Thiskwood climbed in since there were no checks on his passport. One of the two, a woman, informed him they were headed to a new location for 'extra' security.

Thiskwood regretted not sleeping on the plane. The two security officers occupied the front seat of the vehicle and he fell asleep despite trying to fight it. As they arrived at another country estate, Thiskwood was woken by Crippley's voice emanating from the noise of the security guard's radio.

He noticed the 'for sale' sign as they entered the gate. The house had certainly seen better days, it had a look of disrepair, as if no one used it. Whoever owned the building couldn't afford its upkeep, another sign of a country in decline.

The Prime Minister greeted him at the door, a surprise to the General. The car drove away, leaving the two facing each other at the entrance. There was no one else in the house when they entered. Thiskwood followed the PM as ordered to a small dimly lit room and offered him a drink from a small 1960's bar, which was at odds with the antique furniture.

"Another home Crippley?"

"A convenience, I followed your instructions, only those officers out there know I am here. I'm not sure they even know who you are," replied Crippley, pouring himself a large whisky. The General declined when offered a drink, he wanted to keep a clear head.

As they sat in two high backed leather chairs, Thiskwood was glad the fire burned in the grate, the house had a cold, damp feel to it. "How is everything?"

"They have been a lot better, my dear fellow, a lot better. The country fails to understand the need to go through a little pain for the long-term gain. Tell me about your revised plan, you wouldn't give me any details on the telephone."

"Where is your man?"

"McNee? Oh, he might be out of the picture. He didn't return to work on Monday. I can't get hold of him."

Thiskwood sensed Crippley was evasive, "Aren't you worried?"

"A little," replied the PM, "Robbie has been with me for such a long time. He is different to me, sure, he has a great brain but few balls. I think everything has started to worry him. However, I'm sure he won't be a problem."

"Sure?" Asked Thiskwood, "how can you be, do you know where he is?"

"No, look, forget about McNee. Let's talk about the plan."

The General took his time unloading two files from his briefcase. The Prime Minister was drawn out, a haggard hollow of what he had been when they first met. "Here is the revised plan I promised," he said as he handed over one of the slim files.

The PM opened the folder as greedily as a child opening their presents at Christmas. His face twitching as he read it.

Finally, his face crumping. "You're what? What is this?"

"I told you, Sir, you wanted a plan to get you the republic you so want. Of course, the plan will deliver the Crown Estate too."

"I cannot condone this, not at all," Crippley said in a low, wavering voice. "This is wrong, I don't think we need to do it. King Charles, being drugged and effectively murdered was one thing, a necessity. Still, I cannot agree to the murder of children or William and Kate."

"I wondered when your nerve would go. Of course, it is needed. We can't keep the facade up around William and Kate. I've paid to poll your people, the British people, and they are fast changing their attitude to their new King. All the mud we spread with the help of our dear departed Mi5 officer merely dented their popularity. There's every sign they're ready to forgive. I hate to say this, Mr Crippley, your people are fed up with the bad news about their money and their jobs. Their anger is turning against your government and you, in particular."

Crippley stared at him, lost for words. His face flushed and he took a deep swig of the remaining whiskey in his glass. Straightening himself out, he said, "I'm calling this off. We started this so well, the plan was a triumph, we have been successful in many ways, but this is a step too far."

"I'm afraid it is too late."

Crippley stood, a rictus snarl on his face, "No, you won't do anything else. This has gone far enough!" Turning to face Thiskwood directly, he paused, "What do you mean it is too late?"

General Thiskwood tapped his watch, stretching his arm out dramatically. "Thirty minutes ago, a small team of specialists landed on a Norfolk beach. They would have found the family and, all being well, they are on their way back to sea."

"Found the family?"

The General smiled, took his cell phone out of his pocket, looked at the screen and smiled. He pushed a button to delete the text message, the phone made a small noise. Thiskwood regarded the PM with cool ease., "Yes, they're on their way, mission accomplished. William, Kate and the children are dead, there's nothing more to discuss."

CHAPTER 31 - MEETING IN PALM BEACH

After their first night, Heather Taylor-Todd screened his calls, ignored his texts. Radio silence. Even the stream of information regarding the Royal's stopped following their night together.

Amery was disappointed. The sex was great, but he was used to it with other women. Cuddling her, chatting in bed afterwards, falling asleep with Heather made him feel more relaxed and happier than he had for years. The experience wasn't new, the memories of his teenage romance were as vivid as they ever were.

After trying and failing to contact Heather, Amery decided to head back to New York, thinking it might be time Heather needed. Still, Amery, who was used to getting what he wanted, realised Heather might not want anything to do with him again. In many ways, it didn't surprise him. In Heather, he saw a kindred spirit, another person who put their personal life on hold in favour of their work. His heart sank each time Heather failed to answer his calls, going to his house in Palm Beach would help him lick his wounds.

Heather was a celebrity in the UK. She was even being noticed in America, where her Netflix series whipped up a storm of debate. Red Diamond went from strength to strength, so both of them were busy enough to forget the night or, at least, remember it fondly.

After settling some business in New York, Amery made his way to the Florida estate. He needed a rest, Operation Catesby was surprisingly taxing, his own business continued at its usual frenetic pace. The news from Jarrod Crippley regarding the dissolution of the committee was welcome even though he would be needed at a later stage once political events had taken their cause.

John neglected his fitness regime in the last few months, so the first sight of the swimming pool at the house made him feel guilty. He decided to give himself a month in Palm Beach and throw himself into the pool to bring himself back into shape.

Amery called a few swimming pals; they were used to him suddenly reappearing from his trips away and a few of them came over to train with him. They were all much younger than Amery but, usually, he could hold his own with them. The three men and two women, all in their twenties, liked the thrill of being able to swim in the fifty-meter pool at one of Palm Beach's most magnificent estates. Amery loved their company. They were from a variety of backgrounds, but all were naturally optimistic about life. They were genuine people who had no agenda; a welcome relief from the folks he met in business and the art world. His first few sessions revealed how far he let himself go, reigniting his competitive streak. He put in place a training program including gym work to bring him up to pace.

At night he seldom ventured off the estate save for one or two art exhibitions or 'art' parties as he called them. While he was benefiting from the break, he caught himself thinking about Heather often.

Every afternoon he dedicated at least a few hours to business.

Mostly he let Chip manage the day to day operation at Red Diamond from the London office. Still, each of the heads of different units sent weekly reports and updates for him to keep his finger on the pulse of Red Diamond.

Included in the regular reports he received was an update from his Head of Communications. Years ago, he invested in a pretty well-funded PR and Communications Department. Amery's theory was the constant stream of news being splurged out by newspapers, online sites and TV could give him the edge in business. It allowed him to monitor trends, spot opportunities and contact people who might be persuaded to invest or help Red Diamond in some way.

As a matter of course, his PA registered details of people Amery met with the communications department. Their job would be to monitor them for news stories. In his weekly comms report, John looked forward to this section the most. People he met were often flabbergasted John mentioned their latest news, it helped him build relationships and, ultimately, make more money.

After his midday session in the pool, alone this time, John dried off and sat outside the pool house to eat lunch and go through the reports. The sun was shining, he sat in the shade by the waterfall built into the rocks beside the hot tub.

He was pleased with the progress of Red Diamond; profits were even higher than usual, which made him think he should spend more time in Florida. He kept the Comms paper until last in case something came up. While it was the most interesting, it was the least important of the six regular weekly reports he received.

Under the 'News' section, each previous contact was listed under their name. The list was ordered by significance to Amery personally and Red Diamond. If the news was significant and he met the person recently, it would be listed first at the top of the paper. It was two names at the top which shocked John and made his gut tighten: Roger Casement and Ronald Brereton.

As he read the news about the accident which burned the Judge alive and Brereton's suicide, a few days apart, Amery worried about Heather. Did she know? Two members of their committee... he considered the implications. Could he... they... be in danger, too? His heart gripped.

He needed to get a message to Heather. Likely, a text or a call wouldn't work. He called Chip Stourbridge, Chief Financial Officer of Red Diamond, and his right-hand man in London. It would be early in London, but Chip always answered his calls, day or night.

"Chip, I need you to do something for me. Please can you find Heather Taylor-Todd? She's an academic at Oxford University."

Chip replied, "The History Girl, you mean?"

"Yes. Can you drop everything you are doing and track her down? She might not take your call so head on to Oxford where she works."

Chip's natural sense of humour, rare in an accountant, came to the fore when he replied, "If it's ok with you, John, I won't drop the toast I have in my hand but, when it is finished I'll find her."

John laughed, "Don't put another piece of bread in the toaster."

Amery got up, went to get dressed and contacted his PR man in New York to ask for a full dossier on Casement and Brereton. He could expect it in hours. Neither Tim Moss, the Comms Head, or Chip, asked him why he wanted the information. They were used to his unusual demands. Both learned during their first few weeks at Red Diamond Amery preferred action. He would give them more information if and when they needed it. The financial community and staff at Red Diamond regarded Amery as a financial sorcerer who could take information gleaned from a thousand different places and turn it into money.

There was no point in contacting Chip again, he would call as soon as there was any news. Amery became impatient as the day progressed and tried to call Heather again. The call went unanswered. She was one of the few people who refused to have her phone take messages.

To distract himself, John contacted the guys to see if they'd like a session after work in the pool. Three of the swimmers were able to come and they worked an arduous two-hour training session in the pool. Tired from the exercise, Amery apologised for not having them for dinner as he had work to do. While John's fitness levels were back to normal, the fifty-meter sprints at the end of the session finished them all off.

John decided to eat a 'Palm Beach Burger'; his housekeeper's own creation, cooked especially spicy the way Amery liked it. The iPad on the table bleeped with incoming mail every few minutes and John kept an eye out for news from Tim Moss. Eventually, the report came in so Amery went to his study so he could concentrate on its contents.

Unfortunately, the report contained a few relevant details he had not already seen from the original stories and the Google session he conducted earlier. Judge Casement's wife, Celia, was caught on camera on the street the day following her husband's death and the unscrupulous reporters badgered her for comments. With tears in her eyes, she spoke movingly of her husband with grace, dignity, and compassion. The accompanying news reports contained graphic details of how the Judge was seen desperately trying to escape the burning Jaguar by helpless onlookers repelled by the heat.

Given his importance to the security of the UK, Amery was

surprised by the brevity of reports looking into Brereton's death. The Government spokesman ruled out foul play and blamed Brereton's chaotic private life for driving him to suicide. Having met the man a few times, John didn't believe a word of it; the man was cool and calm with a serious demeanour, he didn't often misread a person.

The one item of interest was a reference to Brereton's son, Alex. Tim Moss's team provided links to videos and tweets he posted disputing his father's death. His video became viral not because of the content but because Alex was seen in his tight-fitting rowing kit and he was a handsome man. The video became known as the Sexy Mi5 Kid which was, given the circumstances, a little insensitive.

Drained by the day's activity and with no news from Chip, Amery decided to make it an early night. If he didn't hear anything by the morning, he would call Chip. He was surprised his CFO didn't contact him, but it was too early to give him grief.

At five in the morning, John woke up to the sound of the phone ringing. He hoped it was Chip with an update. His Butler, Serge, was on the internal phone, "Sir, there is a visitor for you."

Amery noted the calm in Serge's voice, nothing ever altered the Ukrainian's demeanour. John did not expect anyone, especially at this hour, but he put on his dressing-gown and went downstairs.

Serge met him and told John his visitor was out on the balcony. "Apparently, she wanted to look at the sunrise and the pool?"

Serge was his Butler, but he was also his personal security, they often travelled together. This allowed John to go out to the deck with confidence as Serge would have searched for any weapons. As he went out, he caught sight of the sunrise, it was spectacular. Silhouetted against the orange light, Amery saw the outline of a woman.

"Heather, I asked Chip to get you to contact me, I didn't expect a personal visit."

One look from her, and that familiar fire ignited again. Her dark hair tumbled over her face and her violet eyes shone, lips pursed. "I saw the news about Casement and Brereton. It scared me to death. I've been hiding out in Oxford not taking any calls. I didn't know what to do."

"You could have called me."

"How could I? I've been ignoring you since, since..."

"Our night together? What made you come?

"Chip came to see me, he's a lovely guy. He found me in some tucked away library in a quiet part of the university campus. He relayed your message and asked me, politely, to call you. I was nervous. I didn't mention anything about the committee or the deaths, but I did say I missed you because everything was getting heavy here and I didn't trust my phone."

"You missed me?"

Heather paused and walked over to Amery and took his hand. "Yes, I did. Try as I might, I couldn't get you out of my mind."

"You've a funny way of showing me, you didn't answer one of my calls, my texts."

"I'm sorry, I'm, just, I'm not used to all this. The last person who I trusted let me down." Heather looked down, trying to find other words. Eventually, she continued, "Chip is a bright man, I think he knows what you mean to me and suggested I take the company jet. I was so worried about the cost, the ..."

"...Look, you're here now. I must give my CFO another bonus; good thinking on his part." He gestured with his arms open to her.

Heather walked over to John and was met with open arms which embraced her. They kissed and held each other for a few more moments. "I think you came to the same conclusion as I. There was no accident, no suicide, I think they were killed."

Heather pulled away slightly to look at John, "I'm scared."

John Amery looked into Heather's eyes, thinking what to say, finally he said, "I am too."

CHAPTER 32 - HARRY - CHANGING OF THE GUARD

Ray went through security procedures at Windsor at pace, co-opting George, the Master of the House. George helped Ray put changes into action around the Castle upsetting several traditionalists at Windsor.

The Changing of the Guards took place at around eleven each day; a centuries-old tradition. Most people only associate it with Buckingham Palace, Windsor adopted the practice first being the older royal residence.

The ceremony is regarded as sacrosanct, acting as one of the many draws for Windsor bound tourists. Ray told me the guards, who are armed and highly trained military men, could bolster security if he made changes. The problem, he pointed out to me, would be they could be neutralised by terrorists given their positions and movements are listed on the Windsor Castle website.

Ray and George took on the might of the Commander of the Guards. They bought in a random schedule thereby destroying one of the spectacles for tourists visiting the Castle. Ray also insisted on combat dress in favour of their red tunics and bearskin hats. According to Meghan, the Castle looked as though it were patrolled by a posse of Sandinista mercenaries.

Windsor closed to the public following Williams' death, so the effect of Ray's changes was minimised. Ray insisted I use my Royal prerogative to close the Castle indefinitely, not only for the mourning period. I asked him to protect us; therefore, I agreed to most of his suggestions. I expected the PM to send a messenger to tell me to open the gates, but he failed to do so. I guess he had more to worry about.

The security systems installed at Windsor were relatively modern. Everything was up to date, given the vast amount of money spent restoring the Castle following the great fire of 1992. New wiring gullies, hidden from view, allowed a constant refresh of the latest security systems to be fitted keeping the building safe and the priceless art secure. Our family... secure. Ray surprised me by asking for further hardware to be installed. It turned out the investment over time was made to protect the Crown Assets, not the monarch or their family.

Large parts of the Windsor operation became dark and silent. Ray and George slimmed down the staff to cut the number of people who could access the Castle grounds. The remaining staff and visitors were personally vetted and approved by the three of us. Crippley, apparently, was delighted given it reduced the running costs. Unlike other Prime Ministers, Crippley didn't use the Castle as a PR machine to impress visiting Heads of State, it meant little to him.

Meghan's event met with Ray's approval. I told him I wanted to meet Virginia Dumont and get a better explanation for the note she gave me. Ray agreed with me about not making any attempt to contact Virginia Dumont. Most embassy staff communications were routinely monitored by the host nation and the country they represented.

At first sceptical, Meghan warmed to the idea of holding an informal cocktail party. With her usual vigour, the list was drawn and redrawn with focus. George ruled a few women by making diplomatic comments such as: "oh, she does like to drink" and "I think you could find Mrs Cane and Ms Tyler don't get along so well." Impressed by his knowledge, I asked him how he obtained his information on the proposed guests. He smiled and said his network of staff employed in upscale houses served him well.

Of course, I wanted the event to take place as soon as possible, but it was two weeks until the day came. I found out more about Virginia Dumont. An American, she married a French diplomat and independently wealthy from a share of a trust her father left her and her siblings. She ran a charitable foundation to help disadvantaged children in France but didn't have any children herself. In her younger days, she travelled the globe with her husband, who climbed the diplomatic ladder with each new posting. Like my family, she loved horses and her large chateaux in Bordeaux included a magnificent eighteen-century stable. 'Hello' Magazine ran a piece some years previously where she spoke of her father and their ranch in Louisiana.

Virginia accepted her invitation to my relief; however, she asked if her sister Carolina could accompany her as she was visiting from the United States. Meghan wanted to object, but I couldn't risk Virginia not turning up. I sent a message to her saying my Aunt would like to meet her sister as, apparently, she was a noted horse breeder. Meghan didn't want Anne there, but I put my foot down telling her we needed as much trusted support as we could muster. Anne supported our move out of the Royal limelight and sympathised with us during troublesome times. It was sad I had to remind Meghan.

In all, twenty-five women were invited; not enough for a party but neither was it an intimate get-together. News leaked out about the event and, true to form, we got roasted in the press for being disrespectful of Williams' death. Tough, they could stick their news where the sun didn't shine.

Meghan relaxed into life at Windsor, I figured she appreciated the break from her hectic schedule in America. Of course, she wouldn't admit it to me. The children were happier, too, with Meghan around more. In LA, I became a hands-on father. I enjoyed it, my bond with the boys was strong. I loved my father, but he was from a different generation. My children enjoy personal moments with me that I never got with my own father.

Relations between the reigning monarch and the sitting Prime Minister were supposed to be one of support, absolute trust and confidentiality. I took to reading my grandmother's diaries every day to find out how she dealt with the PMs during her time at Buckingham Palace. The accounts helped me understand how good and how dysfunctional dealings with the sitting Prime Minister could be. I consumed the journals with a passion, yet I couldn't find evidence of a situation like my own. Crippley was disrespectful, awkward, extremely left-wing and, obviously, a republican.

The least favourite part of my week was my weekly 'audiences' with the PM. I travelled to Buckingham Palace for the sessions but returned to Windsor once the audience with Crippley ended. Informal and relaxed is my style, I couldn't be either of those with the 'Prime Minister'. Crippley's steadfast refusal to bow his head, even in the smallest way, told me more about his attitude than anything he could do or say. He lectured me on spending and spoke down to me as if I were a child. He even suggested the daily dispatch boxes from the government be suspended or 'dumbed down' to save me time and effort in trying to understand the affairs of the state.

Crippley, a consummate politician, never said a word which could be used in evidence of his true intentions toward the monarchy. His passive-aggressive nature oozed out of his every sentence and every gesture. Frequently, he ran late but blamed it on the heavy workload of premiership or, to put it another way; he was busy, I wasn't.

Unlike my father and William, I had no training in Kingship. They'd both been groomed for their destiny. I like the way I could have a casual and intimate relationship with my granny while William's was more business-like. I genuinely believe my special bond with her protected us when we decided to take a different route in life. If it were up to William, I would have lost much more than our titles. Our relationship was toxic for a while, but we mended fences, although our relationship was never the same. My father, I'm told, referred to Meghan as 'the showgirl.' Meghan found out and went ballistic thinking everyone in the family used it. I didn't know if they did or not, but the damage was done.

In the week up to the party, Ray came into his own. For the first time since my ascension to the throne, and the untimely death of William, we were allowing 'outsiders' into Windsor. His security arrangements were in place and I heard some of the junior members of the Guards were in favour of the more professional and up to date security procedures.

Meghan laughed at me saying what on earth could twenty-five women do to harm us when faced by the 'Sandinistas'. She was right, but I saw Ray flexing his muscles, preparing himself, testing if his changes were suitable for the future. Also, Meghan couldn't perceive the threat to us as I; it was better she remained in the dark.

As arranged, the ladies would arrive at twelve noon, allowing enough time for a final security check to be made. Phones were taken away and each visitor screened airport-style. They were also given the once over by sniffer-dogs, trained in explosives; I'm not sure they realised the significance of the trained beagles being part of the reception committee.

Of course, no men were allowed in the room, but I chose a vantage point to make sure I could see all of them arriving, anxious to spot Virginia Dumont. I gave instructions to Ray to siphon off Virginia when they were leaving so we could meet somewhere privately. I'm not sure how we would deal with her sister.

Meghan went into hyperdrive on the morning of the get-together. She made sure the food and wine were plentiful and was still changing place settings minutes before their arrival.

I noticed Virginia and her sister were on Meghan's table, both sisters sitting either side of her. Since I asked for them to be included, I shouldn't be surprised my wife would try to find out why, typical Meghan. I remained calm, Virginia chose to give me the note and her thirty years of diplomatic experience told me she wouldn't say anything. Virginia Dumont was no fool, she guessed I would try to contact her.

"Virginia, so nice to see you and your sister, Carolina, isn't it?" I said when Ray brought them into a small office near the Castle exit a few hours later. I guessed Meghan would want to get back to the children once the event finished.

"I thought it would be a good opportunity to meet your Majesty," Virginia said together with a small curtsy. I noticed Carolina trying to curtsey too with some awkwardness.

"Harry, please," I said. I smiled at Carolina, trying to set her at her ease. "I wanted to discuss a few matters with Virginia." Suddenly, I felt out of place, awkward. "I understand you have a great affinity with horses, like my grandmother. Perhaps you would allow Virginia and I to have a little chat, I have her escorted to you in a few minutes, I promise."

Virginia interrupted Carolina, who was about to answer me. "Harry, I guessed you wanted to talk about the note I gave to you. Carolina gave me the information; it might be better to include her. Also, thank you for not contacting me directly, these are difficult times, we need to be careful."

I noticed the look of concern on her face, "Of course, let's sit."

"Carolina is married to General Arthur Thiskwood."

"I know, I did my research." Again, I smiled at Carolina, still attempting to calm her evident nerves.

Virginia reached out to take her sister's hand, a lovely gesture. She continued, "Carolina contacted me some weeks ago, before the King, your Brother...."

I could tell she didn't know how to introduce the subject of William's death. I said, "It is ok, I understand."

Virginia looked at Carolina who took the cue to continue. "My husband retired from the Army a few years ago, he has a reputation, one of the greatest military strategists by all accounts. You must understand, Sir, he and I have been together for years, but we're not close."

I sensed she was also finding it hard to talk about such matters, I said, "It happens."

Carolina straightened and took a deep breath. "Over the last year, Arthur has made several trips to England. He is a different man; re-energised and happier than I've seen him for some years, since the Army days. I became a little suspicious. He was spending a lot of money, my money, which is not normally an issue, but it was noticed by my accountants. They keep an eye on the books for me. Unexpectedly Arthur repaid a significant amount into one of our accounts, and he also stopped drawing any money whatsoever. I suspected he made some investments which reached a good payoff. Anyway, I wanted to find out more."

There was a knock at the door. "Sir," Ray said, as he came in. "I wanted you to know the party is being shown around St George's Chapel, so there is plenty of time. No one will be missed."

I merely nodded at Ray and he left the room. I said to Carolina Thiskwood, "Carry on."

"Arthur uses our library a great deal. He works at the same desk and, I, well, looked inside when he was away one day. I found a file labelled 'King Charles' and read it." Carolina looked to her sister, who gave a slight nod, and I noticed Virginia squeeze her sister's hand again.

"Arthur laid out a plan to slip a drug into your father's food which would undoubtedly bring about a stroke."

I was struck by the matter-of-fact way Carolina uttered this last sentence. I went through many emotions. I got angry thinking she should have revealed this at the time she found out, my father deserved more. It took me a great deal of self-control not to show my emotions, I needed more information.

Carolina took my silence as a prompt to carry on, "I didn't know what to do. I panicked, I decided to fly here, Virginia always knows what to do."

Carolina turned to her sister, and Virginia continued, "Carolina flew over, I picked her up at the airport. During her flight news came of William's death, the murder of the whole family. She told me about the information she found. I've been around military plots, coups and several wars during my time with my husband. I've picked up a lot from our experiences around the world. I concluded we could trust no one. If I told Phillipe, he might be duty-bound to share it with the French Government. Unfortunately, I couldn't be sure they wouldn't use the information against you or your government."

"I understand," I said, looking from one woman to another, thinking.

"You see, I saw other files in Arthurs desk, a file on William, you, other members of the Royal family. I also saw his diary; he prints it out and leaves it on his desk. From what I could see, he was meeting a few people in the UK." Carolina stopped, looking to her sister for encouragement.

Virginia Dumont looked at me, finishing her sister's story, "General Thiskwood met with Jarrod Crippley each time he came to Great Britain."

CHAPTER 33 - INTERNATIONAL NEWS

"You surprise me," Heather said, her first words after making love.

Still catching his breath, John turned to Heather. They were on the double sunbed on the bedroom balcony. "It was you who suggested coming out here."

"No, I love it out here. I can hear the crickets or whatever the noise is and the humidity too. I like to watch you sweat."

"What?" John propped himself on one arm and traced his fingers through the moisture on Heather's body.

"For a big, strong, billionaire boy, you were surprisingly gentle. I like variety. You are tender just when I need it. Nothing like Charlie."

"The ex-husband?"

"Yes."

"Good. I'm glad I haven't forgotten how." John reached over to a glass of water left outside from earlier, it was warm, but he needed it. "Years ago, I fell in love with a girl called Mia. We were at school. Looking back, maybe it was a schoolboy thing? It felt more."

"Pass me the glass before you drink it all, I'm parched." After taking a gulp of the tepid water, Heather grimaced, "Mia? Should I be jealous?"

"We were at school. She swam like me, we trained together. Everyone liked Mia, you would have." John paused, "She passed away."

Seeing the hurt in his eyes, Heather asked, "How?"

"A stupid accident on her bike. I know we were young, but it has stayed with me," John said, laying back on the sun lounger, "We learned together. At first, our lovemaking was awkward, rushed. But we spent two years together and were honest enough to tell each other what we liked and what we didn't. I've never been with anyone like Mia. I always need to prove myself. I guess it could be the reason none of my relationships ever worked long term. With you, well, it must be right because it feels so good. Thank you, Heather, you've relit something here."

Heather couldn't find a suitable reply. After a few minutes of silence gazing at the Florida night time sky, Heather said, "You've made me realise something. Something I guess I've known for a long time. I've pushed people away all my life. My drive, my ambition isn't money like you, I thought it was a result of my political beliefs. I've been against unfairness and even against my own heritage - the class system - for so many years. Spending time with you here in this Floridian palace has given me the time to think. Seeing you, being with you 24/7, it is the first time I've truly relaxed with a man."

John laughed, "You mean your 'daddy' issues?"

Heather slapped him hard on his side. "Ow!" he screamed.

She laughed, "You're right, I suppose. Maybe you've helped me realise some men are nice. I know, it is early days and I guess you could still do the dirty on me."

"I won't."

Heather continued, "My father was from a different era, nothing I did could persuade him to take more notice of me. My opinions and beliefs, maybe they *are* to do with my... my 'daddy' issues. By attacking the aristocratic system I could be trying to get back at him. I don't know."

John kissed Heather on the lips. "Look, here we are. Poor us. The 'Billionaire Boy' and one of the world's most famous historians; our crappy childhood really fucked us up."

A silence drew out between then before Heather said, "Oh John, you're right," she laughed, "I guess we have turned out alright. Mind you, we've created a real problem for ourselves. Judge Casement and Ronald Brereton are dead, we could be next. Why did we get involved in this?"

John got off the bed and walked to the glass balcony. Looking out across his gardens, he said, "I wanted the money. It's my measuring stick you see. My father, he wanted me to follow him on to become a doctor like him. The more money I have, the more I can prove my dad wrong. I think it sums me up. "

Heather joined him at the balcony, he put his arm around her. "Our job is to survive first, get out of this mess and put everything right. We fucked up, John, and we know it. We can't allow any more deaths."

"Come on, partner. We need to sleep. It's about time we got out of our safety bubble here and dealt with this.

Heather's eyes were closed, she sensed John's shadow on her as she lay on the deck by the pool. Opening them, she saw him standing over her silhouetted by the sun. "Hello, sleepyhead," he said.

"You're looking good in the pool John," said Heather thinking how easily giving a compliment came to her, another change.

"You too. I thought I'd get some laps in while you were still in bed. I didn't see you. Breakfast is ready." John pointed to the guest house and veranda next to the pool where his housekeeper laid out a generous spread.

Heather realised how hungry she was and stood, John helping her from the deck. As he did so, he made her wet from his body, she tried to push him away. He held her tighter and they laughed as she pretended to struggle.

"Come on," said John, let's eat.

John poured her out a coffee from opposite Heather. She eyed the selection on the table and opted for a chocolate croissant and some fresh pineapple. John went for the British bacon sandwich Heather guessed was specially sourced for him here in the USA.

"John, thank you so much for... for breakfast."

He smiled at her, his eyes twinkling. She remained in her dressing gown while he sat, almost naked in tight speedos. "And last night?"

"Eat your sandwich," she said, softly, "ok, last night was special. Incredibly special."

Amery merely smiled back and went for another bite of his sandwich. They both understood their discussion from last night would need resuming, but each happy enough to wait.

He stretched, drawing out a long yawn and said, "One more coffee. Let's go in after and get changed. We need to make plans."

Heather looked at John's fit and toned body. She pulled over the dressing-gown, afraid her own body wouldn't be up to any comparison. He leaned over and pulled the dressing gown back over her shoulders, "You are a beautiful woman, History Girl."

"You aren't bad yourself, Billionaire Boy."

John smiled and sat again; he looked a little worn from his exercise. Heather asked, "How many laps did you do?

"Fifty, easy. The sprints at the end finish you off."

Reaching for another sandwich, John said, "I didn't get to know the Mi5 guy, did you?"

"Ronald Brereton? Not really."

"I liked the Judge, from what I've read, he was fair and considerate. I noticed he kept quiet, but when he did say something, people listened."

"I spoke to him several times. I enjoyed the challenges he gave me. Him being much older, I wanted to make sure I gave him my full attention, my full effort."

"Daddy issues?"

"Ok, ok. Shut it."

"What sort of information was he working on? I know he was looking at the legal ownership of the Crown Estate but not much more."

"We found out a lot about the Crown assets and copies of various documents detailing who acquired them. The Da Vinci drawings were given to Charles II by Henry Howard, the grandson of Thomas Howard, Earl of Arundel. It follows the drawings, arguably the greatest treasure in the Royal Collection, are the private property of the King, not the nation's."

A slight pause, before John replied, "Did you and Casement talk much? Can you tell me anything which might help?"

"Roger Casement didn't share much, I guess Judges have to be guarded. I could gauge how his mind worked by the questions he asked."

He waited for her to finish and when she didn't said, "Where do you think the Judge's mind was headed?"

"Headed? Do you mean did he give me any indication of how he was approaching his task? I don't know. Hang on, he made another request to find out details of actual payments for items, large and small. Each time I uncovered something new, it made him happier."

"In what way?"

"I need to think. He... he, appeared pleased when I found a direct link between payment for an item which could be considered personal."

"Heather, is there any chance Casement could have been building a case for private ownership of the Crown Estate?"

"I don't know John." She paused, "Yes, perhaps he was."

John was blank, as if he looked through her. Heather could imagine him playing out several moves at a time. Eventually, he said, "Given what we already know, why would Crippley want the Judge dead?

That's it John, she could see where he was going with this. "Take Judge on face value. He practised law for over forty years. The press considered him hard but fair. His rise in the judiciary is evidence of the high regard he commanded in the profession. In short, he was objective, to be trusted and a man with a conscience. Crippley's big mistake was to think the Judge would build a case for the Crown Estate to be taken from the monarchy. No, Roger Casement made a case, based on evidence, some of which I provided. John, maybe he was murdered because Crippley couldn't allow the Judge to disagree with his agenda."

"You could be right. But why murder him?"

Pulling her robe around herself, despite the sun, the talk of murder sent a shiver through her. "I think the Judge may have said something, something publicly if Crippley tried to make out a different case regarding the Crown Estate. I can't be sure, but it makes sense."

"Ok, it does make sense, but what about the other one, the Mi5 man?"

"Brereton?"

"Yes. I didn't trust him. I once heard a conversation between him and McNee. I believe he could have been behind all the bad press about the Royal Family. He is, was, sorry, a spy after all."

"If so, why did they get rid of him? Surely having a trained man like Brereton in place proved invaluable. The resources Mi5 can command are considerable."

"We will have to find out a lot more. I saw an online clip of Brereton's son questioning his father's death, claiming it wasn't a suicide."

"How on earth did you come across it?"

"Long story, my team in New York keep tabs on a lot of people."

"On me?"

"You're first on my list."

"Good," said Heather continued, "Let's get to understand why Brereton was murdered. Maybe speak to his son?"

Both were disturbed by someone walking over to their spot

with more coffee. It was Serge.

In his slightly broken English Serge said, "Sir, you look at TV now. There has been some happenings in Britain."

John stood and grabbed his iPhone. An app allowed him to see the live news in any country, an invaluable tool in the finance business. At first, it wasn't clear what happened, John tried to find BBC News, the source he trusted most. He fingered the screen which came alive in his hands, the speaker loud enough to be heard by them both. "...on a Norfolk beach...details still coming through...the bodies have been covered."

John, seeing the pictures, understood before Heather. He looked over to her, "King William, the family, they've been murdered."

CHAPTER 34 -THE FLORIDA EXPEDITION

It required just a single operative to follow his wife, she was so predictable. Based at the Savoy Hotel, Carolina visited her sister several times at the French Ambassador's residence in London. She travelled out to a couple of horse studs near London, he wasn't unduly worried about her until the report of the trip to Windsor. The news came in overnight and, annoyingly, Thiskwood got to it much later than he planned the next day in Louisiana.

He called Carolina as soon as he found out about her Royal visit and was surprised when she mentioned meeting Meghan and the event at Windsor. She explained her sister, Virginia, was invited with some other American women who were based in the UK. Thiskwood didn't like Carolina's sister and avoided her when possible. He didn't like the way her and her husband looked down on him. Both carried a lofty air he often noticed in the French; Virginia acquired the attitude since she's been married to Phillipe for a long time. In the Army, the French were the ones to scupper plans because they insisted they had better ideas. Carolina chatted about the castle and how kind Meghan had been. He would have to think about how he could find out more information.

He had plenty of funds in the Cayman Islands. In retrospect, Thiskwood wished he had not sent the money back to Carolina's bank he borrowed in the short term. The eagle-eyed accountant at Carolina's family investment office headed by her brother probably noticed it. No wonder Carolina went sniffing around his desk in the Library. Still, she could not have found anything there as his papers were safe in her 'daddy's' desk. His wife's visit to Windsor could be innocent, but he didn't like coincidences. There was sufficient doubt in his mind to allow the matter to rest. After all, she was the mother of his children, he doubted she possessed the motive or ability to piece together his activities.

Sitting back on the bed he infrequently shared with his wife, the General considered Operation Catesby. Crippley took a while to recover from the news of William's death. The British PM threatened him and insisted the operation cease. Arthur reminded Crippley he had enough dirt on him to end his premiership and put him in jail. He encountered the problem before, commanders losing confidence in battle. Sometimes all they needed was a little persuasion. Besides, he didn't want to stop. Although Thiskwood didn't tell the PM, he routinely taped all their conversations which could come in useful if Crippley lost it completely. Thiskwood walked the PM through the ramifications of the high profile hit and eventually he accepted the situation.

General Thiskwood got up from the bed, hungry, so he decided to go and find something to eat. As he walked to the Kitchen, he pictured Jarrod Crippley's face as he told him about William. The PM spluttered and blustered his objections but eventually ran out of steam. The satisfaction of having control over one of the most powerful men in the world energised him, it made him feel twenty years younger.

Chewing on some cold pizza, Thiskwood turned his mind to the other loose strands of the plan. Unfortunately, Carolina might become a problem but, for old time sake, he put it to the back of his mind. The next steps were to deal with McNee, Amery and making the 'History Girl,' history.

The General's operatives found McKee's elderly mother in a care home in Leamington Spa and were keeping an eye on her. Robbie McNee visited regularly, but his last visit was days before his disappearance suggesting he may not show for some time. His holiday cottage in Wales remained empty and his only brother was estranged from the family, living in Glasgow. The trail, now cold, worried Thiskwood. The man may not be a problem given his complete disappearance, but he couldn't be sure.

Tracking Amery was made more accessible by tracing his private jet. It was parked at Miami-Opa Locka Executive port in Miami, not far from the Palm Beach estate Amery owned. According to files hacked by his team, the plane landed there some time ago. A call to his office in London confirmed the whereabouts of John Amery who was apparently 'taking some leave.'

Thiskwood considered the likelihood of both Amery and Taylor-Todd together at the hedge fund manager's estate. Given reports of a romance, it was possible. Heather Taylor-Todd was apparently taking time off in Oxford, due to illness. Enquiries revealed her absence occurred ten days ago; the same time Amery's jet arrived at Miami-Opa.

A few days before, Thiskwood established links with a new mercenary unit based in the US. The international outfit used to assassinate William refused to deal with the General again after he arranged for the men involved to be killed by another one of his paid-for operatives. Eradicating potential security breaches was the only way to ensure total secrecy.

Thiskwood made his way to his favourite room in Carolina's large house. On entering the Library, the new desk and metal filing cabinet looked out of place in the wood-panelled room. He punched in the six-digit code on the cabinet's electronic keypad and opened the top drawer. Inside was a new burner phone and the file containing the details for 'Operation Palm.' General Thiskwood smiled as he sat at the desk, he liked the new name for his attack on John Amery's Palm Beach mansion.

The photographs of the house taken by the operatives showed an Italian inspired villa with beautiful gardens leading onto the beach. There were also pictures of Amery, Heather and a big man who looked like a security guard. There were other images of staff, one marked 'Estefania,' the housekeeper.

The new unit was ready, he only needed to give an order to make the problem go away. Thiskwood had all the facts they needed on the value of the Crown Estate and the amounts were fabulous. Crippley apparently arranged for Amery to take a cut of any liquidations in the Crown Estate and insisted Amery remained a vital cog in the wheel. He read the reports Crippley gave him. The young financier compiled not only the most definitive list of Crown assets seen so far but also matching potential buyers - all in code. Repeating this exercise would take months to replicate should John Amery disappear from the scene.

He decided to call the unit head of his team based near Palm Beach. "Good morning Mr Jones," said Arthur using the code name for the unit leader hoping for a five hundred thousand pay-out. "An update, please."

"We've staked out the grounds, it is a pretty impressive place. The drive has a guardhouse, manned night and day. The only other way in is from the sea. There's a security system but we have a solution for that, nothing we can't handle. Staff come and go. Usually, there's the housekeeper, some maids and a Ukrainian named Serge. He has a background."

The General understood. "One of you guys?"

"Not really, but he worked out in Russia and is rumoured to be a freelance guy on occasion though not active for the last few years since Amery took him on. Serge goes with John Amery most places these days according to one or two people we know. He acts as his butler, but it is a security front."

"Why would Amery have heightened security in place?"

"I have no idea, Sir. My guess, John Amery is a rich man who must have made some guys poor to get where he is. A rattled investor, maybe? I am not sure. The fact is the guy has a class one operative serving him cocktails in the evening."

Thiskwood paused. Mr Jones waited until the General said, "The girl, have you seen her again?" The team supplied him a folder of pictures taken at the property in their last daily report. It was clear the two were more than committee colleagues.

"She is here. They don't do much apart from swim, drink and fuck. Oh, they eat occasionally."

Thiskwood laughed, Mr Jones sounded bored and maybe a little jealous. "You need to be in place for action, but I am not ordering it yet, understand?"

"Your money covers us for another two weeks; it is your fucking money. We are fine. I'm keeping my men fresh with exercises and drills."

General Thiskwood frowned, he didn't agree with his use of expletives, it indicated poor discipline. He let it go, "OK, stay alert and let me know of any developments."

"Yes, Sir.".

General Thiskwood wondered how best to work this situation. His first taste of money, his own money, made him hungry for more. There was no way he would admit it, but most of his life he fed on his wife's fortune for the lifestyle he led and freedom from Carolina's purse strings would be liberating. Divorce would yield nothing, Carolina's doubtful father made sure of it in his will, her brother was even more guarded about the family money. His no-good son and cold faced daughter got everything, he had nothing more than a tiny prenup and a pension from the Army, sufficient for many but too small for him.

He looked at the high-resolution pictures taken by Mr Jones' team once again. He could see the expressions on the faces of John Amery and Heather Taylor-Todd. He got closer and studied the pictures in detail, their expressions made it obvious they were seriously into each other.

Thiskwood phoned the number again, "Mr Jones, I've given the matter some consideration."

"Yes, sir?"

"Yes, I want you to kidnap the woman. Make it quick. I don't want her harmed or Amery."

"Kidnaps cost more sir, there are complications."

"I will send another five hundred to your account on capturing her."

"But sir..."

"Don't fuck with me, enough."

The General heard Mr Jones remain silent at the end of the line. A trained negotiator, Thiskwood waited. Eventually, Mr Jones said, "OK, Sir. We'll work it out, I will send you more details over the secure link."

"Fine son, you will do a great job, I am sure." Cutting the call, he swore under his breath, 'Fucking Cuban'.

CHAPTER 35 - THE SAKHRA

Alex Brereton decided he couldn't face University again following his father's death. His dream of competing in the Boat Race didn't seem important any more, since finding his father hanging from a beam in their fourteenth-century farmhouse.

He remembered the last time he saw his father. Alex couldn't understand his dad's reaction to the news about drugs being found in his rooms. He expected an outburst or, even worse, the disappointed look on his father's face having let down him and the family. Roger Brereton reacted well; forgiveness came quickly after. In retrospect, his father believed him where many others didn’t.

Alex's father told him to go back to University, keeping him updated on the disciplinary he would face. On returning, he expected a welcome committee, at least a letter informing of his meeting with the Proctor. However, he found nothing out of place in his rooms even though he’d left them hurried, in an untidy state.

Alex called his father, the last time they spoke. He thanked him and told him he loved both his mum and his dad for standing by him. For the first time in days, Alex resumed his training schedule and studies.

Alex decided to visit his father on a bank holiday when the evening training session was cancelled. His mother was off travelling somewhere and, as an only child, his dad could do with the company. It would take a while for him to heal the wounds caused by the supposed drugs bust.

He decided to leave right after his last rowing session and didn't bother to change, there were plenty of clothes at home. He could change there. On arriving home, he saw his father's government Jaguar in the drive. He rushed in to meet him, leaving his Mini parked in the correct spot, as his father insisted upon.

On entering the house, he called out for his father. It was a rare sunny day for the time of year, so he looked around the garden to see if he was cleaning the swimming pool; a job his father hated. The garden empty, he checked his father's study, the kitchen and the drawing-room, his father was nowhere to be found.

Disappointed, Alex wondered if his father was visiting his mother in Spain, who took long holidays in her villa at this time of the year. However, there were signs of his presence; a briefcase in the study, a mug of cold coffee left out in the kitchen, it was as if he left in a rush. Alex opened the fridge and found plenty of snacks, deciding to wait for his father to return home. A cold curry from the fridge in the microwave, he went to change. Upstairs, he saw it; the body hanging from the exposed beams of the hallway leading to the master bedroom.

At six feet four, Alex found even his rower's physique wasn't enough to lift his father's body from the rope wrapped around his neck. Years back, his father showed him the security system, he edged past his father's body into the main bedroom to press the emergency button. This would bring local police and someone from Mi5. His father's engorged blue tongue hung out of his mouth, the mess on the floor from fluids released during and after his death made it clear an ambulance wouldn't be necessary.

The police came and dealt with the situation, there were cars everywhere. Alex was frozen to the spot by the house phone, it was only a kind policewoman who persuaded him to sit and drink some tea. He didn't drink it but, even with the image of his father still firmly in his mind, Alex didn't feel it polite to refuse. Alex handed the woman the note he found near the body. The typed letter said, "I cannot carry on."

The influx of police and noise of the sirens spooked Alex; he felt the need to get out of the house. Still in his rowing kit, he ran to the Mini, but it was blocked in. The media, outside the gates of the house, could see him and shouted to get his attention.

Dazed, he made his way to the iron gates and saw several cameras pointed at him. Without being asked, Alex said, "There is no way my father committed suicide, no way at all. This is wrong, there's something wrong here."

It was a mistake, he understood as soon as he walked back to the house. The police officer who first came to the house grabbed him by the arm and dragged him inside. Unfortunately, his televised plea to the press dressed in the skin-tight lycra rowing outfit became the news, virtually eclipsing his father's death. The 'Sexy Mi5 Kid' received over five million hits on YouTube after going viral in days.

Alex's mother arrived home later in the evening, allowing the specialist family liaison officer to finally depart. They were unable to stay in the house, but the police allowed them to remain in the small cottage annexe in the grounds. Seeing his mother was a relief and she took over everything. Alex's mother couldn't believe her husband of twenty-five years would commit suicide but didn't have the energy to question it as Alex had done. Alex's mother went through the motions over the next few days. She pulled a few strings with Mi5 and they were able to bury Ronald Brereton within a week at a private ceremony. Only Alex, his Mother, Uncle and the Priest were there; that was the way his mother wanted it.

His mother eventually decided to leave for Spain to her secluded villa. Despite his parents spending periods away from each other, they were close. Alex realised he needed to help her get through those dark days and joined her there.

Mi5 officials and the police came to meet them in England and out at their Spanish villa. They were insistent Ronald Brereton took his own life. They revealed a secret gambling addiction and photographs of him with a much younger woman exiting a hotel early in the morning in London's Mayfair district.

His mother had a near breakdown. He asked his uncle, her older brother, out to Spain to help out. She couldn't believe what happened but in the face of the irrefutable evidence, accepted his father's suicide. Alex didn't. He realised it would take some time for his mother to come to terms with his father's death and the villa was the best place for her at the moment. Safe in the knowledge his mother was being taken care of by his uncle, Alex returned to England determined to find out what happened and why.

He returned to the family home. It was eerily quiet and smelled of the disinfectant used to clean up after his father's death. Alex felt his presence everywhere, suffocating him with grief.

His mother and Uncle were surprised by his insistence on going back to England. He placated them by agreeing to return in a few days.

In Spain, he had time to think. He recalled the last time with his father and the strange way he handled the news of the drugs bust. "Remember our boat, Alex, the one you and I spent most of the summer on in, let's see, well, a few years back?"

"Yes, the 'Sakhra'?"

"Yes, you know where it is?" It's still moored in Southampton."

"Dad, you're joking me, I thought you sold it? In fact, you told me you did, I'm sure."

"Yes, I told you. I considered it. I couldn't let it go. We had great times taking her out to sea, didn't we?"

"But we haven't used it for ages. It was my sixteenth birthday."

Ronald Brereton looked at Alex and paused before he said, "You haven't, I have. Occasionally I'll go there. It costs a fortune but, you know, your mother hasn't noticed yet."

"You are kidding me, Dad,' Alex had said.

"No, no, I'm not. In my line of work, you know we all keep secrets."

"I guess."

"No one at Mi5 knows about it. No one in the government knows about it. I'm quite sure your mother has forgotten about it. But it is still there... It is a little haven."

"Dad, you always surprise me."

"If there's ever a time you need to find peace, take time out, go there. Here are the keys."

Alex smiled; his father's trust warmed him. "Can I take, um, invite someone?

"I know what you're thinking. If you find someone you trust, of course. Don't be putting it on Instagram or anything. Social media can be dangerous, I've told you before."

“I-”

"The Shakra may be important to you sooner or later. If you find yourself...alone...go there."

"Sounds ominous?"

Alex's father laughed the comment off and changed the subject. At the time Alex was delighted to have a place he could take a girl for the night or maybe a weekend, they'd be impressed.

It took time in Spain for Alex to figure out his father's coded message. He was sure he would find out what he needed to know on the Sakhra. It might not be what Alex wanted to know but was determined to find out. Maybe he'd discover more about the gambling and even the mystery woman he was supposed to be seeing. Whatever it was, he needed to know.

After locking the house and setting the alarms, he set out for Southampton and the marina at Ocean Village. The drive took over an hour, so he used the time to phone his mother from the car, "Mum, how are you?"

Olivia Brereton sounded distant, quiet, "We're off to Alicante to shop. I'm going to spend a lot of money. Retail therapy, that's what they call it."

"You have been having that sort of therapy all your life, Mum."

"It was the only thing your father and I fell out about. That and the fact he was always away. I used to tell him to 'sod off,' it was my money."

Alex glanced down at the phone on his dashboard, he missed her. "Mum, you go off and spend, spend, spend. Can you buy me something?"

"No, you're spoilt enough. When are you coming back?"

Alex wanted to change the subject, "You'll never guess where I'm off to."

"Alexander...Answer the question."

"I'm off to the Sakhra."

Confused, Olivia Brereton said, "The boat? It... your father sold it."

"No. Dad told me about it the last time I saw him." Alive, Alex thought.

"I guess he hid his secrets well."

"No, Mum, don't go there again. I'm telling you, something is odd about all of this."

"Ok, Alex, let me know you're coming back. Please keep safe and let me know where you are, always . Are you keeping this new number?"

"Yes, it is a temporary phone, only you have the number. Don't give it out to anyone without asking me first. No one. Please, Mum."

"You sound like your father...I know he kept secrets; it was his job after all. But...the secrets he kept from me were..." Olivia Brereton went quiet on the phone.

In a brighter voice, Alex said, "I'm near Southampton Mum. I'm looking forward to seeing the old girl again. Please, relax, stop thinking things through and trust Dad. I do."

"I know. Goodbye Alex. I won't even give your number to your Uncle. Love you."

The last time he sailed in the cabin cruiser was on his sixteenth birthday. He and his father went for a coastal tour and, given he was so often away, it was a great time to get to know his father better. Alex, fluent in Arabic from a young age, named the boat 'Sakhra.' It meant 'Rock.' It amused Alex the vessel could be called 'Rock the boat.' He fought hard to get his father to agree to the name since he interpreted it differently; 'Sinks like a rock.' They often joked with each other on the suitability of the name.

Arriving in Southampton, Alex looked at the massive cruise liners as he approached the city. The large vessels dwarfed the quays. He made his way into central Southampton and felt sad once again remembering their last time here. His father was often missing in his life, but he was a big part of it.

It took him no time to find the Sakhra moored at the end of a quay as his father described. It looked the same as the day he last sailed in it.

The Sakhra had two large outboard engines, a flying deck, a sitting area, small galley kitchen, two bedrooms and a small bathroom which included a shower. Inside, when Alex smelt his father's aftershave, his tears came once again. His grief returned at unexpected times, triggered off by some memory. Olivia Brereton never stepped aboard the Sakhra. The boat was his and his father's space, it didn't surprise him he felt sadder here than anywhere else since his death.

Alex made for the small bedroom cabin at the front of the boat, where he usually slept. Once inside, the triangle-shaped bed looked smaller, he would no longer fit. Alex pulled up the mattress and found the small compartment he was looking for, reaching inside. It was challenging to get his larger adult hands in, something Alex never had trouble with previously. He found what he was looking for, the boat's watertight safe.

Now, sitting at the small table in the kitchen area, Alex set about opening the safe, anxious to see if anything was inside. The wad of papers inside were not filed nor stapled but they were in some sort of order.

Alex found a handwritten note in his father's handwriting first.

Alex if you are reading this, I'm either standing behind you or something has happened. First, let me tell you, once again, how proud I am to be your father and your friend.

You'll be sad and have many questions. Read these papers carefully and take your time. You are smart enough to understand the content of the files and why they are so important.

Your next step is to make a decision about what to do next. On the one hand, you could do nothing. You can lead your life as if you never read the papers in this box. This could be the best option for you and your mother.
You will need to protect yourself now I am gone. Please protect your mother, it's what Brereton's do. If you decide to do nothing, you'll need to disappear without a trace, your mother too.

The other option is to take the information I've provided and work out how to use it. It is, by far, the more dangerous option. With me gone, the people I mention in these papers will come after you. The only way to stop them is to expose them. I can't tell you how to do it or who to trust, you'll be on your own. Do not share these papers with your mother.

Perhaps any other father would give you only one option; to disappear. I know you well, Alex, I know you won't rest until you find out what happened to me. That's why I've included everything I know about 'Operation Catesby.'

Love, as always, Dad,

tadhkarnaa

Alex put the letter to one side. He repeated his father's last word, 'tadhkarnaa' - remember me. He would never forget. He wouldn't let the people responsible for his father's death forget him either, Alex would make them pay.

CHAPTER 36HARRY - THE INVICTUS ARMY

"Please, both of you take care. Can I suggest you acquire extra security? Carolina, can you go to the Embassy and stay there with your sister, you'll be safer. I don't think you should go back to the States yet," I said.

"Why?" Carolina asked, the surprise apparent on her face.

I looked at Virginia who answered, "Carolina, Arthur is involved in some way, you're not safe."

"From Arthur?"

"–I don't know enough about your husband, but I know a little. With what you've told me he must be complicit in my brother's death as well as my father's. If he suspects you, there is no telling what he could do. It sounds to me he has lost all sense of reason."

When I stood, the sisters did too. We were finished here, for now. Carolina seemed to have difficulty and stumbled slightly. I felt sorry for her, but that boiling pit within, over this whole situation, was growing impatient. Angry. Sure, the women were helping me by coming here, but I wanted them gone. Virginia saw our meeting was finished and agreed to keep in touch by letter since all electronic forms of communication couldn't be trusted. As I saw them out, I asked Ray to come and see me on the balcony of the Round Tower.

Although it was cold and blustery, the view from the highest part of the Castle was clear. I could see the London skyline to the East and stared at the vista until I heard Ray's footsteps behind me.

"You'll catch a cold," he said.

I looked at what I was wearing, a shirt and chinos. I hadn't noticed the cold until those words, and shivered. "I didn't want anyone to overhear us."

Ray merely nodded. He waited a while and took in the view himself. Eventually, I told him about my meeting with the two American women.

"The Prime Minister of the United Kingdom?" Ray reserved his anger for the direst of situations, so his growled tone was unexpected.

"We can't be one hundred percent sure, Ray. But it looks likely. I know he is a republican, we've had them before, but no one ever went this far. The question is, what can I do about it? I am a figurehead of this country. I have no real powers; I certainly have no support from the Government. I don't know how deep this goes; how rotten this is. Crippley wants us all gone. Me, my family. Perhaps we should give him what he wants, it would suit Meghan."

"No," Ray said flatly. "I have seen counties far and wide where corruption leads to decay and chaos. If this isn't sorted, it never will be."

I was pleased with Ray saying the right thing at the right time. "Ok, you're right. I think of all those years my grandmother served the country and the kings and queens before her. Great Britain is great for a whole number of reasons, but undoubtedly the monarchy has been good for the country.

Ray read the doubt in my voice, "Don't ever forget, Harry."

"You called me Harry?"

"To get your attention."

"Well." I laughed. "You did. But what next? We know who the enemy is or are. The General is the immediate problem. If Crippley is the enemy, he'll get another General, someone else to do his dirty work."

Ray went silent, me too. We stood silently looking out over the grounds. Eventually, Ray said, "Carolina Thiskwood showed her cards by coming to us. There is no love lost in her marriage. She's obviously close to her sister and, if she took your advice, she'd be with her at the French Ambassador's residence."

"What are you thinking?"

Ray continued, "Could we trust Carolina enough to use her to lure the General to us?"

"And do what?"

"What would you do with an enemy, Sir? We have to neutralise him."

"I...I can't."

"I am here, you don't have to."

I blushed, maybe I called on Ray because he would do what was needed. "Ok, I think she would do it. I will speak to Virginia first and see what she says. We can't afford to have Carolina turn on us at the last minute."

Ray nodded, "The source of the problem is the Prime Minister."

I pointed out the inner courtyard to the guards who were on their way to change posts. "Who can we trust? Our own guards? Will they help us?"

Ray took his time to reply, "I am not sure. The men like the changes we've put in place. They feel more useful; the constant changes keep them fresh. But I am not sure they will help us, no, they would be conflicted. We will need more than the two of us, for sure."

"We have Dak."

"Yes, we can rely on him, but still not enough. We will need at least ten. It gives us more options, allows us to develop a better battle plan."

I sought assurance in Ray's demeanour, looking to him. "We need our own platoon?"

"You, Meghan and your children are in danger. We need a unit we can rely on."

I let the silence stretch between us, before saying, "Invictus!"

Confusion scrunched his face. "The disabled sportsmen from the forces?"

"And women, Ray."

"...And women. What do you mean?"

"I called on you because of our history. We've been through a lot together. Those men..."

"And women," Ray reminded me with a smile.

"The Invictus Games were created with the aim of proving how much they could do. We gave them an aim, a purpose. We re-lit a fire in their hearts."

Ray lightly touched my sleeve, earnestly he said, "You were the one who had the vision, the belief. You made it happen."

I didn't reply immediately, to deny it would look like false modesty. "There are several guys we could call on, some from our own regiment. Sure, they've got disabilities, but they've proven they can achieve above all the odds. Could we co-opt some of them?

"Yes," he said quickly. "Maybe."

"Deal?" I reached out a hand, regardless of the doubt in his voice.

He clutched it back. "Yes, Sir."

I'm not sure Ray believed it was a deal, I'd have to convince him. "Come, let's go to my study. I'll get us something to eat, this could take us all night."

While I knew Ray remained sceptical, he helped me select the Invictus veterans. We agreed on the essential requirement for listing, to be personally known to me. Next, they would need specific skills. I wanted to ignore their disabilities at the shortlist stage, but, at some point, we had to take it into account. Ray challenged me on some veterans I favoured and accepted my concerns regarding others he thought ideal. We completed a list of potential platoon members by eleven p.m. that evening.

CHAPTER 37
ROOM Q1-50

Jarrod Crippley reached for the album he kept by his bedside. His mother left it to him in her will. Always penniless, Elizabeth Crippley left nothing more save for one hundred pounds she mistakenly thought sufficient to pay for her funeral.

It was late, Crippley couldn't sleep. He sat up in bed and re-read the handwritten note stuck down on the first page of the worn and tattered scrapbook.

Dear Jarrod,

No one could be prouder of their son than me. I've added to this album throughout the years as I've watched you rise from a trade union convenor to the leader of the opposition.

I first noticed your sense of fair play when you came home from school one day with a bloody nose from trying to protect little Emila Lincoln, the little black girl you took under your wing.

It came as no surprise to me that you did well at school and gained a university scholarship, a first in our family. You upset me when you turned your back on a legal career, how I would have loved my only son to be a lawyer. I'm sorry I gave you grief at the time, little did I know you had a plan all along!

I've watched you over the years become a man who cares for others and someone who fights harder than anyone I know for what you believe. You have the brains and the drive to make this a better country, I am so proud of you.

Well done, son. Think of me when you have time, I love you.

Mother.

In the early years, his mother took many of the pictures in the album. The later ones were snipped out of the newspaper and were yellowing from age. The first of him standing on a stage after winning his first election took pride of place in the worn book.

He turned the page and stared at himself wearing a yellow hard hat on top of a truck addressing striking petrochemical workers. He promised to nationalise the oil companies and how they cheered when he said they'd get longer holidays and more sick pay. The newspaper cutting featured the headline, "Crippley Ignites!"

As he looked at the picture, he noticed Robbie McNee standing in the background. Although he looked at the picture hundreds of times, it was the first time he noticed McNee and wondered how he had missed it until now.

Putting down the book, Jarrod Crippley looked at his phone, it was after midnight, but he knew McNee would answer.

"Hi, Jarrod. Can you wait a moment, Mary is asleep, I'll go into my study?"

Crippley heard Mary moan in the background. "McNee?"

"I'm here."

"I know it is a little late. I've been going through my dear mother's photographs, God rest her soul. There you were too, behind me." McNee said nothing, he continued, "Everything was easier back then."

"We've certainly travelled a long way." Drowsiness still thick in his voice.

"Robbie, I've been thinking about something you said to me, maybe it was our last conversation. I've been so busy."

"I know Jarrod, we've got a lot going on."

"When you came to me following our last meeting with the General, Robbie, you said you 'never signed up for this'. What do you mean? I brushed you off at the time, I'm sorry."

Robbie's tongue went thick, throat dry. He paused for longer than he should, but Crippley waited. Finally, he said, "We've worked well together over the years. I always had faith in you."

"And you don't now?"

"Jarrod, Thiskwood is leading us along a dangerous path."

"Thiskwood told me he blames you in many ways."

"Me?"

"He said you muddy the waters. Of course, I backed you all the way..."

"Thank you. But Jarrod, don't you see? What we are doing has gone way beyond anything you intended."

Crippley turned his light off next to his bed. Laying in the dark on the soft pillow, he said, "We've always been honest with each other. Be honest, Robbie."

"I...I think we should end it all. The General is poison, don't you see?"

"Robbie, I can't sleep, I haven't been able to sleep for a while. You could be right."

McNee let out a breath he didn't know he was holding. "Thank God. Jarrod, I'll help you. We've been in sticky situations before, this must be the worst, but we'll get through it."

The glow of the phone screen illuminated Jarrod Crippley's face. He held the phone out and looked at it for a moment before he spoke again, "Thank you, Robbie. One thing, what does Mary think of this...situation?"

"Mary agreed with me, she's worried for me, and you, of course." McNee swallowed. "Of course, you know Mary, she wouldn't breath a word to anyone about this."

"I'm alone, I don't have a good wife like you Robbie. Look, it's the weekend. Go to Chequers tomorrow afternoon, I'll send a car for you. I'll meet you there. We'll stay over, we need to build some bridges, find a way through everything. Getting the General to stand down won't be easy. Bring along Mary too. I value her opinions, I like Mary."

"Jarrod, we'd love to come. Wait, we don't have anyone to look after the children. It will just be me. Mary will moan at me; she's used to it."

Crippley could still make out the picture of McNee at the Petrochemical works from the light on his phone. "A single man like me often forgets about children." He paused. "Try to find someone to look after them. If you can't, bring them too."

"Mary would love it, I'm sure the children would as well."

"I'm not due there this weekend, I've given the staff the weekend off. Mary may have to help out with the cooking."

"Ha, ha. I've tasted your cooking; Mary will be essential!"

"Good, I'll see you there around three?"

"Great," said McNee. "Thank you, Jarrod, we're doing the right thing."

The McKee Family arrived Saturday afternoon in high spirits.

It was clear the chauffeured limousine to Chequers impressed the children, even the highly-strung Mary McNee was at ease, seldom the case.

The PM gave Robbie McNee and his family some tea. "Robbie, we've got a lot to talk about, but we can do that later. Looking at the children, he said, "Now, children, you'll be able to tell your children the Prime Minister made you tea at Chequers."

Mary McKee said, "Thank you, Prime Minister."

"Jarrod."

"Jarrod. Robbie told me you've no staff on. I bought some casserole; I hope you like it."

"I wanted a quiet weekend with real friends. The staff were not due this weekend, I told them not to change the schedules for me. A casserole is perfect, good home cooking," said the PM, standing, "first, let's look around. Kids, I'm going to give you a history lesson."

McNee's youngest son spoke, "Oh no. No thanks, I don't like history. I like other stuff, new stuff."

"Anthony!" Mary said.

"It is Ok." Crippley let the smile stretch across his face. "Look here, Anthony and, er, Rose."

Anthony McNee spoke for his sister, "It is Rosemary. R O S E M A R Y."

This time Robbie McNee grabbed hold of his son and gave him a stern look. Rosemary laughed, "You can call me Rose, lots of people do. There are four 'Rosemary's' in my school. They Call me 'Scottish Rose' but I'm not Scottish. It's because 'McNee' sounds Scottish."

Crippley, never good with children, wondering what the little girl was talking about, merely smiled. "Now children,

'Chequers,' is the official country home of the sitting British Prime Minister."

Anthony struggled in his father's arms and said, "Who's house is it when you stand?"

"The House was given to the nation," Crippley persisted, "by Arthur and Ruth Lee; an American Heiress who purchased the house for her husband."

Rosemary looked at her mother, inquiringly, "Mummy, 'a hairy ass'?"

Mary couldn't help laughing, "An *heiress* is someone who is given a lot of money when someone dies, usually by their mother or father when they die."

"Oh, how sad," said Rosemary, who cuddled up to her mother.

"Now, Children. You've seen where you'll be sleeping tonight and this big room of course. I'm going to show you something hardly anyone knows about. In fact, your father doesn't even know."

Robbie looked over to Crippley, "What?"

Stranding, Crippley noticed Anthony spill his tea on the carpet. He tried to keep his voice level; friendly. "Finish your tea, I'm going to show you the big secret."

At the corner of the room, the PM opened a hidden door which opened like elevator doors in a department store.

"Wow," said Anthony while running into the small cubical. "A lift behind a secret door. Cool."

Crippley grimaced. "Anthony, perhaps step out for a while. I will tell you about this house. Your mum and dad would like to find out more, wouldn't you?"

Both Robbie and Mary McNee nodded at Crippley, both

grabbed their son at the same time. Crippley saw Robbie squeeze his son's shoulder a little too hard for it to be a loving gesture. "Now, Chequers is an old house, but some of it is new."

Rosemary looked around. "This is new?"

Crippley laughed. "Wait, I'll show you. Prime Ministers before me got people to dig out underneath the building. There are massive basements hardly anyone has ever seen."

"Basements?" asked Robbie. "More than one?"

"There is a vast set of underground rooms below us. In fact, there are three floors of underground rooms. They call them Q-1, Q-2 and Q-3. Q-3 is the newest, it holds lots of technical equipment which I'm not allowed to show you. But we can take the lift to Q-1. It was built in the 1930s, it hasn't been used for years. Come on, let's go."

The two children gawped. Mary McNee scolded them as they forgot their manners again and rushed toward the elevator. Crippley shook it off. "Children will be children, leave them, Mary. Come on, let's all go and discover my secret rooms.'

Once inside the elevator, Crippley asked Robbie to press the minus one button, Anthony beat him to it, and they all laughed as the doors closed behind them.

A natural hush came over all of them, Crippley touched Anthony on the head and smiled as the young boy looked at him. As the lift descended, Crippley said, "Each of the levels was constructed at different times, it shows in the materials used. The first basement was built before the second world war, the next, Q-2, was constructed sometime in the late fifties with the deepest level coming towards the end of the century. Take care, it is darker on the floor we are going to, remember we don't really use it much."

After the doors opened, they walked into the dimly lit corridor of Q1. The air was stale, it was hard to see where the passage led. Every ten feet, a small electric light appeared out of the darkness. Rosemary clung onto her mother's hand.

Crippley maintained the touristic chatter as they walked along. "Come on, not far. There's an extraordinary room right at the end of this corridor. The room is where the Prime Minister used to keep his secrets!"

In unison, the McNee children said, "Secrets?"

"Yes, governments and people have lots of secrets. Sometimes you have to make sure no one can find them," answered Crippley, walking a little faster.

Robbie McNee, taking after his mother, said, "Are you sure it is safe here PM? Safe for the children, I mean?"

His wife answered for him, "Of course it is, isn't Jarrod?"

Crippley could see she liked calling him 'Jarrod' again. She stopped using his first name when he became the leader of the opposition. "It is fine, look, we are here, see, room Q1-50. Go in, in you go."

When he visited room Q1-50 earlier on in the day, he turned the lights on in the room, but it was still a little gloomy. Reassuring the four McNees, Crippley said, "Don't worry, you'll get used to the light,"

Mary chased her family into the back of the room. She looked around, surprised Crippley didn't follow them.

As Crippley stood at the doorway, he said nothing. The family looked back at him, expecting him to join them. Robbie McNee looked questionably at the PM, "Jarrod?"

Crippley didn't answer. Instead, he grabbed hold of the door and pushed it. The hinges creaked and groaned with the movement, Crippley put his back into moving the heavy door.

McNee stood transfixed to the spot. He called out again, "Jarrod. What are you doing?"

Mary McNee instinctively grabbed hold of her children and looked to her husband for some kind of explanation. "Robbie, what's going on?" She let go of Rose and Anthony and made a sprint for the door. "Stop, what are you doing?"

Crippley tried to avoid Mary McNee's eyes but glimpsed them as the last slither of light disappeared as the door closed shut. He came in the morning to make sure the lock worked. He used some oil he bought with him to Chequers anticipating the old mechanism would need it. For good measure, he bolted the door at the top and the bottom, making the room airtight and secure.

Later in the day, Jarrod Crippley went for a walk around the grounds for the fresh air.

"A nice evening, Prime Minister."

"Indeed, indeed. Did the helicopter disturb you sleeping?"

"No, Sir," the officer laughed. "We saw it come and we saw it go."

"Yes, Mr McNee and his family enjoyed their time here. I thought it would be nice for them to travel home like that. You can't believe how thrilled the children were when they saw it."

"Excellent, sir. Very considerate of you."

"I thought so," said the PM. "Right, I'm off to eat, Mrs McNee brought me a casserole, it smells delicious. I'm looking forward to it, I hope it is better than my mother used to make, she was a terrible cook."

CHAPTER 38 -THE REAL ENEMY

John Amery studied Heather's sleeping; again, it rested on a pillow next to his. Her vivaciousness, her spark, her intelligence shone through even though her eyes were closed. She looked serene with hair dark framing her beautiful features. Wasn't he a lucky man? He thought

He rolled out of bed, carefully, as to not wake her; it was almost as if a new light hung over the gardens, when he made his way out to them. The Italian architecture magnificent, and new again. Somehow. The last few weeks spent together were the best of his life. It had to be her, Heather. Her radiance dappled this place in something new.

The news about King William and his family shocked them both and, somehow strengthening their relationship; they do say that shared tragedy does that. His chest tightened ... they would get through this together ... he would be sure of it. Glancing back from the balcony into the room, she was beautiful in her stillness. He wouldn't lose this, ever.

They both tried to call McNee; an 'honest' broker in their opinion, but it was to no avail. Any contact with Crippley was ill advised. It was time to do something. John loved his time with Heather here, but they couldn't stay forever.

Following the news of the slaughter carried out on the Norfolk beach by 'Islamic terrorists,' John doubled security at the house. Serge was the first person he updated on intel, running through it with a fine-toothed comb, making sure all measure of safety was considered. Leaving Heather in bed, John made his way to the kitchen where he supposed his Ukrainian bodyguard was having breakfast.

John was right, Serge was having a light-hearted conversation with Estefania, the housekeeper. It was nice to hear their laughter as he entered the kitchen, he was sorry to interrupt. "Good morning, you two. It's nice to hear laughter around here."

Serge winked at him. "There's been a lot of it around here for the last few weeks."

"Yes, I guess it has been different with Heather here."

The tiny Cuban housekeeper giggled and smiled. She was about fifty years old, but the smile stole some of those years from her.

Amery said, "Come on, Serge, leave Ester alone. Hopefully she'll make breakfast for Heather and me."

Estefania said, "It's done, I will lay it out near the pool, ok? Mr John, Manny wants to come over and swim with you. I said you were busy."

"Bring him over tomorrow morning. Your son is becoming quite the dolphin, Ester. Make sure he practices when I'm not here, he can use the pool here, of course."

"Thank you, Mr John. He talks about you all the time."

"He's a good kid. Tell him I'll practice in the morning. We have to sort out his breaststroke, fix his shoulder position. Oh, can you take a tray to Heather? Let her lay in. Would you bring something out for Serge and me?" He nodded to Serge, who stood, needing no more encouragement; all six-foot eight of him seemed to loom over the barstool and counter. The

British term ‘built like a brick shit house’ came to mind. He chuckled to himself, his secretary had a way with words.

"Just a coffee for me Estefania, please. I can't fit anything else in because you feed me too much," Serge said.

Unlike many personal protection professionals, Serge didn't have a military background. His training was first in the boxing ring followed by a period as hired protection for one of the most prominent Russian criminal gangs. He climbed the ranks, eventually acting as the chief of security for the mob leader.

Amery unexpectedly came across Serge in St. Tropez, France, when staying with an art collector friend of his. One afternoon the Russian mob leader paid a visit to his friend who asked John to remain by the pool as they needed to discuss a forthcoming art auction. Like Amery, Serge was banished to the pool area and the two got to talking.

Unlike a typical security 'thug,' John found Serge's conversation fascinating and, sometimes, amusing. His size and bulk hid his intelligence to most, so the more they talked, the more interested John became as he told him about his life. Boxing was Serge's ticket out of poverty. He was spotted at a boxing match by a Russian who made an offer to join their organisation.

Personal security suited Serge Kleckenko as boxing at thirty was no longer enjoyable, even though he remained in good form. The gang trained him, sending him to a succession of camps headed by former SAS troops in England and one run by a retired Navy Seal in America. The whole story intrigued John; their worlds entirely different, but still they crossed. They spent over two hours talking by the pool. It wasn't all one way; Serge asked a lot about John's life and how he made his money.

Eventually, the meeting between John Amery's art friend and the mob leader concluded. John thanked Serge for his company before the two dealmakers came out of the house. He left Serge with his card and a promise of work, should he ever need it.

It was a year later when Amery received the call from an unknown number. He didn't answer unknown callers but the persistence - a call every twenty minutes - piqued his curiosity. Eventually, John answered, he recognised the heavily accented Ukrainian. It amused him to find Serge was calling from outside his office in London and he invited him in.

He recalled his secretary's face when escorting Serge into his office. A deer in the headlights, unsure whether or not to leave John alone. It turned out the Russian mob leader 'retired' and the new head of the gang wanted his own man in charge of security. John found it a little challenging to believe Serge left on 'good terms' and questioned him again and again. Serge suggested Amery call the new man at the top; Serge's story was one hundred percent accurate. Also, the mob leader recommended him highly, but 'for obvious reasons,' he wanted his own team around him. John told Serge how pleasant he sounded. Serge laughed and said at the time 'he is a devil with a sheep's smile.' Amery understood the meaning if not quite able to picture a sheep smiling.

Now, sitting by the pool, both dressed in shorts and T-shirts, they sat drinking coffee. Amery said, "It's time to consider our next steps."

Smiling, Serge said, "Your holiday romance is coming to an end?"

"Maybe, but Heather may stay around."

"I win $10, yes!" said Serge, the grin stretching on his face.

Amery looked questionably at him, saying nothing.

The massive security officer looked a little regretful of his outburst and said, "Um, I had a bet with Estefania."

John Amery laughed, "Ok, since you are in the money, drinks are on you when we're next out."

Serge smile fell away. "I don't drink on duty. I don't drink, you know this."

"It's ok. Look, let me outline everything to you." Jokes were lot on Serge, sometimes.

Over the next hour, John filled Serge in with the details of Crippley, their meetings, the news of the King's assassination and even his role and Heather's part in supplying Crippley information. Along the way, Serge asked several questions. John could tell he was trying to assess the extent of the threat and the possible weak points. By discussing their situation with Serge, the danger John and Heather were in became even more apparent.

The story complete, all questions answered, they both looked over to Heather as she approached them.

"What are you boys doing, eating without asking me?"

"I asked Ester to bring you something."

"It's ok, the scrambled eggs were beautiful. But I will take a coffee. Ok if I join you?"

Serge stood and pulled out a chair. John filled her in on the gaps. Heather looked a little worried. John knew what she was thinking; could they put their lives in Serge's hands? "Serge has been with me for a few years Heather, I trust him, literally, with my life."

"I would die before Mr Amery," Serge said from his seat.

The look on his face convinced her. "Ok, it is ok. But this means you'll have to look after me too."

John Amery looked at the new woman in his life. They'd not discussed the future of their relationship. He reached out to her, both smiled at each other and held hands.

Serge coughed quietly, a little embarrassed, he changed the subject. "I have a few questions, both of you."

"Of course." Both John and Heather answered.

"You have options, but it depends on what you want, you know, long term. I protect you. We grow security, but it could go on for a long time. It would have to be here. You birds in cage, trapped, but both safe. Question... you made mistake with British politician?"

John Amery couldn't answer at first. His head of security highlighted the issue on his mind; were they complicit in the deaths of so many people?

Heather answered for him, "You're right to ask Serge. We were in a different world back then. It was exciting to be asked by the most powerful person in the country to help. I thought I was doing the right thing. I've been convinced the class system in the UK was its greatest weakness, it held people down."

"Class, money, politics, the world is like this. I don't think you change it," Serge said, "Sorry, I'm not rude. It is true."

"You have a way with words, Serge," Heather said, "The answer is, yes, I do want to help put this right. I don't want to feel trapped here either. We need to do something."

Heather looked to John for his response, said he was more than forthcoming. "Like Heather, I was excited. I saw an opportunity to make a great deal of money, it blinded my judgement. We were wrong getting involved. God, this feels like a confessional, I hear my Catholic nanny's voice in my head as I speak!"

All three laughed, releasing the tension of the moment.

Serge spoke first, "Ok. So, we talk offence strategy here, not defensive. No use staying in this wonderful palace, we become sitting turkeys, waiting for Christmas. John, your penthouse in London is easy to keep you safe. Top floor, one way in, easy to protect. Then we look at the rhinoceros in the room."

John cut in, "You mean Elephant?"

Serge continued smiling briefly at John's correction, "We have to neutralise this Jarrod Crippley."

Heather said, "Neutralise?"

Serge understood, "Two ways. Get facts, evidence, tell press. Politicians not like the press. Police then do their work. The other is to take him out."

"Heather, we've met Crippley, he is a worm. If we expose him, you can be sure he'll turn it around and put the blame at our door. I know we've helped, but we didn't know how far he would go. McNee has disappeared, Brereton and Casement are dead. Only the General and us two are left."

A pained look formed on Heather’s face. "Two wrongs don't make a right."

Serge saved Amery from having to reply. "Look, I give you options, you don't spend rest of your days here, wait for someone to knock you both off. We go back to London, take our time and make plans from there."

Amery knew he employed Serge for a reason and added, "Heather, I can't spend the next few years here, can you?"

"I guess Serge is right. Let's use our brains, our resources and everything at our disposal and sort this out. We should go back to London but get this you two; I'm an equal partner in this. I'm not some frightened little girl. You have to include me in everything. If not, I'm off."

"Tell me more about General Thisk..."

"Thiskwood," Heather said.

"He is American, no? This General Thiskwood, why is Mr Crippley working with him?"

John said, "I've asked around about him. He has upset a lot of people with his book; 'Balls to the Walls.'

"Great title, I must read it," Heather said, not hiding the irony.

"I have," answered Amery, "It is worth a read. It's as near to entering someone's head as you can get. He is a self-serving prick and doesn't have a good word to say about anyone or anything. He used it as a weapon to malign some brilliant and well-respected people. It sold well, but the reviews were awful. It wouldn't have made him millions."

"So, why was he included?" Serge asked again.

"He was there to plan out the campaign," said Heather. "I asked McNee the question when I met him after our first meeting."

Serge looked at John for confirmation, he nodded. "Serge, General Thiskwood and Crippley planned everything out. Crippley isn't stupid, but Thiskwood appears to be the brains behind it all."

Serge looked at both John and Heather in turn, "The General is your enemy too, more dangerous than Prime Minister."

CHAPTER 39 - PORTOBELLO GOLD

Alex received the full story from his father's papers; the plan for the Crown Estate and who the members of Crippley's Committee were.

A quick Google session allowed him to find more about the committee members. He 'knew' The History Girl from her programs and was a fan, not only because she was hot, he agreed with her theories regarding the existence of a God. John Amery was often portrayed as a 'Capitalist devil' incarnate while the press on the black judge consistently painted him in a good light. The video of Mrs Casement interviewed by an opportunistic reporter brought a tear to his eye; both he and this elegant lady lost someone they loved.

There was more than enough on Jarrod Crippley, it didn't take much Googling given he was one of the UK's most public figures. When the Nation voted for Crippley, Alex liked his ideas and voted for him. The PM demonstrated he was not the man for the job and was systematically killing any hope for young people like him. Unemployment was high, but the under-thirty's rate was even higher at forty-one per cent.

There was little to find on Robbie McNee. He was Crippley's sidekick but rarely mentioned in the press. He would have to try and find out more as McNee featured several times in his father's papers.

General Arthur Thiskwood was a public figure on the 'other side of the pond' as his father used to say of the USA. The information Google spat out focused mainly on his book; 'Balls to the Walls.' He ordered a copy from Amazon, reading it gave an excellent insight into the General's personality. The reviews of the book were mixed, readers' comments gathered from the internet painted a picture of a bitter man. He exacted revenge on many people, especially former Army colleagues.

One of the most relevant papers in his father's files covered Alex's drug bust. In a way he was relieved he found it, it explained a lot about why his father acted on behalf of the Prime Minister, he had no choice. Alex wasn't a fool; his father was no angel. Some of the work he carried out before the blackmail was questionable, especially the smear campaign orchestrated by his father on William and Kate. Alex considered the information on the Royal Family in his father's papers. In a way, it authenticated the contents of the documents left by his father; it included the good, the bad and the ugly.

When he was younger, Alex got some insight into his father's work by watching the TV news with him. Alex received a unique education on the UK political scene. His father would make the odd remark giving the opposite view on the 'facts' as they were given by the news presenters. Occasionally his mother would stop Alex's father mid-sentence, eager to protect their son. Still, he gained a better understanding of the spin put on significant events than most.

Seeing his father hanging from the rope was an image Alex would never be able to erase from his mind; he couldn't un-see it. He went into his family house, a boy and came out a man. The calm of the Spanish hilltop villa and the sunshine, being waited on hand and foot by his mother's staff, it all helped Alex's healing process. His time in Spain allowed him to decide what he should do next. His father said he could go into hiding. Indeed, with his mother's money, it wouldn't be difficult. It wasn't a life he wanted, his globe-trotting mother with her thriving business couldn't stay hidden either.

Another lesson learned from his father was to start at the top. He pondered on this. Who was at the top? Crippley? Alex read and re-read the six pages written by his father covering the psychological profile of the PM. Crippley was a narcissist, according to his father. Alex looked up the word to make sure he understood the definition online:

'A narcissistic personality disorder can mean you have a high sense of self-importance. You may fantasise about unlimited success and want attention and admiration. You may feel you are more entitled to things than other people are. You might act selfishly to gain success. You may be unwilling or unable to acknowledge the feelings or needs of others.'

His Dad's comparison to the late President Trump gave a good yardstick as to how such a psychological disorder can drive someone's behaviour. Trump's complete denial of any mistakes made at the outbreak of the Coronavirus pandemic and the terrible errors made by his administration demonstrated the damage such a man could wreak. Crippley was undoubtedly in the Trump mould even though he was at the opposite end of the political spectrum. For the safety of himself and his mother, Alex couldn't risk engaging with the PM.

One night aboard the Sakhra, it occurred he could be considering the wrong person. The top man could be someone else: the new King? For a moment, Alex was scared he was the one with a disorder in thinking he could contact King Harry. The more time he mulled it over, though, the more sense it made. The Brereton Papers, as he now called them, spelt it out: Crippley wanted the Crown Estate Money and a Republic; Both involved the King.

The problem was, how would Alex contact King Harry? It

might have been possible if his father were alive. Who was he to be able to make a difference? He was a twenty-year-old boy who only a few months before spent his time rowing, studying, screwing or drinking.

Alex took to running each morning and attended a gym in the afternoon, not having exercised for some time. The weather around Southampton was pleasant and he also found working on the boat therapeutic. With each day he grew stronger, muscle memory took over; his body practically remoulded itself, that paired with a decent amount of sweat ... and some tears, but he missed his father.

It was out while he was running one morning the various pieces dropped into place. The previous night's sleep was long and uninterrupted; Alex's first full night's sleep since before his father died. His mother, who desperately wanted Alex to return to Spain, gave him good advice - to take his time and be careful.

With each stride along the docks and harbours of Southampton, Alex planned his next moves. First, he would need to base himself in London. Alex needed to contact a friend of his, Harvey Foxton-Worth. 'Foxy,' as he was called, rowed well but a poor student; he possessed neither the drive nor the intelligence. Foxy's father pulled strings to get him into Oxford. The university found out Foxy had nothing to justify his place there, even his rowing skills couldn't save him from being 'sent down' - expelled from the university. Alex and Foxy studied together at school. No one was more surprised Foxy got a place at Oxford than Alex, save for Foxy himself.

Foxy's family were well connected like many Oxford students. He might be able to help, he lived in London doing nothing much and could be of help. He would contact his old friend and take it from there.

Alex's mother's family owned several residential properties in

London which they rented out. She was pleased when he contacted her and was more than happy to find him a place to stay in Notting Hill. Alex based himself there last summer, he liked the area. Olivia Brereton accepted Alex wouldn't return to Oxford given he missed so much in the previous few months. Alex didn't tell his mother he wouldn't ever return but decided not to worry her at this stage.

The house was off Portobello Road in a small cul-de-sac. He expected to return to the little flat he used before. His mother surprised him with a small mews property with two bedrooms and an ample sitting room and kitchen, adequate for Alex and better than the flat. It even had parking for his Mini outside. When he moved in, he was a little disappointed to find it sparsely furnished but soon found out the famous Portobello market was more than sufficient for what he needed.

He arranged to meet Foxy at the 'Portobello Gold' pub, close to his new house. Foxy worked at Christie's Auction House; another position secured by his long-suffering father who worried about what was to become of his only son.

"I have no idea you liked antiques?" Alex said to Foxy when he arrived, albeit an hour later than planned.

"Turns out I've a thing for the old stuff, who would have known?"

"Are you enjoying it?" said Alex. He was anxious to get to the point but knew it would take several pints to get there; Foxy was a serious drinker.

"I am. I've met a few old school chums and made some new friends. Social life is extraordinary. Would you like me to try and get you in?"

"No, I'm working on a few things since..."

"Yes, tough luck about your Dad. I never met him but, well, you know, tough luck old man."

"I'm pretty much on my own here. Yes, invite me to a few of your parties. I need cheering up."

"Sure. It's why I was late, sorry."

Alex was puzzled. "You've been to a party already, it's only seven!"

Foxy thrust his chin out and pulled his lapels. "I didn't dress like this for you." Foxy thrust his chin out and pulled his lapels. "Mr Brereton. No, the party is in Mayfair. Dorothy Travis-Burke, you know, the girl who played netball at school. It's her folks' place, they're away. There's a few of us going around. Wait, I'll text her, see if you can be my 'plus one.'"

Alex watched his old friend pull out his iPhone from his jacket pocket. Dorothy Travis-Burke was an extremely tall girl with an unfortunate overbite, giving her a horsey appearance. The girl got so much bullying at school Alex often felt sorry for her. Dorothy swerved university and joined her Uncle's public relations business. By all accounts, she was serious about making it there.

"Right, you're in. You'll have to get a move on, you know. You can't wear shorts at Dorothy's. It is a grown-up dinner party," he laughed.

Alex's plan to gradually work on Foxy was ruined. He guessed there would be some interesting people there and someone might know someone who could help him. Besides, he could do with a night off.

"Right, I'll change and join you there. Text me the address would you."

Foxy stood and said he would send the address when he got

there. "I've been there a few times, fuck, I can't remember the bloody address," he said as he put his coat on.

Always the same. "You'd lose your head if it wasn't pinned on."

Alex made his way home and changed. He found his suit a little tight, his intensive exercise in Southampton worked wonders for his body.

Ready, he looked at his phone but found no message from Foxy, Alex's call went to voicemail. Having tried Foxy a few more times, Alex felt he was dressed up with nowhere to go. He made his way back to the Portobello Gold Pub, having decided it was better waiting with a pint in his hand.

When the tourists weren't around, most of the working week, the ancient pub turned into a local. There was a unique mixture of people from different backgrounds. Wealthy people lived in the Royal Borough of Kensington and Chelsea but so did poor people. Multi-Million pound mansions could be found a few streets away from local government-owned low-cost housing. Local people lost all their pretences when they came through the pub door and it was a comfortable atmosphere.

On his second pint, Alex gradually began to lose hope Foxy would come through. He caught a glimpse of himself in one of the pub's many mirrors: compared to others, he was overdressed. It was warm outside; most people wore casual clothes while Alex sweated in his suit. He undid his tie and hung his jacket over the back of the barstool, relieved to be able to breathe a little easier.

Alex got talking to a few people around the bar and it wasn't long before the fourth pint of the local beer was being poured for him. Alex felt a little bit merry but not enough to return home yet. He appreciated the convenience of having a place to live less than two hundred meters from the pub.

On his fifth pint, Alex's conversation with the Spanish barman was interrupted by people in the bar cheering, a few clapped enthusiastically. Turning around to see what caused the commotion, four men were dressed in sports kits displaying the 'Invictus' logo. The barman, Juan, pointed out one of the men as the son of the owner, his picture was on the wall in the men's toilets. Apparently, Bradley Hall insisted on the place his father could hang his Invictus victory picture; it kept him grounded.

Bradley and the other men chose a table near Alex. He noticed Bradley sported a prosthetic leg, his own having been lost in Afghanistan. The other three men were similarly disabled save for the smallest man with a prosthetic left arm.

Juan cut the conversation with Alex short and rushed to pour four pints for the men. Alex turned his stool slightly so he could see the Invictus team. No one noticed. Eventually, Juan returned and automatically poured Alex a pint.

As he nursed his drink, the bar got busier, he suddenly missed his uni friends. The move to London, having to buy new furniture and sort the house out had occupied his mind. He hoped his meeting with Foxy would put him back on track and a wave of disappointment crept over him making him melancholy.

As the bottom of his pint neared, Alex decided to head for home. Tomorrow he needed to get to business given he and his mother could be in danger. The YouTube video raised his profile and, from what he could make out from the Brereton Papers, danger would surely come knocking on his door soon.

About to leave, Alex picked up on the conversation the Invictus men, who were enjoying themselves, were having.

"No, I tell you. I don't know anything. We've been chosen, us four and a couple of the boys from the regiment. In all likelihood, it is some sort of PR stunt. Sure, it's cool all getting together again. Getting a free hotel for the night is great. Sit back, enjoy your pints, there's plenty more although Dad might regret it soon."

The others looked at Brad Hall and raised their empty pints and said, “More,” in unison.

The man with one arm opened the subject again once the fresh pints were in hand. "You all know him, we served with Harry. He's the bloody King for fuck sake. Our paths crossed a few times. Sure, he might recognise me from the games but, but I'm not sure what I'm doing here."

Another member of the gang of four, a heavyset man with some facial injuries, said, "Listen, Eugene. Euuuugeen,"

"Stop taking the piss, call me Gene, I told you a thousand times."

The man continued, "Gene, Harry called us all personally. We're being collected tomorrow and go and see him. It breaks the boredom. We got to train together today; the hotel is top-notch. We have free beer so what's to worry about?"

All four cheered as they drained their pint glasses, trying to outdo each other as to who could finish first.

Alex made the connection despite his alcohol intake. He saw the opportunity and called over to the four men, "Hey, lads, can I buy you a beer?"

The heavyset man looked slightly annoyed, "Boy, are you allowed in here? You look too young to me. Bradley, get your Dad to sling this one out."

The bigger man looked ready to throw Alex out himself, but Bradley put a hand on his arm and pulled him back into his seat.

"I wanted to meet you and buy you a drink, of course, I don't want to interrupt your drinking session," said Alex.

The fourth man, the quietest of the four, said, "Boyo, you don't qualify, no you don't, you'll be having too many arms and too many legs, so you do." Alex barely made the words out as he spoke in a strong Welsh accent. His friends understood him and laughed.

Bradley Hall, the alpha male leader of the group, called over to Alex, "Come on, buy us a drink then. My poor old man can't afford to keep this lot going. And don't worry, we've nothing against able-bodied men."

Alex smiled and moved to their table, squeezing onto a bench already taken by the Invictus athletes. Juan bought over the pints, the men raised their glasses to Alex and said 'cheers.'

It had been a long time since Alex drank so much. The conversation went better after Alex mentioned his rowing career. The Welsh man told him he had to meet their mate 'Kevin', a great rower despite being blind.

On the verge of their next pint, Alex changed the subject by asking, "What are you doing over the next few days? I've just moved here so it would be good to have another few pints with you."

"I'm from here, so fine by me. These boys come from all over. Taffy here comes from a place called Snowdonia. Be careful of him, I've seen him kill more than a few Taliban, he's a trained killer."

The quiet one, with evident pride, said: "We're off to Windsor Castle tomorrow to meet the King."

Alex raised his eyebrows. "Sure boys. I'm going there too, I'm meeting Meghan."

"No, he's right, we are going." Bradley cut in. "Harry is a good bloke. His idea to do the Invictus Games gave us all a purpose, an aim. He is a seriously top bloke."

The others nodded their agreement.

Alex, using all his powers of concentration given the amount of beer he consumed, said, "Wow, awesome. Good on you guys and good on him. I'm jealous, I don't mind admitting it. I know it isn't considered cool to like the Royal Family and all, but I'm a fan."

Bradley Hall's landlord father came over. "Listen, boys, we're shutting soon. You're welcome to stay in and have as much as you like, but I believe you have an important date tomorrow?"

Abruptly all four made a move to exit the pub. Alex stood too, desperate to think about how to make this work for him.

"Dad, I might stay here with you. These boys can make their way back to the hotel. It will be good to catch up with my old man, ok lads?"

The three members of the squad looked at each other, looking abandoned.

"Now, off you go. You'll get a cab outside, better get straight back to the hotel or you'll wake up in the morning with a leg missing."

The three laughed as they went out of the pub. As soon as the door shut behind them, Bradley Hall turned around with a different look on his face.

"Right, Alex, what's this all about?"

Alex's fuddled mind ground out a slow reply, "I, I don't know what you mean?"

Brad stood his ground. His father disappeared from Alex's peripheral vision. Eventually, Alex said, "It is a long story. I'm happy to buy you another pint but if I have one more, I might be sick."

Bradley Hall led Alex out to the room behind the bar, empty of customers. Juan bought in two pints of beer; they remained half full over two hours later.

CHAPTER 40 - HARRY - MY PRIVATE PLATOON

Unable to sleep as my mind churned, bubbled with thought. What I should do about the situation we were in? Crippley's intentions were clear; no doubt he would do my family harm. He demonstrated how dangerous he could be but could I, should I, really take him on? Apart from the constitutional implications, not to mention the law.

Ray and I decided to include Dak in our plans. Over the last few years, Dak and I became close since he demonstrated more than a few times his value to us as a family. Also, being cooped up in the house in LA with the children, I found him a good adult male company. We worked out and drank together often. More than a few times Meghan made a caustic remark about Dak being more of a wife than her. I trusted Dak and Ray, who recommended him to me in the first place, did too.

Living in LA, we became targets for deranged individuals eager to claim the scalp of 'Harry and Meghan' to give them everlasting fame. Dak's organisation gave us all the protection we needed without being too constraining. Dak caught a lone gunman who turned out to be one of the people sending us hate mail regularly. There were other incidents, all handled with expert care. Concerned that Dak would object to Ray heading the security in the UK, he surprised me and accepted

Ray's seniority well and took orders willingly.

At first, both Ray and Dak laughed at my idea about involving the Invictus team. They said they were better off with a fully armed platoon, in the literal sense. At times like these, my natural inclination would be to solicit the advice of others like my father or brother, but they were no longer around to help.

Since inheriting the throne so unexpectedly, I noticed my confidence growing daily; the party boy, the 'lad about town,' a distant memory. I dug my heels in and insisted on co-opting the Invictus team to help us out. Both Ray and Dak argued against it more than once, but eventually, dropped the matter.

I looked forward to meeting the Invictus team. Ray, Dak and I spent hours discussing our plans and swapping opinions on which individuals would work best together. While we spent a great deal of time getting the unit formation right, both of us avoided the most important issue: the mission. Ray raised the subject several times, but I put him off to buy myself some time. While employing an independent unit of trained soldiers to help protect my family and me was a radical step, using it aggressively would be a leap into the unknown.

The day before we were due to meet the Invictus team, I cancelled my weekly audience with Jarrod Crippley. I said I had the flu and didn't want to expose the PM to any infections. I'm sure it pleased him as I know he hated the weekly audiences as much as me. I could only pull this trick once as it would raise Crippley's suspicions.

Still unable to sleep, my mind shifted to Meghan, lying beside me. So far, she hid it well, but she itched to go back to 'normal life.' The issue came to a head last night when instead of making quiet, barbed comments, she asked me outright if we would return to the US. I made it clear to her, perhaps a little too forcibly, our life couldn't go back to her 'normal.'

Meghan said a few things to me in anger, something she'd regret in the morning, but so did I. In recent weeks Meghan kept to herself and the children. A void lengthened between us. She made transatlantic calls to her operation in LA but I noticed they were becoming shorter and shorter. The show's ratings climbed and "Meghan' the show didn't necessarily need Meghan the woman with Michelle doing such a good job.

The children became my wife's focus. Sometimes when I saw them playing altogether, I had the feeling she acted the part; doing what good mothers are supposed to do. Her focus would momentarily shift to some faraway place, her smile fixed.

Although I kept the note from Virginia Dumont to myself and revealed nothing of my plans, I made it clear the mourning period in the castle kept us safe. Meghan agreed the children were best protected at Windsor until more could be found out about William's killers.

Since sleep eluded me, I slipped out of bed, taking care not to disturb Meghan, and put on my dressing gown.

As time went by, doubts came into my mind regarding the idea to call on the Invictus athletes. Was I asking too much of these poor and damaged men and women? My decision to deploy them looked flawed. Their bravery displayed in conflict and in dealing with their life-changing injuries could be only skin deep.

Ray and Dak surprised me. As my confidence declined, the more they warmed to the idea. They both said how they'd discussed it between them and agreed on using the Invictus soldiers. Co-opting any form of an official team from the forces or the police to help me would be a massive conflict of interest for the serving men and women involved. They would undoubtedly be honoured to be invited by me. Still, their reporting lines to the government and ultimately Crippley made it a non-starter. If the PM agreed to strengthen my personal security, I couldn't trust those who joined us. I couldn't order them to go against Crippley's Government if it came to it. Ray and Dak also ruled out the option of hiring professionals as their loyalty could not be guaranteed.

At first, I thought Ray and Dak were humouring me. Their careful consideration of alternative sources of skilled manpower led them to the same conclusion as mine; to use the Invictus soldiers. Still, we agreed the crunch would come when we met the proposed team.

Security being paramount, we couldn't conduct a standard selection process. We needed to ask only those we were fairly sure would agree to join us. They also needed the right level of expertise and be able to perform notwithstanding their disabilities.

We compiled a list of over forty men and women from regiments I served in or from service personnel I met through the Invictus Games. Ray vetted the list further and came back with a shortlist of twenty-two. While he refused to give me details on how he researched them, Ray said the eighteen failed on specific criteria, I shouldn't judge them in future.

I phoned each person on the list surprising all and delighting many. I said I wanted to 'touch base' with them. My actual reason for the call was to get a feel for their current situation and potential for the task ahead. Unexpectedly, I found it rewarding when I received so many words of support for my new role as King.

I made my first call to the man at the top of my list; Brad Hall. After a lengthy conversation, I found it easy to put a tick to Brad's name even though told me to 'fuck off' three times before he believed it was me.

Another call was answered by the husband of one of the

women who served with me in Helmond. He called over to his wife, and I heard him say, "Oi, it's your boyfriend on the line." I chatted with her for a while and put a tick next to her name too.

Some of the calls didn't go so well. Of course, they were polite and respectful, but I didn't get the feeling in my gut they would be right; their names remained un-ticked. After I made the last call, I reviewed the names again and put it to one side. The selection from the calls gave me twelve names, but I crossed off four more after further consideration overnight.

Ray did another more in-depth check on the eight names after I gave him the list and returned it to me with one further name crossed out. I said it was looking more like a small coach party than an offensive force. The number was fine. The list wasn't exactly a permanent, unchangeable fixture, he'd said. I called the final seven people back to invite them to Windsor today, they all accepted.

Megan insisted on installing a small 'Tassimo' coffee machine in the study, so we didn't have to have staff in our private apartment early in the day. Sitting in the study with the coffee, I reviewed the list of who would be coming later.

Bradley Hall topped the list, I'm glad he got through Ray's checks. I met Brad in training and watched him get into a lot of trouble. I was amazed to see him in Helmond but pleased because he had more about him than many colonels I met. While he wasn't a great one for the rules, something about his personality made him a natural leader. He lost a leg in Afghanistan and his sense of purpose until he signed for the Invictus Games where he won a Silver medal. He became Great Britain's Men's Captain.

I once heard someone call **Flo Gummer** a 'sassy bitch,' never was there a more apt description of a woman. Flo, blinded in one eye, was a tiny black woman from an underprivileged background. Raised in care, she developed a mouth which could destroy a six-foot commando with a few words. While her shooting was excellent, she had a knack for computers; certainly the right choice for our comms controller.

I met **Eugene Foulks**, Gene as he liked to be called, a few times. He was quiet but not outwardly confident. I saw him win a Gold at the games and a Gold medal at the 50M Rifle event at the Olympics - not the Paralympics - after he lost his arm, a real achievement. His value to the team would prove itself given his specialism as a sniper in the Army.

Rob Wickland passed all of Ray's checks which surprised me given he had three small children. Ray found out Rob split from his wife and he had limited visiting rights. The Welshman, known as 'Taff,' was a good all-rounder despite his small stature. I put him on the list because he went on many patrols with Ray and me and we had a good relationship; I could trust him.

Simone Weller lost her leg from the knee down in Helmond. I was the one who found her lying on the ground after the landmine exploded, killing two others in their Land Rover. I got to know her in the years following, and she helped in the Invictus organisation. Like many women who served in the Army, she found it hard to fit in with civvy life and found the Forces called to her. I worried about her following her discharge because she would flounder without something to work on. I persuaded her to join the Invictus operation before the first games took place. Her brilliant organisational skills would strengthen the team as well as her ability to fight.

Andy Witting is a great bull of a man, and another Invictus Games medal winner in the shot put. He lost a leg in Afghanistan. Like Taffy, Andy came on many of our patrols. He had a nasty side to him, bottled up aggression. Our team needed men like this; I knew he would do anything to protect his colleagues.

Chris Gerard was one of the most handsome men I ever met, the Yorkshireman also oozed charm. He admitted to me once he thought it was a mistake in joining the Army but found out he loved it and the camaraderie. He couldn't wait to get away from home where his parents bullied him and forced him to work in the milking shed on their farm from an early age. Of the whole group, his disability was barely noticeable. His missing left foot, caused by another landmine, enabled him to lead a reasonably normal life. I asked him to head the PR for Invictus, and he charmed the socks off a lot of women and a few men who, I suspected, he secretly preferred. In the field of battle, Chris was a machine; he went on and on. When we were all lagging from a long and dangerous night patrol, Chris showed little sign of tiring. He was useful with a gun as well.

The list was good if maybe a little short for my liking, but it had Ray and Dak's approval.

A shower to clear my head, today would be a long one. I'd spoken to Brad the previous evening, I wondered how his first mission went.

CHAPTER 41 - LAYING A TRAP

Estefania Hernández put her coat on, ready to leave. Unlike Serge, she didn't live on the property and it was a long drive home. She was anxious to see her son Manny who would be picking a fight with her mother by now.

The job at the house was often dull and undemanding since there were long periods when John Amery wasn't in residence. However, with John and his new lady staying, she was working longer hours than usual. She didn't mind, most of the time there was nothing to do. Still, her feet ached, and her head throbbed with a headache. Her plan was to get home, see Manny for a little while if she could take him away from his PlayStation and give her mother some food and her medicines.

Even Estefania had to accept her mother was a bitter old woman who rarely thanked her for anything. She moved in over three years ago when she became ill. Her medical insurance was minimal, Estefania struggled to pay for her and keep Manny at school. Since his father left, Manny became a handful. Diego disappeared one morning never to return. He hated Estefania's Mother being in the house and resented the money being spent on her. Manny took it badly; the miserable Mexican didn't even leave a note for his son who was asleep when he left.

The decrepit Chevy screamed when she tried to go faster, like Estefania's Mother, it went at its own pace. Some time ago, the car developed a fault making it difficult to start. Still, once she got it going, it usually got her home. The traffic was heavy as some sort of festival was taking place. The twenty-year-old car looked hideous surrounded by the foreign high-end European vehicles favoured by the residents of Palm Beach. The drive took twenty-minutes longer than usual, so Estefania was pleased to finally turn into the trailer park as dusk turned to night.

Drawing up to the trailer she owned for over twenty years, Estefania saw a black SUV Suburban parked out of the front. There were hardly ever any visitors, Estefania wondered what sort of trouble her missing husband had gotten himself into this time. Slamming the brakes on her Chevy, she came to a stop narrowly missing the late-model vehicle.

The front door was difficult to open, the result of an argument between Estefania and Diego. He broke the handle when he slammed it in her face after he came home with 'the boy's' drunk as skunks. Estefania used all her strength to open the door where she expected to see law enforcement officers.

Inside, Manny was restrained by a big swarthy man dressed in jeans and a black T-shirt stretched over his bulging muscles. Her heart stopped, then started thumbing hard. He was holding a gun to her young thirteen-year-old son's head. Her little boy stood there, trembling, tears streaming down his face. He looked ashamed as Estefania glanced at his trousers which were wet with his urine. Estefania's mother screamed, or attempted to, as her throat was being held in the crook of another man's arm.

Estefania froze; the scene was too much to take in. "What the hell! What do you want from us? We have no money! But take it all! Take what you want. Give me my child, my baby!" She was frantic, ran at the man, who turned the gun towards her. She froze.

The man holding her mother said, "Hello, Estefania, did you have a good day at work?"

His tone mocked her, making her want to slap his smug grin. She didn't answer as she was transfixed by seeing her son in danger.

"I said, DID YOU HAVE A GOOD DAY AT WORK?" The man shouted at her, tightening his grip on her mother's throat.

Estefania felt her knees go weak. Used to men shouting at her, the edge in his voice frightened Estefania. Diego raised his voice at her every day but nothing like this, there was evil in the man's tone. Finally, she said, "Yes."

The other man spoke to her, scaring Manny again as he threw him to the sofa. "We want the keys to the house."

Momentarily confused, Estefania said, "This place? Why?"

"You stupid bitch, Amery's house," replied the man holding her mother. "We need your keys and the codes to get in. Here," he said, throwing a pen and paper to her, "write down the codes. Write the names of everyone in the house and tell me where they are on the property." Her mother let out a strangled cry which drew her attention, the man had tightened his grip; her mother washed white.

The man grinned under her gaze, tightening more. He got his other hand and snapped her mother's head to one side. The sound of the loud crack echoed in the confined spaces of the trailer. Estefania saw her mother's body, already weak, go limp.

Estefania screamed, "No, you can't, Mom!"

The huge man let go of her mother's body, she slipped to the floor, lifeless. He rushed over to Estefania and grabbed her long dark hair and yanked it backwards. Manny called out to her, the other man pulled her son off the sofa to the floor and kicked him in the gut. Manny lay silent, his eyes staring in fright at the big man standing above him.

The man, his grip still pulling her hair, leaned to her ear, "Listen, you bitch. Your mother is dead. Can't you see? This other piece of filth," pointing to Manny still prone on the floor of the trailer, "will end the same way. I WANT THE KEYS. I WANT THE CODES. AND I WANT THE FUCKING NAMES. Understand?"

Estefania's knees went buckling beneath her. Only the thug's hold on her hair kept her upright. She closed her eyes, "Please, I will give you what you want. Leave my son out of this."

The nameless man let go of her hair and Estefania collapsed to the floor a foot away from the young boy who was quietly sobbing. The fact that they still smirked in this situation chilled her to the bone. Appearing to agree on something, they kicked her and Manny again.

"I'll give you anything." Estefania wanted to shout but her words came out in a whisper. The man who killed her mother looked at her. He nudged her with his foot, "Get up, you Cuban bitch."

He stepped back as Estefania struggled to her feet. Her belly hurt and she held her scalp where her hair had been pulled. Her vision doubled, the cheap mascara running down her face from her tears.

Now standing in front of the man, she said, "I have everything. Here," she grabbed her purse. He snatched it away from her and emptied the content out on the bench beside him. Several items fell out, including a bunch of keys.

"Sit, here, on the bench," said the man pushing her onto the soft, damaged cushions which acted as a bed for Manny at night. "Write down the code words for the alarm system. Tell me everything you know about the house; where people sleep, who is there, what they do and what they have in place to secure the building."

"Estefania scrambled for the bunch of keys and, falteringly, tried to ease three keys away from the others.

"Are these the keys to Amery's house?"

"Yes, they're the only ones. I promise. The codes are simple, too simple, really. You need to use these keys, this first one for the outside gates, this second one for the outer doors to the store cupboards and this one is for the main kitchen doors. I don't have the front door key or any of the others. The code is 303030."

The man near Estefania looked once again at the other thug who stood over Manny. He stamped hard on Manny's hand resting on the floor; the young boy cried in pain.

"Stop! Stop it!" she screamed "I gave you what you wanted! Let us go ... please, please. Let us go!"

Again, he approached her and grabbed her hair and struck her around the face. "This will take some time, I need to know everything about Amery's house; the layout, the security systems, everything. Don't leave anything out or the boy gets killed. Hector, tie him up, gag him."

She looked once again into her captor's black eyes. He was Mexican, like Diego, she could tell. The big man's eyes were cold as he stared at her. "You lie, and we'll slice the little bastard in two. When we're done, we might give him back to you. Might, you bitch. If you give us any duff information, he is dead, and you'll be next, you understand?"

Estefania merely nodded. The pain was excruciating, but

nothing like the burning anger in her heart looking at Manny staring wide-eyed at her while being tied up with plastic cable bands. "I'll give you anything you want. Those people in the big house have been kind to me, but I don't care about them. I want my son back, and if I help you, you have to promise to keep him safe.

The man looked at her again. Estefania searched for some sort of compassion and thought she saw it. Maybe she imagined it, but to have Manny back in her arms, she was prepared to make sure these men and God knows who else got into John Amery's mansion if it were the last thing she did. It was her only choice.

CHAPTER 42 - MORNING TEA

Heather felt for John next to her as soon as she woke, but his space was empty; she didn't have to look far to notice the glow of his laptop outside.
"John, come back to bed."

She saw John gently close the screen and come in from the balcony. He wore a pair of shorts and sunglasses.

"I'm working," he said as he entered the room through the large glass doors, "someone has to."

Heather smiled at him, "You look hot."

"It is so hot out there, but I like the morning sun. You were fast asleep."

"No, you look hot."

John laughed and made his way to the bed, kissing Heather as he lay next to her.

"I'll miss this. You. This house. The sex." Heather said, touching her lips, wondering how a simple kiss from him could instantly turn her on, a new experience.

"Me too but it is time to move on. Besides, I need to know this isn't a dream or a holiday romance." He reached up and traced her lips with his finger. He pulled her towards him, they kissed each other again.

Heather gave him a playful shove, "Come on, I'm getting up. We've earned some refreshments after last night."

"Hey." John said, climbing from the bed, "I do have some reports to read. Go. Get some coffee. Brush those teeth of yours - morning breath."

Heather’s pillow missed him by a longshot as he exited the room.

"You throw like a girl."

Heather laughed as she also got out of bed, and made her way down to the kitchen, a cup of tea was in order.

Estefania was busy preparing breakfast and said hello, not catching her eyes.

"Good morning Estefania, have you seen Serge?"

"No."

Heather took her place at the breakfast bar, unfolding the morning paper. "Have you seen the Wall Street Journal? It isn't here, John asked me to take it to him."

Again, Estefania didn't turn around, busy at the cooker. "I stopped to get the newspapers, no Journal."

"Ok, I will let him know. Estefania, can you pour John a coffee and my English tea, I'll take it up."

The coffee machine was on the far counter to the cooker, Estefania walked over to it. Heather watched her and noticed she moved more slowly than usual and, although she glanced at Heather, it was a quick furtive glance.

The hairs on the back of Heather's neck began to rise, her heart rate quickened. The automatic response came moments before her brain engaged, something was wrong. She rose from the barstool as if to not raise alarm and backed away while keeping an eye on Estefania. The housekeeper remained with her back to Heather as she reached for a cup from the cupboard. Heather turned and, as she did, heard a noise. She didn't look back and ran towards the main hallway towards the sweeping curved staircase. She heard someone shouting from behind, "Stop." Abruptly, a blistering heat went through her making her fall to the ground. She lay there convulsing uncontrollably, unable to speak, her vision became blurred. Heather felt her legs on fire and reached to the source of the pain on her bare calf. She noted metal pins now protruding out of her leg, wires running to a gun held by a large dark-skinned man.

Heather felt her consciousness go briefly before opening her eyes again to see the man over her holding her down with his boot. The convulsions were gone but the heat in her body felt extreme. Able to turn her head slightly, she saw Estefania, motionless in the kitchen with a look of horror on her face.

The man bent and came close enough to her face; she could smell his sweat and his breath reeked of stale cigarettes. He put his mouth next to her ear, brushing with it with his lips as he spoke, "Lay still, you cunt, I've got a knife here, and I'm not afraid to use it." Heather felt something brush her neck and saw her own blood drip on her pyjamas top. Terror swept over her, and, before the man could stop her, she screamed out for John. The man hit her around the head and brought the knife to her eyes. "Not one more word," he whispered in her ear, "I'll stick this right into your eye." He moved the knife closer, so close she could no longer focus on its tip. At the same time, he put more of his weight on her side, crushing her, she could hardly breathe.

Unable to move, Heather lay prone on the floor. From where she was laying, she could see Estefania arguing with a second man. They were speaking quietly, but it was easy to see Estefania's distress. Without warning, the other man flipped her around and made a deep slice through her neck from behind.

Estefania slumped to the floor with blood spurting over the white kitchen cabinets and tiled floor.

When her assailant turned his gaze toward Estefania, Heather tried to use the moment to escape but he was too heavy. He called over to the man in the kitchen and stood, sweeping Heather in his tattooed arms at the same time.

Quickly the man carried her outside and headed towards Estefania's car, parked in the servants' space near the kitchen doorway. Heather was thrown into the back seat bumping her head against the door handle, making her shout with pain again. Heather's neck wound tore open with a searing pain covering her top and the window nearest to her with her blood.

Trapped by her assailant, Heather heard the turning of the motor, the engine failed to fire up. The man next to her in the back said, "Get Moving!" He loosened his grip on Heather, but she was too light-headed to try to escape again. Her vision faded and the men's faces looked further away as if looking through a long tunnel.

"Start-the-goddamned-engine!"

The driver looked back, "I can't, the maid must have done something. I can't start it. We'll have to..."

Heather felt her stomach convulse as her assailant shook her. "Right, we'll get one of theirs. Come on, we don't have much time. You," he said, looking at Heather, "where's your car?

Heather felt herself lurch to the left. The man shoved her violently, the movement refocused her a little, enough to see him pulling her back out of the car. He pulled at her forcefully and Heather felt more pain as her bare knees scraped painfully over the gravel of the parking space.

Heather lay on the ground, her head once more spinning, making her feel sick. She vomited, clearing her vision a little and was surprised to see the men arguing again, squaring for a fight. The man who stabbed Estefania drew his knife, still wet with the housekeeper's blood. Forcefully, he made a stab for the other man who he jumped out of the way. They proceeded to circle one another, both getting ready to fight.

"You weren't supposed to harm her, we were told to kidnap her," Estefania's killer said.

The other man replied, "Why kill the fucking housekeeper? She was supposed to drive us out of here. At least she was able to start the fucking car."

Their words became harder to hear, Heather's strength ebbing away. Despite still having her hand on her neck wound, she could feel the blood pumping out of her body with every beat of her heart.

She heard a noise and saw another man getting out of his car. He yelled, "You two, stop it, get her in my car, NOW."

Surprised, the men turned towards him and lowered their knives in tandem. Heather's vision was failing, but she noted the change in their expressions. The boss had arrived. Without saying a word, they turned towards her. About to lift her together, Heather saw a small red dot appear on one man's forehead. He slumped, narrowly missing landing on Heather. Moments later, the second man's forehead was similarly marked. He fell right on top of her so she couldn't move.

The last thing she heard was the boss' frantic shouts. Heather closed her eyes finally succumbing to the pain and the strange feeling in her head. Her hand still on her wound, her breath left her body, her world disappeared.

CHAPTER 43 -HARRY - NO PRISONERS

It shocked me when Carolina said General Thiskwood met the PM, so much so, I didn't ask who else he'd been meeting with in the UK. A few days after, I received a letter from Carolina who remembered another name; Ronald Brereton. I Googled him and found the Deputy Head of Mi5 committed suicide. The video of Brereton's son outside the family home appeared in the search results.

The first time I watched the video, Meghan looked over my shoulder and let out a small wolf whistle. She said the lad was hot and asked who it was. I said it popped up on my laptop. With a satisfied look, she continued to nurse her JD and Coke; something I noticed she was doing more of recently.

I decided to watch the video again before I met Alex Brereton. It showed him at his family home dressed in his rowing gear. While the boy looked distressed, he shouted at the press, "My father wouldn't commit suicide," twice before a policeman dragged him inside the house.

I gave Dak the task of finding him. It wasn't easy; Alex Brereton left University with no forwarding details. I'm not sure how he did it, but Dak eventually got hold of some airline records which reported his trip to Alicante Airport on the east coast of Spain. Alex returned a few weeks later. Dak lost track of him again until he researched Alex's mother. Her family owned several properties in London and in Brighton. There were over forty properties listed under the 'The Bearwood Family Trust.' Mrs Brereton was listed as one of three beneficiaries, the others being her brother and elderly mother.

Dak checked the voter registration documents of each residence and, by process of elimination, he found only three showing no occupants. Dak personally visited each of the three houses and struck gold with the house in Notting Hill. He observed Alex several times buying furniture and making a home in the house off Portobello Road, an area I knew well.

Ray, Dak and I discussed how to tackle the young man. For all we knew, he was just an angry teenager. Ray had a feeling something was going on in the lad's life. He paid cash for everything he bought for the house. In the local Tesco supermarket, he was one of the few who paid in cash.

Ray said I couldn't risk overtly contacting Alex Brereton because we didn't know if he was on Crippley's payroll. Although unlikely, I trusted both Ray and Dak to check knowing their attention to detail kept my family and me safe. Nevertheless, we agreed it would be useful to speak to Alex.

I suggested to Ray the idea of asking Brad Hall to see if he could make contact. I remembered Brad telling me once his father ran the pub on Portobello Road. It was one of our first conversations as it turned out I visited the 'Portobello Gold' pub with friends occasionally. Kensington Palace was less than a mile away. I found Notting Hill, used to the rich and famous, an ideal place to socialise; the local people were too cool to make a fuss over my presence in their midst.

Brad's father was on standby to call his son if Alex came in. Dak discovered from Alex's friends at University he liked a drink, so it was a possibility he would visit the 'Portobello Gold'. Of course, the timing was spot on, my mother used to call it 'serendipity.' Mum used to consult astrologists too, but the idea of a 'lucky coincidence' was as far as I went.

Dak received the text from Brad yesterday evening about meeting Alex. There were no other details. Still, I could wait as I agreed it could be useful to bring the boy when transport was arranged for the team.

Now I was anxious to find out more about Alex. Ray told me it was a waste of time and could possibly be a danger to us if Crippley found out. If there was a spy in the Castle, Alex's arrival in the coach sent for the Invictus athletes would be a good cover. Ray joked there were plenty of cells in the Windsor dungeons if we found out Alex was Crippley's man.

I dressed informally in jeans and another t-shirt, a plain one this time. God, I was getting staid. Kings were meant to be boring, Meghan said to me when I complained, she was having a dig at me when she said it.

The butler announced the arrival of the coach and I made my way to Windsor's Crimson Drawing Room. Ray preferred it if outsiders were kept away from our private apartment.

On entering the ornate red and gold room, I expected to find the Invictus team. Only Ray and Dak were present, so I asked them where the other athletes were.

"We thought you'd like to meet Brad Hall and Alex Brereton first."

"Ok, but I don't want to keep them all waiting."

"They'll wait," said Dak, "You might want to spend time with Alex, he's got a lot to say." Ray and Dak looked at each other, then at me again.

Something about the way the men looked made me change my mind, "OK, we can't meet in this room, it is too big. Ray, on this occasion, can we bring him to my study?"

Ray grimaced, "We can't be sure about Alex, or totally confident in Brad."

Dak, usually at one with Ray said, "From what Brad told me, we will be ok this once. Besides, Meghan and the children are in the swimming pool and the study has its own access. I can be on hand outside."

"Ok," Ray relented, "anyway, I personally swept your private rooms this morning."

Momentarily confused, I laughed. A vivid image of the Gurkha with a brush came to mind. "Ok, thanks Ray."

Ray clearly didn't know why I laughed, but Dak did, and he said, "Come on, Ray, the room is secure. Sir, I'll bring him along then take the others on the Windsor tour to keep them busy."

I nodded and made my way to our private rooms which would be free from listening devices.

Within ten minutes, there was a knock at the door and opened it. Dak remained outside, giving way to Brad and Alex. Both looked nervous.

"Come in, Brad, great to see you."

Brad Hall held out his hand, "Good to see you, Sir."

I pushed his hand to the side and gave him a man hug saying, "Brad, I've seen you shitting in the desert, you can call me Harry."

"Harry, good to see you." Brad grinned. "This is Alex Brereton.'

The young man stood in front of me, ill at ease in a tight-fitting suit. "Alex," I said, extending my hand, "Thank you for coming." As Alex shook my hand, I said, "Next time we meet you don't have to wear a suit, ok?"

Alex shook my hand firmly. "Thank you, Sir, Harry."

Despite my efforts, he remained tense. I pointed over to the two sofas opposite each other and sat, they followed. Brad's metal leg protruded from the bottom of his tracksuit, I found myself looking at it. "How's the leg, Brad?"

"I'm not sure, probably still in Afghanistan."

Alex let out a laugh. "I'm sorry, Alex, I forgot Brad's sense of humour. Do you both want something to drink? Service here is excellent."

"I could down a coke, to be honest."

"Ok. Brad, what about you?"

"Same, thanks."

"Me too. I'll just sort it." I pressed the bell for the butler. After asking for three cokes, I turned to Alex again. "So, you met Brad here at the Portobello Gold, my favourite pub."

"Yes. I saw Brad and his mates there and..."

Brad rescued Alex. "He bought us a drink."

"We've been trying to find you," I said, "you're a hard man to track down."

"Find me?"

"Yes, I'm sorry about your father. It seems there has a lot been going on behind the scenes here in the UK while I've been away."

Brad turned to Alex, "Harry asked me to see if I could contact you. I was impressed you made the first move. That showed some initiative. I like it. You're a brave kid."

"Thanks, Brad. I didn't know it was a setup."

The butler was all but a shadow that brought in drinks and disappeared again. "You can take your jacket off if you like. It's warm in here."

Alex looked relieved as he took off his jacket. Despite his nerves, I could tell he was a confident young man. Leaning forward on the sofa, Alex said, "My father didn't kill himself, Sir. I know my dad, and he wouldn't do it. His whole life, he made sure he put his best foot forward. Oh, sorry, Brad!"

Brad smiled, he patted the young man on the back, encouraging him to continue.

"Tell me more about your father, Alex. From what I've managed to find out he did well to get to the position he held given his start in life. Your grandfather was from Saudi Arabia, right?"

"My grandmother met my grandfather in Saudi. He was an Arab working as a waiter in the British servicemen's club. Grandmother was the daughter of a Captain in the Army. To cut a long story short, they met and fell in love. My English great grandfather didn't approve. Eventually, my parents eloped, fled to England, and set about rebuilding an entirely new life. Before long, my father was born, they struggled financially after being disowned by the family and all my grandmother's friends. Of course, this is what my dad told me. I don't know the whole story. Bit by bit his folks made their life work by opening a shop on the King's Road, importing Arabic goods like rugs and so on. Even so, it was difficult to make a living. Dad was bilingual, I am too..."

I cut in, "Arabic?"

"Yes. I've got an ear for languages. I speak Spanish, French, Dutch and German. Oh, and English, of course."

"I'm impressed. I struggle to be honest. My grandmother was fluent in French, bless her."

"I'm still struggling with English," Brad said. I liked his sense of humour. It got him into a few scrapes in the Army.

"Carry on Alex, but talk slowly for Brad."

"Dad was lucky to get scholarships to a good school and University. He was approached by Mi5 there and went straight to work for them. He climbed the Mi5 ladder, but I really don't know much about what he did there. Once I saw him shaving, he had been away a long time... Sorry, is this too much detail?"

"Carry on, I'm interested," I said. We met so many people who became tongue tied in our presence. I often found allowing people to talk about themselves a little made them more relaxed, a trick of the Royal trade.

"Ok. Dad was shaving... I saw... I saw fresh scars on his back, they looked like gunshot wounds. He was a brave, resilient and a loyal man. He loved this country, my mother and he loved me. He had a lot to live for. He did not commit suicide."

I noticed tears welling in his eyes. He sniffed and tried to compose himself. I said, "Alex, from what people have told me about your father was an asset to the Nation." I was sure Alex loved his father dearly, but no one got to be senior in Mi5 by being an angel.

As if reading my mind, Alex said, "I found the papers after he died. He was good to mum and to me, and he did everything asked of him by the government. The papers don't paint a flattering picture of my father. These last few years he did what was asked of him, but he didn't do any favours for you or your brother."

"Papers?" I was confused.

Alex reached into the briefcase I noticed he bought in with him. I'd bet my crown Ray, Dak and even Brad checked the contents, so I wasn't worried when he reached inside and took a wad of papers about one inch thick. He placed them on the table next to the drinks tray.

Alex looked to me, "In there, you'll find out about everything Jarrod Crippley has been doing and what he asked my father and others to do for him."

"–Alex gave me a summary of them last night.” Brad cut in. “I scanned them on the way here. It would be better if you read them and digested them on your own. I've read through them; its best you do, too. Quickly."

I looked at each of them, they discussed this ahead of meeting me. I said, "I have to meet the team, get moving."

Brad was solemn. "They'll be fine, I'll get them sorted. I expect Dak will help me with accommodation etc. The papers are worth a read. They are the only copies." He looked to Alex. "Right?"

Alex nodded, but stayed his gaze on Brad, waiting. Brad continued, "Oh. There's one more thing, Harry. Alex wants to join us."

"Join us?"

"I want to join in with whatever plans you have to sort this mess. I owe it to my father..."

Brad cut in, "We have a problem with this young man Harry. You'll soon see this set of papers are more powerful than the dynamite laid underneath Parliament by Guy Faulks himself. We can't let him go anywhere, we can't let him talk to anyone, and... we're short of men. It would also be good to get a fit able-bodied man on the team. I'll keep an eye on him, so will Dak. I'm sure we can make use of him."

As Brad spoke, Alex’s eyes bore into me. A fire behind them. My natural inclination was to agree, but I wanted to get Dak's opinion first. Although it wouldn't surprise me if Brad cleared it ahead of our meeting.

"Alex," I said standing, I towered over him and Brad who remained seated, "I could trust you but I can't yet. You can join in on our effort and strengthen our team. Do whatever you're told and don't be smart."

"Yes, Sir."

I looked at Brad, "Brad, I am trusting you on this. If Alex fucks up, sort him out, you know what I'm saying?"

Brad and Alex, both rising from the sofa, stopped and looked at each other.

"Alex, this is serious, I can't afford to take any chances. You, Brad and everyone else need to know this was my war. My family's safety and the Nation's future depends on what we do next. I won't take any prisoners."

CHAPTER 44 -DEAR, SWEET, CAROLINA

The cold metal of the field glasses felt good in Arthur Thiskwood's hands. The touch of them bought back some of his best memories; in battle, overseeing manoeuvres, directing his men.

Finding a good vantage point over the property was unexpectedly difficult. The General scouted around for an hour the previous day until he found a spot with a good view of the rear of Amery's house.

'Mr Jones', the mercenary he employed, called him several times over the last few days. Increasingly, Jones sought the General's advice to the point of worrying him. Mr Jones came highly recommended by someone he trusted, but now he doubted the referral.

During their last call, General Thiskwood and Mr Jones finalised the plan. The General praised Mr Jones for tracking John Amery's housekeeper and, at least, this gave him hope; they weren't scared of playing hardball.

The spot he chose to watch the house required him to stand. Thiskwood found his legs tiring to the point where he got a cramp in his left calf muscle. Nevertheless, he told himself, he was trained for this no matter what his age was. He forgave himself a few rests and took a piss twice close to where he was parked.

Although he shouldn't have been anywhere near the operation, let alone watching it, he couldn't resist travelling out to Florida to take a look. He missed the cut and thrust of his Army days; the times when he could watch professionals in action carrying out the manoeuvres, he devised.

Arthur Thiskwood arrived before six in the morning. It was over one and a half hours before he finally saw the housekeeper's car pass him and turn into the drive of Amery's House. It didn't surprise him Mr Jones wasn't in the vehicle or didn't appear to be. The woman looked tense behind the wheel of the car, which made an unhealthy noise even from where Thiskwood stood watching.

Amery's house was obscenely large, complete with a guard post at the entrance. A lone guard, bored after a long uneventful night, merely waved them through when he saw the car. The object was to get into the house unseen; so far, this had been a success.

When the vehicle parked, Thiskwood saw the woman step out. She went around to the trunk of the car and put a key in to unlock it. Two men got out. They were big; lucky Amery's housekeeper drove such a large old Chevy.

Focusing his binoculars again, Thiskwood could make out the faces of the two men. The woman looked even more stressed as she made several hand gestures anxious to get them inside. Mr Jones wasn't there, his absence made the General's stomach tighten, he should be.

Arthur cursed his leg, a shooting pain in his ass made him want to pee again. He held the field glasses even tighter, determined to keep watching.

It was forty minutes later when Thiskwood saw both men come out of the house. This time one was carrying a woman.

There was blood on her neck, it spread over whatever she was wearing. She might be hurt, but she was still alive. The back door of the Chevy was opened, the woman was thrown inside. One man got in the driver's seat while the other got in the car after the woman. The General smiled: it was Heather Taylor-Todd.

Even at a distance, the sound of the engine turning over could be heard. It was clear the car wasn't firing. There was some sort of commotion before all three got out, Heather dragged out by the taller man, stumbled, a dazed mess on the floor. The blood still slicking out of her neck concerned the General; they were not supposed to harm her.

Inexplicably, the two men drew their knives on one another. Heather remained motionless on the ground. Thiskwood didn't notice Mr Jones until his car came into view. He breathed deep, hoping his operative would get the two thugs under control; someone from Amery's security could arrive at any time.

The two men stopped arguing, surprised by Jones' arrival and looked at Heather. As soon as the men froze, Thiskwood knew what was wrong, he'd seen a laser-guided sniper shoot dozens of times. They both toppled over like rag dolls thrown to the floor. The first landed next to Heather and the other straight on top of her.

Mr Jones, clearly in view, took a step back when the back of his head exploded. The man stood motionless for a split second, then fell into a heap of his own arms and legs, a large crimson flower where his head should be.

Thiskwood dropped his binoculars and almost stumbled into his car at speed. His stiff legs refused to bend, and he had to physically lift his knee to get his right leg into the car. The late-model Toyota started instantly, he put his foot on the gas and took off, his tyres causing a dust cloud.

Speeding away, his heart beating in his chest, he cursed Jones. The operation couldn't have gone worse. All three of his operatives were dead and Heather might be fatally wounded.

Coming to his senses, the General slowed, trying to calm himself. Rapid breaths turning into calm, controlled ones. He hit the button to open the window and tossed the burner phone out into the bushes surrounding the Palm Beach Golf course he was passing.

Operations seldom go as planned, there were always other options. Even so, plan B was for another day, his main priority was to get out of Palm Beach and Florida as well.

He headed for the International Airport in Miami. He could rescue the overall operation, but it would have to be from London. He wasn't afraid of Amery, but it was best to put some space between them to give him time to regroup.

Loose ends played on his mind; though, his age was beginning to show, he admitted, and caused him to make mistakes. The thought of dropping it all for a good book came to mind, but he couldn't. However, Operation Catesby being unsuccessful, his last big campaign wrecked, was unpalatable.

Clear of Palm Beach, he increased his speed and entered the ramp to the I-95. It was time to really put some effort into Catesby. He didn't care about the money, but it would be the proof he needed to convince himself he still had what it takes. General Thiskwood wanted to know if his planning and operational abilities were skills he still possessed.

As he neared the airport, where he'd get a tourist flight if necessary, Thiskwood vowed to get tough. He couldn't give anyone the benefit of the doubt anymore, including dear, sweet, Carolina.

BOOK THREE - HARRY'S REVENGE

CHAPTER 45 - SELLING THE FAMILY SILVER

Sat in bed, Jarrod Crippley looked at the latest economic data delivered the evening before at Chequers. He reached for his phone and asked for the Chancellor of the Exchequer, Guy Storrar. "Why have you sent me this pile of shit?"

Storrar answered, "Good morning PM. Which particular pile of shit are you referring to?" His broad Scottish accent adding to the bluntness.

"Don't play it cool with me, the economic data, the forecast in this morning's red box. This will be out today; the press will have a field day with it. Why didn't you give me the heads up, you must have known how bad it was days ago?"

"Prime Minister, you knew it was going to be bad, I've been warning of this for a long time. Your policies..."

"OUR policies Storrar, our policies. This is a government, led by me AND the cabinet."

After a slight pause, Storrar said, "Jarrod, the government needs more funds. The treasury bills issued by the Bank of England are gaining 'junk' status on the markets, new issues are undersubscribed. Even the promise of generous margins on the bonds is not enough. Investors have lost confidence in the British economy and sterling."

"You're the chancellor..."

A sigh at the other end of the phone stretching out another pause. Eventually, his chancellor answered, "Aye, I am for the moment."

Jarrod got out of the bed, went to the bathroom, and told Guy Storrar to wait for a second while he peed. Finished, he picked up the phone and continued, "The economy is in trouble because governments before us, conservative governments, didn't put enough money aside to invest."

"Jarrod. I've told you many, many times before you've created your own mess. You're making us all suffer it."

Jarrod held the phone away and looked at the receiver as if it were a foreign object. He placed it next to his ear again, "I knew it was a mistake to keep you around. You're the chancellor, it's your economy. That fancy school, education, I should have known you weren't real, you're not a true socialist."

"Let's face it, Jarrod, you can't get rid of me, you're afraid to. If you do, you'll lose your Scottish voters and a good number of your MP's who are fed up with you already. Your 'spend, spend, spend' mentality produced this situation. I'm waiting around until you call time on your premiership."

The phone went dead. Swearing under his breath, Jarrod fell into a coughing fit. He waited for it to subside, but it left him feeling weak. Only the prospect of breakfast got him dressed.

The newspapers were waiting for him in the dining room. The PM's appetite left him momentarily with a glance of the headlines. His surname was a delight to the headline writers; 'Crippley Cripples UK.' Hardly original, the same line had been used before.

The pile of newspapers told their own story. The 'Crippley

Cripples UK' lead in the Daily Mail was obviously the work of Guy Storrar although he wasn't quoted as the source. The day before Crippley sacked his second Governor of the Bank of England against the advice of the chancellor. Appointed only a year previously, the fresh-faced Governor promised a revival in the fortunes of the beleaguered Bank and to re-energise the economy. The man, an academic plucked from Leicester University, came recommended by Storrar. Professor Humphry proceeded to tell the Crippley what he was doing wrong. His suggestions to roll back on nationalisation were impossible. Humphrey wanted to incentivise entrepreneurs and rebuild infrastructure. Every idea the professor had was diametrically opposed to Crippley's views. Crippley felt relieved when he summoned Humphry to sack him. Storrar heard and he flew into a range hence the secret briefing to the Mail journalist.

The smell of bacon and eggs laid out on the hot tray made Crippley's mouth water. He threw the papers to the floor and pushed the bowl of fresh fruit laid out in his place setting to the side. His doctor nagged him to eat more healthily and take exercise, but he hated fruit. With great care, he built himself a sandwich loaded with crispy bacon, scrambled eggs, beans, and mushrooms. He took a large bite making the tomato sauce he smothered on the bread run down his chin.

Reaching for another two slices of bread, Crippley realised he missed McNee. Discussing problems with his right-hand man was a benefit he finally appreciated after McNee was no longer around.

After finishing his second sandwich, Crippley decided to return to his room for another hour before General Thiskwood arrived. The breakfast made his eyes heavy and hoped a short power nap would revive him. If it was good enough for Thatcher and Churchill, it was good enough for him.

Two hours later, Crippley woke to the sound of a helicopter landing, indicating Thiskwood's arrival. The General demanded the PM send the aircraft to meet him at Gatwick airport. Apparently, the only flight he could get to the UK was a tourist flight full of returning families, fresh from their stay in Disneyworld, Florida.

The PM's personal secretary knocked gently at the bedroom door, Crippley told him he would be there in five minutes. He needed to put a fresh suit on given his was creased from his nap. Last time he met Thiskwood, the General commented on his appearance and asked if the PM was lowering his standards. Crippley was keen not to disappoint the General and, if he rushed, he could smarten himself before they met.

Crippley entered his study, surprised to see the General in casual gear. He decided not to comment as the General had done, it would only unleash some sort of new insult.

"I flew eight hours to get here, Crippley, the least you could do was meet me when I landed."

Crippley couldn't imagine Thiskwood sitting in a tourist class cabin surrounded by children with Mickey Mouse ears on their heads. "I'm sorry, General, I expected you a little later. But look, sit here, make yourself comfortable."

Thiskwood walked over to the couch and sat slowly, wincing slightly.

"Are you alright, General?"

The General looked to Crippley and said nothing, he merely pointed to the sofa opposite.

"Heather Taylor-Todd is severely injured, she might be dead for all I know. I'm not sure what John Amery will do next."

The PM looked at General Thiskwood in horror, "Dead, what...how?"

"Don't worry, I'm fairly sure she's dead, you would be better not to know anymore. You don't have to put out a press release on it," said the General stretching out his left leg, the pain creeping onto his face.

Crippley made a fuss of pouring himself a tea, trying to buy some time while he absorbed the new information. The General helped himself to a coffee before he entered the room.

"Where is John Amery? I need him. We must make sure we move on The Crown Estate. It looks like the International Monetary Fund and the World Bank want to put some draconian restrictions on us if we continue on our plan of renewal for the British people."

The General leaned back. "To be frank, Crippley, my role here is to deliver what we planned. I can't help the 'fuck up' you and your government are making of the British economy."

Warmth flooded into Crippley's face. "Your plan is going well despite some issues along the way, but you said it might need the odd change here and there, didn't you?"

The General stared back at the PM. The man lacked character; not even 'man' enough to push back on his comment about his premiership. He snarled at Crippley, "Listen, Crippley, I have an idea for you. It cuts out the need to rely on Amery, it could be a lot faster."

Jarrod Crippley leaned forward, eager to find out more.

The General continued, "Of course, it changes the plan a little, a successful campaign needs some flexibility. The information Amery supplied us is the key. At over seven hundred pages, it is the most comprehensive list of Crown Estate assets ever compiled. It has descriptions, market benchmarked valuations and even includes a model which puts an additional value of the Royal family's so-called 'brand' associated with each of the assets. Let's take Buckingham Palace. In prime real estate terms, it has a value of over $1.2 Billion, at today's exchange about £1Billion, maybe less. His paper suggests, at auction, this should be the reserve price. There are more than fifty people in the world, perhaps more, who would bid higher to see themselves installed there. The place is a gold mine."

"Oh," said Crippley, a little confused, "that's the plan, you want to change it?"

"Given events, we may have to speed up our plans. Besides, you need the money, don't you?"

Crippley smiled, anything which got more money into the nation's coffers would help. "I'm all ears."

"We could sell the lot in one go, lock stock and barrel. There's plenty of money in the world, not in Britain but Europe, Asia; the USA is flying financially. Since the financial system breakdown and especially after the Coronavirus disaster, the whole world is rebuilding. There's a greater focus on wealth accumulation. The number of world billionaires has doubled in six years. It's not just oil money, its money out of China, venture money, there are buckets of the stuff. I am proposing we sell the whole lot. We won't get as much as selling it piecemeal, but we can reach at least £150 Billion. After the title is passed, those who buy it can sell pieces off, we give them the problem. Politically, it will look like you've pulled off a masterstroke in at least cutting the national debt by, what, twenty per cent?"

"More like twelve per cent. You're telling me there is someone with £150 Billion to spend on this?"

"I've been speaking to some Venture Capitalists, in outline, of course. They said we could put the whole lot into a newly formed company and the government could sell shares in it. Pension funds, sovereign wealth funds, family offices; they'll all want a piece of it. The company itself would be able to take more time to sell off the assets. Hell, they could even retain some assets like the off-shore wind farms which generate a lot of cash."

"I see," said the PM, "And I would look like a hero once more to the British people!"

"Yes," said the General, glad he included the political spin to his argument. "Don't forget, I want the one per cent you offered to Amery."

"John Amery is on his way over here. How will we deal with him?"

Thiskwood was caught unaware. He hated that, damned it. "He is?"

"Yes, some time ago, McNee organised something which lets me know where John Amery is at all times."

"How?" This was all slowly getting out of his hands.

"McNee was a clever man. He gave all the committee members a phone. Each day I get notified of the positions of all of you who were on the committee. The phone gives away the GPS locations of each of the phones."

The General was impressed. "You could have told me; it would have saved a lot of time and expense. So, you know where I am at all times?"

"Yes, but you tell me anyway, I trust you..." said Crippley. "Given Amery is on his way here, we may have some sort of problem. He got close to Heather Taylor-Todd. The man could be trouble."

"Don't worry. I will deal with Amery. Besides you and me, there's no one left from the committee is there?" The General caught Crippley's previous reference to McNee in the past tense.

Jarrod Crippley, looking at General Thiskwood as he spoke, didn't answer the question. He merely lowered his eyes and took a drink of his tea even though it was stone cold.

CHAPTER 46- WARNING; CHILD ONBOARD

John Amery entered the trailer park in his Porsche. Curtains twitched and some children, playing on a burned-out pickup, stopped, and stared at his bright red car. Feeling out of place, he drove slowly along the one road twisting in and out of the trailers. Scarred and rusted, they looked as though they housed several families over the years. Estefania looked after her mother as well as her son, she could afford little more on her wage.

Serge wanted to flee the Florida house as soon as possible. He was right; it wasn't safe considering what happened. An hour after the horrendous deaths, Amery was still in shock. He was glad Serge kept a cool head and took control of the situation.

It was the sight of Estefania, throat cut, which delayed Amery. In all the confusion, Estefania's son came to his mind. The little fella sometimes accompanied Estefania to work, and John taught Manny to swim last summer. The lad showed promise, but it was easy to see he suffered at the hands of his absent father and lacked the attention a boy needed. Estefania initially declined John's offer to give Manny swimming lessons. John didn't push it, he didn't want to interfere, after all, he wasn't his son.

One Saturday afternoon, Estefania came in to prepare a meal for him and five of his 'arty' friends. Estefania cooked well, she liked to impress John's guests. Estefania said she was ok to prepare the meal for his art world friends but would have to bring her son in, saying he could do his homework on the kitchen counter. Manny looked bored to death; John suggested a swim. Estefania said no, but Manny pleaded with her and she finally agreed so she could get on with the cooking.

Manny took to the pool with ease and started to come with Estefania regularly. John found himself looking forward to the sessions, disappointed when he needed to move back to London for the busy financial season when summer was over.

Finding the trailer was difficult, they weren't numbered. Amery drove along the road until he saw Manny's bike. He remembered Manny complaining bitterly about the bike his father bought him as it was pink and 'very gay' as the kid put it. John wanted to buy him a new one, but Estefania declined, too proud to accept charity.

The pink bike lay prone outside the trailer and John parked. A large black SUV stood outside, empty. He noticed a face at the window of the next trailer interested to see who the Porsche owner was. No doubt it had been an exciting day for the neighbour.

He pulled at the door, but it appeared to be locked. He pulled it again, a little harder, and it opened, releasing an unpleasant smell. John walked into a chaotic scene; furniture and items from the kitchen strewn over the floor.

Lifeless, the boy's hands and feet were secured by black cable ties so tight they cut into his skin. Manny's eyes were shut, his tear-stained face was blank.

John kneeled beside Manny, gently putting his hand on his chest to check if he was breathing. John called out his name and, gradually, he came around. Manny moaned as he opened his eyes, a bewildered look in them. The briefest of smiles came over his face when he recognised John.

"It's ok, Manny, we'll get you free from these in a second."

"My mom, where is my mom? They killed grandma. Did they kill my mom too?"

John ignored the question for later. His little swimming buddy would have to deal with the loss of his mother later. The priority was to get him out of there in case anyone else came back. He looked around for a knife to cut the boy loose. As he turned around, he saw an elderly woman with her head bent at a strange angle. He bit down on any reaction, the boy needed him to be strong.

John found a knife and delicately cut each of the bands. Manny rubbed his wrists, the pain showing on his face.

"We have to get out of here. Whoever did this to you could come back. Do you understand?"

Manny remained silent as John helped him stand. Amery was able to shield the boy from seeing his dead grandmother by standing in front of him when they exited the trailer. John could feel the boy shake when he held his hand.

Outside, Manny looked at the car and let out an involuntary 'wow' as they descended the steps. John opened the door, and Manny got in. When he closed the door behind him, he saw the boy staring around in wonder. Amery felt guilty again. What he took for granted every day was out of this world for a boy like Manny.

Amery put the car into reverse. The throaty noise of the engine roared into life and he sped off, passing open curtains and open mouths as he left the park.

Manny went quiet in the car and looked at all the buttons and displays of the Porsche Macan, John's favourite car. Serge said coming over here would be dangerous and would delay their departure. John couldn't leave Manny to his fate and insisted he made the trip out. It took less than thirty minutes to get back to the house, considerably faster than the journey Estefania took in her car every day.

Approaching his house, Amery noticed the guard, last seen hanging out of the gatehouse window with a shot to the head, was no longer there. Serge obviously removed him or at least put him out of sight. John's remote worked the gates and he sped along the driveway, checking to see the gates behind him close automatically.

Serge came out to the main entrance to meet them. He opened Manny's door and asked him to get out. Manny looked to John for approval, John nodded, and he did as he was told.

"Wait here for a minute, Manny, inside the front door," said Amery, pointing to the small alcove where Manny would be hidden from outside view. "I have to talk to Serge here. You can trust him. Remember him? He is here to protect us."

As John walked away, he heard Manny shout behind him, "Where is my mom?"

"We will be out in a few minutes. Look at the fish tank, see how many different species there are," said John, "If you look closely, you may see a tiny shark." Manny smiled, it was one of his main reasons for wanting to come to the big house where his mom worked; there was awesome stuff everywhere.

"I am fine, don't be too long though. I want to see my mom."

"We won't, a few minutes, you'll be ok there so don't move."

John and Serge found a place away from Manny, so he couldn't hear.

"Have you told anything him? His mother?"

"Nothing. My main concern was getting Manny here so we could protect him. How are you getting on with the arrangements?"

"The Jet fuelled, ready. The standby pilots there, ready. We need go."

"Estefania's body, is it still in the kitchen?

"No, moved to storeroom."

John went quiet, he didn't want to ask the next question. “Heather?”

Sensing John's hesitation, Serge said, "She recover now. Nasty scar on throat, maybe always there. I stitched it, I not get award, like surgeon. She sleep now but safe only when on plane."

"Thank God, so she'll be fine?"

"Heather, strong lady. She lost blood but not so much she need transfusion."

"Are you sure?"

"She be O.K, I think. No guarantees. Seen worse and they live. John, sorry. My job to protect, I failed."

"We all failed to appreciate how quickly that bastard would act. I underestimated him."

"General Thiskwood?"

"Yes," answered John, "He's behind this, I'm sure..."

"I promise, do everything...."

"Enough, there's no time for apologies. Come on, let's go."

John turned towards the main entrance, "You help Heather into the car. I have to talk to Manny and tell him what's happened."

"Heather can sit on front seat, I put seat back, make comfortable. John, we wait too long already. We don't know if more people come. The two security guards we employ, no good at guarding, bastards. I've put thugs in guardhouse too; it isn't pretty sight."

John recalled hearing the noise from downstairs. The sound penetrated his deep concentration on a business plan he was reading from the new Hong Kong operation. Something made him rush to his safe and remove his gun. As the noise continued, there was no confusion about what he was hearing, anguished screams and shouts from Estefania and Heather. He climbed down the outside of the house. The lattice work supporting the wisteria plants covering the back of the house made it easier to climb.

John Amery's personal insurance costs were astronomical by most people's standards. The insurance company made the cover conditional on him learning how to shoot so he could protect himself. To be fair, it was no hardship as John liked the gun range, he turned out to be a good shot. He also appreciated the advanced driving tuition he had to take because it included anti-kidnap driving techniques.

John's gun, loaded and ready, had never seen combat before; he didn't think it ever would. When he turned the corner and saw the two men towering over Heather, he didn't hesitate to shoot. The laser guide on the semi-automatic made each shot easy, both took a bullet to the forehead.

John noticed a new limp in Serge's gait. "Are you ok?

Serge answered, face washed of warmth. "They clipped leg it is nothing. I sort it on plane. It stings like hell but O.K to drive. You care for Manny. The kid is handful. "

"Ok. Look, I phoned the airport. A doctor is waiting for us to make sure Heather is stable enough to fly. If not, we will go to a private hospital nearby."

"Good. Not safe to stay. John, I sorry, I failed. John, you killed two men, you O.K?"

"I guess it will hit me at some point but when I saw them with Heather..."

"No choice."

John left Serge to get Heather ready. As much as he wanted to be with her, the look on the kid's face when he picked him up told him to make sure he was ok too.

John made his way towards the giant aquarium in the main entrance. Manny stood transfixed by the colourful fish passing in front of his face.

"Manny, I have to tell you something."

"Mom's dead, isn't she?"

John looked at the boy, tears ran down his face. "Yes. She's gone. You know she did the best she could, she loved you."

"What will I do? Grandma's gone, Mom's gone, I don't know where Dad is. I wouldn't want to live with him. WHAT WILL HAPPEN TO ME NOW?"

"Calm down. We're still in danger, try to keep quiet Manny." John didn't want to frighten Manny, but they were all still in danger.

Manny pounded the thick Perspex glass and, gradually, slid to his knees, falling silent.

John looked at Estefania's son, usually so bright, ready with a quick retort. The boy was scared and afraid and alone. John made a decision which could alter the rest of his life, "You won't be alone. You're coming with us. We have a plane waiting, and I will promise you this, Manny." The boy looked to John, waiting. "I promise you I will look after you from now on, you're coming to stay with us. Come on, let's go."

Reaching for John's hand, Manny pulled himself up and put his arms around John's waist. John put his arm around the boy and promised he would look after this poor lost soul. He needed to make sure he lived long enough to fulfil his promise.

"Come on, let's get the 'Hell out of Dodge'."

It took less than an hour to get to the airport. Heather slept most of the way. Serge drove silent and fast, fixed on the mirrors, making sure no one followed. They drove to the waiting aircraft. John phoned ahead and made sure the Jet was full of fuel, stocked with food and ready to take off the moment they boarded.

The doctor met them on the plane. He recommended Heather go to the hospital but Heather, awake, said she wanted to get out of the USA. The doctor agreed and dressed her wound and gave her some sedatives. Although it delayed their departure, he set up a bag with her own blood type to bring her blood pressure up to avoid haemorrhagic shock. Reluctantly he gave the go-ahead for them to depart, making sure Heather signed a release form to protect himself. Before he left, John asked the doctor to bandage Serge's leg despite his protestations.

It wasn't until they were headed towards the runway John, sitting next to Heather holding her hand, relaxed. Heather fell asleep before they took off for London. John closed his eyes, exhausted. He replayed the conversation with Manny; he said the boy could live with 'us.' It wasn't until then he realised what he really meant; he and Heather should be together for the long run and would take care of Manny. Hopefully, Heather felt the same.

CHAPTER 47 -TYING UP LOOSE ENDS

Virginia and her husband, Phillipe, made sure Carolina was made comfortable at the Embassy residence. It was not what she has envisioned for herself, and felt rather more like a prisoner than anything, but it had to be done.

Visiting the King had left her in limbo. Unable to return home, she was at a loss for her next move. Virginia said Harry appreciated their visit. However, Harry made it clear he didn't want to involve either of them any further unless it was necessary.

Carolina didn't feel safe. Her marriage to Arthur was over. They'd sailed into old age on different ships. For years, Carolina and her husband occupied different worlds, it suited them both, until now.

Laying on the four-poster bed meant for visiting French dignitaries, the doubts swirled around Carolina's head. What did she really know? Why would coming to England help her? Why couldn't she leave Arthur to his world and stay in hers? Why was she compelled to offload the things she knew to the King? She's American, why is she even involved with the Brits?

Carolina swilled the gin and tonic as she stared out over at the pallid vista – she didn't know whether it was actually dull or whether that was her outlook. The decision to call Pierce Brice weighed on her mind. A few days before, she placed a call to the General's former attaché who went out of his way to lend an ear and concern. A day later, Carolina questioned her motives behind the call; why involve anyone else, especially Pierce who she had grown fond of over the last few years. He was considerate, yet he was no 'pussy' even though Arthur called him that after he 'came out'.

Of all the people she could call, Carolina knew why she chose Pierce. He understood Arthur better than anyone. His advice to her was she should return home and stay at Pierce's ranch until it was all over. Arthur wouldn't look for her there and she could find enough to do helping out with the horses.

Initially, she accepted Pierce's advice and was set to fly to the US. In the morning the following day, she couldn't face a return to America or to Pierce's ranch an hour away from Arkle Wood. Carolina felt exhausted and wanted to take stock for a while. She waited until Pierce would be awake and informed him of her decision. His tone dripped with disappointment when she'd told him.

Still on the antique French bed, Carolina felt more confused than ever. Within hours of her call to Pierce, she received a message from Pierce's partner, Lance, that his husband already boarded a flight to London and would be there in a matter of hours.

Lance told her the flight details and she asked Phillipe if someone from the Embassy could collect Pierce. She told Phillipe Dumont who insisted Carolina shouldn't leave the house and said he'd ensure his own security would bring Pierce safely to her. The Ambassador joked the Embassy was becoming a little overcrowded and Carolina wondered how long she would be welcome there.

Phillipe was a generous host, but she was well aware the French people were paying and, knowing the French, they'd hate it if they knew. She discussed the situation with Virginia who reluctantly agreed it might become an issue. Although

Phillipe was keen to help, he made it clear he could have no involvement in the situation as an officer of the French Government. The French and the British, never the best of neighbours, were not exactly on best terms at present since the fall-out over the ownership of the Channel Tunnel. Phillipe could not become involved in British internal affairs.

A few years before, Virginia sent Carolina a link to 'Spring Cottage' on the Cliveden Estate, run as a five-star hotel and country club outside of London. She raved about it and suggested Carolina stay there when visiting London, as it was comfortable, private and thirty minutes into London. Virginia visited the cottage once during a summit meeting held for European Ambassadors resident in the UK. Not sure why it popped into her mind, Carolina googled the hotel. The price of the separate cottage was a little excessive at two thousand pounds but she wanted to treat herself ... needed to. It was available for a month. Spring Cottage had two bedrooms so Pierce could have a room if he decided to stay on. It wouldn't surprise her if he did, at least for a few days.

Carolina booked the house before telling either Virginia or Phillipe. She wanted to do something herself, she wasn't used to being 'looked after.'

Earlier Virginia told Carolina she would be out for most of the day but should be back by five in the afternoon. Carolina left her room to go and find her sister given it was well after six.

Virginia was on the terrace on the roof of the embassy residence. There were great views from the small garden planted there by an Embassy wife years before. The small garden on the terrace, planted by a former ambassador's wife, was Virginia's favourite place to sit and read. It was the only spot uninterrupted by Embassy staff continually coming in and out of their home.

As she came out on the terrace, Carolina couldn't see her sister.

"Virginia, where are you?"

"I'm here, under the pergola, walk around."

Carolina walked along the small path made of ornate multi-coloured marble tiles. She found her sister with a blanket around her legs, smoking. "Virginia! You're smoking. I didn't know you still had that disgusting habit."

Virginia looked skywards; her sister was a nag sometimes. "It calms me."

"You always have an excuse. Here, give me one."

Virginia sat up, the blanket falling from her knees. "What? My saintly sister wants a fag?"

Carolina laughed at the term used by the British for a cigarette. "No, he is coming later on." she joked. "Pierce Brice, I've told you about him, he's coming over from the States. He knows Arthur as well as I do, better maybe, and I can assure you there's no love lost there. Phillipe is sending someone over to pick him up and take him to the hotel."

"Hotel?" said Virginia, passing a cigarette and lighter. Carolina lit it, taking a long drag.

Breathing it out, Carolina said, "I have to admit, I smoke about ten of these a year. Only when I am drunk or stressed."

"The amount you drink I'm surprised you don't have ten a day."

Her sister’s company was like being wrapped in motherly arms. However, it was time to move on, "I've booked Spring Cottage at Cliveden. Remember you told me about it a few years back. It looks perfect. No one will be able to find me there."

"Yes, I remember. It is a good place to take time out. Are you sure you want to go?"

"I think so, the place has an office, there are a few bedrooms and it is right on the Thames, it's lovely."

"Yes, it is perfect. In fact, I've often thought a small cottage would be great for Phillipe and me once he retires," said Virginia wistfully.

"And the one-thousand-acre estate in France?"

"You're right, a girl can dream, can't she? I'll text Phillipe. If I go down, I will be given a list of things to do. You know how organised he is."

"Thank you, I'll pack and come find you. Thank you so much for being there for me. I'll call an Uber," Carolina continued, "I'm going to lay low. I can run Arkle from there. A month should be enough, I'll be able to take my time and reassess the situation. I have a lot to think about."

"Uber is a good idea. You'll check in every day? If something happens, if you get worried, come back, won't you?"

Carolina leaned over and put her cigarette out in the ashtray by her sister's side. Impulsively she hugged her sister. Although close, neither hugged much. As she pulled away, Virginia was crying. "Now stop it. I'll be fine, Pierce will look after me. He'll help me sort out how to get out of this, I'm sure."

"What are you going to tell Arthur?"

Carolina spoke to her husband the night before. He was making his way to London for more 'business', and he arrived this morning which is why she wanted to leave London. Even though Arthur sounded reasonable on the phone, she remembered her throat tightening when she replied. "I said I was considering going to Spain to visit some ranches there. To be frank, he didn't seem bothered. He told me he had a lot to do. I didn't feel right on the call though. I hope he didn't notice."

Virginia looked at her sister, "It will be fine. I'm sure it will be. You're on edge, no wonder. Maybe the time at the cottage will help you relax. He shouldn't be able to find you there."

Carolina was gone within the hour, relieved to be free of the Embassy although she'd miss her sister. It was hard to be dependent on anyone, she knew the four-poster would still be waiting for her if she needed to return.

As an extra precaution, she reserved the cottage under the name Miss Ryan.. An invented alias made her feel safer, even if it wouldn't be effective; If asked, she was to be a writer doing some research into the Astor family, the former owners of the historic house.

The bright sunny day made the car warm and Carolina relaxed in the back of the vehicle. At first, the Uber driver chatted away no doubt anxious to get a good rating from his passenger who clearly had money and connections. Carolina's one-word answers soon made him realise the higher scores would come from his silence.

A few minutes before they turned into the Cliveden Estate, she phoned the hotel for directions to Spring Cottage, so she could go there directly and bypass the hotel reception. It occurred to her when she booked the cottage to pay upfront to reduce the need to meet people. Although she was ready with her alias, it didn't feel comfortable yet, she'd only just been born into this new life.

The Uber driver offered to help her with her bags but she said to leave them at the door. She wanted Spring Cottage to herself and was anxious to build her temporary nest there. The stress of the last few weeks weighed heavily. Carolina now regretted allowing Pierce to come and stay given she was looking forward to solitude. Perhaps he wouldn't stay long once he knew Carolina was safe.

The inside of the cottage was the same as the pictures on the hotel's website. The kitchen had a stove called an 'Aga' which would take some figuring out. The cupboards and the refrigerator were stocked as she requested and she was glad to see they put a bottle of Bombay Sapphire Gin and ice in the freezer.

The bedroom was adequate but a lot smaller than she was used to. When Carolina visited Europe, it struck her that everything was two thirds the size of its American counterpart. Nevertheless, she was happy with the room, even the shower was powerful enough; a rarity in British hotels.

Pierce would be arriving in a few hours, so Carolina changed, poured herself a gin and sat in the sun outside. The birds sang and the water flowed by at the end of the garden. 'My little Paradise' she said to no one but herself.

She must have fallen asleep because she woke with a shiver, the sun long since disappearing behind the woods on the other side of the river. Carolina looked at her watch, Pierce would be due. She gathered her things and went inside.

"Good afternoon Carolina," Arthur said as she came through into the kitchen.

Carolina, surprised and more than a little shocked, dropped her empty glass and it shattered on the floor. She wore no shoes and remained stationary. "Arthur, how, what are you doing here? You could have rung, you scared me to death."

"I thought I'd surprise you, dear, sweet, Carolina," said her husband in a mocking tone. "You've been quite the busy bee. You must have seen far more about my little campaign when you broke into your Daddy's desk?"

Carolina remained silent. Her brain was screaming at her to move, to run. Ignoring the reference to the desk, she said, "Arthur, it is so nice to see you. Tell me, how on earth did you find me? I was going to settle in and call to let you know my plans to fly over to Spain were cancelled. The stud owner over there cancelled on me, he has the whole stud in quarantine because one of the horses contracted the..."

"You weren't going to call me, were you?"

"Yes, I.."

The General cut her off again. "No, you weren't going to call me. YOU WEREN'T GOING TO CALL ME!"

A shiver ran down her spine. "Arthur, let's talk, I'll clean this up and we can sit and talk. Pierce will be here soon."

"Oh, I know." Arthur turned and shouted, "Pierce, you can come out, the surprise is over."

Pierce came out of the small sitting room, smiling. "Carolina, so good to see you again."

Carolina was confused, why were they both there?

Arthur stood, went over to Pierce and kissed him on the lips. Putting his arm around the man, Arthur turned towards Carolina, still standing among the broken glass on the floor. "You see Carolina, Pierce and I got, um, close in the Army. His being my attaché was the perfect cover. We went everywhere together. You were too busy with your damn horses to notice."

Pierce couldn't meet Carolina's eyes. Quietly she said, "I trusted you. I helped you build your Stud, you confided in me about hating Arthur... you're married to Lance for god sake."

Pierce stared at the floor, embarrassed. She could see his cheeks were red, his breathing laboured.

Arthur spoke for him, "You see, dear, sweet, Carolina, I know everything you've been doing. I used some of your money so Pierce could open a stud near our, sorry, your ranch. Marcus nearly found out but I sorted it."

"But you said Pierce was a monster, you hated him for his homosexuality and his decision to come out."

"A cover my love, a cover. I know you messed around with the odd ranch hand to satisfy your sexual needs, mine were being met by Pierce. In fact, moving him to the place near us made it convenient for me. Of course, Pierce has been his usual helpful self by letting me know where you were and what you talked about."

Ignoring the glass shards on the floor, Carolina walked towards the small armchair, unsure her legs would support her any more. The glass gouged her feet, and spots of blood appeared on the carpet. "Arthur, please, let's..."

"I don't want you to talk, I want you to listen. I came over here to sort out several loose ends. You've stirred the hornet's nest; you've caused nothing but trouble for me."

Pierce regained his composure, "I'm sorry, Carolina, you've been so good to me. You have to understand; my life has been so hard. Thanks to Arthur, I was able to stay in the Army. Of course, I love him. You don't, you've told me as much."

Carolina felt sick, sickened and scared. "But Lance, what about him?"

"Weren't you surprised he was often away? Arthur paid for him to be with me. He agreed on the condition he could spend one week in every month with his girlfriend."

"His girlfriend? Who are you, Pierce? What are you?"

Pierce looked over to Arthur who rushed towards Carolina and slapped her hard across the face. She was stunned and the side of her face turned red from the swelling.

"Now listen to me, Carolina. You thought you were the queen

of Louisiana, didn't you? Your money, your connections and your classy family. You know your father hated me? Ask your sister. You never gave me anything I wanted, even our children are ungrateful. Don't, I mean don't... ever... speak to Pierce like that again. You hear me?"

Her agreement got caught in her throat, she merely nodded.

Arthur ran his hands over Pierce’s back, stroking him, as if to pacify. Gently he said, "Pierce, would you move her stuff out of the big bedroom. I'll make sure she can't do anything; did you bring those cable ties?"

Pierce smiled at Arthur and said, as if still in the Army, "Yes, Sir." Carolina saw Arthur turn toward her again, a smirk on his face; the bastard wanted to drive the message home. Tears came and she buried her head only to see Arthur securing her arms and legs to her chair.

Getting close to her ear, Arthur said quietly, "If you want your sister to live, Carolina, there is something I want you to do. If YOU want to live, you need to do what we say."

Weakly she replied, "What?" Her spirit was broken.

"Contact with Celia Casement and tell her you can't find me. I know if you're not convincing so don't try anything. I want you to ask her to come here. Let them know you're in the same boat, you can't find your husband and you're worried I may be in danger. She will sympathise since she also lost a husband."

Carolina looked up, "Who?"

"Roger Casement helped me in what I was doing here in the UK. Don't bother saying you hadn't an inkling of what I was doing. For heaven's sake, you've been blabbing to Pierce. Casement's wife knows too much, she needs removing from the equation. Pierce you’re up to it, aren’t you?" said Arthur looking over to his lover. "You need to call her; tell her you've lost someone too and you want her help."

"What about me?"

"Simple. If you do what we say, we'll let you go back to Arkle. You stay there, say nothing, be a good little daddy's girl and we will leave you alone. Oh, and if you don't do as you're told, we'll kill every damn horse in every one of your fifty stables and burn your daddy's house down. By the time I finished, there won't be anything left of him to remember."

Carolina let out a sob before her husband of forty-five years stuffed a rag in her mouth to gag her. Once he was sure she couldn't move or speak, Arthur grabbed Pierce's hand, "Come on, my boy, we need some R and R, let's go upstairs."

CHAPTER 48 - THE LAST ACT

Jarrod Crippley called Felix Goldberg from Goldman Sachs and explained the General's idea. The finance expert said he would consult with his team and come back to the PM as soon as possible.

Felix called the PM back the next day. Crippley took the call despite being late for a Cabinet meeting. "Felix, you've come back to me fast, more questions?"

Felix said, "Jarrod, how are you?"

Crippley answered, "As well as I was yesterday, get on with it."

Felix Goldberg got the message. "Logistically forming a company and selling off shares will be difficult but not impossible. Who provided the list you gave us of the Crown assets?

"It's none of your business."

Felix, used to more pleasantries, said, "Oh...OK. Anyway, the list is comprehensive. I've had a few of my people double-check some items on it, they're impressed."

"And?"

"The list is as good as it can be since we have tight timescales. The team's only concern is the 'ownership issues' as they put it. They'd like to commission some experts to make sure the

Government has the right to sell off the assets."

Crippley anticipated the question. "Don't worry about. We have it covered; I will send you some information compiled by my people."

"Ok, if you are sure. We will need to make sure…"

"Look, the British people own everything on the list. Your organisation stands to make five per cent of the sale revenues, a hell of a lot of money. The Crown Estate is the peoples' to sell, not the King's. Public opinion is with me on this, trust me. Now get on with your job."

"We're on it, Prime Minister," The conference phone went dead. Looking around at his team in the Goldman Sachs offices who heard the exchange, Felix said, "ok guys, you heard the PM. We need to sort this. We've not earned a bonus for some time; this could be one of the biggest deals in this firm's history. Mr Crippley needs the money to satisfy the International Monetary Fund demands. The Government will be able to borrow more money with the liquidation of the Crown Estate. I have to say, I don't see it lasting long in our Prime Minister's hands. Still, we stand to earn over nine billion. If we get this right, each of us in this room will be several million richer, so let's get moving."

Many of the Socialist Labour Party MPs were new to Parliament. Years before, Crippley set out a plan with Robbie McNee to destroy the old labour party and rebuild it along socialist lines. The Crippley doctrine caused fundamental disagreements at the local constituency level, leading to the resignation of many of traditional labour supporters. Crippley replaced many of the sitting MPs and candidates with his own men and women dedicated to the socialist cause. Crippley's strategy was ultimately successfully evidenced by the change of name from 'Labour' to 'Socialist Labour'.

The new MPs came to Parliament with vigour and enthusiasm. Many were 'true believers,' most supported Crippley in the early years of his Government by voting along party lines. As time passed, botched nationalisations, dramatic increases in taxes and bloated government spending resulted in even the most fervent believers gradually losing faith in their leader. The result was support for Jarrod Crippley in the Houses of Parliament were at an all-time low. Even though the Socialist Labour Party maintained a healthy majority, many of his MPs voted against Government proposals. Consequently, Crippley found it increasingly difficult to get anything agreed. The political system was in crisis, if Jarrod called a fresh election, he would lose.

The Crown Estate Disposal Act was drafted as a 'white paper' to be tabled to Parliament four weeks after the PM invited Goldman Sachs to No.10. Considering the complexity of the Act, preparations should have taken far longer but Crippley knew he was against the clock.

Rumours about the proposed Act rippled around Parliament, causing a great deal of discussion. Crippley was delighted with his MP's reaction as most of them supported the idea of raising funds by selling off the Crown Estate. It reflected their original socialist ideals and they also saw the potential of such a large amount of money pouring into the nation's coffers. Ultimately, it was their one last chance to strengthen their appeal ahead of the next election; it was about their survival.

Unfortunately for Crippley, a list of every estimate got leaked online. One or two of the more serious newspapers, notably the Times and the Guardian, published multi-page articles pointing out the weaknesses in the Crown Estate Disposal Act. Of most significant interest was the valuations put on the art and the palaces.

The team Crippley put in place to deal with the sale and work with Goldman based their deliberations on John Amery's reports. Amery's analysis deliberately undervalued the assets, erring on the side of caution. Also, the 'fire sale' nature of the disposal would inevitably result in lower bids made by people trying to take advantage. This resulted in a twenty-percent discount for protection.

Harry Winston's, the International Jeweller, said the Crown Jewels were listed at 'scrap' value with no recognition of their historical significance. Saville's, the high-end real estate agents, said they'd easily be able to sell Buckingham Palace at twice the listed value. Day after day, items from the list were plucked out by reporters and there was even a hastily produced TV program on the BBC entitled, "Roll UP, Roll UP Crown Going Cheap!"

While Socialist Labour MPs would vote in favour of the Act, Crippley was genuinely surprised by the reaction of the people. The PM expected positive headlines but The Crown Estate Disposal Act was seen as a raid on the nation's assets. The media branded it a fire sale and a desperate attempt by the PM trying to mend a broken economy.

It was also a surprise to see several commentators supporting the ownership rights of the King and the Royal Family, a reaction Crippley didn't expect. Former Law Lord Simon Mapry published a well-considered paper expressing doubt about the ownership rights to the Crown Estate. Crippley read it and tore a strip off Goldman's for missing a few points identified by Mapry.

The PM was relieved to see reference material made available to Judge Casement wasn't included in Mapry's considerations. The General was right to take the former Committee member out of the equation. If the report Judge Casement submitted ever came to light, the Act would never be passed. Also, the ownership of the Crown Estate, a question of some debate over three centuries, would finally be resolved and it would be a disaster for Crippley.

Without McNee as wingman, the PM felt uneasy with the headlines. He was confident his left-wing MPs would vote for the Crown Estate Dispersal Act but so much could go wrong. He decided to contact the General to ease his mind.

"Good Morning General, how are you? Also, if I may ask, where are you?"

"Crippley, why are you calling me? Can't you do anything you're told?"

Crippley swallowed hard, "I'm so sorry, I wanted..."

General Thiskwood yelled, "GET THIS CRIPPLEY. I... WILL... CALL... YOU, OK?"

The phone went dead in his hand. He looked up and caught his reflection in an ornate mirror. His face was red, his heartbeat thumped his chest and he was taking short breaths. Who else would he turn to?

The phone rang, it was the General, "Right, you get the point. I will ring YOU in future."

"Yes, yes, I understand. I'm sorry, General."

"I'm in England. I've been watching the news and reading the online comments. I can't say you're handling this well. The list, what those jewellers said, it makes you look like an absolute prick."

He agreed. Trying to still the shakes in his voice, Crippley asked, "How are your 'loose ends' going?"

The General laughed, "If I have a few loose ends, your situation looks frayed at the edges."

Crippley replied, "I'm sorry, General, it is why you are so important to me."

"Don't you forget it." Thiskwood's tone softened, "Now we have everything off our chest, let's talk business. I found Celia Casement. She's coming over to meet me soon."

"How did you manage it? What reason did you give?"

"It doesn't matter. I'll be seeing Mrs Casement shortly, I'll interrogate her on what she knows about Roger Casement's conclusions like we discussed."

Jarrod Crippley dreaded to imagine what sort of interrogation techniques the General had in mind. He remained silent, hoping to keep Thiskwood calm.

The General continued, "I'm pretty sure it will all be fine. From what I've seen of her on TV she is a nice simple woman. She hardly looks the type Roger Casement would discuss legal matters with. Anyway, I'll soon find out."

"How about Alex Brereton? Have you considered what I said?"

"You don't think he is an issue?" said the General, "I told you 'thinking' is not in my vocabulary. I need to know. The problem is I can't find him. I need to contact his mother, she's in Spain somewhere. I'm sure she will let me know where her boy is. I need to see what he knows."

"Ok, thank you, General, I do appreciate it. The timescales are getting tight, and I want to make sure the Act goes through without a hitch."

The General smiled at the other end of the phone. Jarrod Crippley, Prime Minister of the United Kingdom, finally understood his new position; Arthur Thiskwood's bitch.

CHAPTER 49 HARRY - SEE YOU NEXT TUESDAY

The Crown Estate Disposal Act finally made sense of the last few years. My father and brother were put to death by a Prime Minister so desperate for money he would do anything.

In a way, I was relieved to see the PM's endgame. I could scarcely believe the 'Brereton Papers' after Alex gave them to me. While everything slotted into place, I was reading a dead man's papers, so there was a margin of doubt in my mind until now.

Crippley cancelled our weekly audience. Initially, I welcomed it as it would give me more time with the Invictus team. The meetings generally lasted no more than forty-five minutes. However, they took a great deal of preparation on my part as Crippley would test me on papers I should have read and if done my homework.

Meghan woke me in the morning. She was a light sleeper and an early riser most days. With Meghan, as soon as she was awake, she was 'on it' as she would say. She nudged me sharply, "Harry, you better read this."

I was annoyed. I hated being woken, I liked to take my time. Meghan's nudges had many different meanings. If the push was soft and we were both under the bed covers, it could mean sex. It was my favourite way to start the day, but Meghan didn't really like it. She used the soft nudge tactically as, when we finished, she would use the time to suggest something she wanted; it was the best time to get me to agree. I knew Meghan used sex to her advantage, but, I liked the sex! A mid-level nudge meant it was my time to get out of bed and look after the children as she would be busy writing emails and writing her daily 'to-do' list. I wouldn't mind but Meghan's 'to-do' lists mostly involved someone else 'to-doing' for her. When we were a couple, not married, the soft nudges came frequently. I was lucky to get one soft 'nudge' a month these days.

"What's wrong?" I asked.

Meghan threw her iPad my way. The site was the Daily Mail, her favoured early morning read. I'm not sure why. She once sued the newspaper and often took issue with it. The headline shouted at me 'Crown For Sale.'

Of course, I shouldn't be surprised. The papers Alex gave me spelt out precisely what Crippley's plan was but was alarmed by how soon Crippley played his hand.

"It looks like I might be supporting you and the family," said Meghan and I wondered if there was at least a little smugness in her voice.

Her tone was typical. Meghan is what I call an 'I told YOU' sort of person. I fully expected her to say 'she knew' and 'I told you so.' when we come out of this, if we do. To be fair, however, I shared nothing with her about the Brereton Papers, the deaths or the note from Virginia which set everything off for me.

"Meghan, this is serious. I've told you about the Crown Estate Assets. I look after them while the Crown is on my head, someday they'll pass on to Archie and on to his heirs. The Royal Collection is of historic national importance as are all the sovereign assets. Buckingham Palace is internationally recognised as the centre of the British Monarchy. If it is sold to Hilton, the Emir of Qatar or some other rich Billionaire, it will be seen as a further sign of Britain's decline. Buckingham Palace is where the nation meets in times of celebration and commiseration. This isn't about money, it is about the fabric of our society."

Meghan looked at me, she moderated her tone when she said, "Harry. You can't take this lying down. Get up, man. Sort this out."

I put on my robe, ignoring the children as they ran into our room. Meghan called them over while I made my way to the study.

I placed a call to Jarrod Crippley only to be answered by an assistant. I never swing my weight around, or rarely at any case, but I insisted Crippley answer the telephone. I heard mutterings on the other end of the line and the same person who answered the phone said, "I see the Prime Minister is available, Your Majesty."

"Is this why you cancelled our meeting, Crippley."

"Good Morning Sir, I'm sorry, what can I do for you?" replied the PM.

"The papers this morning. Please tell me they have it wrong."

I could picture Crippley's creepy smile, "I'm not sure what you are talking about..?"

I heard my mother's voice; 'Count to 10 Harry' whenever I became angry. It was the advice I used more and more as I got older. I paused before replying, "The Crown Estate Disposal Act."

"Oh, yes, if our meeting wasn't cancelled, I could have discussed it with you."

1,2,3... "YOU cancelled the meeting. YOU didn't include anything about the Act in my red boxes. YOU have been planning this for a long time." I stopped abruptly as I didn't want Crippley to know how informed I was about his and the General's plans.

"Your Majesty, don't worry. It is merely a case of prudent financial management. We have identified the sale of the Crown Estate will be in the people's interest. I guess it may work like the National Trust in some way, you know, where we allow some families to live in a few rooms of their former family home."

I swallowed hard. I needed to consider what I said next... 4,5,6.... I changed my tone, "I'm sorry, Mr Crippley, this all took me by surprise. When will you be putting the Act to parliament for a vote?" I needed to get an idea of how much time we had left.

"Fortunately people have been accommodating on this matter within our government and elsewhere. It looks as though we are going to put this before the house within the month."

I paused ...7,8,9...," Thank you, Prime Minister. Thank you. Please would you send over a draft of the white paper so I can peruse it before our next meeting."

Crippley answered, "Of course, Sir, I will send it over today, and I'll see you next Tuesday?"

I recognised the phrase, it was common in the Army. 'C. U. Next Tuesday' meant he called me a 'cunt'. The PM underestimated me, most people have over the years to their cost. The PM had no idea of how much of a cunt I could be, but he would soon.

CHAPTER 50 -A BRITISH PASSPORT

The moment John Amery's plane landed, a private ambulance, with doctor, was there. Heather's condition worsened on their flight; John phoned ahead to make sure everything went smoothly when they landed.

The ideal place to land would be Farnborough. Serge recommended John ask the pilot for an alternative on route to improve security. They changed flight plans to Biggin Hill, the famous wartime airfield used as a base for private jets.

The pilot nearly aborted the night-time landing due to the weather. Rain pelted down, soaking them as they exited the aircraft, walking to the waiting ambulance. John held Heather as tightly as he dared while Serge carried Manny. By the time the four reached the ambulance, they were soaked, shivering.

"Christ on a bike, who the fuck did these stitches?" the doctor asked, "It looks like someone has been watching Nightmare on Elm Street by the state of these."

John couldn't help but smile. The irreverent Australian doctor made them all a little less stressed.

Serge confessed, "Me. Not expert."

"Don't worry, mate. You saved this lovely lady. She might have to wear a scarf for a little while, but it is sure better than wearing a coffin I'd say."

"Sorry, what's your name, doctor?" said John.

"Me name's Liz Bandy. Good to meet you all. Now, listen, the little lady ain't going to bleed out, the Russian boy here has seen to it."

"Ukrainian," Serge said, he hated being called a Russian.

"Whatever. Anyway, the little lady has a temperature, an infection looks like it is setting in. I'll hook her up to a drip. It will work, I'm sure. Whose Sheila is this?"

John understood and answered, "She's mine."

Heather, sleepy but still awake, squeezed John's hand.

"We're off to a private clinic, It's all sorted so relax. Everything is going to be fine. It will take about thirty minutes so we'll be there before you can say Billabong..."

Manny, quiet since he climbed into the ambulance, whispered, "Billabong."

"Ah, he speaks. What're you called, Joey?"

Manny looked at the woman doctor, "No, my name's not Joey, it's Manny."

"Well, hello, Manny. Pop over here and let's take a look at those wrists of yours. Maybe we could put something on them to make them heal a little faster."

John looked over to Manny, who looked cold and miserable. His concern over Heather made him forget the boy's injuries. Manny moved confidently over and sat next to Dr Bandy, holding out his wrists.

"Wow, you've been in some wars, mate," said Doctor Bandy

Manny looked up at the woman, slowly. "No, no wars."

"What happened? Was it these guys?"

Manny looked back at John, a little confused. When he turned back, he said, "John, Heather, Serge, they rescued me. Some men came in and..."

"He's been through some stuff Doctor." John cut in. "I can assure you; it wasn't us, was it, Manny?"

"No, they're the good guys."

"Alright," Doctor Bandy said, eyes falling on John, "You know I have to ask. There are some wicked people out there and I ain't going to have any kid in danger under my watch no matter how much I get paid."

"How much do you get paid?" Manny asked.

"Manny, you don't ask anyone questions like that," said Heather, speaking for the first time.

Bandy laughed while she finished dressing Manny's wrists. "I'm paid enough to be quiet but not enough to see kids get hurt."

A silence drew out in the ambulance, watching Dr Bandy attend to Heather's wounds. Before long, they felt the ambulance come to a stop. The doors were opened from the outside where another medical professional in a white coat beckoned them inside.

John watched as the team inside transferred Heather to another bed and wheeled her off. "Where are they taking her?" he asked Dr Bandy.

"They'll sort out our Russian, sorry, our Ukrainian friend's stitches and neaten them a little. The main thing is to bring the infection down so she doesn't develop sepsis. Joey here will be fine with what I've sorted for him. You three can make your way to the rest area, follow the signs. There's something to drink, maybe you can all get a little sleep.

"Thank you, doctor. It's been a rough day," said John.

"I'm paid not to be a nosey bugger. Make sure you look after the little guy here." She turned to Manny, kneeling slightly to meet him at his eye level. "Manny, are you happy with this, these people?"

John went to answer, Manny beat him to it. The boy took John's hand and answered the doctor firmly, "Mr Amery will look after me. He's all I've got."

Amery felt for Manny and squeezed his hand, unable to speak without fear of his voice cracking. Dr Bandy looked convinced and said her goodbyes and John, Serge and Manny walked off to find the waiting area.

It was six in the morning when John woke with a stiff neck having slept on two armchairs pushed together. Manny was next to him, curled up. The warmth from the boy carried a whole new feeling ... somehow; total responsibility for another human being.

Serge was awake, he said he slept for a while although John didn't believe him; his eyes were bloodshot, twitchy, but he remained vigilant.

"I'm going over to see what's happened to Heather, Serge. Keep an eye on Manny, will you?"

"Sure, I've checked everything out here, we're safe."

John found the nurse's station where a solitary nurse concentrated on an online course wearing earphones, looking at a screen. She noticed John approach and took off the earphones. "Can I help you?"

"Yes, Heather Taylor-Todd. How is she doing?"

"She's still asleep. She's in room eight along the hallway. You can go in but maybe let her sleep."

"I'll look in on her," said John. He found the room and saw Heather inside, laying on a bed hooked up to a drip. John stood there, looking at her, hoping she was going to be alright. His heart ached, he wondered if this was what being in love was all about. He would do anything for Heather.

As John turned away, he heard Heather say, "John."

Their eyes met with the usual spark. "How are you, John?"

"I'm fine, it's you I am worried about." He grabbed her hand.

"I have a little bit of a headache, my throat is dry, but I'm fine. I... will be fine."

"Here, drink some water," said John passing a glass over to her. "I love you, Heather."

There was only a slight pause. "I love you too, John. I want this to be over. I know we can't hide, we have to face this, but how?"

They were disturbed by Serge who entered the room. "I just talked police at Palm Beach, very angry. Said warrant for arrest put out for us, don't know about Manny. Interpol also, so British Police look for us. Time is running out."

"Shit!" John said, "This can't get any worse."

"It can. I made call to cop who I know, friend. I wait to tell you."

Heather, a little more alert, pulled herself up on her pillows, asked, "What did he say?"

"Big search in area, check many cell phone records. Dog walker saw old man. He watched house at Mitzner Close, over from the gatehouse. They find binoculars."

"Cut to it, Serge."

"General Arthur Thiskwood's prints on binoculars. Burner phone find mile away, in ditch. General's prints on phone. Cop says calls traced to man dead at John's house."

"Serge, you were right, the General is after us. The bastard," said John.

"W-why are they looking for us?"

"They have to make sure the facts check out, after all, we were all there. Serge, you told them what happened?"

"Yes, all details. But not happy, want us back. John shot two men. I killed one."

Heather looked at John, "You shot those men? You?"

"I'd do it again." John said, "Serge, we need to sort this ourselves."

Heather looked concerned, caused more by John's anger than what he said. "John. We can't do anything. Let's go to the Penthouse and let this blow over. Or maybe go back, face the music?"

"We can't, the bastard has made me, us, wanted criminals in our own country. Serge, we have to get some more men, you're great, but we need numbers. Even you're not safe."

Serge didn't answer, something was on his mind.

"Serge?" Heather said, "what is it?"

"USA, UK, not my country, I Ukrainian."

They all laughed, Serge knew how to cut the tension in a room. "We need to sort it out, John," Heather said, "let's make sure after this Serge gets a British Passport."

Serge smiled, "Deal! I still Ukrainian, but safe British passport holder."

"I'll call Chip at Red Diamond. He'll sort out some money and transport for us. You rest."

Heather looked at John, "John, you killed those men, are you OK?"

"Yes."

Heather took his hand, a determined look came over her face, "John, thank you for ... thank you. But there's something else I want you to do."

"What?"

"Get Thiskwood, kill him if you have to."

Amery bent to kiss Heather on her forehead, "Deal."

CHAPTER 51 - GONE FISHING

Carolina was handcuffed to the bed in the Cottage's smallest room; she could hear Arthur and Pierce through the thin walls. Arthurs voice, deep and husky, rang out as he had sex. Pierce called him 'daddy.' Every grunt, moan and knock of the bed against the wall between them humiliated her as she listened. Unable to sleep or cover her ears, she heard Pierce begging for more. His voice assumed a child-like tone. At one point it sounded like Arthur was beating Pierce who said to Arthur, 'I'm sorry daddy, please don't hit me.' Arthur played his role in their strange game predictably, repeatedly saying to Pierce, 'Son, you've been bad, you know what daddy does when his boy has been bad don't you.'

At one point in the night, Carolina called out for them to stop. Arthur came rushing into the room, naked and hit her around the head, making her ears ring. He went out and returned with some silver duct tape and put it over her mouth. Her chest fluttered as she drew each breath difficultly.

At some point, Carolina supposed she must have fallen asleep out of sheer exhaustion. She woke to the morning chorus of birds singing, not a sound coming from the room next door. Her wrist ached from where it was tied to the bedpost by the handcuff. She could see her hand and fingers looked pale; she could hardly move them. Carolina's face hurt so much; tears came to her eyes through the pain.

After some time, Arthur's voice came from behind the wall. Carolina prepared herself for a repeat of the night before, but their voices were normal. She guessed Arthur and Pierce were tired as well.

Pierce's voice was loud enough for Carolina to hear, "What are we going to do with her? At some point, the hotel staff will want to come in."

"I've been giving it some thought. There might be a silver lining to this. I'm pretty sure when she is found dead, I get to inherit some money and live at the Ranch until I die. How would you like to come and run the Arkle ranch? Carolina won't be there of course, but she's helped you with your stud. It should be easy enough."

Carolina found against crying out, what use was it now? Arthur wouldn't get any money whatsoever. Her brother Marcus constructed their family trust so only her children would benefit. Arthur didn't know that, she hoped her children would throw him out. It occurred to her she was accepting her fate, it made her angry, determined to escape.

Pierce spoke, "Carolina's Ranch is the best. We can send Lance packing; he's done his job. His wife will be happy."

Arthur continued, "Go and make me a coffee. Phone the hotel and tell them we don't want to be disturbed by anyone. Tell them you're Carolina's assistant, she gave you strict instructions to make sure no one comes near this place."

Carolina could hear Pierce leave the room. Arthur made a call when Pierce was gone. She couldn't hear the other end of the conversation. "Hello, Sitton...Biggin Hill, and where next? Ok. Are they still there? ... What? ...They must know we're on to them. Look, I'll need you to find out where they've gone. Find out what car they took and see if you can trace them through the police. The British have more CCTV cameras than any other country on earth; they'll be able to trace them through registration plate recognition... ok...Yes, not yet. I want to use Pierce while he is here...He can be useful to us. When it is over, we'll have to deal with him too...ok? Martin, you'll get the money. No, remember, I know where you are too and you could end up dead like him and all the others if you try to blackmail me, understand? Ok...Yes. Good.... I'll call you later. I can hear Pierce coming."

She hated the pang of guilt she felt for Pierce... everyone was expendable to Arthur. But she stopped herself, Pierce could go to hell.

"Here you go, just as you like it. I phoned the reception, there's no problem, they're used to people wanting to shut themselves off here."

"Thank you, son," said Arthur, "nothing like a good strong coffee in the morning. You better be ready; I'm getting my strength back."

"Good."

"Now hop back into bed."

Carolina could hear Pierce getting back into bed as it knocked against the wall again.

"I got into Carolina's email again and used it to contact Celia Casement," Arthur continued. "We don't have to ask Carolina to call the Judge's wife. She replied. Her email said she would come out to the Cottage." Arthur let out a laugh, "She said she knew how it felt and would help Carolina find me if she could. Bless her. She'll be here later. I sent her an email from Carolina's account, I asked her not to call as I was worried who was listening in, 'I' being Carolina. She'll be here after thirteen hundred hours; we need to get ready."

Guilt rolled over Carolina as there was noting she could do to warn Celia.

"Now, Pierce, I need to make a call to someone. Be quiet." After a pause, Arthur spoke again, "Good morning, forgive me for telephoning you out of the blue, so to speak; my name is General Arthur Thiskwood... Yes. I know, sorry... I knew your husband. We worked together several times... Thank you... Yes... I have to tell you; Army Intelligence respected him in my Country. I am so sorry for your loss... Well, I remember Ronald talking about Alex. When I heard the sad news, I wondered what he was doing? He's at university, isn't he?... No? Ok, I can understand him wanting time off... Your husband told me how bright Alex is and, now he's gone, I might be able to help Alex in some way... Yes... Of course, it will be up to him. I know, time will heal and, through experience, I can tell you it is better to be busy ... No, I understand. I wouldn't expect... Look, why don't I give you my number, I'll text you so you have it to hand... Thank you. If he decides not to call, I will understand perfectly. He might like helping out on my next book... Thank you, Mrs Brereton."

Pierce spoke next, "Do you think he will call?"

Arthur Thiskwood replied, "Oh, yes, he will. Did you see him on the YouTube video?

"You know I did. Alex Brereton is one hot looking guy."

"Now, now, this is business. Alex is young and impulsive. He's been shooting his mouth off all around town about how his father was murdered. Sooner or later, someone might take him seriously. We'll have to deal with him. We can't risk anyone finding him while this is all going on."

CHAPTER 51 - WANTED

John Amery was called out of Heather's room by Dr Bandy. "Heather is recovering, helped by plenty of sleep plus the antibiotics which have calmed her fever. She's doing well."

"When can we get going? There's a lot we need to sort out."

Bandy replied, "Yes, I've seen the newspapers, the TV News did a great little piece on you all last night, did you see it?"

Amery wasn't surprised. "Yes."

"Don't worry, you get what you pay for with us; discretion. Besides, from what I've seen, I have to agree with the little fella, you're the good guys."

John blew out a long breath, "Thank you, Dr Bandy."

"Liz."

"Liz, we do need to get going."

Looking at the charts in her hand Dr Bandy replied, "It would be better for Heather to rest for a few days. However, she'll be right as rain, don't worry By the way, the stitching job your mate did saved her life. I saw him on TV, some old clips of him boxing. I'm guessing he learnt how to stitch from the cuts and bruises those guys get used to. It looked horrible when she came in but it has been sorted."

"Serge is full of surprises. I won't be asking him where he learnt it, though," Amery laughed.

"Neither would I," Dr Bandy replied, "I'll sort out some paperwork and some medicine she'll need to take. You can't allow the infection to come back. Make sure you get her to rest."

"Thanks once again, Liz."

As Dr Bandy went along the corridor, John saw Serge and Manny at the vending machine. He called them over and went back into Heather's room.

John sat next to Heather and held her hand while he waited. "Heather, we're going to have to leave here. Can you manage it?"

"I feel a lot better."

"Good," said Serge as he entered the room. "Good, you are perky."

Heather smiled at the big man, "I've never been called 'perky,' but thank you, Serge, I do feel a lot better."

Manny ran over and jumped on the end of the bed, and quietly started eating a Mars bar.

"Cops look for General Thiskwood, cop call me." said Serge.

"So, they're looking for all of us?" asked Heather.

"Yes. Must leave hospital quick." Serge looked over to John, "O.K?"

"The doctor said it was OK if Heather takes it easy."

Serge looked uncomfortable on a small stool opposite, "Mayfair penthouse not possible, they look there first."

"Why not turn ourselves in? It will be far easier. The CCTV footage will exonerate us. Hell, the scar on my neck gives them enough proof!" said Heather putting a hand to her neck.

John was about to say something when Serge cut in, "Two problems. General Thiskwood find us or Police find us."

"Yes, both might be dangerous. Thiskwood could get the Prime Minister to help him, ultimately the PM can get the Police to do anything he wants. Going to the Police could be the most dangerous option we could choose. We can't go to any of my houses here or anywhere else. The warrant's cover the USA and UK. I reckon even my boat will be under surveillance in Lanzarote," John said, ruffling Manny's hair.

"I'm sure we could find somewhere. The problem is; do we want to hide and wait?" Heather said.

"We can't. It might be days," John answered. "Weeks or even years. If we hide out, we won't be able to do anything. Nothing is stopping either of them waiting for us; they'll find us in the end. Besides, none of us are 'do nothing' people."

Manny spoke for the first time. "You guys all have funny accents, especially Serge. I miss speaking American. Anyway, why can't we go after them? You know, wipe them off the planet. They got my mom and grandma killed. Miss Heather, look at what they did to you. I've watched enough police stuff on TV; it is what they all do."

All three looked at Manny, sitting on the bed. Turning to each other, they digested Manny's words and nodded their agreement. Heather spoke first. "We need to find the General."

"John," Serge said. "Why you have two phones?

John reached in his pocket and pulled two phones out. "McNee gave me this one. It didn't occur to me they might be tracking it. If they are, they'll be able to find us."

"Jeez, don't any of you watch TV? Police 101; track their phones!" Manny said scowling.

Serge looked at them. "Need burner phones. Manny, go get paper and pen from nurse. John, Heather, open contacts, write ones you need when Manny gets paper."

"It will be easy," said Heather, "there are only six contact numbers on the phone McNee gave me."

Manny ran back with a handful of pens and paper, smiling. "No one was there so I grabbed these."

Both Heather and John copied the numbers from the cell phones McNee supplied.

"Finish?" Serge said. When they both nodded, Serge turned to Manny, "Right kid, you know what to do."

Manny grabbed the phones and took the SIM cards out, snapping them in two by biting on each. He threw the phones on the floor, smashing them. Using the fire extinguisher in the room, Manny smashed the metal cylinder on each phone; both were beyond repair.

"Good kid," said Serge, looking at Manny. "See Manny, you part of team now. Do same for mine. You have one, kid?

"Mine cost me a thousand bucks, no way," said Manny. All three looked at him, he laughed, "Like I would be able to afford a phone, you doofuses."

Serge laughed along with the others; the kid was showing signs of getting over his trauma. Growing more serious, he said, "We need do again with own phones. Copy the numbers you'll need."

John and Heather copied numbers furiously. Serge turned to Manny again when they stopped writing. "Right, Kid." Manny destroyed John and Heather's personal phones, leaving a mess of mashed iPhone on the floor. He used his trainer to push the debris to the side of the room.

"We haven't got much time if they're tracking us. Heather, are you well enough to move?"

"Yes, John. If you Gentlemen can leave the room, I will get changed."

"Come on, Serge, I've got a few ideas. We'll leave Heather to make herself pretty."

They headed to the nurse's reception area. John said, "Since we have nowhere to stay, I think we should buy a motorhome. I googled a dealer, there's one nearby. I'll call Chip and get him to wire the money over."

"Motorhome?"

"A caravan with a motor, Serge." John smiled. "A step down from my usual standards but it will serve a purpose. I'll call Chip from the nurse's phone, there's no one at the desk, I'm sure they won't mind. We'll find a phone shop on the way."

"Can I have a phone too?"

"Yes," John answered, a smile lighting Manny's face.

"Once we sort it out, we will have to meet the General head-on. Serge, do you know anyone who could help us? We'll need guns, they're not easy to get here, maybe some men too. The General isn't the sort of man to take down easily."

"No problem. How we find Thiskwood?"

"We phone him when we're out of here. I'm not sure yet how we'll play this but having met him, he won't be able to resist a confrontation."

Heather entered the reception room. "You were quick, for a woman," said Manny.

Heather pulled a face at him. "You cheeky little bugger. I got a quick shower and made the most of the clothes the nurse gave me."

"You look great," John said. "Now let's get this party started."

John set about calling his Chip and barked out orders. The owner of a dealership arrived fifty minutes later in a new seven-metre motorhome. As instructed, he left the vehicle outside the clinic with the keys in the ignition. He walked away without looking back, another condition on the deal negotiated by Chip.

"What the f...?" said Manny.

"John, you're not the camping and caravanning type of guy?" Heather laughed at the idea. "Why a motorhome?"

"It came to me. We don't know how long we'll be at this and we're going to get caught if we check into a hotel."

The four piled into the vehicle. Serge looked around, "I will sleep under the van. There's no room for me in here!"

Heather and John looked at each other and raised their eyebrows. Manny spoke first, "Cool. I'll sleep under the van too."

"It will be cold, Manny," Heather warned him.

"Maybe I won't. Serge, you'll get cold."

"I sleep many cold places, I'm good." Serge took the driver's seat and put the vehicle into drive and set off. The others found the places in the back apart from Manny who roamed the space opening cupboards and playing with all the switches to see what they did.

As they sat across from each other, John and Heather locked hands on the motorhome's small table. John leaned forward and kissed her lightly on the lips. "I love you, History Girl."

"Ditto." Looking around the vehicle, she continued, "You pushed the boat out with this. It is like being on holiday save for the Ukrainian boxer and the random trailer kid!" She squeezed his hand, "What's the plan?"

"First thing is to get out of here and sort out some phones. I'll try phoning the General when we have them, but I'll get to a landline, we can't let him have our new cell phone numbers."

"But what next?"

"We have to meet him head-on. Serge will sort some man-power once he has a new phone."

Heather looked concerned, "Are you sure you're right? I could call my brother; we could go to his estate."

"They'll find us eventually. No. Hang on, your brother."

"What about him?"

"He's an Earl."

"He is."

"Well, doesn't he move in highfalutin circles?

Smiling, Heather replied, "A strange word to use. But yes, I suppose so. Why, what are you thinking?"

"Does he know Harry, the King?"

"I'm not sure. Oliver attended Eton; he knew William."

"Could he reach Harry?"

"I suppose so. I wouldn't have thought they were friends on Facebook," said Heather, "Harry and Meghan are still at Windsor, the mourning period isn't over yet. If Oliver called, I'm sure the message would get through. I don't know if the King would call back. Are you serious?"

"Look, we can work it in two ways. Let's see if we can reach General Thiskwood but hedge our bets. God, I wish we weren't involved in this."

"Me too. What would we say to Harry, King Harry, what good will it do?"

"We've been focusing on ourselves, our safety," said John, "Harry could be next. If William's death was anything to do with Crippley and the General, we should warn him. It might go some way to making amends...put things right."

Heather remained silent for a while. They both turned to Manny, who was climbing the ladder to the bed above the front of the truck.

"Hey, can I sleep here? It's awesome. I can see where we're going at the front."

Both Heather and John both answered, "No."

John leaned forward to Heather and whispered, "Did you have the same idea as me? The curtains on the little cabin could make it relatively private."

Heather, on the way back to form, said, "Maybe..."

John laughed, "Look, when we get our new phones, something to eat and park somewhere for the night, we can talk to Serge and make some decisions."

Serge must have heard them and called over from the driver's seat, "I'm hungry!"

"Don't worry, Serge," Heather said "We all are. I will see if I can sort out a bed for you inside. I'll make your bed and get you something to eat. I'll make sure you sleep like a baby."

"Hang on; I thought I was your favourite!"

Heather leant over and kissed John again, "No, I tend to go for the type of man who can stitch a major blood vessel these days."

Manny made a whistling sound to get their attention, "Hey.

Your police cars are tiny. One of them is behind us. He's got his lights on. Damn, there's a police bike too. It looks like they want us to stop."

Serge raised his voice, "Guys, they flash me."

"There's nothing we can do," John answered. "I'll climb upfront with you. Manny, you go up to the bed and shut the curtains, they don't need to know you're here. Heather, you ok?

"Yes, great plans, eh? I was looking forward to our road trip."

John felt the tremor in Heather's voice. "Don't worry. Serge and I will handle it. Keep quiet and try and stay out of the way. Serge, let me do the talking, with your accent they might shoot first and ask questions later."

CHAPTER 52 -HARRY - PLAN OF ATTACK

I read the draft white paper outlining the plan to sell off The Crown Estate. Of course, I knew about the proposal from the Brereton Papers but seeing it spelt out in black and white in the official Government document hit home. The next logical step would be to turn the United Kingdom into a Republic; I could be the last King of Great Britain.

Sitting in my study, I glanced across to photographs of my father with William and I. My grandmother looked at me as did Queen Victoria from portraits hanging on the study walls. They were private pictures, never seen by the public but, they too, could have a for sale notice on them.

After reading the Brereton Papers, I contacted Farrer & Co., the Royal Family's law firm for over three hundred years. I told Meghan about the PM's plans after I read Alex's papers about this part of Crippley's plan. More commercially aware than I, Meghan pressed me to take pre-emptive action. With this White Paper, the full impact of the government's plans could be considered by the firm.

When I spoke to them before, they recommended they co-opt a fleet of corporate legal experts and other professionals who could help. The cost would be considerable. I owed it to Archie, to my brother and to my forbears to do as much as I could to protect The Crown Estate, the art, property and Crown Jewels.

I realised the British people might support Crippley's plan. To them, it was a simple equation: the country needed the money. While the amount raised would be substantial, Crippley would go through it quickly, in doing so, he would destroy his country's heritage.

John Crossley, Farrer and Co's Managing Partner, was a seasoned legal expert. The rest of the Brereton Papers remained hidden from Meghan, but I needed her laser-like brain on this. Meghan, initially sceptical, gave the firm her seal of approval when they bought in some corporate experts from the USA.

Meghan joined me in a conference call to the teams of lawyers based in London and in New York. Farrer and Co instructed all parties to sign non-disclosure agreements and, in this instance, I was reasonably sure of confidentiality.

John Crossley opened the call and summarised the draft white paper. His team outlined the primary strategy needed to defend The Crown Estate from being plundered.

John Crossley said, "We will put aside every argument and concentrate on one principle; The Crown Estate is not the government's to sell. Also, previous monarchs acquired the Royal Art Collection with their own money. Fortunately, it is easy to prove due to the excellent records kept over hundreds of years. Other assets, notably the Crown Jewels, some twenty-six thousand artefacts, can also be traced back as purchases or recorded gifts. The Crown Estate includes; land, Palaces, properties in London and around the UK, the shoreline wind farm assets, and so forth. We have to go back to Charles III for most of the assets which were part of the King's private property. There are masses of detail, but we have a strong argument for His Majesty being the rightful owner of the entire estate. The government has been busy since they listed everything in the papers, they don't realise how this has helped us."

I felt an urge to contribute, but Crossley seemed to have it covered. He continued, "We will concentrate on these significant assets even though there are thousands of other items and rights which we will include in our petition. I don't want to take time on this call discussing them."

Sitting back, I glanced at Meghan, her full attention was on Crossley. He continued, "The Civil List Act of 1760 was a deal which suited both parties and has stood the test of time. King George III and the Government agreed on the principle The Crown Estate would be 'lent' in exchange for a sum of money paid to the monarch and their family. With each new King or Queen, the government at the time would seek agreement to extend the arrangement. Theoretically, any monarch had the right to refuse, but, of course, none ever did. The Sovereign Grant Act, relatively recently signed into law in 2011, changed the situation. Our interpretation of the wording of this Act further supports the argument the monarch owns the Crown Estate. A formula was put in place to pass over a fixed percentage of the profits to the Royal Household.

"We will, therefore, seek an injunction against the UK Government, preventing them from progressing to an official White Paper. This will avoid any discussion of the proposed Act in the Houses of Commons and Lords. We have, as you already know, successfully applied to the courts for a complete press blackout notice on the White Paper draft you have all seen. Fortunately, Mr Crippley, in his haste, shot his gun too early by supplying His Majesty with the White Paper draft ahead of its official publication.

"We will argue the Crown *in persona* owns the Crown Estate, the Art collections and every single item on the list so helpfully supplied as an appendix in Crippley's white paper. By assuming ownership, the government has nothing to sell."

Assuming he was finished, I said, "Thank you, Mr Crossley, you and all those on this call have done an excellent job.

"One more thing if I may, Sir?" said John Crossley.

"Yes?"

"As you know, we co-opted PWC, the international accounting firm to look at this from a financial point of view. They are not on this call. However, I have their analysis in front of me; I will send it around after this call. It appears we will have a claim to significant back payments where the 'deal' resulted in an underpayment to the Crown dating back to the original Civil List Act."

"Since 1760?"

"Yes, the Government will owe the Crown, owe you as an individual, some thirty-seven billion pounds."

"My God!" .My own sharp inhalation of breath echoed in the others present. Meghan tapped me on the arm, she smiled at me and raised her eyebrows.

Crossley continued, "This is significant. I will explain why. The amount is so large they will not be able to pay the amount, such are the UK finances at this time. It, therefore, acts as a huge deterrent in opposing our lawsuit."

The amounts were mind-boggling, "I know you want me to believe, and I like positive people, we'll win. How likely is this in reality?"

Crossley paused, I prepared myself for bad news, "I am neither a positive nor a negative person Sir. However, I wouldn't be a good lawyer if I weren't a little bit of a negative individual. After all, it is my job to plan for the worse; it is yours to hope for the best."

"So, how likely?"

"I am extremely confident; we'll get the right decision. Your

Majesty will be one of, if not the, richest people in the World with some one hundred and sixty billion pounds of assets."

"It's madness. Really?" I realised my voice gained an octave. Calming myself, I said, "I never planned this, I don't need that much."

"Indeed, Sir," John Crossley answered. "Once we prove your claim, it is yours to do as you like. For example, you could agree on a new 'deal' with the UK Government. We could agree on an iron-clad legal structure ensuring the spirit of the original Civil List and Sovereign Grant Acts remain. This brings me to the final point; possibly the biggest gun in our armoury."

He let his last sentence hang, then continued, "As I mentioned. Each new King or Queen has to formally agree on an extension to the arrangements surrounding the Crown Estate. In the past, this occurs typically within the first six months. Your Majesty has not agreed to the extension, meaning there is a clearer path to you claiming ownership of the entire estate."

"Thank you, gentlemen," I said to a muttering line of approval.

"Do you want to push the button, Sir, shall we file the case?"

I didn't answer. Perhaps I should wait until the plans I already agreed with the Invictus team were complete. I couldn't depend on them; the operation may fail. I had the future of the Crown to consider. With a glance to Meghan, she muted our line and looked at me, nodding. "Go ahead. Make sure you win!"

I pressed the button to unmute the call. "Well done, Mr Crossley, go ahead." I ended the call, still a little shocked with what the lawyer said. I leaned forward to kiss Meghan. She pulled me in.

Alone in my study, I let everything sink in. It wouldn't be easy to fight Crippley and the government, nevertheless, I felt optimistic.

Sitting there for half an hour, staring into space, I mulled over the future. Windsor's walls were like a prison. Ray told me we needed to stay put, but the public would expect to see us both out and about soon. According to reports, public sentiment towards the Royal Family and me, in particular, was steadily improving. My negative views about our popularity may have been mistaken. I needed to build on this as soon as possible.

The mourning period would be over in a week, I couldn't wait. I'd been busy with Ray and getting involved with the Invictus team, something to focus on dear to my heart. I hadn’t felt this optimistic since William’s passing.

The telephone rang again; it was my private secretary. He told me Alex asked to speak to me urgently. I didn't go back to Meghan and the Children as promised, I could meet Alex where the Invictus men were staying, he would be with them.

When I arrived outside the Arm's building, Alex, Ray and Dak were waiting for me.

"Alex, good to see you again, what's so urgent."

"General Thiskwood has made contact."

I went to speak, but fumbled my words. I didn't want to talk in the open, so I suggested we go into St George's Chapel, it would be empty.

Once inside, I made my way to the Royal Stalls at the end of the building where we could talk in private.

"Ok," I said, pointing to the pews, "Take a seat. What's happened, Alex?"

"When I left Spain, sorry, my mother owns a house there, when I left, I said to her not to tell anyone where I was. She arranged the house for me in Notting Hill. I've been phoning her regularly."

Ray and Dak glanced at each other. Alex anticipated what they were thinking, "It is alright, I bought a cheap phone, no one but her has the number. Anyway, she called me this morning and said General Thiskwood was trying to get in touch. Thiskwood gave her his number and my mother told him I would call him if I wanted to. She didn't want me to call him and asked me to fly back. Don't worry, I won't. Go to Spain, I mean."

Dak spoke, "Perhaps you should." Out of all of us, he was the one who expressed most doubts about Alex. I was getting comfortable with the young man. He handled himself well, he impressed me when he reached out to Brad in Notting Hill. It showed initiative. However, Dak was right to be cautious.

"So," I said, "you have his number?"

"He does." Dak scratched at his chin. "I've checked it out already. I've found out where General Thiskwood is."

"You've been busy."

"He is at the Cliveden Hotel."

"I know it well. 'Been there a few times. The place has quite a history."

"Using the GPS data from, err, a friend of ours, we found him located in a small building in the hotel's grounds."

I surveyed my team, the determination in their eyes apparent now; it was time to move. "Right Gentlemen. It is time for action. Alex, you've done us a great favour. It is time to go and look after your mother," I said.

"No. I won't, Sir. I've come this far. I'm not leaving you or the team."

Ray spoke first, "He has worked well in our exercises. As I mentioned the other day, he is strong and, it seems wrong to say and I mean no criticism..."

"What he is trying to say is we have only three able-bodied men," Dak cut in "We will need someone like Alex, it looks like we can trust him."

I looked at all of them in turn, "You have FOUR able men."

I put my hand up stopping Ray, about to speak. "Right, Alex stays on the team. Alex, let us know if it gets too hairy for you. And you two," I said firmly looking at Ray and Dak, "I'm the boss. I'm going to get this bastard; I will be right there with you."

All three nodded, none of them tried to speak.

Crippley and the General, the brains behind everything, wouldn't take this without fighting back. I had to save my family and the future of the United Kingdom. Standing, I said, "Right, we've finally found our mission, I want to capture Thiskwood, bring him here. Let's plan our attack. It needs to happen tonight."

CHAPTER 53 -BY THE THAMES

General Thiskwood slammed down his phone. The iPhone screen cracked as a result.

"Careful."

Thiskwood looked at his lover of over twenty years, "Watch that tone with me."

"I'm sorry, Daddy."

"Save 'daddy' for the bedroom."

Pierce turned toward the kitchen without saying anything. The role play was fun, but in the cold light of day, the General wouldn't pay attention to the safe word they agreed on. Arthur could be dangerous. Once, in the heat of the moment, he saw Arthur Thiskwood grab a soldier's throat so hard he died from his injuries. As usual, Arthur managed to keep it from the authorities. Pierce knew he best stay out of Arthur's way in this sort of mood; it happened frequently.

"Where the fuck are you going?"

"To make you a drink. A coffee?"

The General would be easier to handle if he gave him time on his own. From the safety of the small cottage's kitchen, he said, "Who was that?"

"It was Alex Brereton's mother. She played it cool. She must be abroad somewhere; she wasn't for playing ball. Mothers! They're schmucks sometimes. Women let their little boys manipulate them. Carolina is the same with Bernard. Alex Brereton must have warned her. She wasn't for giving me his number."

Pierce paused before he spoke, hoping to keep the General's temper in check, "You're right. What's next?"

"I gave them my number. Alex will get in touch. He is young, hot and angry. He'll reach out to me soon."

"Is he a real danger?"

Arthur, still ruffled, answered, "He is a loose cannon and a loose end. There's no telling what he will do. For all we know he will talk to the press again."

"Is there any other way to track him down?"

Pierce took the boiling kettle from its stand. In the early years of his relationship, an affair so covert and secret he sometimes wondered if it were real, Arthur Thiskwood was careful. As the years went by, Arthur became more brazen, increasingly he took chances. He became more and more dominant, often hitting him and causing him pain.

Pierce decided to change track, "What about Celia Casement?"

"Her body is already in the trunk of the car. Everything's been sorted."

"I know, but you can't leave her there."

"No," said the General coming into the kitchen, so close Pierce could feel his breath on his neck as he made the drinks. "Here are the keys. Go and sort out the body. The rental is not in my name, no one can trace it. Drive it somewhere and dump the car and the woman. Don't be lazy; choose somewhere a good way away from here."

Why did he love this pig so much? "Arthur. I don't know England. I don't even know how to operate their cars, the gears and all."

Arthur laughed. "You are useless. Don't worry; I got an automatic from the airport. You'll be fine. Drive it into London and dump it. Clean the prints off and make your way back here. You can handle it?"

"I don't have any money."

Thiskwood put his hand in his pocket and pulled out a large wad of British currency. "Here, take this and get in the fucking car."

As Pierce reached for the money, Arthur grabbed him. "IF you do this right, we can have another night here on our own."

Celia Casement came to Spring Cottage in the morning. At first, she was surprised by Arthur's presence but he explained Carolina had come down with the flu. He told her Carolina tended to panic; it was his fault for not keeping Carolina informed as to his whereabouts.

In the garden, Arthur made Celia Casement comfortable serving her tea. "You've been through a tough time, I'm sorry for you and your family."

"Thank you," said Celia, making a noise of pleasure as she sipped the tea. "You make a good cup of tea for an American."

"This biggest compliment an American can receive from an Englishwoman," said Arthur, smirking. "How have your children been?"

"They fussed around me and insisted on staying over but they have their own lives. Eventually, I sent them off packing. The last few days alone has helped me come to terms with Roger's death. But it is hard."

Seeing her teacup empty, Arthur said, "Come, let's take a walk around the garden. It is lovely here. British people have beautiful gardens, we have yards."

Celia smiled, "Yes, we love the garden for what it is. The flowers, the beauty, the peace."

"And we like it if we can play ball in it," laughed Arthur who was trying to remain patient but struggled with the time it was taking to find out what he wanted. Celia eventually offered the information without any coercion.

"I have some files you may be interested in. Come, let's sit there by the river, I have them with me."

"I wondered why you brought your briefcase."

Celia collected the briefcase as they passed the bench where they drank tea, "Roger told me about your meetings with the Prime Minister. He said how important Mr Crippley's mission was. To be honest, Roger was left of centre himself, given his background. He was so poor when he was younger, the memories stayed with him for a long time. I was so proud of my husband. He was a great man."

"He was a good man, Celia. What do you have there?"

"You see, Arthur left me all sorts of notes and instructions. He was such a caring man. Anyway, I only recently got around to visiting his safety deposit box. You should see what was in there; our first wedding rings, they only cost a few pounds. He even kept our letters to each other. It was so wonderful to see. I wish I'd gone to the bank straight after he died. It was such a bad time for me."

"So, why bring me the files, what's in them?"

"Arthur was working on the details of The Crown Estate. Who

owned it. I've never seen him so focused. I didn't get to see the output of all the effort until I got these from his safe deposit box. You see, Roger found out so much. These papers, I've read them, I understand most of them. They have a brilliant conclusion; so clear, so precise, so Roger."

He gave her another smile, false as it were, moments away from striking her, "So, Celia, what did he conclude?"

Celia held out one of the files. "It's all in here. I've read these and reread them. Someone said the King, Harry, doesn't own Buckingham Palace, the jewels, the Crown and everything. But my husband proved them wrong."

"Perhaps I could take a look? Come, let's sit by the river."

As Celia made herself comfortable on the seat made out of a fallen tree partly submerged in the river, Arthur flicked through the file and skipped to the end. The summary was surprisingly brief. Celia was right, one of the most senior judges in the United Kingdom concluded the current King, Harry, owned full title to the Crown Estate and all the royal assets including the art collection, everything.

"Your husband was a clever man. Can I keep these for a while?"

Celia said, "I haven't made copies. I'd like to keep them. How about I get them copied and send them on?"

Without warning, Arthur Thiskwood grabbed Celia's hair, pulling her towards the river's edge. Celia Casement screamed, her eyes filling with fear. She tried to stand but Arthur kicked her over. Leaning down, he grabbed her hair once more and forced her head into the water.

Celia was a small woman, the General found it easy to hold her head in the water as she thrashed about. Her plain underskirt rode up, exposing her thighs. As she struggled, her red painted fingernails dug into his hands, drawing blood. Annoyed, Arthur stepped into the shallow edge of the river and pushed her head down further, her face disappearing in the river's muddy bed. Even though Celia Casement stopped fighting, Arthur made sure she was dead by holding her head under the water for another minute.

Now wet himself, Arthur climbed out of the river and carried Celia's body to the trunk of his car. As he started to close the boot, he stopped, fascinated by the look of her eyes staring at him through the wet mud caked on her face.

Arthur Thiskwood slammed the boot shut and looked down at his wet trousers and cursed, he'd have to change into something dry.

He watched Pierce drive away with her body, pleased with another job done; his phone rang and his eyes widened at the sight of an unknown number.

"General Thiskwood."

"Hiya, Mr Thiskwood. My name's Alex Brereton. You called my mother today?"

"Ah, yes. Thank you for calling back. I appreciate it."

"What did you want? Is there something I can help you with?"

"I knew your father."

"You did?" Alex's tone was surprised. "Who are you? Did you work for my father? No, your accent, you're American right?"

"Your father was a true friend of mine. As I said to your mother, I wanted to help now he has sadly passed."

"Thank you. I appreciate it. What did you have in mind?"

"Why not come here to see me, we can talk about it then. If you could come tonight, we could have one of your British beers at the hotel. Where are you? I'm outside London at a place called Cliveden."

"I've heard of it. No, I'm busy. I'm free tomorrow afternoon."

Arthur couldn't believe how casual the boy sounded. Clearly, he was over his father's death. "I am flying back to the States the day after so two in the afternoon tomorrow looks good. I can send a car."

"Tomorrow it is! Can you send me the postcode so I can find you? I have a car.

"Sure. Thank you, Alex."

The two would meet, but not on the General's terms.

CHAPTER 54 -THE SOUND OF SUMMER

"So, Prime Minister, the legal action prevents us from publishing the White Paper. There is a Section 'D' notice in force so none of this can be reported on by the press. It won't stop them speculating though, whoever leaked The Crown Estate list made sure of that."

Jarrod Crippley regarded at the Attorney General and the team of lawyers gathered around the Cabinet table, he remained speechless.

Jenny Fairbrother continued, "There is another issue here, Prime Minister. We've never encountered this particular issue. The King is the Crown, and I report to the Crown. Since the King, and therefore the Crown, is bringing legal action against the government, I can no longer advise you on this matter. The government will need to employ independent counsel. There is a conflict of interest I am afraid."

"You what? I appointed you. I-GAVE-YOU-YOUR-JOB," the PM spat.

"I am afraid you did not appoint me, Sir. You recommended my appointment to the King," replied the Attorney General firmly.

Crippley walked up to the table. "That was to William, he didn't last long."

"Indeed, Sir. All appointments made by the monarch remain in place until changed. You have yet to recommend me or anyone else to the new King. To you, this may be a technicality, however, it means I cannot speak further on this matter as I report to him. I've already created a conflict which I'll have to report to the Law Society in due course."

Crippley rounded on her. He invaded the space behind the Attorney General, forcing her to turn around in her chair. "Ms Farebrother, you are out of order here. You're using this so you don't have to become involved. I will replace you; I should have done this before. Look at how you've handled all this civil unrest in Newcastle. You're a jumped-up lawyer. I should throw you out of this room. Consider yourself fired."

Jenny Fairbrother looked straight ahead, away from the Prime Minister to address her colleagues. "I can assure you, Prime Minister, as I have informed you and everyone here; you cannot fire me. Of course, you can make a recommendation to the King, but I'm not sure he will be anxious to help you out on this or any other matter."

"All of you, get out, GET THE FUCK OUT," screamed Crippley.

The six lawyers, led by the United Kingdom's chief law officer, calmly closed their files and stood to leave. Jenny Fairbrother paused at the door while the other lawyers made their exit. Turning to the red-faced PM, she said, "One of the powers I have, Mr Crippley, enables me to point out to the King he has an unsuitable Prime Minister. I will call the King in the next few days once I've retained counsel myself."

"Get-OUT, leave!"

The lawyer smiled at the PM and turned to leave. As she exited the room, she heard Jarrod Crippley shouting after her as did the lawyers and the private secretary to the PM gathered outside.

Crippley waited a few minutes before returning to his office. He knew he lost it with the lawyers, he needed to calm down. Sitting alone at his desk, he made a call to General Thiskwood, "It is getting out of hand. This whole thing."

"Good afternoon Crippley. What are you going on about? I am getting annoyed with your constant whining."

"Harry. The boy who couldn't even pass any basic exams at school. He's fighting back. His lawyers claim The Crown Estate, the art, everything, belongs to him, personally. Moreover, he is claiming income dating back to 1760 the Royal Family never received."

General Thiskwood found it all funny. "You have yourself between a rock and a hard place, don't you? You asked me to help you, Operation Catesby is a success, you're the failure. The one thing I can't help you with is your archaic laws and customs. You were supposed to wait at least six months to file the White Paper. Why did you shoot the gun? "

"But...You don't know what a mess the government's finances are in. No one will lend us more money without massive alterations to our plan for the economy and oppressive conditions."

"Crippley, shut up. I've delivered on everything I promised; you will get yourself a republic. The Royal Family is on its knees. The only thing, ONLY, you had to do was to sort out this stuff, and you've failed."

Jarrod Crippley replied, the desperation evident, "General, you have to help. I can't see myself getting out of this mess. You won't either."

"Are you threatening me?"

"No, no," Crippley stuttered. "I'm not... I'm sorry, General, I don't know what I am saying."

Thiskwood smirked as Crippley let out a sob. Pathetic, he thought. "You're a weak man. Come here. I'm at Cliveden. Get in your car. Dismiss the driver; you'll find a way. Come on your own, we'll figure this out."

"I know the place. But... I can't come. My security follows me everywhere. It is their job."

"Sort it and get down here. I'm staying in a house on the hotel grounds called Spring Cottage. By my reckoning, it will take you less than ninety minutes once you have your guards out of the way. I expect you to be here by six this evening."

Jarrod Crippley replied, almost inaudibly, "Yes, Sir. I'll be there."

General Thiskwood put his phone in his pocket. Crippley was on edge, his veiled threat was a concern.

The General ran through the critical aspects of Operation Casement, satisfied with his input and the success of the plan. Crippley's primary objective was to help turn the UK into a republic. By removing two Kings, destroying their reputation in the process, he made significant progress, he admitted. Harry's reputation had ebbed and flowed over the years.

As the UK finances worsened, Crippley became more interested in the money from The Crown Estate. Thiskwood watched Crippley's attitude and demeanour crumble to reveal a frightened man who blamed his mistakes on others. His chaotic management of the economy was that of watching an addicted gambler lose it all, as they often did. Crippley's only solution to his debts was to find more money so he could win everything back.

Arthur Thiskwood went outside and sat on the bench overlooking the river; the spot where Celia Casement sat before.

The sun shone and the air humid, making Arthur Thiskwood calm down and relax. The sound of summer was different from his in Louisiana, every sound muffled, a delightful white noise.

Thiskwood used the peace and quiet to consider his next steps. He would have to deal with Carolina; Pierce would help him so no one could trace her death back to him. He would leave the house tomorrow after dealing with Alex Brereton. Pierce could stay with Carolina's body and make out to the hotel staff she was still alive. Pierce could make a noisy exit for the staff to remember and check in to another hotel in London. The General smiled. He would meet Pierce and set up his 'suicide'. Pierce would think it was another roleplay except for this time no safe word would save him. The hotel staff would lead the police to Pierce, who would be found hanging, a note confessing the murder of dear, sweet, Carolina.

Pierce’s sacrifice was the only option. His plan for his wife and his long-time lover sorted out so many loose ends. If Celia Casement's body was found, Pierce could take the wrap for it as well.

His telephone buzzed in his pocket; it was Martin. "Sir, we have the motorhome in view. It looks as though there are two of them upfront; I can only assume the woman is in the back."

Martin Sitton, the General's top operative in the UK, wasn't cheap. Still, former British Intelligence officers willing to sell their services were like finding gold. Sitton sorted out the Judge and Brereton to a satisfactory standard, save for the incident surrounding his son and the press. Sitton organised the hit on William and his Family through his connections and even found someone to slip the drug to King Charles. He wished he could have helped in Florida given it ended in such a mess.

"A motorhome? Ok. Pull Amery over; it will scare them because they know the police want them. Put the tracker on the vehicle as I told you. Ask to look inside and tell me if Heather Taylor-Todd is in the van. Make sure you plant a bug so you can hear what they're saying. Give them a warning over their speed or something. I want them to carry on; see where they are going, follow the motorhome from a distance in an unmarked car."

"Yes, Sir. I know where I can borrow a police car and uniforms."

"Good, do you have the explosives ready?

"I have them, we are..."

Thiskwood cut Sitton off, "Good, are you able to plant them on a vehicle? I didn't figure on a motorhome."

"Yes. I noticed a small door at the side of the vehicle, storage space for bicycles. I went on holiday in one of those things once. It was one of the most miserable weeks of my life."

"Right," said Thiskwood, wondering why Sitton added the story about his holiday, "fix them there. Oh, and Martin, well done. The idea to track the aircraft paid off."

"Thank you, Sir; it is why you pay me the big bucks. Remember, it is near the end of the month, there should be another one million pounds in my account in two days."

General Thiskwood smiled, he liked a man who worshipped money, they'd do anything for you. "There will be, don't worry. Remember, if you manage to sort out Amery and his new girlfriend, there's a nice bonus due."

"Good. The only concern I have is regarding your safety there. You only have Pierce with you."

"I am fine here at the moment. No one knows I am here and I am pretty sure no one other than the police are looking for me. I've scrapped the phone McNee gave when I landed in the UK. By the time the British Police find me, there will be a cold day in hell. After this is all over, I will escape, everything is ready. I'll disappear from the face of the earth."

"A shame, General, you're a good customer."

"Right," Thiskwood said, "get on with it and make sure the bug is in place. Relay any conversations which may be important. Text me if you can't get hold of me straight away."

Arthur raised his face to the sun and closed his eyes. The warm rays felt good on his face. Age was Thiskwood's greatest enemy, one even he couldn't defeat. Carolina must be suffering in the bedroom, she couldn't escape, so he decided to lay on the tree trunk bench by the river where he last spoke to Celia Casement. He listened to the gentle rippling sound of the river in the warm sun and drifted off to sleep.

CHAPTER 55 - ARISTOCRATIC CONNECTIONS

"It is unusual Sir. I am not sure what he wants."

My gaze washed over George, my Head of Household. "It is kind of people to contact me with words of support. I know, they all want to get in with the new King, I'm not stupid. Why speak to me about this message? Usually, you normally send it in my notes for the day."

"The Earl was at Eton School with William, Sir. He knows a lot of people and, by all accounts, is fairly switched on. The family fortune is safe with him, he runs the family's investment company. He is one of the few members of the aristocracy to increase the family fortune. The Earl sounded anxious to talk to you. The tone in his voice wasn't as desperate as such, more persistent and urgent."

"Today isn't the best of days, there is a lot to do." I'd returned from speaking to Ray and Dak who were briefing the men. I needed to be with them in an hour, I owed it to Meghan to visit her and the children. I didn't intend to tell Meghan what we had planned tonight. The least I could do is say to her face to face, I would be otherwise engaged later.

George paused, then said, "Earl Hazlehurst's sister is Heather Taylor-Todd."

Does he know more than he should? "What do you know about Lady Heather, George?"

"I saw the papers mentioning her today. Apparently, she has been in some trouble in the USA. The article I read mentioned Earl Hazlehurst. It can't be a coincidence."

"No. I guess not. OK, call him, put it through to my phone in the study. Can you advise him I am busy and won't have much time? Thank you, George."

"Of course, Sir." George bowed his head and I made my way to my study. Ahead of the call coming through I telephoned Meghan who, as predicted, wasn't happy. I messaged Ray I'd be thirty minutes; we had a big night ahead.

The call came through from Earl Hazlehurst. "Good morning."

"Good Morning, Your Majesty, thank you for taking my call. I appreciate it," said Oliver Taylor-Todd. Without a pause for my reply, he continued, "I'm afraid I have reason to believe the matter I have to discuss with you is urgent."

Surprised, I asked him why?

"My sister, Heather Taylor-Todd, called me. She is with a gentleman called John Amery, a hedge fund manager."

"I know, the History Girl. She's caused a stir in the US with the program about God, or lack of one."

"Yes, yes, she has," replied Oliver. "I'm afraid she is in a lot more trouble now, Sir. It has to do with your Prime Minister."

I didn't want the Earl to detect anything off in my tone. "I am not sure I can comment on our Prime Minister."

"Jarrod Crippley asked Heather, John Amery and a few others to join some sort of committee to investigate The Crown Estate. I am not sure of the details. They mentioned someone called General Thiskwood, an American, it looks as though they've all fallen out. Actually, I am underplaying this. They believe the General is a danger to them and," Oliver paused, "you sir."

"In what way?"

"That's just it, Sir. Heather was in a frightful state. She's usually the cool one in our family. She wondered..." I heard Earl Hazlehurst pause. Not for effect, he struggled with his words before he said, "She has something important to tell you and she won't do it on the phone. Heather would like to see you."

"I'm sure I can get someone to arrange something."

"Sir... my word, I find this deeply embarrassing. She said it was a matter of 'life or death,' she wants to speak to you, in person, today."

I let his urgency fall away from me. "Oh, dear. I am going to be busy today. I can't. Life and death, you say?"

"Yes. Trust me, Sir, if Heather is anything, she is not one to bolt at the slightest hurdle. She is full-on, always has been. Of course, there's no reason you should trust me. However, I think you should see her."

Our operation against the General would commence after dark. It would be dangerous; every piece of information was important. "Alright, can she make it here before this evening? I'm at Windsor."

"Sorry, Sir, I meant to say. They are in a motorhome, parked a mile from Windsor Castle. You are still there, aren't you? Heather sounded nervous. Is there any way you could let their vehicle in and see them there? She warned me; the Castle might be bugged. It is most unusual, I know. She isn't unhinged because I know my sister. Heather doesn't panic."

"I will make arrangements. I only have a few minutes. Ask

them to come to the Nelson's Gate entrance immediately. It will take them longer but there's less chance they will be seen. "

Earl Hazlehurst let out a breath. "Thank you, Sir, thank you."

Giving Heather Taylor-Todd a few minutes of my time could prove useful. Her name appeared in the Brereton papers, something Hazlehurst didn't need to know.

"Ray, a slight change of plan. Heather Taylor-Todd and John Amery are in Windsor. Her Brother, Earl Hazlehurst, called me. She wants to come and see me."

Another sharp intake of breath over the line. "What do they want?"

"It is a matter of life or death in Earl Hazlehurst's opinion. I have a feeling we should talk to them ahead of tonight. They have information on the General; they both feature in the Brereton Papers."

"Ok, Sir."

I have to tell Ray, but not in here. Maybe in the courtyard. I could hear Meghan and the children, their excited voices echoing about the apartment following their swim. "Look, they're in a motorhome. It might be better to let them drive into the Castle grounds, direct them to the west car park. It will be better as I don't want anyone seeing them here. We're still not sure how secure the Castle is."

Again, I had to wait for Ray's considered reply, "Ok, can you get here right away?"

I smiled to myself, Ray was full of respect for the Crown, but, in 'operational' mode, he had no time for the niceties. "I'll be a few minutes."

Megan was in the children's room, getting them dressed after their swim. "Meghan, do you have a minute?"

"Yes, come in here. "

"No, let them finish off themselves. Can you come into the drawing-room?"

Her face was the picture of misery. "For heaven's sake, Harry, you were supposed to come for a swim. What is it with you these days?"

"Lay off, Meghan. A lot is going on."

Meghan beckoned me to sit beside her as she took her seat. "I'm going to be busy all day and maybe tonight too. I'm sorry."

"You're sorry? You promised me the children would always come first. You've barely seen them since we got hauled back here."

I looked at my beautiful wife. Her mood, progressively belligerent over the last few weeks, reflected on her appearance. Gone, these days, was her radiant smile, replaced by a sombre look. It was time I told her everything; it might change her demeanour. "Since we came here, I have become aware of some worrying events, we are in danger from people who want the monarchy to end with me. It wasn't Islamic Extremists who killed William and his family. A lot is going on in government. It's not all to do with The Crown Estate."

"Why didn't you tell me?"

"I've been trying to find out more. It turns out Crippley is not only after The Crown Estate. He may be, I stress, maybe, going a few steps further, and he is working with outsiders. He may be after the Crown itself."

"What do you mean?"

"There is a plot to destabilise the monarchy. He wants a republic."

"You're saying Crippley's involved? How?"

"We're forming the picture, but it is why I bought the Invictus team here. It's why Ray and Dak are here too; to protect you and the children. "

"And you, Harry," Meghan said as her face softened into concern for me.

"Yes. There's enough to suggest Crippley and a small number of people, including an American General, might be involved in the death of William, Catherine and the Children. They might even have had something to do with my father dying, I can't be sure. However, we're on the front foot, it's why I have been so distracted."

"An American General? Let me help."

I was firm, "No Meghan. I need to sort this out. You have to stay with the children. Don't trust anyone, not even the Nanny, no one. "

"Harry, you're scaring me."

"Trust me, Meghan. I have to go. Hopefully, Ray, Dak and I will be able to sort this out. Keep your phone near you and only trust us. Do you understand?"

Meghan hugged me. My wife is full of contradictions, sometimes I never knew where I stood with her. The hug felt good, she whispered in my ear, "Take care, H."

I hugged her again and left her there. Before I left the apartment, I said, "Trust no one. We have only a few days to make sure you, the kids and I are ok. This...plot...needs sorting and it could be more about the future of the country, it could determine how we live our life."

"Or it could mean we don't live at all?"

I looked her in the eyes. "Now, you understand."

CHAPTER 56 -A STROKE OF LUCK

"You're joking! They are in Windsor?"

"The town of Windsor," Martin Sitton replied. "They are obviously trying to contact the King."

"And you have them on tape?"

"No, Sir. They made a stop and bought new phones. We've heard some conversations from the bug, I don't know what they're saying when they leave the van."

"How do you trigger the bomb on board the motorhome? What is the range?"

"Anywhere in the world," Sitton replied slowly, trying to anticipate the General. "A call to the mechanism triggers the device."

"Assuming they are trying to get access to the King, how will they do it?"

"I don't know, Sir. Since they are mobile, there's a possibility they will drive it into the Castle grounds."

The General paused again. He was always careful with his words. "Will the guards check out the motorhome?"

"They should. They could look in the storage space, but the device is next to the gas cylinder, it will be hard to detect but not impossible."

"An explosion near the Castle will trigger a massive security lockdown. Speak to me before you do anything. Be ready to set the device off at a moment's notice. Remember, do nothing until I give the go-ahead; it may be better to let it play out without setting off the bomb. Where are you staked out, in Windsor?"

"Yes, Sir, we're monitoring the chatter inside the van, they're not saying much."

"Will you be able to see them if they get into the Castle grounds?"

"No, the place is a fortress, literally. If I may suggest, Sir. You may as well give the go-ahead; the bomb will get rid of them all in one go."

"There would be havoc, terrorists might not be the best excuse. The investigation could lead them to Crippley, maybe me. You should have called me before they got to Windsor." Thiskwood said, cutting the call before Sitton could reply.

Pierce noticed Arthur in the garden near the river when he arrived home, laying down. He wasn't sure if the General was asleep or on the phone.

Pierce went to check on Carolina, deciding not to let the General know he returned; it would probably annoy him if he was busy.

Carolina's suffering hurt more than he'd tell Arthur, their friendship wasn't faked. He took her some water, knowing Arthur wouldn't bother. On entering the room, Carolina opened her eyes and stared at Pierce as he brought a glass of water to her lips.

Out of habit, she said, "Thank you."

All he could do was smile, awkwardly so. Still dressed in the clothes she had on the day before, Carolina's usually immaculate hair clung to her head and her hands looked black from the lack of circulation.

"Pierce, let me go. I won't say anything. You should come with me."

"Don't you see, Arthur and I, we..."

"I heard him on the phone when you were downstairs earlier. You'll be next." Carolina said, "You have to believe me, Pierce. He is going to kill you too, he asked Martin Sitton."

"Carolina, I know you're desperate. Arthur wouldn't. He loves me."

"He uses you; don't you see? Even in the bedroom. How can you stand to be treated in such a way?"

Warmth flooded Pierce’s face, realising Carolina heard him and Arthur in bed. Unable to answer, he moved away from Carolina and went to leave the room.

Carolina continued, "As far as I can figure out, Pierce, you haven't been responsible for any of this. Arthur is evil. He is deranged. Haven't you noticed how Arthur has changed since leaving the Army? Arthur is slower. He forgets sometimes. He is more morose, insular."

Pierce nodded. However, he said, "He has me to look after him."

"No, Pierce, I heard him talking to Sitton, he is the one who is doing his dirty work here in the UK isn't it?

Pierce knew Sitton, words escaped him. Sitton was several years younger than himself and good looking. A knot of jealousy tightened in his chest.

Carolina continued, pleased she still had Pierce's attention. "He spoke to Martin when you were making coffee. The guy was at Biggin Hill airport, he found someone the General was looking for. He said to this Sitton guy he only needed you for a short while, he asked him to get rid of you." Carolina continued, lying to Pierce, desperate to win him over, "Pierce. You and Arthur had sex, he sent you downstairs and immediately called this Martin Sitton. He finished the call by saying 'I love you, Martin, I can't wait to see you again."

Pierce remained silent. He wanted to run away, out of Carolina's sight. Arthur had a high sex drive; Pierce suspected the General had over men besides him. He'd met Sitton a few times and noticed a vibe between him and Arthur. The man was better looking and fitter than Pierce.

Carolina could tell her message was getting through to Pierce. "Look, Pierce, Arthur is in some heavy shit right now, it can only get worse. I know him, his grip on the whole thing is rapidly going. He'll strike out at anyone. Pierce, you can get out of this. Let me go and come with me. I can't be your friend again, but I won't say anything."

He couldn't help himself, he needed to know more. "Carolina, you'll say anything to me to get out of this." Tears ran down his face. "Arthur needs me. He needs me." The repetition more for himself than Carolina.

"Yes, he will use you because it is what he does. He doesn't like loose ends, Pierce. When he has finished with this, he will tie up those ends, he will make sure you can't lead anyone back to him." It occurred to her Pierce was a submissive character, and she changed her tone, "Now get these straps off me and get ME OUT OF HERE."

Pierce turned and left the room. She considered calling out but Arthur might hear and any chance of getting free would be lost.

Carolina closed her eyes, sobbing. The pain in her bladder became unbearable, she buried her face into the pillow as warm liquid pooled around her legs again.

"Carolina."

Caroline looked up as Pierce returned. Silently he used a kitchen knife to cut through the plastic straps holding her arms and untied her feet. He lifted her from the bed and grasped her tightly as they left the room and edged their way down the stairs. While Arthur wasn't in the cottage, she heard his voice from outside, causing her to jump.

Pierce put his finger to his lips. He whispered, "When we get to the bottom of the stairs, there's a chance he could see us. Just crouch down if you can, we'll slip out of the kitchen door."

Arthur Thiskwood's voice grew louder as they descended the stairs, *I am fine here at the moment. No one knows I am here...* Carolina grabbed Pierce's arm as they crept to the kitchen and through the open door.

Pierce helped Carolina into the car. She remained silent despite the pain in her arms and legs from where they were tied. Pierce started the engine and drove away slowly to avoid being heard.

As they left the hotel grounds, Pierce looked over to Carolina, "I heard him on the phone talking to Martin Sitton. He talks to him the same way he speaks to me. I'll get you out of here but after you won't see me again. Keep your end of this deal and don't come after me."

Carolina looked at Pierce, "I won't. Take me to my sister's house. I'll direct when we get close but head for central London first."

"I will drop you off close by. I can't risk anyone finding me."

Carolina nodded, saying nothing. When she was safe, Arthur apprehended, she would do everything she could to find Pierce and make him pay despite this act of kindness.

Arthur Thiskwood regarded empty bed with disdain, and checked the window; he caught the sight of a car Pierce must have rented after he disposed of Celia Casement's body. He called out to Pierce and cursed him. Arthur knew it could be the last time they saw one another.

Lifting a phone to his ear, Thiskwood said, "Get as many men to Cliveden as you can. I need protection."

"Yes, Sir. I have some men on standby. What happened?"

Thiskwood wasn't sure what happened between Pierce and Carolina. He had to give his wife credit for managing to convince Pierce to release her. No doubt she would head straight for her sister, there was no way he could take on the French embassy staff. Crippley couldn't be contacted as he drove to meet him so the British police might raid the house if she called them. His instincts told him she wouldn't, but he couldn't risk it. "Pierce took Carolina. Don't bother with them. Send your men here. Has anything happened at your end?"

"The motorhome is in the Castle grounds. I can't see them yet but I think I'll be able to if I move up into the town. It looks as though I might be able to see in from one of the top windows of a building."

"Wait there. Send the men as soon as possible. The tables might be turning. I will need to get out of here as soon as I've dealt with Crippley."

CHAPTER 57 - NELSON'S GATE

I rushed to meet Dak and Ray to update them; anxious looks greeted me.

"This could be a trap," Ray Said. "Anything could happen."

"I've given the guard at Nelson's Gate to direct them to the west car park," said Dak, "I asked George to clear all the cars. I want them to park in the middle so we can surround them. I won't use the team; they're ready to set off to Cliveden as are we. Let's get this sorted first.

We walked to the car park. "I will go and ask them to get out of the van." Ray prepared himself. "We'll carry out a search and bring them over to you. According to the guards at the outer gates, the motorhome has two men in the front; Lady Taylor-Todd must be in the back."

It was only minutes before I saw the large motorhome. I stood behind a wall just around the corner from the car park and could see most of the vehicle, Ray insisted I remain there while he approached it. The Royal Guards, all in combat dress, numbered some twenty-six men and they trained rifles on the vehicle. Their orders would be replayed by Dak who wore an open link to Ray as did I in my earpiece.

Ray walked up to the motorhome; the driver's window went down. Ray said, "Please state your name, Sir. Tell me who this is beside you and who else is in this vehicle."

I could see the expression on the man's face: confident despite the situation. The passenger leaned over and said, "I am John Amery, this is Serge Kalinko. I have Heather Taylor-Todd in the van."

"Do you have any weapons?"

"Yes, Serge does."

Ray aimed the gun he was holding at Serge, "Sir, take out your gun with two fingers and drop it outside the vehicle." Ray's voice was so loud I barely needed the earpiece.

The giant man behind the steering wheel did as instructed and threw the gun to the tarmac.

"Now, slowly step outside the vehicle, one at a time. Walk ten paces towards the wall," Ray said, pointing to it with his gun, "Lay face down with your hands at the back of your head. Big guy, you first."

The man unfolded himself from the wheel, following his instructions to the letter. John Amery, who I recognised from pictures seen while Googling, followed. Finally, Heather Taylor-Todd got out of the van from the door at the side. I could see her bandaged neck and her clothes were dishevelled; she'd been through a lot. She paused when she got out and turned to Ray, who held a pistol and point-blank range in her face - she wasn't following the precise instructions he gave.

"I need to speak to the King," I heard her say. I guessed, correctly as it turned out, they decided Heather should be the spokesperson as her brother arranged the meeting.

"Go over," Ray said, shaking his head. "Lay next to them."

I could see Heather's face and decided, against all advice, to walk towards Heather.

Heather's eyes turned to me but returned to Ray as he raised his voice, "Sir, back off, we haven't checked out the van."

"Heather, do you have any weapons?"

"No," she replied.

"Ray, search Lady Heather and let her come over to me."

Dak moved forward to hold another gun in Heather's face while Ray put his weapon in his holster. Ray completed a full body search. Eventually, he turned to me, " Sir, can I advise you not to make any bodily contact at all and stay at least two meters apart."

I understood, Ray saw danger in everything, a deadly virus was another type of weapon. "Lady Heather, will you approach me please."

I noticed Ray leading some of the soldiers towards the van. I walked towards Heather. She made her way towards me, briefly glancing at the others laying on the floor. Heather had a formidable reputation, but she looked drained from her neck injury and understandably nervous. Nevertheless, she remembered her etiquette when she spoke to me, "Your Majesty." She even performed a small but noticeable curtsey.

I saw Dak approach the van behind her, Heather turned to look too, having seen my stare. A young lad rushed out of the motorhome, screaming. Heather turned and ran towards the van, shouting," Stop!"

Ray raised his gun to aim at Heather, the guards also sprang into action with two of them diving on James Amery and the other man.

The motorhome seemed to rise slightly moments before it blew up in my face.

CHAPTER 58 -BBC NEWSFLASH

It didn't take long to get into London as traffic was light. Pierce drove the car within the speed limits, anxious not to attract the attention of the police.

As they drove, Carolina resisted the temptation to speak to Pierce. Information on their affair and what Arthur really was up to could wait until she was safe.. Although her wrists hurt, the blood was making its way slowly to her fingertips, tingling.

Pierce focused on the roads ahead, silent. Occasionally, Carolina saw Pierce's eyes well with tears, but he blinked them away. She trusted him enough to take her to London but wanted the car to go faster as she couldn't be sure he might change his mind.

"Pierce, why the change of heart? How come you helped me?"

"I love Arthur."

Carolina looked at Pierce, his eyes focused on the road. She pitied him and hated the man at the same time, "But you've helped me?"

"Arthur is a great man.I-I don't know. Martin Sitton, I suspect they..."

Carolina waited, there was more to the story.

"He treats me… me… he treats me like a dog. "

Carolina persisted, softly, "I thought you liked it, am I right?

Pierce glanced at her, then to the road ahead. "Yes. But he is different. He… He made me do stuff I didn't want to do. But… If Arthur…? If he wants someone else? It isn't worth it anymore. I don't know, Carolina, he is not the man I met in the Army."

Carolina just watched him. Pierce deserved little pity. With nothing left to ask, she relaxed in the chair, rubbing her wrists trying to regain feeling in her blood starved hands. Carolina kept her hand near the door handle of the car for fear of Pierce changing his mind again.

"Carolina, I value our friendship. You've helped me so much these past few years. I am sorry."

"Pierce, surely you can't believe I can forgive you. Drive on, I want to see my sister. Please."

"It was Arthur's idea to set me up in a ranch, near yours. He wanted me to make friends with you, to keep tabs on us both, I think."

"He certainly knows how to plan, move the pieces into the right place," said Carolina, willing the car to go faster. "What will you do?"

"Do? I don't know what I'm going to do." Pierce said, raising his voice. "I've felt like ending it with Arthur so many times since I left the Army. He planned that too. I didn't want to leave. I've nothing else, no parents, no brothers or sisters, no friends… Don't you see, Arthur was everything to me, now I am alone. "

"He's moved on to this Sitton guy, is he American?"

"No, British. Don't worry, I'll take you to your sisters. I know you made it up about Sitton."

"So... why did you decide..."

Again, in a loud voice, Pierce said, "To rescue you? I needed an excuse, an excuse to end it all. That bastard doesn't love me, or you, or anyone. I warned you to stay away, you wouldn't listen. I'm not so stupid, I've worked alongside Arthur for years. It wouldn't be long before he got rid of me, I was just one of the loose ends he needed to tidy up. Getting you out of there, it... it gave me the push I needed."

Despite herself, Carolina could see Pierce's torment, "Whatever the reason, thank you."

By Hyde Park Corner tube station Pierce remained silent, he didn't look at her as she opened the door. Carolina got out, quickly realising she had no shoes. It was a short walk to the French Embassy, the least of her worries.

Looking inside the car where Pierce sat, eyes forward, anger rose within and she didn’t try to bite it back down. "Good luck, Pierce. Now fuck off." She slammed the door and running away as quick as she could.

The front of the ornate French embassy came into sight within minutes. Carolina didn't care Londoner's staring at her; they were used to stranger sights. She continued to run until she arrived at the entrance to the French Embassy and Residence.

As she climbed the steps, Carolina could see the French soldier look at her. Using the little French, she spoke, she informed the soldier she wanted to see her sister; the Ambassador's wife. The man nodded and bent to help her enter the building into a large lobby used as a waiting area. He showed her to a leather seat and asked her to wait while he made enquiries.

Carolina felt embarrassed and out of place, she smelt, her clothes were soiled. She leaned back into the chair and looked at the TV. She noticed several people staring at the screen. There were pictures of Windsor Castle with a plume of smoke rising from the middle of the building.

At the base of the screen, he saw the headlines: 'King Feared Dead in Explosion at Windsor'.

CHAPTER 59 - RIVER CRUISE

Marin Sitton watched the smoke from the explosion rise from the Castle walls from his vantage point. Perfectly executed, if he said so himself.

Immediately after the bomb exploded, Martin Sitton worried what the General would say, he didn't explicitly tell to set the bomb off. In fact, Thiskwood explicitly told Sitton not to take any action without his permission. Unfortunately for the General, Sitton liked the idea of an explosion inside the oldest inhabited castle in the world, he wouldn't get another chance, after all.

Now on the road to meet Arthur Thiskwood, he turned on the radio. The news of the explosion replaced all regular programming. It was twenty minutes from Windsor to Cliveden and information came through in short bursts as the news organisations struggled to find out the facts.

Only five minutes from the hotel the newscaster, in a sombre voice, said, " According to reports, the explosion has not damaged the infrastructure of the building. The Queen and the Children are known to be safe. Unfortunately, we have received unverified reports the King was killed together with several guards who were close by. It is not known what caused it. An explosive device may have caused the accident but, as yet, this needs to be confirmed."

Sitton tried to figure out if the King's death would fit in with the General's plans, his death may have come too early. He put it to the back of his mind and got on with calling various free-lance men who he knew could come at a moment's notice.

"James, can you get Abdul, Sami and Clive to Cliveden House Hotel? I'll send the details by text."

"Clive isn't available, but I have a couple of others who will be OK?"

Sitton, trying to keep the concern out of his voice, said, "Are you sure we can trust them?"

"Yes, I've used them before. Most of the guys are in London any-way. They've been on another job."

"I don't want to know. I'm on my way to the hotel. Let me know when they are close. I want to meet them before we go to the cottage, it's on the grounds of the hotel. We can't make a show of it so we'll assemble somewhere and I'll work it out with the client."

James, another mercenary, replied, "Ok, Martin. By the way..."

"It is normal rates with a bonus. Ten grand each and another five on success."

"I trust you, boss. What is the nature of the client?"

“I can't tell you much. He is a good customer, there's plenty of money to be made for all of us. We have to protect him tonight and for most of the day tomorrow until he can get out of there and fly back."

"Fly back? Another Arab gent?"

"Stop digging. Anyway, the client is American; he knows his stuff, ex-Army. You won't be able to fool him, watch what you say if you meet him."

Sitton hung up and tried to text details he promised James while driving. Eventually, he gave up and pulled over.

As he finished texting a call came through, it was General Thiskwood. "I told you not to pull the trigger. For fuck sake, can't you follow basic instructions?"

"It went off on its own; they must have found it and set off the mechanism."

"You've caused me a lot of problems, boy. "

Sitton didn't care for his tone, letting the reprisal go ignored. "I'm on my way to you, I'll be there in about ten minutes. I've got the men. We'll meet outside the hotel and make our way to the cottage without causing any fuss with the hotel staff."

"Good, get here as soon as you can. I have an important visitor on his way. I want you in place before he arrives."

Martin set off in his car, while continuing with the call. "Can I ask who it is? Will they be alone or with security?"

"You don't need to know who it is. He is a prominent man, and he is leaving his security behind so don't worry about him."

"Ok, Sir. I will see you shortly."

The phone went dead. His moment of madness in setting off the bomb was an annoyance to the General. He couldn't have a cowboy on board, he'd had enough of them in the army. Though, Sitton videoed the whole thing, it would be great to watch it later; one for his collection.

When Sitton arrived at the hotel, his phone rang, "It's me."

"Where are you, Carl?"

"We've found a way to the cottage. Believe it or not, there's five of us on a boat a little way upstream from the location. The house has a dock so we can be there in two minutes. Call us when you are ready.

"Only five of you?"

"Yes, it is short notice."

"The six of us will have to do it. If the client asks, let on you have another four men covering the perimeter."

"Sure. I will if you pay us for the 'four' men."

Sitton rounded a bend in the road, and the massive frontage of Lady Astor's former home came into view. Spring Cottage had a parking area so no one would stop him driving straight to the property accessed via a small road at the side of the building.

General Thiskwood stood outside, waiting for Martin as he parked his rented Ford. He got out and said, "Is everything clear? Where is Pierce?"

"Forget Pierce. Where are your men?"

"Let me call them; they can be here in a minute."

The General's face crumpled. "I thought you wanted to let them in one by one? The hotel staff might ask questions."

Sitton didn't answer, he made the call, glancing at Thiskwood, who was rattled. Experience taught him the General could turn on him as he'd seen before with other men who worked for him. finished, he said, "Let's walk towards the dock, they're coming by boat."

Thiskwood merely nodded and walked across the garden, not waiting for his operative. As they reached the river, the boat came into view. The small craft was low in the water, weighed down by the heavy men dressed in jeans and T-Shirts.

The boat docked and a man jumped out to tie the line to the dock, the others followed him.

"Not exactly dressed for combat," Thiskwood said as he

turned towards Sitton. "Get them inside, we need to talk first. I don't want anyone else seeing your goons."

Sitton indicated to the men with his head, and they made their way inside the small cottage.

"Sir, we need to know what we're dealing with here."

Thiskwood looked at Martin Sitton, his eyes narrowing, "The goddamn bomb went off way too early. What the hell happened? I've been lucky because the PM is already on his way and he is alone."

"They must have set off the device themselves. The Prime Minister? He will have heavy security."

"Crippley will come alone. I can't reach him as he is on his way ALONE. He doesn't have a phone. Crippley is the least of my worries. Carolina's disappeared; I don't know what she will do next. She may call the police, but she's more likely to run and get out of the UK. Since you seem to have killed the King, we need to be careful."

"It isn't confirmed. Harry could be alive. Why not get out of here now?"

"Because I have the Prime Minister coming and I have to sort one last loose end. If the shit hits the fan before then, we'll get out, go our separate ways. I have to admit, I've achieved what I set out to do."

"The Prime Minister, that raises the stakes..."

"Don't ask me for more money," Thiskwood snapped.

A silence laid over their conversation before Sitton continued, "Can I go in and brief the men and get them into position?"

"Yes. We'll be fine, of course, but there's nothing like being prepared. The police are after me but I've covered my tracks well.

The river could be a good escape route if I need one."

"...Can you confirm you've deposited the funds?

Thiskwood replied, "For FUCK SAKE, SITTON."

"Sir, I have to remind you, we're not in the Army, we don't come for free."

If he could have spat poison at Sitton, his look would have killed.. He missed the simplicity of command. "I will sort it. Don't disappoint me, I will make sure you'll never get another job. I'll make sure people knew you fucked up."

"I'll make sure you get out to give me another commission," Sitton replied, knowing his Plan B was ready for him and his men if needed. The General was a valuable customer, but there were others.

CHAPTER 60 - PHILLIPE DUMONT

Virginia took one look at Carolina and rushed over to her. Visitors in the lobby at the French Embassy stared at her; she couldn't care less. As she reached out and helped her sister stand, she noticed the welts on her wrists and ankles and the stained and torn clothing.

"Oh, Carolina, whatever has happened?"

"Virginia, I, I..."

"Shush, come with me, we can talk upstairs. Come on."

As they were exiting the lobby, a gasp from the people huddled around the TV caught their attention. The two sisters stopped and watched the newsreader's announcement:

'We are seeking more information on the events at Windsor, but some news just in. The Prime Minister cannot be reached and is thought missing. Apparently, he dismissed his security team citing the need to visit his mother's grave in private. This is highly unusual. Speculation is rife at Westminster and in Government circles. Rumours are coming though there is a sustained terrorist attack on the UK. To be clear, this is entirely speculation at this time. Police are appealing for information on the whereabouts of the Prime Minister. Anyone with information should call the police. The Chancellor of the Exchequer, Guy Storrar, is assuming the Prime Minister's role with immediate effect and has declared a 'State of Emergency.'

All aircraft apart from the RAF have been grounded. The authorities have suspended public transport and traffic cannot leave or enter the London metropolitan areas. BBC News will be broadcasting permanently on all BBC channels and will bring you the latest information.

"I know where Crippley is going," Carolina said as they climbed the stairs to the first floor.

"Let's go in there," answered Virginia. As they entered a room, Virginia paused to speak to an embassy official. Quietly she said to her, "Please ask my husband to come here, immediately."

"I'm sorry, Madame, he is in an emergency session."

"Ask him to come here, this is an emergency!" said Virginia. The petite embassy culture liaison's face froze; she was used to Virginia being the epitome of cordiality.

"I will inform him, Madame."

Virginia continued into the room generally used for meetings between the Ambassador and important guests. Carolina collapsed into a sofa.

"Carolina, if you can, tell me what happened."

"Can I have some water?" muttered Carolina.

The door to the room opened. Phillipe Dumont rushed in, anger clouding his face. "Virginia, what is this emergency? Don't you know what is happening out there?"

Carolina spoke first. "Jarrod Crippley isn't missing nor has he been kidnapped. He is on his way to see Arthur."

Phillipe, noticing Carolina's distress, altered his tone. He took a place on the sofa next to her. "Virginia, get Carolina some water and see if you can find a first aid kit. Don't invite anyone else in here. Carolina, tell me what happened. First, tell me where Mr Crippley is, I will have to inform the UK authorities if we know anything which will help."

"I understand," said Carolina, who held out her hand to take the water from Virginia, "but first I need to tell you the whole story."

"Acting Prime Minister, thank you for taking my call. This must be a worrying time for you, your government and the British people. Please be assured the French people will do everything in their power to help if we can."

"Phillipe, thank you for calling," said Guy Storrar, "It appears the information you gave me when we last spoke is correct. At this moment, it might suit me not to pass the information on. I'm sure you'll understand the need for calm and consideration at this time. If you are correct, Mr Crippley has some explaining to do."

"Yes, indeed. Perhaps when things have settled down, we can resume our discussions regarding the Channel Tunnel. I'm sure you will look on the French claim a little more sympathetically when we do," answered Phillipe Dumont.

"You have been very helpful in keeping me informed. I'm sure I can repay the favour sooner or later."

CHAPTER 61 HARRY - RECOVERY

I lay still on the ground, my head throbbing from the blow. The guard still on top of me from his dive for my safety. He stirred, muttering apology as he came to.

The scene was one stolen right out of hell, people scattered about, fire burning, all but the wheels remained of the motor-home. The plume of smoke drifted high over Windsor's Round Tower. I looked around, thankfully no one seemed severely injured although several people were walking around dazed.

The guards surrounded John Amery and his man, guns trained on them. Heather Taylor-Todd, cradled the boy, on the ground, guns pointed at them, too.

Dak rushed over to me and helped me. "What the hell is going on?" I said, shouting at them all.

"We didn't know," Heather shouted. “We didn't know."

Dak sprang into action and began to drag me away, I struggled away from his hold. "Calm down, everyone," I said at the top of my voice. It had the desired effect, so I took advantage of the silence. "Heather, what in the hell is going on?"

"Sir, it is dangerous to stay here,” Dak interrupted. “Please come."

I refused to budge. "Heather come here and bring the boy with you. Ray, detain those men but take them to the barracks out of the way and clear the area. Dak, we'll go inside and let Heather explain what is going on."

I saw the guards pile into John Amery and the other man. One of them punched Amery, he doubled over in pain. Another repeatedly kicked the larger man. Neither of the two would look a pretty sight; I couldn't be concerned with them at the moment.

"Heather, follow us. No questions." She hesitated a look to Amery. "No, leave them, they'll be fine, move."

Dak frogmarched Heather and me with the young lad, obeying my instructions. St George's chapel was the closest building, we were inside in seconds.

Dak started to say something to me, but my stare told him to keep quiet. I turned to Heather. She was comforting the boy, stricken with fear.

"Heather, tell me what's going on."

She was almost too scared to look me right in the eye. "We were followed by police when we left Biggin Hill. It might have been when we left the clinic; I'm not sure."

"Slow down. Take it step-by-step; we're safe in here." I hoped it was true. "Dak, phone Meghan will you and make sure she is OK. I don't want her to be worried, tell her I am fine. Make sure she isn't near the courtyard, near any windows. Come on, Heather, let's sit over there."

Dak stepped to one side and took out his phone. Heather seemed to calm a little. I needed to get the story out of her, but something told me I'd get more if I slowed down a little. "First off, introduce me to this little fella."

The boy looked at me and stuck his chin out, "I ain't so little."

"Ah, you're an American I see. What's your name?

"It is Emmanuel Juan Hernández. These guys call me Manny."

"You're Mexican?"

The boy looked at Heather and raised his eyebrows and before turned back to me, "No, I'm a Cuban American."

I smiled, a little amazed how calm I was... Heather regained her composure and said, "Manny, here, was the hero of the day Sir. We got pulled over by the police. They got us to leave the van and told us we were speeding. Manny hid in the van on the bed above the cabin. He saw the men come in and planted a listening device under the table. Manny heard them talking."

"They weren't police. They were fake," Manny cut in.

"They were talking about finding out where we were going and keeping an eye on us," Heather continued. "They let us go but we decided the best thing to do was to come straight here, that's when I phoned Oliver, my brother, to ask him to call you. We had no idea there was a bomb."

Ray bounded back into the church. "Sir, there was a bomb, planted right next to a full gas cylinder. The gas didn't go off, that's why the explosion didn't cause more damage. Whoever planted the device made a mistake, thank God."

"I should have listened to you; I am sorry Ray. We never should have them into the Castle."

Ray looked satisfied with my apology, "No, Sir, but we're all safe. Meghan and the Children are safe."

"Ask George to come here immediately. I don't want any news getting out yet. Is the Castle locked down?"

"Yes, the fire engines are on their way, the police too."

"Good," I said, "Go, get George, tell him NOT to issue any news whatsoever."

"On my way, Sir."

Back to Heather, again. "Look, things are going to move fast. I'll have to believe you didn't know about the bomb."

"We only made one stop to buy some new telephones. We had no choice but to come here. If we stopped anywhere, there was a chance they'd catch on we knew about the bug. Also, the real police are looking for us so we may never have been able to reach you."

As she spoke, Heather held Manny tight. I wondered where on earth the boy fitted into all of this. There would be time later to find out. "It might not be the best idea to bring a bomb into Windsor Castle."

"I... I'm so sorry," Heather said with a sob.

"Continue, in short, tell me it all. We don't have much time."

Heather's breaths were still shallow. "Your Majesty, we didn't know you'd come to meet us, Sir. Our mistake. We parked the motorhome in the middle of the car park in case. We couldn't say anything in the van because they had the listening device. We came to warn you."

I sat next to her and rubbed my head; it still hurt. "Warn me about what?"

"We believe a man called General Thiskwood, a retired American five-star general, was instrumental in the deaths of your father and your brother and his family. He tried to kill us but we managed to get away."

"In Florida," Manny said. "They got my mom and my grandma too. They're dead. They killed them."

"I am sorry, Manny, you're a brave lad. Heather?"

She took a deep breath. "We're pretty sure he is working with Jarrod Crippley, Sir."

"The Prime Minister?"

Heather lowered her voice. "The PM asked a few of us to look into The Crown Estate. He needed me, John, Roger Casement and Ronald Brereton to see if he could take it away from you. Judge Casement and Brereton, the Mi5 man, are both dead. He tried to kill us next. The General is a wanted man because he was outside John's Florida house where they attacked us."

"The General is still working with Crippley? If he is, aren't you?" I was trying to take this all in. I wanted to trust Heather but her admission made it a difficult.

"No, I promise. John and I checked out of this early on. Being asked by the PM to help him was an honour. I'm ashamed I became involved."

I stared at her, until Manny spoke again, "She's one of the good guys, so are John and Serge. Serge is a giant!"

I couldn't help but laugh; Heather smiled at Manny. I turned around and asked Dak to have Heather's friends brought to us and stressed no one approach the motorhome and to make sure the area remained clear.

John Amery and the man called Serge walked in. Each had bruises on their faces and walked slowly, evidently in pain.

"John, are you OK? Heather said. I clocked the look between them.

John Amery failed at smiling and said, "We'll live. Sir, has Heather told you what happened?"

"Yes."

"I am sorry, I..."

"–There's no time."

"You and your family are in danger, Sir. You have to believe us."

I was still sceptical, "Why should I?"

"Crippley needs the money, Sir, it's plain to see. He's involved with the General who, frankly, is a rogue player. He won't stop at anything. We have to find the General and question Crippley, Sir, else Heather and I, you and your family, we'll be in constant danger for our lives."

"What about me?" Manny said, his little eyes glistened as he looked to John.

John, lowering his voice, said, "And you, Manny."

Ray bought the two men in and had been following the conversation. I looked over; he said, "It makes sense Sir; your father and your brother. I'm not sure about this General, but Crippley couldn't have achieved this with official resources. Mr Crippley has a clear motive. I have difficulty believing he would go this far."

"We have to find the General," John said. "We are sure he is in the UK.

"He is," I said, surprising them. "Thanks to Roger Brereton's son, Alex, I know a lot more about him than you know."

Amery's eyes went wide and he tried to say something but Ray interjected, "Sir, I have an idea. It will buy us some time and will possibly keep you safe for now. "

I raised my eyebrows, indicating he should continue.

"A news blackout will keep the world guessing about you and your family. You may not like it, but it means the General will see it. It will give us time to make our plan work tonight. We don't have much time, though. It could give us the advantage we need."

I looked at Dak, who nodded in agreement. I remained silent; I knew they would wait for my answer. One of them didn't; Manny said, "You Brits, have you got balls or what? What are you going to do? Wait until the bastard comes for you?"

Day, Ray, John, Serge and Heather looked at me.

"Manny, we Brits have been around for a long time. You'll soon learn what we are made from. Heather, you, John, Manny and Serge come to my apartment with me. Ray, come too, keep an eye on this lot, I'm not sure I can trust them yet."

CHAPTER 62 - CLIVEDEN

The small van carried the six Invictus men, Serge, Alex and Ray. Ray insisted Dak stay with the King who they eventually persuaded to stay at Windsor.

Alex and Ray dressed in the Invictus emblazoned tracksuits. Alex Brereton suggested the cover which impressed Ray. He expected some hot-head, driven crazy by revenge. Still, Alex's careful analysis of all the options showed a depth and a level of calm seldom seen in someone so young. Only Serge dressed in black jeans and a T-shirt since nothing would fit his giant frame.

Alex phoned the Cliveden Hotel in the morning having suggested the idea to book rooms in the hotel to gain access to Spring Cottage without raising further questions. Ray heard Alex speak with confidence to the manager and all rooms were secured despite the short notice.

Harry negotiated the team's exit from the Castle which was locked down by the security forces. The Bomb, as expected, caused little damage to the Castle but generated a great deal of smoke making it look worse from the outside than it was. Since the great fire of Windsor of 1992, the emergency services prepared for another disaster and there were fire engines and police everywhere. Joining in were Army trucks and RAF helicopters flying overhead.

While Alex drove the small minibus, Ray turned around to

face the team. "Now, we've been training for this, we know the territory. We're expecting the General to be alone or, at most, with one or two people. You've seen pictures of the General but remember, he won't be in uniform and may look a little older than the images you've seen. Thiskwood may be approaching his seventies, but he is a fit man with decades of combat experience. Do NOT give him the benefit of the doubt on anything if you come face to face with him."

Brad Hall spoke as the unofficial leader of the Invictus team. "You've told me, and I'm not sure all the men heard it from your lips, Sir; You DON'T want us to kill the General?"

Ray looked at each of his platoon in turn. "The mission is to capture General Thiskwood. We don't want him to escape and we don't want to seriously harm him unless we have to. The aim is to take him back to Windsor so Harry can question him before he hands him over to the authorities. Do you all understand? You have a choice here. If you disagree, we'll stop and let you off. There's no shame and no questions will be asked. If you accept my orders don't nod, tell me."

In unison, they all said, "Yes, Sir."

Ray noticed Alex Brereton and Serge Kalinski both said 'Yes Sir' as well. "Alex, these people are trained, they've seen combat. It could be dangerous; we don't know what we are going to find. Understood?"

Alex replied, "Of course, why are you picking me out? What about Serge here?"

Ray smirked at the large man cramped in the back of the van, the others did too. Serge raised his eyebrows and everyone laughed. Ray turned back to Alex, "We better not ask Serge too much about his experience."

Ray grew more serious, "The perfect situation is to capture Thiskwood by overpowering him. Brad, that's your team's objective. As a backup we need Eugene in place. I want to find a position for him which gives him a sight of the house. If necessary, we can clip the General in a sniper shot. Gene, demobilizing shots, please; anything which will bring him down. We need him alive until Harry decides what to do with him. Do you understand, Gene?"

Eugene Foulks answered, "Yes, Sir."

Turning to Rob Wickland, Ray said, "Taffy, your job is to watch out for Gene. Make sure he is covered at all times. Check?"

The small Welshman answered loudly, "Yes, Sir."

Chris Gerard, the handsome soldier with the missing foot, looked at Ray anxious to have his role confirmed. "Chris, I want you to keep the hotel staff away and do the talking. If we need you to back up the others, I'll give you the order."

Taff chirped in, "Chris, it's fine; you can keep out of trouble and save your pretty face."

Ray caught the slight reddening of Chris's cheeks. "Stop it you lot. We're going to need to think on our feet. Chris has the gift of the gab."

“Chris can only think on one foot,” Simone joked. The quiet laughter fraught with nerves; capturing someone could be more dangerous than killing them at the first opportunity.

“Simmer down,” said Ray, “Chris is there to protect all of us and get out of this mess alive. We'll need someone with brains to deal with the hotel staff and nosey guests. Chris, be armed and ready if needed, understand?"

"Yes, Sir."

Out of the corner of his eye, Ray saw Alex go to say something. "I'll talk to you in the end, Alex, alright?” Alex merely nodded in response.

"Flo, are we set to go with the earpieces?"

The small black woman, with an eyepatch over her right eye, said, "Yes Sir. We did a check right before we left and will do it again once we are at the hotel, in the rooms and again when we're all in position. There shouldn't be a problem but we need to check."

"Brad; You, Simone and Andy work with Flo who will coordinate. You'll lead the team on the ground. You have the map for the hotel grounds, check?"

Brad Hall replied, "Check Sir. We will surround the Cottage. You will call the order if we have to enter the premises, OK?"

"My biggest concern is the General may have a back-up, Brad. The news about the King and the missing PM will raise all sorts of red flags and, if I were him, I'd make sure I'd have protection. Remember, we are relying on the General being in place because he is meeting Alex tomorrow morning. Listen, make sure you understand what I'm about to ask Alex, it is a slight change to what we discussed. Park in the lay-by ahead. We're two minutes away and I want to make sure we have this part of the plan spot on."

Alex parked and turned the engine off. The small bus was silent.

"The General is expecting you tomorrow, Alex," Ray said. "When we have all checked in, I want you to call Thiskwood. Call him and tell him your plans changed and you decided to see if he was free tonight. Tell him you decided to treat yourself to a night in one of the best hotels in England. By the way, Chris, make sure only Alex's name is on his hotel room reservation. The General will check for sure. Sounding good so far, Alex?"

"Yes, Ray."

"Here's the part which could be dangerous and I need you to be happy with what I have in mind. Ask the General if he would come to the Hotel for a drink and a chat. I'd expect Thiskwood to decline and will counter your offer and invite you to the Cottage. If he does, I want you to go there and meet him; it will be our only opportunity to do reconnaissance."

Alex cut in, the others in the vehicle looked surprised, it wasn't good form to interrupt, not in the Army at least. "If I call him, he'll have time to prepare. If there are any others around the Cottage, he could warn them. How about I walk to the Cottage and surprise him."

Ray paused, "No, too dangerous."

"It makes sense. Look, the bastard is responsible for my father's death. I want to make sure he is dealt with. You keep referring to how young I am and inexperienced. He won't expect me to have a team of professionals waiting for him."

Brad Hall spoke, "It does make sense if the lad is prepared to do it. If Alex gets in trouble, we can get him out of there. As you walk to the cottage Alex can talk us through what he can spot. Even Alex should be able to see if there are armed guards or anything out of the ordinary. If you get to speak to the General use your head to let us know what you find inside the Cottage. Flo, you can make sure we all hear what he is saying?"

As Flo said she could, Ray turned to look at Alex's reaction. "Alex, are you sure? It does make sense."

Alex flicked his gaze to Ray. “Yes.” He turned to face the team and added, “You’ll keep me safe guys, right?

Intuitively, most of the team in the back of the van turned to Brad who said, “You’re in good hands. You can handle yourself, take care and don’t take any risks.”

"What do you want me do?"

"Your team isn't big enough, Brad. Can you use Serge here?"

"Are you happy to follow my orders, Serge?

"John and Heather wanted me come. They trust me you trust me too. I have no problem following order. I'm handy when comes sorting people out."

Ray smiled; his team was ready to take this on. "Right, the plan is settled. Flo, you make sure we are all connected at all times."

"I'm up for it, you can depend on this little bitch for sure," Flo said, and the others laughed. "Alex, a warning, the microphone won't be able to detect what others are saying to you, anyone you meet. We will only be able to hear what you are saying."

Ray spoke, "Right, Alex. Let's get going. Remember guys, you're the Invictus team here, visiting for one night. Let Chris do all the talking when we reach the Hotel. Serge, keep quiet, if anyone asks who you are, let Chris answer, he'll cover for you."

Chris Gerard said, "I already have Sir. Serge here can be our Russian colleague."

"I Ukrainian."

Chris looked over to the Serge, “If you say so."

As Alex turned into the main gate at Cliveden, Ray said, "Look, guys. Keep cool. Check-in and get into your rooms. Alex, make sure you are wired correctly with Flo. Stay in contact through your earpieces at all times. Leave it thirty minutes until you set off. When you do, I want a running commentary. Tell us about everything you notice and describe anyone you see. If you see someone describe them and tell us what they have on and if they are armed. If you can guess who they are, tell us; they could be guests, staff or one of the General's team. The more we know, the more we get right. You others, you know your roles. Brad, check in the same room as Serge, I'm sure he can look after himself but tell him exactly what you need him to do. When I say go, we will congregate in reception. If not, I'll let you know. Chris, tell the staff the team is taking a stroll. Again, play it by ear. Are you all clear what you have to do?"

Ray noted the team's confident replies in unison, the sign of a tight team. He wished he was as sure of the success of the operation as they were.

CHAPTER 63 - TAKING FLIGHT

Jarrod Crippley turned off the radio when he got into the car and found the drive more soothing than expected, even though he faced meeting the General at the end of his journey.

Getting rid of the security wasn't easy. Jarrod eventually got his way only by threatening his head of security with his job, something which he tried not to do too often. He suspected someone might follow him, but he switched cars at the last minute to cover his tracks.

The hour drive to the hotel was the first time Jarrod Crippley had been genuinely alone for years. Leaving his phone at No.10, as directed by the General, made him feel uneasy at first but it was good to be free of its constant interruptions. The General said they'd track the device and perhaps the official car as well.

Jarrod Crippley drove slowly along the drive to the hotel. As the minivan in front turned left to the car park, he took the small lane to the right of the property as instructed by General Thiskwood.

As he approached the cottage, his stomach tightened, making him belch loudly in the car. The smell of his own stomach gasses fouled the air so much he opened the window to let the fresh air in. The drive gave Jarrod Crippley time to reflect on his relationship with General Thiskwood. As the Prime Minister of Great Britain spotted the small cottage, Jarrod Crippley, without a phone or security, finally accepted who was calling the shots; it wasn't him.

Crippley parked the Jaguar outside the cottage where lights shone out of every window. The General told him beforehand to wait in the car until he came out to meet him.

After a long wait, a tap on the window made Crippley jump in surprise. Outside the car, the General laughed at him. He peered through the window, "Crippley, get out of the car. You're afraid of your own damn shadow."

As the PM got out of the vehicle, another man came out of the shadows and searched him. "He's a clear General."

"Do you know who you're addressing, young man?"

The man dressed in black jeans and a black t-shirt turned to the side of Crippley and spat on the floor. He didn't answer the PM.

"Now, Crippley, you're coming indoors. We need to talk." As he spoke, Thiskwood turned around expecting Jarrod Crippley to follow him. He did.

Once inside, the General looked even more imposing to Crippley in the small sitting area of the cottage. "You've no idea how difficult it has been to get here alone. I trust this has all been worth it. I can't stay out of contact for much longer. They'll be wondering where I am. I've been waiting in that car outside for forty-five minutes."

General Thiskwood sat and pointed to the chair opposite, expecting Crippley to follow suit.

As Crippley sat, the General said, "You bet your ass they'll be looking for you. Have you seen the news?"

"I didn't even turn the radio on in the car, it has been a while since I last drove myself. The peace and quiet..." Crippley stopped when he saw the TV news on the screen in the corner of the room, "What have you done?"

"I followed the plan Crippley, our plan. True, the explosion at Windsor came a little earlier than I expected. I guess we got lucky with the King."

"You're mad. Everyone will be looking for me." Crippley tried to stand, but Thiskwood kicked out his leg connecting hard with the PM's knee. Crippley collapsed into the chair, in pain.

"No, Crippley. I've done everything you asked of me. The monarchy won't survive this, all you have to do is kick it home."

"You've achieved nothing but mayhem you bastard."

Quicker than Crippley expected, Thiskwood stood and kicked the Prime Minister hard on his other leg, inches below the knee. Crippley cried out, his face crimson.

As Crippley choked back his sobs, Thiskwood said, "My part in this is over. I'm going to disappear. You are going to help me. I want you to arrange for me to be taken to an airport. I want a plane capable of flying direct to South Africa where I have some friends who will help me out a little while this blows over. What happens to you next will depend on what you do and if you've got the guts to do it. But let me make this clear. Every conversation we've had, every email and every message between us are stored online in the cloud. I can make it rain on your parade at any time I want. You'll help me get out of here. I have you by the balls. Frankly, I don't care what happens to your country. Great Britain isn't great anymore; you are the man who finally brought down the British Empire."

Crippley, his face gripped with pain, said, "And if I don't?"

The General smiled, "My friend Martin out there will come in. I've ordered him to kill you on my command. To add to the fun, he won't do it straight away. He borrowed the gardener's tools so he could chop little pieces off you while you watch. We've been discussing it while you waited outside. You'll die eventually but not slowly and not without a great deal of pain."

CHAPTER 64 HARRY - THE FAMILY OFFICE

From the outset, Ray and Dak didn't want me to join them and take on General Thiskwood. Both John Amery and Heather Taylor-Todd added their concerns when I told them of the plan. It was Heather who finally persuaded me. Her reputation for straight-talking proved apt when she said to me; 'If you die, your family could be next. It will be the end of Great Britain as we know it. Drop your pride and let them do it for you. If you're found anywhere near the hotel, the republicans will wrap your Crown around your neck.'

After the commotion of the explosion, I grabbed Heather, John and the cheeky little kid. I disappeared into the private apartments without anyone noticing.

On the way I called George, I needed to manage the situation to my advantage. "George, are you OK?"

"Sir, I'm OK, what happened? Are you, the Queen..."

"George," I said, interrupting him, "we are all fine, we don't have the time to go into everything. I need to act fast."

"Of course, your Majesty."

"Don't allow anyone into the private residence, blackout all communications from Windsor and Buckingham Palace."

"The people will be concerned; we need to let them know."

"Look, George, you'll have to trust me on this. There's something I need you to do. Tip-off someone in the press, maybe Sukie Watlingham of the Daily Mail, they'll get the message out faster than anyone."

George looked confused, "Tip-off?"

"Yes, tell them I've been injured, no, tell them I am feared dead."

"Your Majesty!"

"Don't worry, George. I need to buy some time here. A lot is going as, no doubt, you've picked up. Please I need you to play your part, I trust you."

"As you wish, I will let you know when it is done."

The move would be unprecedented in modern times; however, George would eventually understand the importance of a news blackout.

As we entered the apartment, Meghan rushed over to me and hugged me tightly. The children followed her, and we stood there in a close group. "It is alright; we're all safe. I'm unharmed. Archie, you're a brave little man, aren't you? I bet you looked after your mum."

My little Archie replied, "Sort of Papa. Mom made us all go in a cupboard. It was really, really dark. Philip cried, but I didn't, did I, Mommy?"

Meghan regarded Archie with warmth. "They were both brave." Meghan pushed away from me a little as she noticed John, Heather and the little boy looking on, a little embarrassed to be in the room. "Harry, you'd better introduce me."

I made the introductions and led Crippley's former helpers to the drawing-room, asking them to make themselves comfortable.

I returned to Meghan and the children. "Archie, Philip, would you like to see what's happening. You know Philip's bedroom, the window near the bed. If you go there, you can peep out of the window and see all the police and fire engines. Make sure no one sees you, only peep." I saw Manny by the door, watching us. "Manny, can you make sure the lads are alright?"

"Sure. Hey Kids," he said, looking at them, "Can you show me the fire engines too?"

Archie looked to his mother for reassurance, Meghan nodded and Archie grabbed Philip's hand. "Come on, Philip, let's go and see the blue flashing lights."

I asked John and Heather to wait for me and turned to Meghan and asked her to come with me to the Study. Surprisingly, it only took me a few minutes to give her the full, if edited story. Unlike Meghan, she didn't interrupt me until I finished.

"Why did you keep this from me, Harry?"

"Rightly or wrongly, I made the decision early on. At first, it was a suspicion, based on something someone told me."

"Virginia Dumont?"

I was surprised, "Yes, you knew?"

"I saw her pass you a note at the funeral."

"Why didn't you ask me?" When she looked down, I continued, "Meghan, did you think something else was going on?"

"I don't know, you've been so preoccupied. Sure, I understand it hasn't been easy, but since everything happened you've shut me out. You haven't discussed our future; you've assumed I would agree with everything you wanted to do. Harry, less than a month ago I was playing in the sea with you and the boys thousands of miles away. Now we're here with some sort of plot going on while we live in a Castle for heaven's sake. I can't tell you how many times you've turned around to me in the last few weeks and told me to look after the kids. I feel like I've slipped back into the nineteenth century. This place doesn't help."

It was true, I had to admit. "I guess I wanted to spare you everything."

"Spare me? You're making me a spare part, don't you see? I have a brain, Harry; I could have helped you deal with everything.

"I'm sorry," I said, and I was. However, as I said the words something in my brain kicked; why was I always apologising to my wife?

"Now you've bought those strangers into our PRIVATE apartment."

"I'm sorry we had to get out of sight."

Meghan paced the room. "You don't get it, do you, Harry? Every day, the children and I live our lives in a corridor. People pass through; most I've never met before. Our privacy means nothing to anyone. What do you mean, 'we'? From what you've told me, those two out there were helping Crippley."

I wanted to tell Meghan to 'calm down,' if I did, the opposite would happen. "Meghan, I promise you, when this is all over, and I'm talking days, we'll sit and talk this through. We'll go to Sandringham House and lay down some rules about where our servants can and can't go. We will lay it all out and find a way forward for you, me and the children. Are you with me?"

"I will have to be," she answered unconvinced.

Worn out and dejected, she was a picture of everything I'd put her through. I loved my wife but she was so used to calling the shots and being in control. Life in the palace took away her independence.

I stood to face Meghan, putting my arms loosely around her. "Now, look, we're a team again. I'll tell you everything. Come and talk to those two. I need them to do something for me, you'll see.

Meghan nodded and held me tight. " Harry, I love you too, but I'm arranging a trip to Sandringham as soon as we've finished with them."

George knocked on the door, and came in without a response. "I'm sorry to interrupt, I wanted to update you on the situation. News has broken, and there is..." George seemed to notice Meghan for the first time. He said, diplomatically, "There is speculation that you have been injured in the explosion. Some reports are suggesting you have been killed."

"No. I want to remain silent on this." Megan looked to me first, and went to speak before I stopped her by saying, "I expect the Prime Minister to call, if you can, avoid him."

A stricken look washed over George. "That's just it, Your Majesty, it appears Mr Crippley can't be tracked down. The Chancellor of the Exchequer has taken temporary control of the government. He has called several times. He has declared a state of emergency."

Meghan's face mirrored my feeling. "Where do you think he is?"

"Cliveden?"

"I don't think so, but the timing is strange. I will try calling him."

"I've been told he left his phone at number 10. Apparently, he decided to visit his mother's grave and insisted on being alone. The other ministers are not happy. Are you sure we shouldn't issue a statement?"

"We need to buy some time for the Invictus team. As soon as they are clear, we will make an announcement. Prepare one for me please George. Something about us being taken to a secure location. Have something ready, please."

"As you wish, Sir."

We joined John and Heather in the drawing-room, where they sat together, his hand resting on her knee. An array on untouched teas and coffee in front of them. "I see George has made you comfortable. Please, help yourself to some tea or coffee."

Meghan, in hostess mode, said, "Harry, I don't know about you, but I'm having a proper drink. John, Heather, will you join me?"

John answered for both of them, "We're both gin drinkers." He looked at Heather. "Neat Heather?" She merely nodded; still visibly shaken.

As Meghan went over to the drinks cabinet, she said, "It sounds like you two need a drink, everyone's been through a lot already. Harry, I'll pour you one too."

I looked at John; I needed to get to business. "As I told you, Ray is organising everything, soon they'll put their plans into action at Cliveden. I've got a comms link with the team; I want to listen in."

John Amery said, "Of course, sir."

"I wanted to talk to you about something urgently. Events are moving quickly; I need to know where you stand on certain matters before the end of the day."

Heather sipped her drink, letting John speak, "You can be sure of our support, Sir."

"As you've said, Crippley wanted The Crown Estate to plug the hole he created in the nation's finances. To cut it short, we've been working on this, everything points to us being successful in preventing it. To make sure this never happens again, I need to act fast. I've instructed our lawyers, Farrer & Co, to prepare the case for my family and me to bring an action against Crippley's government. We need to make sure Crippley doesn't get his hands on everything. I plan to formally transfer The Crown Estate, the Art, the Crown Jewels, everything, to my personal property."

John raised his eyebrows, understanding the magnitude of my proposal. "You're talking billions, Sir."

"I know. However, let's make this clear; some of the greatest minds, even poor Judge Casement's analysis, make a rock-solid argument for this. The assets never belonged to the state in the first place. The accountants even believe billions more are owed to the Royal family, having accrued over three hundred years."

John leaned forward, showing his complete engagement. The reaction I wanted. "Yes, but it is a brave move."

I stared at him, pausing as I wanted to make sure he understood I was resolute about regaining control over my family's assets. "Yes. I hope I can use Crippley's treacherous actions to get him to make this easier for us. He has a massive majority in the house and it would be better for all concerned to pass a permanent Act which recognises my title to everything."

Heather spoke for the first time, "You'll let him get away with everything in return?"

Meghan, next to me, narrowed her eyes. I sensed she was about to go into combat, I put my hand gently on her arm, "Meghan, can I have another drink, please."

"Look," I said to both Heather and John, "I've no intention of Crippley getting away with anything. I intend to do this in stages. Ultimately, Crippley will pay the price. Remember, we all believe he was behind the death of both my father and my brother. He will pay."

"Why tell us all of this, Sir?" said Amery, a little perplexed.

"How rich are you, John?"

"I'm s-sorry, what do you mean? Why?"

"They tell me you're worth in the region of ten billion pounds?"

John briefly glanced at Heather before he answered, "It is above twelve billion, Sir."

"I've been thinking about The Crown Estate if we manage to rescue it from Crippley's hands. The answer came to me from something my father said to me years ago about how he selected people to head his charities and various business interests. He told me he chose the best men and women from the commercial world; people who had proven themselves in business. Unlike his predecessors, he avoided the aristocracy and 'jobs for the boys'. His organisations were staffed with determined and capable men and women. His approach underpinned the success of The Prince's Trust, the charity helped tens of thousands of young people get a start in life.

"Yes. When I was looking at the Royal finances, King Charles impressed me with his management of The Duchy of Cornwall, his private estate."

"Yes. Look, I have a proposition for both of you. I want you, John, to become the CEO of my Family Office. You will form a Board and take over all the existing infrastructure of the Crown Estate replacing the Crown Commissioners who presently manage the organisation. The brief will be simple; I want you to make it double in value over fifteen years without taking undue risks. Each year I want us to decide how much we give to the government; not the other way around as is currently the case."

A smile drew slowly across Amery's face. "Wow. You're turning the whole deal on its head. Currently, they give you and your family a fixed amount, a percentage. If this works, you will provide them with a payment. Brilliant, I like it.

"Good."

"However, I have my own plans. I agree with what you're proposing but I have my operation to run, Red Diamond is a big corporation."

I looked at him again. He didn't understand what I was telling him. "John, I'm sorry. Let me make it clear. You will do this. You have no choice."

Amery went silent. I could see his mind whirling and the look on his face as he realised I had him cornered. Given the assistance the financier provided Crippley, I could make a good case for him to be prevented from trading in the UK again. If I didn't have enough evidence, I had the connections to make sure he lost his authority to trade in the UK and around the world, I wasn't afraid to use them. Nevertheless, it was time to dangle the carrot. "John, I'm sure you see what I mean but look at it another way. You will effectively be in control of one, if not the largest, family office on the planet."

Heather jumped into the conversation. "What's a family office?"

John answered, "It is like a corporation or investment company. The only difference is it belongs to one person or a collection of people who are related. They are surprisingly common. The Rockefellers, Rothschild, Bill Gates, the list goes on. Oliver run's your family office."

I could see John working for time in answering Heather; he was considering my proposal and looking for a way out. "You could employ someone far more capable," he said, his attention back on me.

I merely looked at him and kept silent. I waited for John to continue. After an awkward pause, he said, "It sounds interesting. However, ownership of Red Diamond, my investment company, means there will be a conflict of interest, the Financial Services Authority wouldn't allow it."

"I don't want any conflicts of interest; sell Red diamond. With all your money you shouldn't be tempted by mine."

John looked ashen. "I... I can't."

Again, I needed to be tough with him. John knew I had him. "John, you're not losing a diamond, you're winning a crown."

Despite himself, John laughed, but I could see him thinking it through. He said, "Instead of selling Red Diamond, can I merge its fund with yours? Although separately identified, I could manage them together. Our interests would be perfectly aligned. In return, I will use my key staff around the world to run the Windsor Family Office."

I leaned forward, "John, I even like the name. Here's to the Windsor Family Office." I held out my hand, we shook on it.

Heather spoke again. She said shyly, "You said 'both' of us. What do you want me to do?"

"Heather, I want you to manage the Royal Collection and, importantly, increase it. Together with John, we'll decide how much we want to spend on replenishing the Royal Art collection each year and what our objectives will be."

"Wow!" she said, enthused by the idea.

"It comes with some provisos. Your TV career would need to

end, I don't see you managing the Royal Collection nor the Crown Jewels while holding down a job as a professor at university."

Heather turned to John. It was her time to squirm.

"Heather, you are enormously talented and managing what would be the biggest private art collection in the world will be a full-time job. Besides," I looked her in the eye, "I guess you are in a similar position to Mr Amery here."

John looked at Heather and held up his hands in a defeated gesture, "He's got us both. If he can't have us, we'll have nothing."

John looked at me. "You've summed it up well," I said.

They looked at each other, something I couldn’t quite spot happened between them, then they looked back at me. Heather spoke first, "I look forward to the challenge."

John spoke again, "Me too. It could be interesting." Changing the subject, he said, "How do we get Crippley to agree to this?"

Meghan, silent for most of the conversation, said, "I guess it depends on how the team gets on at Cliveden."

CHAPTER 65 - CHECKING IN

Chris Gerard headed the Invictus platoon as they made their way into the hotel. The team looked the part save for Serge who lagged behind them in his jeans and t-shirt.

As expected, Chris rose to the occasion and organised the team. The hotel receptionist fluttered her eyes at Chris, who told her a wealthy supporter treated the team to the stay at the five-star hotel. He said to the receptionist they'd settle into their rooms followed by a walk around the grounds.

"Will you be dining tonight?" The hotel manager said as he rushed out from behind a door to greet the team.

"Sadly, we won't," Chris said. "We've eaten. We might stop by for a drink later."

"Please do, of course, the Cliveden House Hotel would be pleased to meet the bill should you decide to have a drink with us. We are all grateful for the sacrifice you have all made for the British people." Chris noticed the man glance at Serge, obviously, he was the most out of place. It could present a problem, but he brushed it off. They'd planned it too meticulously.

"Kind of you to say. We've all got our keys, everything is fine. Thank you for coming out to meet us. It is appreciated. By the way, I was surprised we got rooms on such short notice, how come?" said Chris trying to find out about the hotel's occupancy levels.

"Alas, we have plenty of space tonight. Um, we made a mistake when someone rang to book the hotel for your group. I'm glad we were able to do everything for you. We host a lot of corporate bookings; the entire hotel is full tomorrow and the next three days."

"Good, we'll have plenty of room and, if we do have a drink later, we won't be disturbing many people."

"Indeed, Sir. Please make use of our excellent spa and feel free to use all the grounds."

"We will, thank you."

Ray was thankful the exchange was over; he was anxious to get out of the reception area. The team needed to get settled in. He wanted to spend a little more time with Alex ahead of his reconnaissance mission.

Once in the room allocated to Ray and Alex, the Gurkha asked Alex to sit while they spoke.

"Are you sure you are willing to do this?"

Alex, complete in his Invictus training gear, said, "Of course. It makes the most sense."

Ray tapped the device in his ear, "Team, confirm you are ready in your rooms."

A series of replies came. Ray spoke again, "Team, Alex is one brave man. Remember, he is not in the Army, we have to make sure we protect him as far as possible. Brad, you've set out positions with your people. Listen carefully as Alex talks us through his walk to Spring Cottage. Alex knows what he has to do. The microphone is sensitive. Alex, speak normally, and we'll hear you even if you have to whisper. Flo, copy that."

Flo Gummer replied, "Alex, we'll hear everything. Don't

worry."

Ray continued, "Alex, if you get into any trouble, I mean if someone threatens you or you feel in danger, I want you to say KING. Brad, do you copy?"

"Yes, Sir."

"Brad, if Alex says 'King' it is your job to get Alex out of there. Alex, you must talk us through everything you see. I want you to walk there slowly; half your usual speed. Look to each side, describe the bushes and any landmarks, a flower bed, anything. It will help Brad and the others figure out exactly where you are. Most important; look carefully for anything unusual. If the General has people protecting him, they will most likely be hiding. We need to be ALERT!"

Alex nodded. "Yes, Sir."

Ray noticed the signs of nerves, he'd seen it enough times in the past. "Say the word and we'll get you out of there, safe. Don't be afraid to use it. If you get spooked, withdraw and we'll figure it out from there. Understand?"

"Yes, Sir," Alex replied before saying 'King' quietly.

"Alex, your objective is to find Thiskwood. With the right information, Brad and his team will be able to extricate him. Gene is there as a backstop if we need to take down the target. However, we are here to capture the General alive. Team, do you copy?"

Serge's answer was the first to answer through the earpiece, closely followed by the others.

"Alex," Ray said, "work with Gene. While he can make a shot from a mile or so off, the nearer he gets, the better the chances of him being able to take down Thiskwood without killing him if we encounter difficulties. If you find a good spot, make sure Gene knows where it is. As you get to the cottage, see if you can draw the General outside. Brad, that's when you have your opportunity to seize the target. Gene, get ready for anyone who may be protecting the Thiskwood. Try not to kill them, OK?"

"Yes, Sir," Gene said, clear and loud.

"Brad, to repeat. You and your people fan out behind Alex. As he gets closer to the cottage, you follow on behind. Not too close. Be prepared for anything. Serge, you make sure you follow Brad's commands. No heroics."

The deep Ukrainian voice came over the earpiece equally firm, "Yes."

"Chris, go ahead of Alex to the reception. If you see any guests or staff, get them the hell out of there. Use your pretty blue eyes."

"Yes, Sir!" Chris replied.

Ray looked out of the window. The evening was dark outside, apart from the spots of light dotted around the grounds. "Andy, Simone, Rob. Are you clear what you have to do?"

"The members of Brad's unit answered in unison, "Yes, Sir!"

"Right, we're ready. Make sure you have your guns in your bags and don't take them out until you're outside. The hotel manager will shit his pants if he sees them. Chris, please make your way to the reception. Make sure the coast is clear. Let Alex know when you're ready.

"On my way, sir."

Ray looked at Alex, he was the only one unarmed, yet he was the first to go in. "Alex, are you ready?"

Alex stood to his full height, towering over the Gurkha soldier. He took a deep breath and answered his commander, "I'm ready, Sir, I won't let you down."

Ray slapped Alex on the back. "I know, son." Despite his reassurances, Alex had to be the weakest link in the chain but the tactics were sound.

Ray gave his final instruction, "The plan is to get right back in the van when we have finished the operation, but this might need rethinking. Those hotel staff are all over us."

"Taff, Serge, Alex, get to the van once the operation is complete. Take General Thiskwood with you. Take everyone's weapons. Make your way to Windsor, understood?"

Alex nodded, "Yes, sir!"

"I would like the rest of the Invictus team to go back to your rooms, change and make your way as soon as possible to the bar. I would like you to get drunk. After all, it will be on the house. Make sure you're seen and try and get as many staff around to join you. I want them to remember the night in the bar after the attack as much as possible. If anyone gets injured, they get in the van with Alex, Taff and Serge. Do you copy?"

The team replied in the affirmative. Ray continued, "the alternative plan will be for all of us to pile into the van if there are injuries. I'll make the call as we see how this pans out."

Alex turned to Ray, "What about you, sir?"

Ray said, "I'll need to get back to the King. If I get noticed, there's going to be a straight line to him, we can't give anyone the reason to connect Harry to our activities here. I'm going to leave the hotel and listen in from the road. I'll be near enough to stay in touch but able to leave. The hotel staff will see me leave with a bag shortly after Alex meets Chris in reception; Copy?"

"Yes, Sir," came the reply.

"I'm in Reception, Sir," said Chris.

Ray looked at the young man in front of him; he admired his courage. "Off you go Alex."

As Ray closed the door behind, he sincerely hoped he would see the young man again, but realised he could be sending him to an early death. Well, it was an occupational hazard, he thought, turning back to his duty.

CHAPTER 66 - PROFUMO

The pain in Jarrod Crippley's knee was excruciating, barely able to speak, he said, "Why bring me here? I can't arrange anything from here."

Thiskwood paced around the small house, looking out of each window in turn, on edge. "You needed to see I mean business. I wanted you to come here and meet Martin and take a little pain."

Crippley watched the General repeatedly go to each window. The pain in his legs made him want to be sick, bile rising to the back of his throat. "Why did you choose Spring Cottage?"

"I didn't. I found my wife hiding here. Why does it matter?"

"Your wife?"

The General, still distracted, replied, "Yes, a long story, you don't need to know."

Crippley continued, desperate to occupy the General to avoid any further attack. "This is one of the most famous houses in Great Britain, or was, back in the nineteen sixties," As Crippley spoke he tried to stretch out his knee to relieve the pain.

The General merely looked at Crippley with a quizzical expression.

"In the sixties, the government was brought down by something they called the 'Profumo Affair.' Stephen Ward, a sort of 'Mr Fix it,' leased this house and held parties here. There were government ministers, aristocracy, drugs and prostitutes. A rumour went around Prince Philip attended a few parties. Apparently, they were wild. The trouble was the guest list also included Russian diplomats, spies. The Minister for War made a statement to the house denying press reports about his relationship with one of the models only to confess a few months later. The models who came here were said to be feeding information to the Russians. Macmillan, the Prime Minister at the time, eventually resigned. The conservative party took years to recover from the scandal."

The General laughed a bit too hard, clearly enjoying every moment of this. "This all happened here? Well, how about that? There's something poetic about it all. Your government hasn't got long to go, has it?"

"No." Crippley bowed his head. "I suppose not."

The General slapped the PM hard around the head, Crippley reeled from a blow he didn't notice coming. "No, you're not beaten yet. I want you to get in your car and sort OUT MY DAMN PLANE."

Thiskwood noticed something out of the corner of his eye. He didn't hear Crippley's answer because he rushed from the room and went outside.

CHAPTER 67 - RADIO COMMS

ALEX: OK, I'm just walking around the side of the hotel. I'm just passing our bus.

FLO: Good, Alex, all is clear. Everyone should be able to hear you.

RAY: I'm going up the drive. I will be in position in three minutes. Alex, slow down. Stand by the bus until I tell you. Brad?

BRAD: We're at the side of the Hotel. We can see the path to the cottage from here. Men are ready on your mark Alex.

RAY: OK, I'm here. Alex?

ALEX: Check. I am walking along the path. Every ten feet there's a small garden light on alternate sides of the path. I've just passed one light. Now I'm passing the second... now the third. There are fountains and an illuminated pond on my left; you can't miss it. There are bushes all around. There are thick woods on my right. I can't see anyone yet.

BRAD: OK. Gene, follow two lights behind Alex. Keep it cool, don't look like you're following. Take it slow. Hold the rifle close to your body if you can. Check?

GENE: Check.

BRAD: I'll walk to the right of Alex, there's a route to the cottage through the woods. Serge, you follow Gene, sort out any trouble, try not to make a noise if you do. Check?

SERGE: Check.

BRAD: Taff, Simone, Andy, start walking. Make sure you fan out as you go. Use the trees as much as you can. Check?

TAFF: We're on our way, Check

ALEX: Light four...light five...

RAY: Slower Alex, let the team get into position, I want them close enough.

BRAD: Chris report.

CHRIS: Quiet here; no one is outside the Hotel.

FLO: Alex, keep talking, do you see anything else, give us landmarks. As soon as you spot the house, let us know. Check.

ALEX: Yes, I'm sorry. There are four benches on my left. I'm turning sharp right. The road leads to the cottage. Trees each side of the path. Now I'm walking through an archway. Hang on, yes, I see the house. Gene, check?

GENE: Check, I'm three lights behind, I've passed the benches now. I will see if the arch is a good position.

ALEX: *'No, I'm sorry. I'm Alex Brereton, General Thiskwood is expecting me.'*

FLO: Alex has met someone. Alex, can you work something into the conversation, let us know how many people. We can't hear what they are saying. Check.

ALEX: *'The General is expecting me, but that's tomorrow. I thought I might as well come now because my plans changed. He didn't say there was going to be anyone else, nothing about the two of you.'*

BRAD: Gene, do you copy. Where are you?

FLO: Alex, let us know if you see anyone else, I have you with two people. Check

ALEX: *'Listen, get your hands off me.'*

'Take me to the General, I promise he is expecting me.'

' *No, there's no one else with me.'*

GENE: I have the two men in my sights. One is a small chap, black clothes, same with the other; both are white, the second man is much taller. The taller of the two has Alex by the arm.

BRAD: Ray, shall we get Gene to take them out?

RAY: Cool it. We need to get to the General. Any noise and he will run, he probably has an escape route. Cool it. Alex, remember the safe word. Gene, keep your rifle trained on them. Check.

GENE: Check. I have the big man in my sights now, he is holding on to Alex. I could take him and not hurt Alex.

ALEX: *'Look, it was the General who wanted to see me. I'll come with you; there's no need to manhandle me.*

Thank you, now lead the way.'

GENE: They've let go of Alex. All three are walking to the cottage.

BRAD: Andy, Taff, Simon, change of plan, make your way to the cottage as soon as you can. Surround it. I'm making a guess there aren't too many people. Check.

SIMONE: Check, we have a view of the cottage.

BRAD: Alex, keep talking. Can you see anyone else?

ALEX: *'Is the General in the cottage?*

Yes, let me go. I can walk right in.

Oh, OK. You have more men there. OK, I'll stay with you.

SIMONE: Andy is running out to the left and he will be near the back door soon, I'll be able to cover the other side of the building, I'll wait there.

Taff, check-in.

Taff, check-in.

Taff?

I can't see him. Assume man down

BRAD: Serge report.

SERGE: I've passed by the benches; I can see Gene.

BRAD: Simone, flash your light so Serge can see where you are. Check

SERGE: Found Taff. Throat cut.

RAY: Brad, Serge hit the ground. Make an Army crawl to the house. There's someone or some others out there.

ANDY: I've taken one out. He came from Taff's direction; he might be the one.

ALEX: *'Good evening General Thiskwood, quite a reception you have waiting for me. I'm sorry, I'm early.*

RAY: I can see Alex talking to someone. Confirmed Thiskwood. The two men are moving away. The General is pointing, looks like he's giving the men instructions to go around the house. Simone, check?

SIMONE: I'm in position by the kitchen window. Andy?

ANDY: I'm under the window out the back. Check

SERGE: Goddammit. My leg.

RAY: Gene, are you in sight? Serge, are you mobile?

SERGE: Leg, no, shot.

GENE: The General is taking Alex into the house.

RAY: Damn. Gene. Take the two out if you can, stat.

GENE: One down, one missed, he's gone.

ANDY: I see him. He's down, good shot Gene. Simone? SIMONE?

BRAD: Simone, do you copy? Simone? Chris, get here, I need you. It sounds like we have three down.

CHRIS: Check, on my way.

RAY: Flo, can you triangulate on Simone, Serge and Taff. Make your way here but slow, OK? Bring the first aid too. Leave the comms on, concentrate on our men. Check?

FLO: Check

BRAD: I've seen their sniper. Hang on, Gene, report.

GENE: I'm trying to get a fix on the General inside.

BRAD: Look up to your right, the boathouse has a sort of tower. Their man could be there. Check.

GENE: OK, I see the tower... I see the sniper... He's down. Not sure he is out, might have clipped him. Check.

RAY: Brad, find the other man who took Alex to the house. He is out there somewhere. We have Alex inside. You need to look out. No prisoners, understand.

FLO: I've found Serge. Bullet to the leg. He can't move.

RAY: Check. Is he conscious?

FLO: Yes.

SERGE *Good, Simone, move. I got it.*

RAY: OK, Flo. Serge is on his own for now, get him to tie his own tourniquet. It looks like Taff is down and out. Go to Simone next; she's by the house. She may not be out. Check.

FLO: Check

BRAD: I can see two men. They look like they are getting into a boat. They're trying to make a getaway. Chris, can you see them, Gene, you?

CHRIS: I'm down near the house now, sir. Simone is here, still breathing. Flo, can you find us? Check?

FLO: I'm on my way soon.

SERGE: I'm OK. I can stop the blood. Flo, move.

GENE: I've taken shots at the men in the boat. Not sure if I got them. It is too dark on the river. Check

RAY: Keep in position. Alex, you've gone quiet. Check? Alex?

ALEX: 'King, KING'

CHAPTER 68 - POKER FACE

The General tripped Alex as they entered the cottage, placing his boot on his head before he could get up. "Crippley," he said. "Stay put."

The PM couldn't steady his nerves. "I can't be part of this. I heard shots outside. I can't be part of this."

Thiskwood sneered at him. "You are not part of this, you are this. Shut the fuck up. Alex, what's going on?"

Alex kept quiet. Thiskwood raised his foot and stomped hard on his head. He couldn't help but let out a yelp. Kneeling to the floor, still holding on to Alex, the General put his mouth close to Alex's ear. "I saw your video. I've got one too; how my men strung your father from on the beam in your house. He begged them not to, you should hear him, begging for his life. As they tightened the rope, piss ran down his leg. I didn't tell my man to do this, but he played with your Dad. Just as he was passing out, they let the rope go slack and let on it was a warning. Then they tightened the rope again. They did it three times. Your Daddy cried. He called out your name. I guess it was wrong to play with him, but, shit happens, eh?"

Alex, let out a sob.

"You cry like your precious father."

Alex muttered, 'King,'

Thiskwood stopped talking; he wanted to hear what Alex was saying. He leaned closer, "What did you say? King? He's gone, moron. You, too, soon."

Alex was quicker, younger, stronger than Thiskwood. He grabbed the General's collar. Before he could react, Alex had him on the floor. Stunned, he didn't move. The General started to struggle but Alex struck him as hard as he could with his fist.

General Thiskwood, pained, "Crippley, don't just sit there. Get him off me."

Out of the corner of his eye, the Prime Minister was frozen like a deer in headlights. Thiskwood took advantage and punched Alex hard in the stomach, the pain making Alex release him. He shoved Alex sideways and tried to stand. Alex was quick enough to grab his ankle as he stood and pulled his legs from under his. He smashed his head on a glass coffee table, blood trickled down his forehead, the glass shattered around him.

Alex saw a poker hanging by the fireplace. He rolled over twice allowing him to grab the poker's cast iron handle. In a quick sweeping motion, he used all his strength to bring the poker down on the General's head. The General lifted his arms to try and stop the blow. Alex struck him again, connecting with the General's head. Blood splattered all over him, the floor and the walls. He could see the General's head turn red and, with his next strike, Thiskwood's left eye burst out of its socket, dangling by a nerve. Alex went to strike again but the poker got snatched from his grip.

Brad looked at General Thiskwood's body, motionless on the floor with his head a mess of blood, the eyeball hanging loose from its socket. "Alex, it's alright. We're here. Stop, Alex."

When he looked down, he could only see blood, covering him. He tried to speak but the words wouldn't come. Brad hauled him to his feet, grabbed hold of him and dragged him away.

Behind them sat Jarrod Crippley, Prime Minister of Great Britain. The PM sat still as if in a trance. Still holding on to Alex, Brad said, "You have a meeting with the King. You have a lot of explaining to do."

CHAPTER 69 -9.6 MILES TO WINDSOR

"I'm so sorry we have to leave. One of my colleagues has taken ill. We have to take him back to the veteran's hospital straight away, we're going with him," said Chris Gerard to the Hotel Manager.

The Manager looked at Chris, who had mud smeared over his clothes, "Your walk must have gotten a little boisterous."

Chris smiled, "You see, we might be disabled, but we're still Army nutters in the end. One of the team came a cropper. I've already asked Flo, from room 66, to get everyone's stuff from their rooms. She has all the keys."

"Do you need any help?"

"No, no, we've sorted it, thank you. The credit card we gave you will be good for all the rooms. Alright?"

"Thank you, Sir. Let me come and help you all get sorted outside," the Manager said as he moved from the other side of the desk.

"No, it will be fine. Please don't. We can handle it. My mate is a bit embarrassed, to be honest. He doesn't want to be seen by anyone in his state," said Chris, desperate to stop the Manager from following him.

Flo walked into the hotel reception, then. "Chris, everything's loaded, ready to go."

Chris said goodbye to the Manager, who remained behind his desk. Chris hit the number on the phone in his pocket, and the hotel phone rang. The Manager turned around to answer it as Chris and Flo set off through the hotel doors and jumped into the van.

"Flo, did you sort the video?" asked Brad, driving the bus.

"Yes, all deleted, there won't be coverage of any of us either inside the hotel or out. I've deleted the hotel records, blanked the whole system, it will fuck them for a while," answered Flo putting on her seatbelt.

As they drove slowly out of the hotel and onto the main road, they stopped a few hundred meters further along to pick Ray up.

He got in the car to total silence. Turning back to Brad, he said, "Drive on. Let's take stock. Brad?"

"Taff is dead. Simone is injured, she'll make it. Serge is conscious, but I'm a little worried about him. Chris, Andy, Flo and Gene will be fine, a few cuts and bruises but fine overall. I'm all in one piece too."

"Where are you taking me? You have no right." Crippley called from the back where he was handcuffed and squeezed in between Chris and Andy.

"Andy," said Brad, "shut him up."

Ray looked back again and saw the big man place his giant hand over the Prime Minister's mouth. "Simone, how bad is it?

In a low voice, Simone replied, "One of them knocked me out, I'm shaken, a little bloody, but alright. I'm sorry about Taff."

"Me too," Brad said, looking at the lifeless body of the Welshman, "Fuck, fuck. The man survived everything Helmond had to give. I can't believe one of those pieces of filth managed to get him."

"I'm sorry too, it happened under my command, Ray said, "I'm sorry I let that happen. What about Thiskwood, his men?"

"Um, the General is dead, you should see his face," replied Brad glancing in his rear-view mirror to look at Alex, who didn't stir.

Adjusting the strap on his kit bag Ray asked, "What happened?

"Sir, it was me."

"–Alex; you had no choice," Brad said. "Don't worry."

"The General's men?"

Gene spoke this time, "Two got away for sure. There might be more we didn't see. The lot of them were men for hire. The General and three others are dead. We put them all in the house as you asked."

Ray turned around, "Well done, guys. We're on our way back to Windsor. They have a full medical team there, I've already made a call to Dak, and he is sorting everything there. There's nothing we can do for Taff. I'm sorry it got messy there. We didn't expect the General to have an army with him."

"Hired hands," Andy said. "Not an Army."

"True, but they still caused us a lot of grief. Can you all make some noise back there for a few seconds? I need to ask Brad something, I don't want Crippley to hear."

Brad leaned forward so he could hear Ray. "Did you set the device?"

"Yes. It is ready to go. I reckon we could leave it until we get into Windsor."

"No, let's set it off, pass me the phone."

Brad handed his phone over to Ray, "It is open, phone the number under 'The General.'

Ray called the number but cut it off as soon as the call went through. As they drove along the road, the only sign was a flash in the rear-view mirror. A low *whump* followed and, those who could, turned around to see Spring Cottage ablaze. Taff's body sagged against Jarrod Crippley in the next seat, blood dripping on the PM's suit.

CHAPTER 70 - HARRY-THE GENERAL'S HAND

Dak urged me to send the minibus into London where the injured could be treated. He didn't want the incident at Cliveden linked to Windsor or me. Windsor has a small surgery and hospital facility, staffed by a medical team I could trust. Since they were only a few minutes away, it was their best option. While he was not my man, Serge also needed treatment as soon as possible, given the amount of blood he lost.

I asked George to fetch John and Heather from their guest suite. The children were asleep, Meghan was with me as we waited in the drawing-room.

As they came in, I said, "I'm afraid Serge is injured. They had a reception committee waiting for the team, there have been a few casualties. One of my own died. They are on the way back. Ray will take them to our medical facility straight away."

"We should go there, see how we can help," said Heather, tightly clutching John's arm.

"My thoughts too but Dak said we were better letting them sort out the injured and they could do without any more people there," I replied.

John led Heather over to a chair, it was easy to forget her injury. I could see the events of the last few hours had sapped her energy.

As Heather sat, John asked, "You have a doctor, nurses?"

"Perks of the job."

"Harry," Meghan said from next to Heather, "ask George to bring in some tea."

"I already have. I guess we've all forgotten to eat, he is bringing something. How is Manny, John?"

"He is fast to sleep. It is peaceful here."

"John, take a seat." I sat opposite, "Let me bring you all up to speed. I'm not sure if Thiskwood got wind of the team going there but they were more than ready. Alex's surprise trip a day before he was due didn't work. I'm glad we prepared but hey shot Serge in the leg. He will get treated first. We lost Taff, sorry Rob Wickland."

"I'm so sorry, does he have a family?" asked Heather.

"Yes, a wife and kids. He is separated, there have been a few issues there. Still, he was a father, so some kids won't have one anymore because of what he sacrificed for me." Meghan, next to me, squeezed my arm in support. I continued, "The others are battered and bruised so they'll all need some care. Simone is injured but, apparently, it will be alright. They're a brave lot; I owe them."

John looked directly at me, "What about Thiskwood?"

"He is dead. It isn't what we planned, but, in many ways, it simplifies the situation."

"Was he killed before Alex met him?" asked Heather.

I looked to John and Heather wondering how much I should share with them.

John noticed and asked, "What?"

"Alex decided to go to the house alone. It looks like it got out of hand. General Thiskwood is dead."

"Alex?" asked Meghan.

"According to Ray, who filled me in by phone, yes."

"Wow," said John, "Bloody hell, he's only twenty, twenty-one? Traumatic."

"There is a witness, he's on his way here," I said. "Jarrod Crippley will be here in a minute."

"The Prime Minister?" said Heather. John looked at her noticing her raised voice.

"Yes," I said.

"Should we leave?" Heather asked.

"No, I want us all to be here. We all have unfinished business with the PM. I want you three to witness our conversation now your part of my team."

A nod from Heather was all John needed. It was clear they had discussed our previous conversation. "We're on board. Sir."

"You'd both better start calling me Harry."

"You're a good man." Heather's face softened. "I know it hasn't been easy for you."

"Good. Crippley is coming and, while we may know he is complicit in the death of my brother, his family and my father's death, it will be hard to prove. He is still the Prime Minister, a powerful man. He's an arch politician, I'm afraid he could get out of this if we don't play it right. When he arrives, let me do the talking. I know this is last minute but could you all record the conversation with your phones? I want to make sure there is a record of this."

It took longer than I expected for Crippley to come into the Drawing room. I was anxious to get this done so I could go and see the team. When he came in, I was struck by how dishevelled and pale the man looked. George showed him to the seat near me. Crippley walked stiffly, obviously in some pain. Were they too heavy-handed with him?

I remained quiet as did Meghan, John and Heather. We stared at Crippley.

Eventually, he spoke, "You have far exceeded our authority in getting your private army to kidnap and bring me here. This, this is, it is an insult to the British People and to me."

I was glad the others remained mute. I continued to stare at the PM.

"This is an affront to democracy and the common rule of law. I demand you let me go."

We remained quiet; I wanted to see the windbag flounder.

"I'll tell you, and you better listen, I'll bring the full weight of the parliamentary authority on you and your family...for God sake...let me go."

Eventually, I said, "Mr Crippley, we have documentary evidence to prove you orchestrated the plot to murder members of my family."

"I did no such thing. You can't prove a thing. You come back here, from the country you turned your back on and expect to be treated like the returning hero. No, Harry, you can't. Nor can that bitch," said Crippley looking at Meghan.

He was trying to press my buttons, and, despite the bile reaching my throat, I forced myself to remain calm and mentally counted...1...2...3.

"Your family sucked the life out of this country for tens, no, hundreds of years. When the people hear about tonight, they won't want anything to do with you or your disgusting half breed wife."

5...6...7

"Your father, look at him. Look what he did to your mother. I'll tell you; he had a hand in killing your mother. I know it."

8..9...

"William couldn't keep his dick in his pants. He wasn't a King at all. You lost all respect when you married this American half bread and deserted the country."

10...

My first instinct was to hit Crippley. No, I wanted to get hold of his neck and strangle the life out of the disgusting twat. I could see Crippley's surprise when I said nothing and walked over to the phone to ask George to let Flo Gummer in.

As she came into the room a few silent minutes later, I said "Flo, before we get to business, I would like to thank you for everything you have done. I will say the same to the rest of the team after this. I'm sorry about Taff. Please, come and sit with us. You can put the laptop on the table, we'll need it, does it have enough charge?"

Discomfort riddled Flo's face, but she soon lost her inhibitions as she made herself busy starting the computer. She looked around and connected the power lead to a nearby power outlet while we remained silent.

Once she was ready, I said, "Flo, if you don't mind, please tell me what you have there."

Flo looked at Crippley, focused on him alone. Her confidence restored; she addressed the PM. "General Thiskwood is known for making comprehensive notes on every campaign he ever led. His library in Louisiana was the subject of a fascinating interview published some time ago in the 'Army Magazine.' The General was proud of the collection of battle plans and campaign descriptions; I read an account of the General's library. It fills an entire chapter of his book; 'Balls to the Walls.' His Majesty," she paused and winked at me with her single eye, "remembered my skills in obtaining information. The King asked me to see if I could access General Thiskwood's computer files on 'Operation Catesby.'

As she said 'Catesby' I noticed the twitch in Crippley's left eyelid. Everyone has a 'tell,' I learnt playing poker in the army.

Flo continued, "At first there was nothing I could do. I wanted to, and Harry is a good man, sorry, His Majesty is a good man. It was difficult as I needed Thiskwood's computer. Now I've got it," she said, looking at the Dell laptop opened in front of her.

The Brereton papers together with everything John and Heather could give me would be useful, but not great, evidence of Crippley's part in Thiskwood's activities. Flo grabbed the computer from Spring Cottage earlier. The contents of the laptop were a mystery, I could only hope they were enough.

"Thiskwood was security conscious, and you'll see the Dell computer has a fingerprint reader for security. Luckily, I've got his fingerprint here."

Flo reached in the bag she bought with her and pulled out a clear plastic bag. I heard Meghan gasp next to me, Heather looked away.

As Flo took the severed hand out of the bag, John said, "Fucking hell."

I tried not to show my shock. I looked at Flo, the tiny black woman who still wore her Invictus tracksuit. She looked back at me, I nodded at her to continue.

Flo placed the index finger of the severed hand on the machine. I could see the screen change to show a picture of a tank littered with small computer Icons.

Flo looked over to Crippley again, "We were in a rush. The only choice was to bring this with me," said Flo, looking at Thiskwood's severed hand, on the table. "When I have more time, I'll reconfigure everything, so I can throw this thing away. You see, Thiskwood was a precise record keeper. His file structure is a dream - everything listed in subsections; Documents, Videos, Audio Files. There's even a spreadsheet showing every meeting and conversation he ever had with people involved in the campaign. Mr Crippley, I did a quick search on your name; you feature many, many times. Here, I'll turn the screen around so you can see. Here's one audio file. I haven't listened to it yet but let's do it now. That ok, Harry?"

I nodded, and Flo clicked the pad on the computer and the speakers sparked into life,

THISKWOOD "How are things Prime Minister?"

CRIPPLEY "They have been a lot better, my dear fellow, a lot better. The country fails to understand the need to go through a little pain for the long-term gain. Now, tell me about your plan, you wouldn't give me any details on the telephone."

THISKWOOD "Here is the second part of the plan needed to clear the path to a Republic,"

CRIPPLEY "You're what? What is this?"

THISKWOOD "I told you, Sir, you wanted a plan to get you the Republic you so want. Of course, the plan will deliver The Crown Estate too."

CRIPPLEY "I cannot condone this, not at all. This is wrong. We don't need to do it. King Charles being drugged and effectively murdered was one thing, a necessity, but I cannot agree to the murder of the

Children, or William and Kate."

THISKWOOD "I wondered when your nerve would go. Of course, it is needed. We can't keep the facade around William and Kate. I've paid to poll your people, the British people, and they are fast changing their attitude to the new King. All the mud we spread with the help of our dear departed Mi5 officer merely dented their popularity. There's every sign they're ready to forgive. I hate to say this, Mr Crippley, it looks like people are fed with the bad news about their money and their jobs. Their anger is turning against your Government and you in particular."

I was close enough to touch Flo on the arm, "Enough. Play us one more conversation, any. Crippley, raise your head and look, you bastard."

Flo said, "This is an earlier file." She clicked another file, and the speakers rang out in the room again,

THISKWOOD "You're going to have to tell me what's on your mind, Crippley."

CRIPPLEY "We need a hammer blow, something which is going to end it all."

THISKWOOD "What you mean. A hammer blow?"

MCNEE "We feel despite all of the furore around William and Kate's decaying marriage, the public remains stubbornly committed to the King and his family. William has three heirs. Harry and Meghan have cleared off and are doing well on their own. The people, according to the polls, have no time for Harry since he made that famous 'step back' comment years back. All they see is someone who turned their back on the beloved Queen and an American actress who used her marriage to further her position. She is one of the richest actresses in the World with her TV show. The British don't like it, not one bit."

I asked Flo to pause the recording, "Who is speaking?" I stole a glance at Meghan, who looked embarrassed.

Crippley answered without thinking, "Robbie McNee." On muttering the name, I could see him regretting the outburst.

"Carry on Flo."

THISKWOOD "You want me to come with something to deal with William?"

CRIPPLEY "Yes, if we could engineer a way to get, no force William to abdicate and rule out his heirs, there's no way they'd settle for Harry and Meghan."

THISKWOOD "Are you sure your polls are correct? Harry comes across really well. He seems to be popular in the States. They've navigated their exit from British Royal Life well, some say."

CRIPPLEY "The United States of America is a country obsessed with celebrity. The British people tend to be a little more cautious where celebrity is concerned. They are not popular here and never will be again. They walked away; the British don't like people who throw in the towel."

THISKWOOD "Let's be straight about this. You need me and probably Brereton at Mi5 to create a shitstorm the King, Queen Katherine and the three children can't ignore to force their hand?"

CRIPPLEY "If that's what it takes, yes."

John, Heather and Meghan looked at Jarrod Crippley who lowered his head and looked at the floor.

The air in the room froze. "Here's what we are going to do Mr Crippley. I'm sure Flo here will find file after file implicating you in the most serious crimes against the British People and my family ever committed. Not only have you caused the deaths of good people, people I loved, but you have also sought to raid all the assets you could get your hands on, including The Crown Estate. John, Heather, take note of what I am about to say next."

I got up, standing over the Prime Minister, a pitiful excuse for a man whimpered beneath me. "Mr Crippley, you will continue with the Crown Estate Disposal Act."

I saw John Amery about to cut in, I held up my hand to stop him. I continued, "Publish the White Paper with one significant amendment. You will formally recognise The Crown Estate as mine. Use the documents Judge Casement authored to support the claim. You will put this amendment to the house. You will also outline how I, and my heirs, will make a yearly grant to the British Government from the Crown Estate equal to eighty percent of each year's profit. Effectively this improves the deal between the Government and the Royal Family. There are some other details. Most notably, the Crown Estate Commissioners will no longer be necessary, it will become a private asset managed by a board of directors. John Amery here, you'll be the first CEO of the Windsor Family Office. The Royal Collection and all other assets, including the Crown Jewels, will also be passed to this new organisation. I will own everything and, when I pass, the entire estate will become the property of my heir provided they assume the crown. As is currently the case, there will be no inheritance tax. Do you understand."

"This is nothing but a robbery." He'd regained a hint of a back bone.

"You can't steal something you already own. You fool. DON'T YOU THINK I KNOW ABOUT WHAT YOU FOUND OUT?" I was angry with myself for finally showing my emotions.

Crippley looked as though I'd hit him with a hammer, "I ...I won't be able to persuade the house."

"You will. Once you have, you will call a general election. I want you out of power. I've got everything I need on you to send you to jail for the rest of your life. In fact, I believe treason remains the only crime you can still get hanged for in England. Do you understand what you have to do?"

We all stared at Crippley and waited. A range of emotions crossed his face. I saw range, indignation, anger and, finally, resignation. Finally, he said, meekly, "Yes, Sir."

"Good, now get out of here. I will ask John and Heather here to stick to you like glue from here on to make sure you do what you're told. OK?" I said, looking over to them.

"Yes, Sir," John said.

"Good. Flo, have you backed up all the files on the computer to our Royal Cloud?"

"You bet Harry. It's all there."

"Good, make another copy and send them to Mr Crippley here. I want him to know what we have on him. Thank you, Flo, will you ask George to arrange a car for Mr Crippley."

Flo, storing the laptop, looked behind her, "Crippley, get up."

I watched Crippley struggle out of his chair. "Issue a statement as soon as you can through Number 10. Tell them you were with me all the time to explain your absence. No public speeches, only written statements. Tell them I am fine and I will be speaking to the press tomorrow."

Crippley looked beaten, these last hours aged him ten years or more. "Yes, Sir. Also...thank you for allowing me..."

"–Flo," I cut him off, I couldn't trust myself to answer him, "Can you ask Dak to come in?" I looked at Crippley, hoping for the last time, and in a low voice, I said, "Get out of my house."

Once we had the room to ourselves, Meghan said, "You're going to leave him in power?"

"I'll explain. John, Heather, thank you. Can you leave us alone?"

Dak came in as they walked out. "Dak, I have another job for you. You can refuse this request; I want to make this clear. Is that alright?"

"Yes."

"Talk to Flo, find out what drug they used on my father. As soon as Crippley does what I have asked of him, I would like him to get some of his own medicine."

"It would be my pleasure, your majesty."

CHAPTER 71 -HARRY - CROWN ESTATE DISPOSAL ACT

"John, it is great to see you again, how is Heather?"

"Good evening, Harry. It is good to see you've moved to Buckingham Palace. She's fine, blooming you might say."

"Thank you. Meghan doesn't like it much, but I've earned my place here haven't I. Buckingham Palace has a King in residence again. How did it go?"

"I've just come back from the House of Lords; they've finally passed the Crown Estate Disposal Act. It was touch and go. I've been at Crippley's side every day, he's an animal but a brilliant politician. He pushed through the new Act and convinced enough people to support it in the Commons. By the time he finished, the change in ownership and the prospect of the grant to the government sounded like the wisest financial move he ever made. You have to hand it to him."

I passed him a whisky; we were alone in the room. "I'm not sure I want to hand anything to the bastard. So, what happens next?"

"The Act will come to you for your approval and become law. I've told Crippley to call you."

I took a sip of Whiskey. "I know the PM doesn't have to be here for me to give my Royal Assent but, on this occasion, I will ask him to report to me."

"I will pass the message on. I'm sure Crippley will come."

"Good. John, you have a lot of work ahead of you. Have you liquidated Red Diamond?"

"Yes. As we agreed, I will manage my money alongside the Crown Estate Assets to make sure our interests are aligned. "

I stood and shook John's hand. "John, Thank you. Tell Heather I'd like to talk to her about the Royal Collection if she's 100 percent."

John finished his drink and said, "More like 110 per cent."

"110 per cent?"

"She's pregnant."

"Congratulations!" I said and shook his hand again. His face was beaming, it suited him. "Tell Heather, I said so. Now you'll be a family."

"Already happened. It looks like we're stuck with Manny."

"John, does Heather still want to head the Royal Collection?"

"Try stopping her."

As John left the room, I called for Dak, and he came to the phone. "Dak, I said my goodbyes to Ray last night. Did you manage to see him?

“Yes, we had a drink or two, he doesn’t drink much. Serge joined us. He’s not a drinker at all. That said, we had a laugh.”

“Good, I’ll miss Ray, but it was only right he should go back to the Hurlers. He’ll find he is promoted when he returns. I haven’t told him; you know what he is like.”

“Yes. I’m sure our paths will cross again. Thank you, Sir, for the new position."

"You deserve it Dak. You heading up security makes me feel secure, no one else could after all we've been through."

"Dak," I said, changing the subject, "Mr Crippley will be travelling to Windsor soon. The Act has passed. I will need to give it my ascent. Can you make sure you're ready?"

Dak replied, "I will be, Sir. I will travel back to Downing Street with him, as we discussed."

CHAPTER 72 - HARRY - THE HOUSE OF WINDSOR

I returned from Crippley's funeral late in the afternoon. Meghan refused to come with me; I didn't blame her. She went to Windsor in the morning and I decided to head there before we all set off for Sandringham.

On the journey out to the Castle, relief came over me. Seeing Crippley put in his grave and the dirt thrown upon his coffin finally brought an end to the nightmare we'd all been living. For the first time since arriving in the UK, my shoulders relaxed, the break I planned in Norfolk would be good for my family, we could all do with it.

Amongst all the mayhem of the last months, Philip concerned Meghan and I. His communication skills were not progressing. Only Archie seems to understand him and we agreed we'd address it after our return.

The sheer brilliance of John Amery astounded me. His brief was to preserve the Crown Estate first and enrich it second. The Crown Assets were already flourishing, it looked like my first grant to the nation would be substantial at the end of the year. In just a few months, Amery made more than it would have under the former ownership. Heather's new role would fit her like a glove. Her ability to assemble the right team would produce results way beyond my initial expectations I was sure. I liked the couple and invited them to Sandringham for a few days. They declined as Heather was due.

The news about The Crown Estate and all the other assets generated a lot of press coverage. Apparently, I was one of the wealthiest men on the planet. Of course, I didn't consider the assets mine, but I would look after them better than Crippley ever would.

Crippley's stroke and subsequent death came as a relief. I wanted to make sure my family would never be in the same position again. He lived for a few hard months afterward, but his ability to communicate was gone. Although Guy Storrar took over as Prime Minister, the government crumbled, quickly; an election was called earlier than planned. It looked as though the Socialist Labour party was dead in the water and the conservatives would take over the government.

While I was looking forward to seeing the children, I needed to build my relationship with Meghan. My workload throughout the passing of the Act was immense; I spent more time with the lawyers, John and Heather than I did with Meghan.

When I arrived at Windsor, I rushed in to find the apartment empty. I rang Meghan, but there was no answer.

I called on Dak, permanently stationed at Windsor. "Dak, have you seen Meghan and the Children?"

"No, Sir, I thought they were with you at the Palace?"

My heart skipped a beat. "Dak, they've, where are they?" Panic addled my voice.

Dak went to answer, but my phone rang. It must be Meghan. The screen displayed an undisclosed number. My heart beat so hard I could feel it. "Meg?" I wanted it to be her.

"Your Majesty, my name is Morgan Lederman. I act on behalf of your wife, Meghan Mountbatten-Windsor."

I was confused. "Who? Where did you get my number?"

The man on the phone answered, "I act on behalf of your wife, Meghan Mountbatten-Windsor. She is on route to the USA and will land in Los Angeles in hours. The Queen consort has instructed me to handle her divorce; the 50-50 claim on all community property and full custody of the children."

I began to panic. "What? What's going on? Where are my children?"

"Oh, they're safe with her. From what she's told me, they've been in some danger. Your wife is adamant; her children remain under her protection in the USA."

END

Look out for **Windsor v Windsor Inc.**, the next book in this series.

Cover by Cherin Parry

The Crown Estate is Published by Uber Publications Ltd.

Uber Publications specialise in works of fiction which are time sensitive. Our authors create works of fiction which reflect events of the day. Unlike many publishers, Uber Publications work with authors to produce and distribute creative works quickly and efficiently throughout the English speaking world in days, not years.

www.Uberpublications.co.uk

Printed in Great Britain
by Amazon